Sirens of Manhattan

Benjamin Buchholz

BP

BRADLEY PUBLISHING INC
NEW YORK, NY

ISBN 978-1-7330551-3-0
Buchholz, Benjamin (September 2021).
Sirens of Manhattan.
Bradley Publishing. Paperback Edition.

Now the Sirens have a still more fatal weapon than their song, namely their silence . . . someone might possibly have escaped from their singing; but from their silence, certainly never.
—Franz Kafka

CONTENTS

PROLOGUE: SNOW

By the time the old woman makes her way out into the copse of elms on the hill in the middle of Morningside Park, there beside Columbia's campus on the boundary of Harlem and the Upper West Side, the torrents of snow from that day's storm have nearly stopped falling. She knows more is coming. She's got a sense for snow, having grown up around it out in Idaho and, after that, having lived a good portion of her life in New York. These are snowy places, cold places. The people who live here are accustomed to dealing with it, living with it, being hemmed in by it.

More snow will come, later this same day perhaps. Or early next morning. The old woman knows this. She can feel it. But for now, tonight, she's caught a break in the downfall and she intends to use it to her advantage.

She's got a walker, one of those robust aluminum types that look like they could support a small building, tennis balls cut to fit over its back feet, wheels on the front. She leans on it to hobble her way up the curved parkland sidewalk until arriving at the edge of the wooded hill. At that spot she sets the walker aside, a pace or two away from a park bench beside which a green metal trash can has been bolted down onto the sidewalk itself. The upper faces of both the park bench and the trash can hold thick white blankets, courtesy of the snowstorm, spread evenly and comfortably to a depth of five or six inches.

It's a beautiful scene. Soft. Crystalline. Even warm, in a charming, Christmas-like way.

The omnipresent noise and bustle of New York City swirls around, near at hand, with cherry taillights on passing cars just

1

beyond the wood line of the park, also the honking of horns, a whoosh and grumble of engines, and even—if the old woman listens deeply enough—the sound of occasional voices, distant but perceptible, human noises from always-present multitudes of New Yorkers going about their business not too far away, yet unaware of her or of her little quest. Above, at the edges where the darkness of the woods meets the brighter nighttime glow of the city sky, buildings peer toward her. They do so uncaringly, uninterestedly, as if they are gods assembled in an Olympian hall, alive but frozen and no longer troubled by the bawdy happenings of mankind.

Nearer, nearer than the buildings and the roads and the sidewalks, sound seems muffled. No smell disturbs the scene either, as the blanket of snow settles claustrophobically over the old woman's senses like a bell jar. She feels encapsulated. It seems like the entire scene has been constructed inside a snow globe, one that was shaken vigorously and then forgotten, with a few last bits of confetti falling from the sky.

The woman takes a hesitant step off the shoveled sidewalk path.

The snow cushions her footfall, making her feel like she is walking on a pillow. Tufts of it collapse around her ankles, over the tops of her galoshes, brushing against the hems of her dress so that her gray winter under-leggings rub against it.

She has thrust her hands out to either side for balance, tenuously, one higher than the other, as if looking for a handhold among the crisped, brown, barren branches, or as if she is preparing to brace herself against a fall.

One step becomes another.

She's slow. Wobbly. But she manages to close the distance between the walkway and the edge of the copse of trees. There she stops and looks over her shoulder once again at the snow-covered park bench, at the nearest buildings, at her abandoned walker. She looks back at the trees and squints at them, through them. She seems to be triangulating her position against them and against the edge of the woods and the path and especially against the park bench with its accompanying trash can.

She nods to herself, a satisfied nod, before taking another five or six steps. Then she stops to push aside some waist-high brush.

She says, to no one in particular: "This is it."

Reaching into the front pocket of her overcoat, she produces a little shovel-like tool, a garden trowel.

She bends one knee, sticks the trowel in the snow, sinking down with it, allowing it to stab the cold ground, to become fixed there. As she leans downward her other knee also buckles under her. She slumps, her weight no longer supported by her legs, so that she finds herself, unexpectedly, in a kneeling position. She tries to stand but fails. She tries again, then laughs, waving the trowel in front of her at the bottom sides of the bushes where they stick up at odd, colicky angles from the snow.

"This won't do," she says.

Looking upward through the tree branches toward the clouded, orangish glow of the city sky, she rolls her eyes, either at heaven or at her predicament. Then, having cast one more calculating look about her to make sure she has chosen the exact right place, she simply collapses forward to lay fully prone on the ground, the snow pillowing around her.

After a moment of stillness, like a lumpy or cocooned snow angel, there with her skirts and her jacket splayed out about her, she wriggles onto her side and uses one arm to prop her head and shoulders above the snow. She transfers the trowel to her free hand and begins to dig.

First, she clears all the snow within her reach, an arc that increases her resemblance to a snow angel, although one that has, at this moment, only one wing outlined.

Then, inside the arc of this wing, she churns through the underlayer of the little wood's decomposing waste—mostly leaves and twigs and unidentifiable muck—quickly reaching the wet, heavy dirt below. This she removes as well, piling it up, scraping it aside to form a bulwark against the bank of cleared snow she has shoved down toward her knees.

She's breathing hard but doesn't seem to mind the work. She focuses on the soil, even as her labor continues for ten minutes, fifteen minutes. In the folds of her coat and all along her long, pleated dress a little veil of snow—a shroud of snow—begins to collect, a last gift from this day's storm. The old woman doesn't notice. She just continues digging.

"There it is," she says at last, shutting her eyes as the trowel strikes something in the dirt.

She digs more vigorously for another minute or two, clearing away a space about the size of a dinner plate, lifting globs of soil up and out of the way of her excavation. When enough of the object has been exposed, the woman turns her trowel upside down and uses the trowel's hilt to explore it, knocking its surface—once, twice, three times. The tapping resonates with a deep, hollow sound. The old woman listens for a moment, seeming as if she almost expects an answering thump in reply.

No answer comes. The hollow-sounding surface contrasts with its surroundings, a green splotch in the snow, inanimate and solid while everything else is white and imbued with a drifting dreaminess. The snow continues to muffle sound, so that the thump of the trowel's handle doesn't echo, doesn't even seem to escape the hole the woman has dug. Individual snowflakes flutter down, settling—building up little geometric mounds and walls and dunes of white—each flake whispering with a pixie-like shushing sound as it settles from the sky into a temporary repose on snowbank, sleeve, face, hand, or the green flat surface the woman has unearthed. That shushing sibilance sweetens the air, a counterpoint to the silence of the woods and the stillness of the trees, a melody above and beyond the rasping cadence of the woman's breath and heartbeat.

She sets the trowel aside, reaches down with her hand, and places the flat of her palm against the surface of the partially unearthed object there in the hole. It's dirty, but in patches it seems shiny, as if it had once been lacquered. Along one edge a band of leather extends like a binding. Rusted bronze-colored rivets fasten the band to the wood. It's a case of some sort, or a trunk, much bigger, much more extensive than the little hole the woman dug. Perhaps it's an old-fashioned traveling trunk like those used by the rich, once upon a time, to bring their bowler hats and boas and gingham suits on grand tours of Europe, hotel by gilded hotel; the same sort employed by magicians to mystify crowds and secret away the bodies of sequined assistants they pretend to cut in half.

It's a trunk or a box or a coffin or a case or the top of a buried palace. Who exactly can say? Whatever it may be, it isn't going to be any further revealed. Not at this moment. The woman has stopped digging. She's placed her trowel to one side. She simply lies there, in the snow, with her hand on the green surface.

She even lets her head rest on her arm, supporting herself in a fetal position that curls toward, yearns toward, even protects that mostly buried, age-old object there in the ground.

She does not see me standing in the woods with her.

She does not notice me watching, as she settles herself to sleep, letting the snow fall where it may.

I wait there a long time, an hour, two hours, something like that.

When the old woman does not rise, when after a very long, very patient period of waiting she does not rise, then at last I turn away and leave the little park. I do not go near where she lies. I have no need.

Throughout the rest of the winter, the months to come, I sometimes return to check on her, never leaving footprints in the snow, but looking from a distance to see the undisturbed little mound beneath the copse of trees. I go no nearer than the walkway. I just monitor her, and let the snow cover what it will, at least until spring thaws the snow, the ground, and her peaceful resting place.

Part I
Unavoidable Movement toward the Center

One entered the city like a god; one scuttles in now like a rat.
—Vincent Scully, Professor of Architecture, Yale,
upon the demolition of Penn Station

CHAPTER 1

The year is 1960.

Dixie Jane Hawley stands on the train platform in Pocatello, just in the spot her mom said she never should stand—too close to the edge, out from under the canopied passenger depot, too much in the wind, too exposed. Dixie holds her hat on her head with one hand. Behind her, Pocatello's orange-brick depot building rises up, almost pretentiously tall and thick, as if it is trying to set its city solidly on the map, there in the morning sunshine, as the first monument to a new Rocky Mountain metropolis. Dixie feels the setting is perfect for her, how the heavy old boring building opens up right there onto the impermanence of the wind and the impending reality of the onrushing train; how she can occupy this spot, right on the tittering edge between one possible life—cramped there, uncomfortable, limiting, always seeing the same people, the same problems, day in and day out—and another new and eager and wide-open existence that approaches her as if it is a dervish of unpredictability.

Dixie wants to dance, at that moment, there on the platform's edge. But she can't. She's too encumbered. Again, like the contrast between the train depot's solidity and the wildness of the wind,

Dixie's own composition contains this multifaceted tension. She stands right on the edge of the platform, but also right on the edge of herself.

Beside her she has set her valise on the herringboned brick pavement. The bag anchors her a bit, not too much, but it does mark out a place at her foot, forbidden for dancing or swirling. More significantly, a few steps further back, a bigger and more serious chest, a portmanteau almost waist high—green lacquered wood bound in leather straps, with brass rivets all along its edges—stands guard as if to prevent Dixie from returning to the depot building, or to Pocatello itself. The edges and seams of this chest have been wrapped in a layer or two of tape, waterproofing it, holding it together even though it seems completely capable, all on its own, to maintain its shape and protect its contents. Written on the portmanteau in perhaps a half dozen places, each time in a bold copperplate hand, are three words that combine possession and liberation in equal measure. These words are simply Dixie's name: her first name, her middle name, and her new married name—Dixie Jane Hawley. The trunk is Dixie's trunk. The journey to this point, here on the edge of the train platform, marks the starting point of Dixie's escape, her escape from life in Pocatello, but it also serves as her anchor and her backstop. Her portmanteau, and even more so her name, are the things that will help her leave but also the tethers that tie her down, full of grounding earth and centering calm. Dixie is surrounded, shepherded, chattel to the worldly treasures packed in her chest and in her bag. She knows this. She can sense this. And so, as if in revenge, she has chosen this particular spot, all alone out here in the cold morning sun, right on the edge of the tracks where the wind tugs at her hat and at the hem of her dress.

She might find herself tied down a bit, but—if so—she's decided to make sure she's at least tied down to danger, brushing up against the truly ineffable edge of the onrushing train and the onrushing wind.

That's Dixie.

And this is Dixie's moment at the rails of the train station, out in the wind, out from under the portico's shelter.

Dixie wants to dance, but she can't. She can only wiggle the toe ends of her shoes over the platform's lip. Her bags stand guard beside her. One of her hands holds her hat to her head, and her other arm, an arm that might in similar situations find itself thrust out in front as if striking fourth position prima donna all on its own, she keeps close and strangely tucked away, sheltered from the wind and from the train even as the greater part of her leans forward into the rush.

Why is Dixie's arm not upthrust? Why is it not leading her on her charge out of Pocatello?

Well, it's not just the portmanteau and the valise that hold Dixie to her spot.

No. She holds a little figure in that crook of her arm—a boy, a baby boy swaddled mostly in white but with a bit of minty blue fringe around his red-cheeked face. Dixie has turned him, the most natural way to hold him, so that his cherubic gaze looks upward toward her, toward the sky, a fixed and cold-pinkened stare, slightly glassy and unblinking, that makes it look, at first glance, as if the baby is a doll rather than a living child.

It seems strange that Dixie is standing so close to the edge, with that baby, and with the warnings of her mother so resonant in her inner mind. It seems strange too, after having a bit of a closer look at her, to note that she's been crying.

Not recently.

This isn't a today-cry type of look, no runny makeup, no burst little capillaries in the outer whiteness of her eyes. Rather, the crying shows itself in half-moon circles shadowed above her cheekbones. It shows itself in a stiffness along the side muscles of her neck, instead of in the more immediate hunch of her shoulders. It shows itself, or makes itself heard, the few times she speaks—asking the conductor to verify her ticket, asking someone else for the time— in the thrombosis of her voice, a starlet huskiness that doesn't quite come natural to her, not at this young age, not yet.

Today Dixie revels in the wind. She's not crying now, but for the past week, whew, it's been nonstop, an out-of-body experience for her, just as if some alien creature had taken over all her otherwise freewheeling senses.

Who is this person I've become, who is this ninny? she asks herself. *It's not me.*

Yet the crying won't stop.

It isn't her baby doll's fault. He's done nothing wrong. Whenever she looks at him, whenever she touches him, puts him to her breast, she feels the full warmth of love and tenderness, just like everyone told her a mom should feel. Indeed, she feels that love. She just can't, or couldn't, control herself when the feeling of tears came. Couldn't control her tear ducts. Not until yesterday when she decided to step away, step outside herself, and force some decisions to happen. Once she did that, and had an element of action about her, then the crying subsided. The old Dixie came back, though the crier remained just under the surface, like a flood being held at bay by an earthen dam eroded by the gnawing of a million little mice.

Because of this crying, and because she's pulled herself almost, but not completely, together, only subtle marks of sufferance show on Dixie's face. Struggle appears in the little details of her, makes her hands shake a little, her lip quiver, though her body language also shows how earnestly and conscientiously she fights against it.

She's leaning forward, forgetting all about Pocatello and babies and crying for a minute. She's leaning forward because she's old enough now and she's made up her mind about leaving home. She's out here at the edge of the platform, right in the midst of the

Pocatello switching yard that's been used by everyone coming and going, from Wild Bill Cody to way back before even railroads when Lewis and Clark came through, switching from plains to mountains, following the river upstream. So many folk have passed through Pocatello: men with long gazes and frightful aloneness, husbands and wives in stagecoaches, fat bankers, cattlemen driving their herds, leathery hands in the rail yards who spit tobacco at the edges of brimstone embankments and lounge in the shadows of saloons. So many people have come through here, heading west, heading east, that it feels natural. The natural starting place. That's what Dixie tells herself. *If all those other people come through Pocatello and keep going, then why should I feel stuck here? Why should I let this place pin me down when it hasn't pinned anyone else for near as long?*

Decision made, Dixie spends a frantic day packing that chest, her portmanteau.

She digs into her cigar box of treasures, opens the envelope Gary left her to free up the bit of spending cash he'd set aside, just for her. With that money she marches down to the train station and buys herself a ticket, coach class, passenger plus child, from Pocatello to Manhattan, via Salt Lake, Cheyenne, St. Louis, Cincinnati, Pittsburgh, and half a hundred other smaller towns between.

Dixie has been crying for a week, ever since Gary left her at her mom's house. It wasn't nasty, their parting. It all went according to plan: Gary, off to grad school without her, without their child, because Manhattan wasn't their idea of the ideal place to raise a family. Pocatello was, and is, and always will be, and that's what they have all agreed on, Dixie and Gary and Dixie's parents and even her Uncle Paul, who lives with them in a room upstairs. A whole family conference, coming up with this plan. Perhaps Gary's parents should have factored into the decision-making too, except he doesn't have any, not anymore. They died when he was young, and since then he's lifted himself up by the bootstraps, first by enlisting

5

for the Korean War, then by putting himself through college. That's how the decision for Gary to go and Dixie to stay behind is made: Gary is so thoroughly accustomed to making hard choices and doing hard things out in the world, while Dixie by default occupies the traditional role, waiting for him once again, only now with their baby too, and with the blessing of Dixie's family surrounding her and making the whole endeavor safe, sanctioned, and stable, keeping her close where they can help her and look after her. It's the right choice, fair and good and taken with the best of intentions all around. Gary leaves Dixie at her family's house, taking his GI Bill and his good grades from undergrad at BYU so that he might go get the key to their happiness, their future happiness, which is—as he sees it and as Dixie's family sees it—a graduate degree from Columbia.

That means New York City.

That means Manhattan.

That means far away.

No place for a young wife and new family, Dixie's parents tell her.

You'll be lost and alone most of the time, Gary says.

And you should have help with the baby, Uncle Paul says, pointing to the immobile lump asleep in Dixie's arms. He's pacing behind the couch in the family room, while all the rest of them sit in a semicircle around the glowing embers of a fire no one has stoked since the conversation started. Paul always seems to have more energy than the house can contain. Paul always seems to be an exaggeration, bigger than life, even though he's a small man, thin and wiry and fast. Flamboyant is perhaps the word, trying to seem somehow grander, somehow more professorial than he really is. All of them are used to Uncle Paul—all of them except for Gary, Gary who is newer to the family and who casts a wary glance every time Paul turns another corner in his pacing.

6

New York's no place for a girl like you, Dixie, they never quite come out and say, not outright, though it hangs there between the statements and in the expressions of sentiment oozing from all their actions and words.

The decision, then, made mostly in unison, involves a little suffering, a little separation, but Dixie has the baby to keep her busy, her little doll, Cyril, who by this time is already two months old. Gary will come home on holidays and breaks, whenever he can slip away without endangering his studies. They'll see each other, these newlyweds. That's the plan. It is a good plan. Rational. Smart. Safe. Keeping her in the bosom of her family, the comfort and quiet of Pocatello. Looking forward to the blessings of a sound, prosperous future.

With Dixie's family in agreement, with Gary in agreement, Dixie is really not able to fight it, not then, not yet, not even realizing it is something to fight against. So, she too agrees.

During all of their discussions Gary looks suitably forlorn, with the tallow-like swirl of his forelock drooping down so handsomely over his eyes. He takes Dixie's hands in his own, that last night together on her parents' front porch, and he says his goodbyes, sweetly and smartly and with all the confidence in the world. He is good at making tough choices. He's made so many before, fighting in Korea. In fact, he uses his Korean War sergeant voice now when he speaks with Dixie, which isn't unkind, but is—for certain— louder and more distant, more likely to involve him staring straight ahead at the horizon, like he is addressing an audience rather than just her. Like he is more comfortable with the abstract idea of their separation rather than the specificity of looking her in the eyes. This army voice is a voice that isn't the Gary whom Dixie grew up with but is, without a doubt, still him, just a better, cleaner, clearer version of him, a version of him that has taken on the aura of inevitability.

7

The whole episode of Gary's departure happens just how they collectively imagine it will. And it all seems like it will be okay, that everything will be okay. It seems that way right up until Gary actually leaves.

That's when the alien invades Dixie's body. It invades and commandeers her tears, making them flow uncontrollably forth, putting all the plan, and all the hard choices, and all the love for baby Cyril, and all the support and good intentions of her parents and friends, her Uncle Paul, and all of Pocatello in doubt.

The alien (those tears) invades, and Dixie cries for a whole week without stop.

The first time Gary calls, not yet even in New York, spending a nickel in a phone booth along the way, she bites down on the edge of a towel and barely says anything, hardly sounds herself in her attempt to not speak at all. She just mostly listens to him, which is enough for her, really enough. That's how she stops herself from sobbing like a ninny. That's how she stops herself from making him feel guilty. Oh, he knows something is up, that's for sure. He keeps asking about it: *Dixie, dear, are you okay? If you're hurt, if you're in pain, if anyone is hurting you, you let me know.*

She says yes. Then no. She says no, that's what she meant. She's flustered. He's asked too many questions all at once. She can't sort them out. *Yes* to the first question. *No* to the second, she clarifies. Then she clamps down on the towel again and steels herself to listen to all the things he's seen out the window of his train car: antelopes following alongside just like in the songs, big rivers and bigger iron bridges and a side-wheel ship on the Mississippi, vast tracts where the new Eisenhower Interstate is being built through an Illinois cornfield, progress everywhere, smokestacks and so many people out east, an ever increasing horde—more and more people and more and more smokestacks, more and more factories, more and more civilization creeping in every state farther east you travel. Nothing compared to Korea, mind you, the people flock together

8

so thickly there that they seem to swarm like flies, but still everything out here—out *here*, he says, with emphasis—is a whole world different from Idaho: *Dear, it's different indeed and I just wish you were with me to see it all.*

Dixie wishes that too, of course. But she can't see through her present pain to a solution. She can't get her mind to work for this whole first week of being locked away in her room, or of trying to go about her daily chores and her daily life, though with a hanky held up to her nose and a need to step away to the corners of whatever room she happens to be in—it doesn't matter which, or where, from time to time, hourly or even more often than that—whenever the sobs wrack her hardest. She can't think straight. She doesn't even try, really. She just holds herself together, best she can, doing routine things but not doing them particularly well, not with any gusto, not with any song in her heart.

Dixie's parents watch all of this. For that whole week they watch her.

Dixie's mom tries to say little things to help, tries to do little things to help. She brings her soup and clippings from the cartoon section of the newspaper. She picks a bouquet of early spring flowers for Dixie and puts it at the bedside in Dixie's otherwise spare, eggshell blue–colored bedroom. She does these little things, but they aren't particularly effective. The flowers sit there, rather than getting woven into a crown or a bracelet. The newspaper clippings go unread. The soup is barely tasted, definitely left unfinished. So, by day three or four of that week, Dixie's mom steps back, not in frustration so much as mystification, watching and wondering and fretting, and saying things in a half whisper—a whisper meant to be heard throughout the house, really—whenever Dixie's father ventures near enough to give her reason to speak.

Dixie's mother of course knows about, and has even experienced a touch—modulated with the occasional glass of sherry—of the blues women sometimes get in these situations. But the blues are so un-Dixie-like that she can hardly imagine Dixie succumbing to something so simple and medical (she doesn't know, none of them do, after all, anything about the alien of tearfulness that has taken possession of Dixie's tear ducts).

The things Dixie's mother does at this time aren't much. They don't add up to much. But all of it is well-intentioned. Dixie's mom simply does not have the necessary arsenal of weapons to turn Dixie about. She only has the endurance of her forefathers who crossed the mighty plains and ended up there, in Pocatello, deep in the flatlands between Idaho's mountains, enduring, enduring. So that's what Dixie's mom resorts to, a Donner Party–esque type of fretful waiting, chewing her own lower lip in worry and emotional hunger. She simply keeps on keeping on.

Maybe that's also why Dixie's mother doesn't protest when Dixie digs into that special cigar box for the extra spending money Gary had left her, somewhat maniacally thereafter bounding downstairs, looking a bit feral about the eyes, whirlwind-like in the way her dress and her hair fling about her, announcing to the whole house and half the neighborhood that she will be buying a ticket to Manhattan for herself and for little Cyril too. She doesn't know that Dixie plans to buy it for the very next day. She doesn't know that her daughter will really go marching right out of the house, right that moment, right over that forlorn front porch where Gary had said his goodbyes, right down the street across town those seven or eight blocks to where the Pocatello train depot sits in the spring sunshine. Dixie's mom doesn't have a chance to stop her daughter before she spends her bit of pocket change at the train ticket counter. Nor could she have stopped her afterward, not once the alien inside Dixie shifts gears to make her start singing and dancing at random moments as she loads up her valise and goes down into the cobwebbed basement to bring forth and claim for her own purposes her father's old green-lacquered traveling chest. Dixie's mother can't stop this from happening any more than she can stop a spring thaw. Nor can she make herself sit Dixie down to try to talk any sort of sense into her, any sort of caution.

"But it's so far," Dixie's mother says.

Dixie doesn't hear her.

"And you'll be all alone."

"And what will you eat? What will you wear?"

Dixie hears none of these questions, not as she rushes around, a little bit like Snow White in the oblivion of a newly discovered dwarfish forest, surrounded by birdsong and never seeing the dark depths of the metaphorical woods just beyond this first dappled glade, because of the way the alien's sudden Technicolor artistry plays in her heart, in her tear ducts, the way the decision to buy that train ticket shifts everything from a passive and interminable acceptance to an active and exciting, almost death-defying sense of possibility.

Dixie's mother tries to say a few things but can't get through to Dixie at all.

Dixie's father doesn't bother trying to get a word in edgewise. He knows he can't compete with either of the women in his house, not in terms of words, not in volume or voluminosity of speaking, communicating, not in dancing or singing or even in packing up portmanteaux. He can't compete with Gary in terms of solid, strong, quiet resolve. And he can't compete with Paul's energy and quick tongue.

Dixie's father doesn't say anything.

He simply takes his pipe out to the shed behind the house.

The backyard of his house is a small one, bounded on three sides by a fence in need of paint, with all the grass in between overgrown a little, his hand-pushed mower leaning against a stump while daffodils sprout beside it in the cold spring air. Spare gaskets and grommets and all sorts of rusted whatnots hide in those weeds, leaning against the back shed, menhirs of motors and machines. Dixie's father always has an engine or two laid out in the little shed, laid out on his workbench amid an assortment of other things he's taken apart, some of which in good time he'll put back together, some of which will end up filling little tin cans, bolts and bits and bobs, pins and nails and doodads, there to sit among squeeze cans of oil and cleaner, tools, wire, old magazine advertisements, and random refractory cups and shards of gemstone-like glass.

This is his lair, his space, full of wheezing practical magic, the smell of which Dixie will never forget.

From a jar on a high shelf, unscrewing the lid with a sound like the grinding of teeth, he takes a single playing card, a Jack of Hearts. It's an old card, worn at the edges, and of a style not at all modern. This he brings back to Dixie, still puffing his pipe even though it has been strictly forbidden for the last twenty-odd years that he ever smoke in the house. He comes in with the card in his hands, not saying anything, just going to his daughter and folding her hand in his to transfer the strange object.

He provides no explanation. Dixie asks for none, even though she doesn't know what it means.

I'll explain it someday, her father's eyes say, *but for now this is enough.* Which makes Dixie, or her alien-in-incubation, her tear-duct hijacker, nearly burst forth with a fresh new indecision of tears. She manages to rear back just in time, keeping control of herself, staid and solemn rather than wild-eyed for a moment so that she can kiss him on the cheek and let the smell of his pipe smoke catch and seek cover in her clothes and her hair.

Here Paul enters the scene, coming down the stairs.

"Dixie," he says. "Dixie, I have something for you too."

It's a tone not unlike mockery. It makes Dixie's father and Dixie break their embrace, step away from each other. Dixie takes a single step toward the stairs, toward where Paul waits as if expecting her to come to him.

Maybe this is where the alien is most useful. Maybe this is where Dixie doesn't have to rely on herself, all the time.

The crying starts again.

Paul brushes past her, past her father, past her mother, and out the front door. He's gone. Dixie stands there alone, a very different-looking, withdrawn, shriveled Dixie compared to the one who waits, exhilarated, on the train platform.

All this happens in memory for Dixie as the train rushes forward.

All this happens as she toes the line, near as she can get to the onrush.

She turns slightly so that she shields her baby from it, but she keeps her face full and shining in the train's direction, as if daring it to jump its tracks. She cuts quite a figure there, beautiful but also tragicomic, far too brave, far too poignant.

So much knotted up inside Dixie. So much controlled. So much put together perfectly on the outside, while on the inside—as the train approaches, as the engine passes, as the passenger cars in their unbreakable chain stop near her in a great commotion of industrial screeching, smoking brakes, slowing, slowing, coming down from full blast to a chug and a stop amid the smells of smoke and tar and heated iron—she trembles. She trembles and leaves home even with her father's pipe scent from that last hug in her own hair. So much control as she breathes deeply a last, lasting bit of Pocatello, her former home, there before she jumps into life.

CHAPTER 2

This is how Dixie remembers it: the trip from Pocatello to Manhattan happens without any sort of disturbance, any sort of issue, any sort of momentous or grandiose meaning.

Yet, that is a lie.

In truth everything that falls within the sphere of Dixie's gaze takes on a momentous level of meaning. All her feelings have tuned in and have ratcheted up. The explosion across all her senses creates a full palette of eventfulness, import, and wonder. All of her has sprung alive, the experience of things crisscrossing, one upon another, each upon the next, a synesthesia, so that she feels the sounds, the very vibrations of the sounds (interlinked above the claptrap train tracks), hears the colors (how the whoosh of the passing young and newly sprung aspen leaves creates a leafy harmony), smells the contours of the train cabins (the astringency of vinyl and lacquer and cleaning solutions applied to toilet, seat cushion, common table, plus Brasso on the bronzed railings, and deep inhalations of organ-like, even haggis-like humors wafting from the various pieces of leather or canvas luggage carried by the porters, stowed by the passengers around her). This is living. This is the very definition of eventfulness, at least for a Pocatello girl. This is what it feels like to be woken on all levels. This, plus Gary out there somewhere ahead of her in Manhattan (and her family behind her), the thought of reuniting with Gary, having him and Cyril and herself together as a family: this is why Dixie has decided to travel.

Beyond the living, breathing, thrilling fulfillment of *going somewhere*, the trip transpires without a flaw. Uneventful, really, despite the pace, the sound, the fury of motion and new experience. That's what Dixie remembers. That's what she tells herself.

No tragedies occur, no slipups, no accidents, no real struggle. Nothing like that happens. Or so she tells herself.

Dixie says her prayers, as always before and during travel of any sort, even if her journey only takes her from Pocatello to Twin Falls or Rexburg with its university, prayers asking that she might not just experience new and wonderful things, but also arrive, if it should be the Good Lord's will, without incident or delay.

So, no, on this trip, on this journey to New York City—biggest and mightiest city in the world—Dixie remembers no moment of cataclysm, no chaos, no flash of searing trauma.

Everything goes exactly as planned, exactly as Dixie has dreamed and imagined.

It's peaceable.

It's well-planned.

She's made herself a sack of sandwiches, so that she doesn't have to pay for expensive food on the train. These she manages not to open for the first few hours, holding them in reserve until long after her stomach begins to growl. It's dark already by this time. And Dixie's distracted by her hunger (Cyril having fallen asleep). It's this distraction that prevents her from noticing, at least at first, a bit of paper that falls free from the wrapping of her first sandwich. When she does see it, she thinks at first it may be a napkin her mother added, or an extra sheet of butcher's paper, doubled up when she wrapped her belongings back in her parents' kitchen.

But it isn't.

It has writing on it.

Dixie has eaten a few bites of this sandwich before she notices the writing on this paper, and it's a good thing, because the note—even just the handwriting of the note, before she ever reads the message itself—turns her stomach. She realizes she can't eat anymore, not for a while at least, and so she rubs away a bit of the peanut butter that has smeared over the writing and she takes a deep breath before lifting it up close enough that she can read it.

It's from her Uncle Paul.

I tried to find a moment alone with you before you left.

I wasn't able. Things happened too quickly. You were possessed, it seemed, demonic.

I need to tell you something about how Arlo, your father, how we met . . .

Dixie pauses here. She knows, she's always known, that Paul isn't actually her uncle. He isn't related at all. Just someone they call Uncle. Just someone her father has known for a long while, too long, and who has become—for better or worse—part of the family.

I need to tell you about how ol' Arlo and I met. It'll explain a few things. Your father was in trouble. He'd run away from home. I saved him. He owes me. That's the easy stuff to put in writing. Maybe that's the most important stuff. I don't know. You'll have to decide for yourself, I suppose. I think I've taught you well enough so that you can figure things out a bit. You've probably always suspected something was up. Just think about the songs I used to sing you and the tales I used to tell you when you were a child and I'd come tuck you in your bed whenever your parents went out for dinner or a game of cards. Think about those stories a bit and what it is that Arlo owes me—those stories about tigers and elephants and ladies in sequin dresses, bearded men.

I saved him. Where we met though, and how, and what those circumstances were, well, that's what I need to tell you in person . . .

The letter goes on, but Dixie doesn't want to read it. She doesn't throw it away. She simply folds it in half, just as it had been when it was hidden in the wrapping of her sandwich. She folds it in half and puts it back in her handbag with the other few items of food she's brought with her. She puts it back and tries to forget about it, but when she falls asleep she dreams of the circus stories that Paul used to tell her, the clown tricks he'd perform, his attempts to be grandiose and entertaining despite his weird twitchy energy and his small stature, always like he was trying to impress Dixie, to be bigger than himself, to show her how important he could be.

Dixie falls asleep and dreams of circus scenes, only to wake up sweating a few minutes later with the snuffling cry of her little baby doll the only sound other than the rhythm of the train along its rails.

This seems like it might be something worth noting—different, strange. Perhaps even cataclysmic. But it really isn't. It's what Dixie's used to—Uncle Paul creeping into everything. It's normal, a weird sort of normal, but it doesn't upset her, not outwardly. She maintains her earlier opinion: the whole trip is great, it's fine, there's nothing for her to worry about, nothing for her to dwell on, nothing to harbor in her heart or puzzle over in her mind. It's all good. She's on her way. She's free and headed in a direction of safety and independence.

There's nothing else in this whole trip at all worth commenting about or recording except maybe an encounter she has the next morning with a man who shows her his magic playing cards.

This man isn't on the train with Dixie from the get-go. Certainly not.

He isn't from Pocatello or Rexburg or even Boise.

He isn't from Wyoming or Montana or Colorado or Nebraska, those first few states the train whooshes through, all of them similar to Idaho—sparse, dusty, open-sky places with simple people, simple manners, unthreatening atmospheres. Dixie would have known, and would likely have ignored, any man joining the train in any of those states. They would have reminded her too much of her own people. Too much of her own parents. Too much of Uncle Paul. She couldn't have let that slip past her, wouldn't have let that slip past her, not without noticing. She's alert to that sort of thing. Vigilant.

Nope, this man boards later, and Dixie can't help but notice him almost right away.

She sees him sometime right after the train crosses the Mississippi River, sometime right after Saint Louis, right after the gaping steel-trussed emptiness of a big bridge, the ascent up a far cliff-like precipice, the flattening of the train tracks and smoothening of the journey as the route enters Illinois farm country. Before Dixie and this man ever make direct eye contact, she sees him, once or twice, and notices a riverboat feel to him, a gambler's gambol, a brill-creamed slipperiness. She can't look away from him. He doesn't seem to reciprocate her attention during their first encounter. Or at least he doesn't show it, doesn't change his behavior. He enters Dixie's vision at a moment when he is a few rows ahead of her in the train car. He is, at this time, preoccupied in a conversation with a man a few rows ahead of the place where Dixie sits with baby Cyril in her arms.

The man's laughter draws Dixie's attention, deep but also hollow, somehow fake.

Almost unwittingly, her eyes glance at him as he stands in the aisle making small talk with the seated passenger.

Dixie doesn't look away from him. She stares.

She probably should look away, but she doesn't.

After a moment, the man turns his head toward her and seems to shiver. Dixie thinks this might be a reaction to her stare. It might be that deeply animal response any human, especially any woman (but sometimes also men of the more unconventional sort, the sort like Uncle Paul), will exhibit when they know they are being watched. Though he continues his conversation, his gaze drifts away from the man he has been speaking with, and he allows himself a quick, appraising glance through the whole of the train cabin, up one row of seats and down the other, an inscrutable, terribly dark-eyed flicker of reconnaissance. Nothing in his surroundings seems to disturb the man. His regard of the room is thorough. Similar to the way a very deep pool swallows the ripples of a thrown rock or how the space between the stars on a cold, windless night can be probed without fathom, the darkness—nay, the serenity—of his gaze releases nothing back into the world around it. He absorbs all he sees and does not let the least bit of it go.

His appraisal continues smoothly, without pause or concern, before at last his glance alights on Dixie.

His survey then stops, if only briefly, the most miniscule hitch in its glide path.

Dixie thinks she sees a hint of a smile catch one of the muscles in his cheek, pulling a corner of his lip upward, there at one side of his thin but well-trimmed mustache. Quickly though, the twitch of that smile-muscle fades, subsumed as spontaneously as it appeared, gone, gone, his whole face returning to flatness, his whole countenance personable and undisturbed. Nothing else changes in the man's expression, or his stance, or the flow of conversation he maintains. Only this little hitch in his gaze, as it travels across the room, alerts Dixie that the man has seen her and has indeed taken note of her.

Quickly, too quickly, she looks away.

The man doesn't change anything about his behavior. He doesn't stop what he's doing to approach her. He doesn't wave. He doesn't smile. He doesn't look back at her after that first connection of their gazes. He doesn't approach to say *hi* or *how do ya do*. Dixie thinks the eye contact they made had probably been accidental. She tells herself that the man most likely didn't mean to look at her. He might even have been disgusted with what he saw—a girl like her all alone with a baby in her arms, obviously far from home.

Dixie tries to put the man out of her mind. (She tries to put Uncle Paul's letter out of her mind, his circus tales out of her mind.)

She tries to think of other things: home, what her mother and father would likely be doing at this time of day, midday back in dusty Idaho. But here, aboard the train, the sun has receded already into late afternoon with its light long and slanting through the rows of Illinois corn outside, looking corrugated and blurry as the train speeds along. She tries to think about Cyril, dead asleep again: whether he is happy, what he might need, how she should anticipate and better prepare for his next bout of wakefulness—playing with him, walking him up and down the length of the train cabin, even from cabin to cabin across the precipitous and rattling divide between cars. She tries to think of stories she'll tell Cyril when he's old enough to understand, ones that don't involve circuses, peanuts, clowns, or pretty ladies on jeweled and feathered horses. Stories that don't involve Uncle Paul, or her father.

Dixie even tries to sing a song or two, quietly as she can under her breath, looking down at Cyril as if he is listening rather than deeply engaged in the almost-snoring mindlessness of a newborn's slumber.

None of these things really work. She tries all of them, but none work.

Dixie's thoughts return to the man, the new man she has seen aboard the train. Her thoughts return just as if he is at the end of a rope she twirls around and around in the air, a ring on a hoop, a boomerang, a trapeze, all of it with a gravitational pull, inward, tighter and tighter, wrapping and raveling together faster and faster, closer to the center, which is her. She tries to give this new man a name, but she fails. He seems nameless, with neither any sort of biblical moniker—Peter or Paul or Luke or even, say, Jedediah—nor any sort of newfangled appellation, like Bugsy or Kip or Joe or whatnot, seeming right. She tries to give him a history too: he's a riverboat gambler of course, she thinks, but she doesn't know what this means (she's not letting him be a member of the circus, though that's the obvious thing—she's not letting that happen at all!). Maybe he's a small-town lawyer, the type that takes up charity cases even against the better judgment of his peers or his family (she's not thinking of the circus advance teams, their promotional schmucks arriving at cities a day ahead to plaster up posters and rally the farmhands). Perhaps he's a newspaperman, with a pencil chewed to the quick and a way of scribbling shorthand while never breaking eye contact, having conversations on the street corner and in the barroom with baseball players and bankers and mafia hit men (she's not thinking of strongmen, or acrobats, or sword-swallowers. She knows she's got to pick something else, otherwise he'll be tainted, *verboten*, a part of her nightmares).

She thinks of all these things, and she does a very good job of *not* thinking about the circus, but still, of all the professions she tries to provide for this man, none seem right.

Without giving it a definite label, she continues to feel unsettled about it—his name, his history, his background, his qualifications, even the fittingness of being associated, though only through the merest fleeting glance, with such a man. She needs to put it to bed. She needs to end the dialogue inside her own head. She knows it is driving her crazy, repetitively thinking about and through it. So, she forces herself to make a choice right then: she decides the man is a professor (definitely NOT a ringmaster, the ringmaster). She decides he's a professor who has probably been schooled in some obscure and maybe even slightly scandalous subject—mummies or transistor radio waves or evolution, God forbid *evolution*—and that's what she'll call him, in her mind, in her most private thoughts: the Professor. Maybe even *her* Professor. That's what she decides will be his name and his history and his reality. She decides all this, with certainty, and she feels better about it, having made a decision.

She doesn't even doubt herself, a little while later, when this same man again appears in her train car (even though he looks, somehow, even more like a ringmaster than he had before, changed into an old-fashioned velvety dinner jacket with threadbare cuffs and an embroidered lapel). He enters through the far door, with the whistle and clatter of the open space between the train cars his harbinger.

He wends his way carefully but with a somewhat slipshod aura down the length of the train car. Perhaps he's drunk. Or perhaps he's been hit on the head. Or has made an escape from robbers and kidnappers. Dixie doesn't know. But her mind whirls. She watches him as he picks his way along the aisle of the train car and lays his hands here and there on the shoulders or even the heads of passengers who have, by this time, settled deeply in their seats, well after the noon meal, well after the midday round of drinks, far into the long, somnambulant afternoon. Using the interruptions his touch and his presence create, he again looks in on the conversations of these passengers, striking up a few discussions of his own, saying *hellos*, though the man he had laughed with before is no longer there, three or four rows to Dixie's front. This means that the Professor (Dixie's Professor) remains a bit farther away, too far to look at directly, too far for Dixie to even consider any sort of remark, embark on any sort of direct approach. She simply tickles Cyril a little, cooing at him, while keeping watch on the Professor from beneath her downturned eyelashes.

It's coy of her, Dixie knows this.

She isn't trying to be coy. She's just off her game a little. Nervous perhaps, though she doesn't know why.

The Professor takes his time coming down the length of the train car, and so Dixie has a long while to analyze his motions.

The style he uses, for instance: she notices there's something practiced to it, something not quite honest, or at least not fully natural and uninhibited. Dixie feels a certain rehearsed smoothness in everything he does, a bit of performance. She notices that he seems to revel in the moment just before his somewhat careless actions, his backslapping and his stagger, allow him to meet someone, to bridge a gap, to cross that precipice of awkward interjection, of bumping into, of saying something, anything, that might help him make of these strangers an acquaintance or two.

Dixie is predisposed to feel that this is a good thing. She thinks: *Perhaps he is lonely.* She thinks: *Perhaps this is how people in big cities, people out east, learn to deal with being anonymous among so many millions of souls.*

But also, she can't help but notice, it's all a little fake.

This turns her stomach somewhat, just as her stomach had turned when she found the letter from Uncle Paul. It's not so bad that she shuts him from her mind. It's not so bad that she can't finish reading him, like what happened with the letter. It's not so bad that she has to shunt him away. In fact, the opposite happens. She looks at him again, quickly, conspicuously, and with more than a little negativity flowing toward him from the fount of her eyes.

She feels him draw near. One step. Two steps.

The train hammers away at the rails beneath her, squealing.

Dixie looks down at Cyril and says, "You're feeling nervous too, aren't you, baby doll? Just what your mommy feels."

Dixie checks on the Professor's approach once again. And again, for the second time that day, their glances connect.

Now it's too late.

Now she knows he's coming for her.

She can't get up, can't leave her seat, can't leave the train car, can't leave the train. All that would be too obvious, impractical, impossible. She's stuck. She's helpless. There's an obligation for her to be polite, to be nice.

He pauses to distribute another congenial pat on the back to an anonymous passenger's shoulder, using his handhold there to lever himself away from any conversation that may ensue, intent to be away, to keep moving, swaggering down the aisle—swaggering, he *swaggers,* that's the word—then lets his mouth fall open and his jaw work side to side as if physically chewing on the words he might say, the words of introduction or condemnation he's preparing for Dixie. *What will he say?* It's as if he's tasting, or silently auditioning, the various handy crackerjack platitudes he's accustomed to using, silver-tongued, part of his repertoire, always on the ready. It's as if he's measuring the weight of his words to choose just the perfect ones for her.

He approaches.

Good Lord, Dixie thinks, *this is unending, this is unavoidable, this is fixating.*

Dixie's never seen anything like this, not even with Uncle Paul and his odd and all-pervasive energy.

The Professor nears within just a step, mouth open, hands moving out wide as if to embrace the air—or Dixie, as if to embrace Dixie.

But then, suddenly and with a lack of assurance he had not revealed up to that point in any of his previous interactions in the train compartments, or with any of his previous interlocutors, he backs down, bottles up his words, and passes by her without saying anything.

Dixie knows why.

Right on the edge of that first civility, right on the edge of his manufactured introduction, the man's gaze darts from its connection with her to fasten, again, briefly and calmly, coolly, on Cyril. Dixie has moved her baby doll close to her shoulder, backward, burping him and letting his fat-faced, wide-eyed, barely heads-up jouncing flow with the railcar's rhythm. She holds him so naturally, and so closely to herself, that she supposes Cyril must seem part of her, a part that a man such as this collected, calm, perfect Professor likely wouldn't see, wouldn't expect to see, if he were only thinking he might meet and speak with a single, vulnerable, all-alone girl, a girl from Idaho, a girl without much experience of life. A girl who is running away from home by running for the safety of her husband.

It seems that Cyril's presence makes the Professor reconsider the situation, there in the railcar. It seems that Cyril, and nothing other than Cyril, causes the man to move on past Dixie, on past her row of seats, on through the door behind her into the next railcar.

Dixie notices a strange thing then, when the man passes. Well, maybe not so strange, but worth mentioning at least. Worth thinking about. A thing she could not see, or did not see because she wasn't expecting it, when this man had been farther away, earlier this afternoon. In each of the man's ears, a wadded ball of cotton protrudes, as if he has had a long-standing rupture of the eardrum, a sickness, tinnitus, a disease or condition for which he has found a treatment, a long-time-ago sickness that he has now grown so accustomed to that the permanent presence of the wads does not bother him or make him self-conscious. He seems not to notice the cotton balls. He gives off no sign that he bothers about them. He's as uncaring of the cotton in his ears as Dixie is of her own ears, or her nose, something that just doesn't get thought about much, until an outside force turns attention that way. The man, Dixie's Professor, moves without regard to them. He does not reference them in speech or in action. He is careless, though these wads of cotton are—Dixie notes—undeniably present, undeniably real. Whatever it is, she concludes, it adds a flavor of wounded mystery to him.

What? Dixie thinks. And *why?* And *what could it mean?* It's not part of the circus. It's not got anything to do with Uncle Paul's circus, the stories he's told her.

As much as Dixie didn't want, doesn't want, to call this man a ringmaster—as much as she has already invested in an idea of him that is somehow crucially different—as much as she wants and needs it to be something, anything, different, these wads of cotton are *soooo* different, *soooo* unexpected, *soooo* weird, that she's thrown for a loop. They don't fit her idea of a professor. They don't fit the idea she's choking down either, this possibility that he's a character dredged up from one of Uncle Paul's uncomfortable stories.

Dixie can't help it though. The circus tales from her youngest days are such a bedrock part of her, such a dark and delicate corner of her, that she's having a hard time *not* connecting the wads of cotton to Paul's circus. It's weird. And it means that she tries even harder, saying the name she's chosen for this man over and over and over again this evening as she waits for Cyril to wake:

Professor,

    Professor,

        Professor.

            He's a Professor.

CHAPTER 3

Nothing bad happens on the train trip from Idaho to Manhattan.

Dixie can't remember a single thing she should be worried about, ashamed of, or self-critical over. Nothing to repent. Nothing to remember. There are no turning points, no signposts in the road, no momentous situations that send her life thereafter spiraling in strange, unforeseeable, troubling directions. No skeletons are put in Dixie's closet. She's following iron rails directly in the direction *away* from her skeletons, her family's skeletons back in quiet, cold, windy Pocatello.

Though the cornfields do not seem to change overmuch, the train in which Dixie and this Professor are encapsulated must cross at some point from Illinois into Indiana, maybe Kentucky too, probably Ohio—she's not sure which of these comes first, which second, or where exactly she might be at any given point, though the consummation of time continues, and with it the locomotive drives through mile upon mile, its progress broken and measured only by the stops it makes in strangely identical flatland towns.

Thus, night begins to draw a cloak over the world, Dixie's second night aboard the train.

The smell of food—mashed potatoes and perhaps warm bread with butter—calls her to the dining car from the semi-connected confines of the coach where she's spent most of her first full day. Sandwiches are great. They were a great idea. But she can't bring herself to open her handbag and dig them out again. She doesn't want to read the rest of Paul's letter.

She enters the dining car and is shown a table. Cyril, asleep in his bassinet again, fits neatly wedged between her and the window to the outside world, so that he is guarded by both the wall and by Dixie's body. He's somewhat invisible there, all his everything tucked in, his body deeply snuggled (and deeply motionless, shaken only by the train's repetitive staccato on the rails). Mother and babe together neatly occupy one side of their dining table, with the other side remaining free.

Dixie orders from the menu. The food comes. She eats. All the normal things in a dining car happen, even up to the point of Dixie receiving her bill.

Then the Professor arrives.

He sees this open space at Dixie's table, across from her, directly interfacing with her.

He does not hesitate this time.

It's almost as if he and Dixie are old friends by now.

"Draw one," he says, as he slides onto the bench seat across from Dixie and little Cyril. He does not glance at the bassinet but holds Dixie's somewhat startled gaze. The man's body is tall and angular, which makes his act of folding himself up into a sitting position both awkward and unexpectedly real, as if all the sense of rehearsal Dixie noticed earlier in his motions has been washed away by this action, replaced by a boyish incorruptibility. He has long fingers, big hands that fill up those threadbare cuffs of his dinner jacket. The cotton balls she had seen earlier in the day remain deeply

29

planted in his ears, wedged in but also spilling out like mushrooms or cauliflower. His hand has stolen into the breast of his dinner jacket, even as he sweeps into the seat, probing the jacket's inner pocket. From it he extracts a deck of playing cards, flashing them outward, back sides facing Dixie in a peacock pattern as he repeats those two words: "Draw one."

"I don't bet," Dixie says. "Or gamble."

A long moment passes where neither Dixie nor the Professor budges, neither moveable, but neither of them antagonistic toward the other. It's stasis. Stalemate. Neither of them gives off the impression that they are upset. No aura of unpleasantness emerges between them. They're two passengers, each in transition between place and time, caught floating above the earth on the train's system of jangly iron rails, jostled, captive, but also strangely free. They've broken through the barrier of their initial meeting, the silence of true strangerhood. They are on speaking terms but also a little stuck, impaled on the bold but strange choice the Professor has made to approach Dixie with his playing cards drawn. An impasse has presented itself, and neither Dixie nor the Professor feels certain how to get around it. A look of worry creases the Professor's features, strange after so much calm and confidence, but also strangely real and, again, boyishly open. Dixie, though having struck such a puritan tone with her statement about not betting, not gambling, also seems amused, contentedly so, and does her utmost to send this man across from her all the indications she can muster of kindness and interest despite the intervening deck of his faceless, unfortunate cards. Akin to a cloud passing over water, an expression flickers across the man's face, uncertainty now, the opposite of confidence. It's as if the dark sparkle of some impious fire has been lit, then snuffed, then lit again, sputtering on the edge of flame.

"You don't bet?" he says. "Everyone bets."

"No, I don't," Dixie says, and she lets that statement sit, heavy in the air.

She wonders what sort of Professor he is. She wonders what sort of Professor takes his amusement from betting, from sharking at cards. Maybe all Professors do? She doesn't know many Professors at all. Actually none, not personally and directly. Rexburg has the university, not Pocatello. So, Professors are an oddity for her, semi-mythical beings who live a hundred miles away, or farther, out east, and in bigger cities. Maybe, she thinks, his is a mathematical study, a focus on probabilities and random encounters. Or maybe his card playing is just a coincidence, either a passion unrelated to his core academic pursuits or a misreading of him altogether: he's no Professor—he's a thief, could be a thief, a riverboat gambler like she first suspected, a hooligan, a ne'er-do-well. She can't think about these choices though. They open up too much possibility that she might backtrack and assign him a circus role. That wouldn't be good. That wouldn't be safe. Still, the possibilities surrounding his true nature seem to be endless in Dixie's mind, with his confident sense of oddity simply one of the ephemera of his trade. His approaches, to her and to others, will certainly reveal themselves to be both a sale and a severance, the con man's swindle, the magician's bait and switch (the ringmaster's appearance in the sudden spotlight when all the big top lights have been snuffed).

All this Dixie thinks, and continues to analyze, as they face off with each other. She's wary. But she's also rather proud of the situation. He's older. Wiser. Worldly. But she's got him on his heels. She's thrown him for a loop.

He doesn't know what to make of her, she thinks, and she feels a confidence of her own rising up in her heart, her throat, her head, so that all the sensations of this momentous incident (nothing she needs to worry about afterward, of course; nothing worth dwelling on, thinking about, repenting for—nothing happening here, just look away . . .), all these sensations start to make her feel a little dizzy. She tells herself: *Hey! All those talks Uncle Paul gave me, all those lessons and prayers he made me say about doing what's right and good and moral, maybe they're paying off. Maybe I am good enough, no matter what Paul says. Here I am being my very best self, staying true to my beliefs and my heart and my principles, not falling for his gambling tricks, and just see here how it is making me, little old me, an even match for this very interesting man, making me worthy, worthwhile. How perfect! How fun!*

Entranced by this newfound power, Dixie holds her hand out across the table from the man, her Professor, who has by this time grown tired of wafting the spread deck of cards in the air and, with another practiced flourish of his hand, has fanned them out onto the dining car table, equidistant between them. Dixie holds her hand out above the cards, upright. She presses her fingers firmly together, each one against the next, palm sideways, the whole hand vertical, a knife-edge. She offers to shake hands, just like a man would do when first meeting another man, just like a man would do with an equal, a peer.

"And hi," she says, still looking directly into his gray eyes. "Hello. I'm Dixie. Dixie Jane Hawley."

They shake.

It's strangely satisfying. Well, actually, there isn't too much strange about it at all. Dixie knows exactly why it feels so satisfying—first because of the way it makes them equal in the egalitarianism of the gesture, and second because it allows the first bit of physical contact between them. It allows a nonthreatening touch, a formal and accepted method of connecting skin to skin. In Dixie's mind this leads nowhere. Their shaking of hands serves as an end in and of itself. It's nothing to worry about, nothing to write home about, no sort of major event worth dwelling on in the future for years and years and years. It's the sort of greeting exchanged between bankers. Or businessmen. It's got nothing to do with circuses, clowns, or anyone having to rescue her father.

She's good. Dixie's good. Everything's fine. Nothing major happens on this train trip out to Manhattan. Nothing she needs to tell Gary about. Nothing she needs to tell her father and mother about, Arlo who will say nothing, Gladys who will pretend not to hear. Nothing is wrong with the situation. Nothing at all.

As they release their hands, the Professor seems as if he's about to say something significant, again working words in his mouth. But he does not actually speak. He swallows whatever thoughts he had been mustering, and for the first and last time in their acquaintance he allows himself to touch his ear—Dixie wonders if he'll remove the cotton wad. She imagines a geyser of blood and maybe brains too, all of it pouring forth. She knows if he did remove the wad it likely wouldn't be something so gory, so gross. It likely wouldn't result in much of anything at all. But that's where her mind goes, even as the man merely scratches at his earlobe, a tic, and then pushes at the cotton wad, pushes at it so that it is driven deeper into his ear canal, almost so that Dixie cannot see it anymore. That done (and fascinatingly so), the man gathers himself together a bit and says: "I'm going to keep these cards right here, Daisy. I'm going to keep them right here between us."

"Dixie."

"Dixie?"

"Not Daisy. Dixie."

"Dixie, right," he says, a little sheepishly, lifting both of his biggish, boney hands from the table, raising them as if in surrender.

"Daisy bothers me. It's what my uncle calls me when he wants to make me mad. It's what he calls me to get under my skin."

"Okay, Dixie," the man says, carefully now. He shuts his eyes for a second and then returns his attention to the cards, saying: "I think you'll take one."

"I won't."

"This is supposed to be pleasant."

"I never said it wasn't pleasant. I'm having a pleasant time," Dixie says as she smiles at him, verifiably pleasant in all her manners. "Pleasant indeed. Everything here is pleasant. I've got no objections, and I'm happy you've come to sit with me."

Truly, Dixie is having a fine time. The food she ate a few minutes earlier wasn't exactly delicious, but it was warm, a lovely change from sandwiches. The light outside has also passed from loveliness to loveliness, bright and jewel-toned throughout the main part of the day, then shining low and mellow across those endless cornfields that seem even more indicative of an eternal heaven than the high plain scrublands or the stands of aspen Dixie knows from the valleys and canyons of the Idaho hills. Before dining, Dixie had just nursed little Cyril, had put her baby doll to her breast, and that act filled her—still fills her—with warmth and wellness, good things both, having done not just her duty but her purpose, her very molecular purpose, her evolutionary purpose, a flooding of serotonin and goodness.

What Dixie has said is true. Man or no man, Professor or no Professor, cards and betting or nothing of the sort to deal with: Dixie is indeed having a pleasant time. She can't imagine anything better, grander, or more filled with intention and purpose (albeit unknown purpose) than what she is doing right at this moment: headed outward toward the adventures of Manhattan and who knows what else in the world! Heading outward and away from Pocatello and her family and Uncle Paul. She can't imagine anything better, grander, without worry, regret, or a need to apologize to anyone or anything. She can't imagine anything more momentous, even though nothing at all momentous happens on this trip.

Dixie notices the man's bow tie, with a gaudy pinstripe matching but slanted backward from the similar stripe of his three-piece suit. This ornament has come unfastened since first she saw him, earlier that day when he passed through the passenger car. Now it hangs about his neck like a thing discarded, clinging but forgotten.

Somehow that makes her feel sad, as if the bow tie and the man both have lost something. Not something especially dear, but something elemental, nonetheless. Like the feeling a person must have after having their appendix removed. Or after a dentist has put a fake tooth in their jaw, golden or otherwise. It's a clinging aura of unreality, the sense that this man might still exhibit slightly unnatural tendencies, slightly wrong and rehearsed manners, making Dixie feel as if she is looking at the whole scene through water or as if she is watching, from afar, a TV show meant to retell, in a formulaic and inevitably false way, a parable trying to hint at some perfectly intimate and animal experience. A reproduction of reality.

Maybe the closest thing would be deafness—sudden deafness—the robbing of a singular but often ignored sensual experience.

Dixie steals a look at the Professor's cotton-wadded ears again.

Deafness? Could it be?

No, she tells herself. *No, it's not deafness. He hears me perfectly well. And others. He's chatted plenty with other people: I've seen it myself.*

She looks down at his cards, feeling inexplicably like she owes him something. She knows not what. In fact, she knows she owes him nothing at all. But still the feeling is there, persistent, real. He seems imperfect. Partial. And Dixie longs to fill that void.

She looks again at his tie—clinging but forgotten. Empty but not essentially so. Flaccid. Maybe that should be the word she uses for this feeling: *flaccid.*

For just a moment she feels tempted to play the man's game and pull a card from his deck, just to cheer him up. But she holds back. She's never wagered anything before. She's got a thing against betting. It isn't religious, per se, more an animal instinct. Dixie just doesn't feel like she needs to play along. She doesn't see an advantage or even very much amusement in such games. Paul would always try to get her to do things like that. To pick things. To choose things. To back herself into a corner.

"We're at an impasse, then," she says. "A pleasant impasse, but still, we're rather stuck, aren't we?"

The man nods.

"Well then," she says. "Since my baby son Cyril is sleeping, and since neither of us have anything better to do, why don't you tell me a bit about yourself?"

How can a person not bet? Though the cards are laid down before her, all her future is spread out ahead of her along the tracks toward Manhattan, and Dixie forgets completely about them. She forgets about the cards and she forgets about the betting. All of it has left her mind. The cards might just as well have never existed. They are gone, extinguished, subsumed. And she has stumped the man in the professorial suit by asking him about himself.

She can tell that he is afraid to answer her. She doesn't know why.

Most people love to talk about themselves.

When she says those words, asking him about himself, she thinks it will offer an easy way out of their dilemma, a path by which they might ease their conversation and their friendship into safer territory. But it doesn't seem so. It seems like the Professor instead swallows a giant weight, or like an octopus has latched on with all of its tentacles to the insides of his throat. He even turns a little purplish blue in the face. His mouth struggles to form words, which makes it look like he also struggles to breathe.

When he does at last speak, the moment has shifted again—from concrete reality to an insensate minute stolen from, ripped from, time itself. All has dissolved. All has been captured. All, everything, exists within the bubble of their present time, like some quantum reverberation has caught hold of them, right there, and is using this moment as a fulcrum of decision: everything from this point on will choose its spin and its velocity in accordance with these next words, these next actions, these next intentions.

(This is the moment Dixie never can tell if she remembers correctly and truthfully. This is the moment she plays and replays, perhaps giving it that sense of the insensate. This is the moment— she tells herself, now and always—that is uneventful, not worth worrying about, not worth discussing, not worth repenting over. Nothing happens here, to her, for her, with her. Nothing happens of note within the bubble of their time, so Dixie looks away, unable to focus. Or, better, Dixie can't look back, can't—despite trying again and again—review the scene in her memory, not without altering it, the sense and the substance mutable in proportion to the amount and the intensity of attention she puts on it, so that, like quanta, she can only ever determine one or the other: *words* or *context*. Never both together. Never spin and velocity.)

Dixie's Professor leans back, face going slack for a moment, and in response to her question about him, about his history, these are the words he chooses to say: "What would you think about living forever? Would it be a curse or a blessing? Would such a person be nearer a devil or nearer an angel?"

She laughs. "An angel? Like the kind with wings and glitter that we hang on the Christmas tree each winter?"

"Yes," he says. Or, that's what Dixie thinks he says. She's not sure. The memory comes with a halo of fog around it, permanence and impermanence.

He says this, or something like it, something similar, and then he reaches across the table for her hand, the same hand he had earlier shaken in their grip of equals. He takes her hand, palm to palm, placing his other hand over the back of it so that he cups it, and holds it there, right on top of the cards, as if warming it against frostbite. Indeed, Dixie notices, running all up and down her arm, a chill like a winter cold snap thrilling through her skin. She feels no warmth from his embrace, but neither does she encounter the same sort of clamminess that she'd expect from the skin of someone who has the chills. This is different. This is unearthly. This is unright. It worries Dixie. Right away it worries her. And it continues to worry her, as she later (again and again) thinks about it, dwells on it, replays it.

In his defense, this man, her Professor, never says he's an angel. Nor does he say he is a devil, for that matter. Dixie knows this. He's only asked a question. He hasn't made a statement. Even though the whole conversation retains that fog of pregnant time to it, that halo (so to speak) of unreality, of suspended being, she knows what she feels in his touch. And, though maybe she's not sure about the exact words he says, she knows he *hasn't* said anything about his personal state. He hasn't labeled himself as one thing or another. He's just asked her a question, a question that comes as a response to her own question, somewhat evasively, and causes more questions. Questions upon questions. Dixie asks this man about himself, and she gets no answer in return, just a deflection. Just an impermanence that treads in place in the water of that moment: *What would you think about living forever? Would it be a curse or a blessing? Would such a person be nearer a devil or nearer an angel?*

Maybe that's what he studies, she tells herself. *Maybe that's what his professorship and so forth are focused on—a study of angels, a study of eternity. Maybe it's his interest area. That, and betting on cards.* Maybe that's why he asks her about living forever. Maybe that's why he tried to read her fortune or do whatever he planned to do by asking her to draw one of his cards.

The man begins speaking again but Dixie doesn't notice his mouth moving. She no longer hears what he says. Or perhaps, suddenly, the words themselves come out sounding like syllables of locomotion, the rat-a-tat-tat of steel wheels on track, a whistle over bridges, the echoing underpasses through which the train tunnels (all along that great new ribbon of Eisenhower's freeway), the deceleration slowing into towns, the strain of engines gearing up for their steady traverse of the open countryside, the approach in darkness toward the rolling foothills of Appalachia. The Professor's words come to her like the whoosh of air and passing trees just a few feet away, inches away, outside the train's windows. They begin once more to fit and lodge within the warmer tones of conversation and footsteps, the clanking of china and tinkling of wineglasses, the harrumphing of other guests nearby, all joining in anew, rejoining with them, filling up the bubble of that fine dining car, the scents and sounds of a life's worth of context. There's a monotony to this moment. A normalcy. (Nothing out of the ordinary: see?) There's a sense of increase, of fullness, ripeness that hovers around and also within this moment so that the sound of everything in Dixie's ears takes on a quality like the hovering of bees about a hive, stillness amid intense activity, noise that becomes nothing except background. Comfort taken as the edges of life enfold her once again, after she experiences this momentous/non-momentous singularity.

The man speaks, Dixie knows this. But she doesn't hear his words. A spell is upon her.

Just like she has ceased to see the cards that remain spread on the dining car table between them, Dixie shuts away the sound of the man's voice. She has become set apart, almost asleep, as she wakes and wonders and does everything but hear.

Indeed, all Dixie's senses work, everything except her ability to hear him. It's as if she has cotton balls in *her* ears.

All the intensity of trying to cipher his voice siphons down into intense concentration on one thing: her sight of him. Dixie watches the man most intently. She's not lip-reading, but *him-reading*. She's not trying to understand, but to know.

He's a different sort of person than she's ever encountered before. He's older than either Paul or her father—though of course she has met and knows plenty of other people as old as him, older too of course. He's taller—though she knows plenty of tall people too, plenty taller than this man even. He has chiseled features, which for Dixie recalls somewhat unfavorably the prominences of cattlemen: weatherworn, lined, hard of jaw, cruel of eye, unflinching in all exterior elements. Though Dixie has so far spent all her days in Idaho, near and exposed to such men, crossing paths with them fairly frequently, she knows she is really a product of the softer small-town niceties of Pocatello. She knows she's been raised in a hundred subtle ways to appreciate a bit more fat around the edges, a bit more ease in a person's manners than those of the hard-bitten ranchers, a bit less certainty or color than such men (and women) normally provide, a bit more sophistication. This Professor has those qualities, but they are layered over with experience and confidence and culture. They are layered over with the aspect of performance and falsity she first noticed too.

Dixie has seen plenty of features like those of this Professor, this gambler, this (maybe) angel. (She's more comfortable with angel than with ringmaster!) She has even met some men, and a few women too, who manage to mangle together several such elements in a single visage—older, steelier, taller, somewhat learned and prolix and extroverted—but what she hasn't experienced before, or only once before (in Paul's attitudes and energies), is the focus and concentration of all these qualities solely so that they bear on *her*. People of this sort have existed around the margins of Dixie's life up until this point. They have come into her awareness more as parents' friends, as passing strangers, as teachers, bankers, businessmen (and uncles). Dixie's never before met such a person alone, as a stranger to her. And she's certainly never had such a person devote himself, his speech, his manners, his attention, wholly in orbit around her. This is new to her and probably the thing that makes her feel as if she cannot hear him, feel as if a bell jar has descended over her head, so that all this man's actions (and especially all his words, words she isn't hearing at all) float off far away, coming to her as if through water, filtered through water, or something thicker than water—syrup maybe. Or honey. The still and sap-like honey inside the honeyed hive.

Who are you? Dixie wants to ask, maybe as much of herself as of this man. *Who are you, Dixie Jane Hawley, to be having such a conversation as this?*

The man stops talking. Whatever speech he had been giving, he has finished. His manner now shows a certain satisfaction, releasing her clasped hand from his, crossing his arms in front of him, a pose that tries to say: *I've answered your question, Dixie Jane Hawley, even though you may have heard nothing at all.*

What did I hear? she wonders, recalling snatches of words and place-names that will not, cannot, never need to be worried about, dreamt about, dwelled on later.

The man raises his eyebrows, as if to open a space for Dixie to speak. He clearly feels as if he's said something worth responding to. He clearly feels as if Dixie will now reply to him, on her own terms, in her own way, with her own story of a fabulous personal history.

Dixie doesn't know what to say. She hasn't been following along at all. He could have said something completely absurd (and, in fact, it seems as if he did . . . angels and odd places and whatever snatches of daydream came out of his mouth that she just totally, completely, could not process. *Did he say Ashkelon? Did he say Athens? Did he say Ulaanbaatar?*).

He expects something. He expects her to chime in. He expects her to give him some feedback.

But Dixie's got nothing to say in return, nothing that might match the spell he created.

Just like Dixie isn't going to bet, she isn't going to make up a fable either. Not one about herself. So, she stays quiet.

The man looks down once again at the cards between them on the table. He looks down pointedly. He looks down longingly.

Dixie's gaze stays fixed on the man's face: gray eyes with just a hint of blue, thin features, balding in a way where laurels like those on a statue of Caesar or Pompey might fit—a feathered balding, a connection with academia that still seems at odds with the man's slippery edges. Dixie has an urge, suddenly, to touch his hair, to test whether it is really as light and as feather-like as it appears.

The man's gaze lifts from the cards and returns to Dixie's face.

They look at each other.

Dixie feels her hand lift. Of its own accord it stretches forward, into the space between their bodies, venturing toward his head, intending—it seems—to brush his temple, to reposition a stray bit of laurel there.

The man does not recoil from her. Even when she touches him, the man stills himself and waits, a fox caught in the headlights of a hunter's truck, knowing that if it moves—if it moves at all—then the whole pack of dogs behind, in the truck's jalopy bed, will scent it, see it, and certainly come bounding down to break the spell with their barking and their pursuit.

Dixie and the man balance like this for a full second. Maybe two seconds, seconds that seem endless and churchlike, before the train suddenly brakes.

Dixie lurches forward.

Her hand slides from his face, down his neck, down his back, leading the way over the fabric of his dinner jacket, strong and smooth at the same time, leading the charge, lurching forward like the first troops sent to pierce an enemy's entrenchment.

The man catches her shoulder in his own grip, ignoring the fan of cards as they slide toward him, piling up, jumbling into a heap on his lap, leaving the table clean (and his fortune, or his sleight of hand, broken and unread).

He catches Dixie's shoulder in his grip, and as the braking of the train stops, and the car once again jerks forward, Dixie's arm around his back pulls him toward her, cupping him, thrusting him bodily across the tabletop. This is all incidental. All accidental. All caused by inertia only. There's no volition to it at all. However, it is as if they perform a seated tango. It is as if they dance over the tabletop, a formal dance, locked together. The train has not braked completely. One moment after its unexpected hesitation it resumes normal pace, speeding along the track again, hardly having lost steam, only this jerk—forward and backward. Nothing else has changed.

Except for Dixie and the Professor.

They're stuck, both of them up and over the table, pressed against each other. Other diners regain their composure. An older woman nearby who had spilled some coffee begins to complain to the nearest recuperating waiter. Laughter and grumbling in equal proportion ripple from beyond a steward's doorway. The clanking of dishes fills a void of sound. The whoosh of trees again, and of wind, floods through the blackened nighttime windows and underscores the restart of their motionless motion, their floating above the earth on those hardy iron rails, measured and magnificent.

All the world returns to normal, except for Dixie and her Professor.

They remain in the embrace, unwilling, unable to let it go. (Foxes. Foxes circling each other, quietly so, and aware of their innermost dogs.)

They stare at each other, unflinchingly, before Dixie places her mouth over the Professor's lips and kisses him. It's a kiss, yes, but a chaste one, unavoidable almost, and certainly nothing to worry about in the long run. Certainly nothing to write home about. Certainly nothing to trouble Dixie's conscience. Nothing momentous.

The kiss lingers for a moment, heady, and then it is gone.

Beside them, beneath them on the seat beside the window, baby Cyril in his bassinet does not cry. His eyes flicker open, both of them at once, and with a stony, impenetrable expression, it appears as though he watches his mother and this stranger in the odd, telescoped perspective afforded by his upward-facing, frozen, and secret position. He appears to watch but he does not disturb.

CHAPTER 4

Dixie and Cyril arrive in New York City a short time later.

It's the moment Dixie has been waiting for. She feels as if she has been wiped clean, like everything is fresh and new, careless and free. She's got a plan for how to meet up with Gary, even though he's not coming to get her. She's got a plan as far as where to go, how to get there—though her train arrives when he is in class. He has told her it's a long and boring but *very* critical lecture. He stresses how important it is, how much he'd like to get away and come greet her when the train arrives, but how he just can't—not in good conscience—miss it. He tells her this the last time they speak back at a spot where the train pulled into a station somewhere on the edge of Ohio and Pennsylvania (sometime between first seeing the Professor and having dinner with him later on the upward slopes of Appalachia).

"Don't worry," Dixie tells him. "You don't need to come get me. I'll be okay. I've got a plan."

As the train pulls into New York City she repeats this sentiment to herself: she's got a plan, at least the idea of a plan, and she'll make it work. She's got a plan and she's not worried, not at all, not even with the urban canyons of the city starting to close her in, first the squared-off blocks of newish housing, all built the same, little bungalows in rows and neat right angles in the neighborhoods along the train line in New Jersey. These are postwar edifices, now in 1960 starting to show the first signs of age and of the impermanence of their design. As she passes through these areas Dixie can almost hear Gary's take on them, always the pragmatic engineer: *They're just temporary, made for the bubble of housing we needed with our returning soldiers and sailors and marines, right?* And she can hear Uncle Paul's opinion of the houses too, or what she imagines he'd say: *All those little housewives, bored, dreaming the same small dreams. A whole neighborhood, whole cities, of people who are lost!* And now, among these voices she adds the voice of the Professor, imagining what he'd say (though strangely he doesn't want to talk about the houses at all: *Would you want to live forever, if you had the choice?* Maybe the sameness of these houses gives Dixie a vision of repetition, eternal repetition. Maybe that's where her mind goes, and why it returns to the Professor and his strange talk of angels and devils). Such a proliferation of square little houses with square little lawns and square little fences. They present a unified front, at least for a while. Dixie dozes in and out of sleep, watching them pass by.

Then comes a time, a few minutes or miles later, when storefronts and houses start merging, start becoming single indivisible units of blocks, block by block, broken by streets and alleys and sometimes greener and grassier boulevards, all with their storefronts and fancier faces turned away from the train tracks. These townlike neighborhoods too disappear, swallowed into a sudden railyard—piles of what seem to be brimstone, still smoking, stacked beams, rust and cinder, ageless water towers and railway sidetracks that appear to lead nowhere but to do so always with the purposeful and gently concrete intent of industry. Then the houses start back up again, one upon the other, older row houses scrabbled together, close to one another, close to the tracks as well, intruding on any remaining open spaces with graffiti, abandonment, decay, saying: *Nothing is permanent. Nothing is forever. There's no point in gambling.*

Dixie isn't worried about this. She feels a bit trapped, a bit hemmed in by the closeness and continuity of the buildings, but she knows this is natural, nothing to fret about. It's what every person coming in from the farm or the ranch, or—like her—from small cities and towns, must feel. She'll get over it soon enough, she's sure. And everything looks so new, so fascinating, and so without regret, that she just can't help herself from springing up, buoyantly, and loading Cyril and Cyril's items on one arm, her handbag on another, to jump down from the train the minute it begins slowing and stopping at its very central-most point: Penn Station.

There, stepping off that train, Dixie is stunned for the first time during this entire crazy adventure. There, for the first time, she is taken aback.

The masses of people debarking, the flow of humanity around her: she had expected her bigger bags in a pile, greeting her, her green-painted brass-bound portmanteau, her suitcases. But they are nowhere to be seen. They are unseeable, even if they are present, as the crowd surges, flows, eddies, and utterly blocks from view everything she might need to find. She expects, or at least has been hoping for, someone kind to be there waiting. She doesn't know who. Not Gary. She knows Gary can't make it. She knows he has a very critical class to attend. But she holds out the image of a rescuer, or at least a guide, someone to show her the way, to teach her. There is no such person. She is utterly alone and confused and overwhelmed, even though she has, or had, a plan. She's used to the crutch of Uncle Paul, always nearby, always ready to give her advice, to coach her, to make her feel okay. She's lost now, even though she knows, somehow—for Cyril's sake and for her own—she'll figure out a way to make things work.

Amid all this, she knows she should be thinking of Gary. She should maybe even be mad or at least annoyed with him that he would prioritize his class, his lecture, his schooling—even as important as that schooling might be to their future plans and their future life together—over the once-in-a-lifetime moment of meeting her on the station platform, holding her after this long first month apart, and being the sort of helpmeet and guardian and teacher she now realizes she would draw comfort in discovering, here in this moment. She should think about Gary in this situation, but she doesn't.

She thinks about the Professor. She tries not to. She tries to push the image of him down and away from the top layer of her mind. But she fails. He's there. She's looking for him in this moment, there on the train platform with Cyril in his bassinet on her arm and her luggage nowhere to be seen.

As Dixie stands there in the midst of her inner turmoil, the crowd on the station platform at last begins to thin and clear. Dixie sticks out a bit, standing there with her baby doll in his bassinet and her small handbag with its uneaten, somewhat rancid sandwiches. The flow of debarking passengers moves decisively in one direction, all of them, or almost all, heading directly down the platform to her right. She turns her head and watches them go. Every third or fourth person among this throng elicits a little jump from her, a little tingle, as some feature of their featurelessness reminds her of a similar facet or fact or incident or manner exhibited by her new friend, her Professor—not a guilty reminder, per se, nothing to cause her any anxiety, nothing to make her worry or feel a sense or suggestion of impurity. All this is just innocent coincidence: someone with a hat cocked at a jaunty angle; another man tall and thin, carrying himself just so, preoccupied while also watchful; a third in a striped suit like the suit and the bow tie she had first seen the Professor, her Professor, wearing, though naturally that man turned out to be lumpier and shorter and worse for the wear after the long trip on the train than ever the Professor would allow himself to appear.

She hasn't seen the Professor since their dinner together.

She's looked for him, certainly. But she hasn't found him again.

She had watched for the flash of a deck of cards. She had checked out the little medical dispensary aboard the train, just in case he might be there replenishing the cotton balls (and maybe also dealing with the underlying disease?) in his ears. She had taken a meal, this time lunch, again in the train cabin just before crossing over the train tracks' pylons above the Hudson River into NYC itself. Even though she was so close then to deboarding, she had decided to get lunch—a quick bite, no more—simply in the hope that she could recreate that meeting, back miles and hours earlier somewhere-between-Illinois-and-Appalachia, the moment in the early evening darkness when she had dined with him (all of which amounted to nothing, nothing at all to feel guilty about, nothing at all to remark on).

Dixie turns her body to follow the last of the passengers to the right, down the platform to what she imagines is the train station terminal (earlier in her imagination she had thought of this station as just a larger version of the one she'd left behind in Pocatello, a big solid brick building with a wooden porch and a waiting area where someone on the train's staff would neatly place and mark her bags and her trunk). Envisioning this, and operating on the premise of it, she turns and takes a few steps, and then hesitates, hearing something behind her.

She spins around.

"Dixie . . ." a voice says.

She looks down the tracks toward the rear of the train, a place where—in her innocence back at the beginning of her adventure— she had expected to see a little red caboose. Now she knows better. No cabooses exist in the world anymore. Not in the real world. Not on the tracks, functional and working. They're just museum things, one of the conductors had told her. Instead every train now ends with a clean break, like a big dog with a shorn tail, or a snake that doesn't taper at its end, an unnatural thing.

Dixie looks in the direction from which she has heard the calling of her name. Again, she hears it, unmistakably so.

"Dixie. Dixie!"

She sees her baggage there, piled on the platform, the unmistakable green trunk. It's not a big pile, but it's hers. She sees this and starts to move toward it, already filled with thoughts on how to move all her things—her baby, her handbags, her suitcase, her trunk. That's what's at the top of her mind. At the bottom, down in whatever mild darkness she possesses, not quite subliminal but at least unknown and unplumbed by her, the register of her own name brings with it a hope and a mystification. *Is it him? Is it the Professor at last, bidding a final farewell to me, pausing in his own journey just to help me with my things?* This thought floats there, in the recess of her mind, not quite formed into words, not quite formed into thoughts, but present as an upwelling, a longing—yes, a guiltless longing that she forces herself to hold down, swallowing it, depressing it beneath the light and free and unrepentant upper, active layers of her thoughts. That's what Dixie feels. She doesn't take ownership of the emotion. She doesn't judge it. She just feels it and tries to ignore it, focusing her mind on the problem of claiming and moving all her material goods, while unbidden beneath it all she imagines and replays and hopes this calling of her name is, after all, the Professor.

"Dixie," the voice says for a third or fourth time. She sees an arm waving in the mirage of the nearer distance. She sees a hand or a handkerchief swooshing forward and backward in front of her pile of baggage. She sees a body, a flattop haircut, white arms, even whiter elbows protruding from a white button-down shirt, the torso of this figure divided head to stomach by a black tie, all of it floating above black pants that seem invisible, at this distance, parked against the dark and grubby concrete of the train platform.

"Right here, Dixie," he says, and Dixie knows who it is: Gary, resolving from the mist of newness and change, metamorphosis and daydream, that has clouded her eyes.

Dixie walks toward him, then picks up her pace, not realizing until right then, right that moment when she sees and recognizes her own husband, how very frightened she had become. She was going to do it. She was going to figure out a way to do it on her own, get all her gear loaded, off the platform, into a taxi or a bus or the subway or whatever. She was going to pay a valet boy or some thug on the street corner to help. She didn't know how, back a moment earlier when she was forming her plan, but she was certain then, and remains certain even now, that she would have found a way. Yet, the relief of Gary's presence jars all of that loose inside her. Now she doesn't need to worry or work or do anything much at all, and as a result the tension of holding it all together drops away from her like a curtain falling at the end of a theater show.

Dixie runs and reaches Gary, who never moves from in front of her baggage, standing stubborn guard over it. She reaches him and collapses against him, setting baby Cyril's bassinet on the platform beside them, letting her handbag fall farther afield, and with a much more drastic thump than she allows her baby doll to experience.

"Oh, Gary," she says, "you came. You came for me. That's so amazing. That's so *nice*. I can hardly tell you how nice it is, how amazing."

She's crying. She's not sure why, but she is. It's the alien again, erupting from within her, erupting through the shell she had made for it in her traveling heart. She realizes it has never left her, but she doesn't care. She's crying and she pours it all out onto the white shoulder of Gary's starchy shirt, burying her head deeply into his armpit, deeply against his stony chest, before he lifts her face up and kisses her forehead (Gary never kisses her lips, not in public, but this time is a treat, he seems to say, a treat that he kisses her at all, right in public like that).

"You came for me," she says again.

"Of course," he says. "I was just keeping it a surprise for you. I'd never let you try to find your way from here all the whole darn distance to Columbia without me, not on your life I wouldn't."

He's confident. He's collected. He's cool. He's real.

All these things she admires, she knows. She can feel it, even right then.

But he's also about one inch deep. Just like a bad mystery where you know the hero and the villain right up front and never even dream that the story might surprise you. That's Gary. She knows it and she's fine with it. It's nothing to worry about. It's normal and okay and perfect and they're together as a family—far, far from Idaho, but together all the same.

Dixie tries to pull him closer then. She tries to pull Gary's face down to her and to kiss him on the lips in utterly stunned gratitude. She doesn't know it but deep down she wants to reproduce that feeling of equality, even of one-upsmanship, of dominance, brief dominance, that she had known in the train-braking kiss she'd delivered onto the mouth, into the mouth, of her Professor. But she is unable to create either the moment or the necessary impetuous motion. Gary resists her. She realizes the moment is gone and might never return. Yet, right then, right then as Gary rescues her on her first foray into Manhattan, she isn't able to connect the two emotions, or disconnect them from each other. She doesn't understand her own hunger, or the void that her hunger seeks to plug. All she knows in that moment is that Gary pulls away, nicely, matter-of-factly, moving away from her simply so that he might wave and whistle down the long promenade of carved iron columns that hold up the half roof of the platform.

"Porter!" he yells, swirling his hand in the air and then pointing at the mass of Dixie's luggage.

A look of satisfaction fills his face as a maroon-uniformed black man begins walking toward them from a few dozen yards down the track. Dixie hadn't noticed this man, standing in an alcove against the concrete-and-tile bulwark of the station wall. She wouldn't have known to whistle for him. She wouldn't have known to swirl her arm in the air.

"See, that's how it's done," Gary says.

"Yes," she replies, squeezing his arm as a second rush of thankfulness floods into her.

She loves this feeling. She loves the planning and the risk and the calculation Gary must have made, weighing her arrival against his schoolwork. Still, she feels an undefined sort of regret at the porter's approach. She feels like she has been robbed of something, robbed of experiencing the arrival on her own terms, robbed or saved from maybe making a mistake, and robbed of having to learn a thing or two on her own. She feels like she's moved from Uncle Paul's tutelage, from being Uncle Paul's secret student, to being Gary's possession, Gary's thing to take care of, Gary's child.

Gary seems to understand this. Dixie's not sure how. But as the porter approaches them, he takes her face in both of his hands and turns it up to him.

"I'm here to take care of you," he says, almost laughing at the thought of it (even though the statement is probably the exact wrong thing to say to Dixie, at this particular moment of her life). "I'm here to take care of you, and you don't need to worry about anything anymore. You don't need to worry about anything at all."

"Nothing?" Dixie asks.

"Nothing," he says. "I've got you."

Then, without kissing her at all, he turns, takes one of Dixie's suitcases from the ground between them, and strides down the platform with the porter towing Dixie's portmanteau on a cart behind him.

It leaves Dixie with both her handbag and Cyril's bassinet. As well as with a weird thought in her mind: *He never asked how the trip went for me. He never asked about Cyril either.*

And this, as she picks up the bassinet and carries it in the crook of her arm, makes Cyril seem heavier than before.

Part II
Arrival under Fire

CHAPTER 5

Time in the city, at least as Dixie experiences it, does not flow.

It jerks forward and then seems to swoon, slipping past with an unexpected easiness, so that between the two extremes of timelessness and trauma life vacillates, a composition not unlike the motionless motion and sudden stops that jolted Dixie during her train journey. Dixie's first weeks should be more of that herky-jerky, explosive cadence, what with everything new and fresh and experiential. But they are not. They are the slowness. They are the timeless hypnagogy of the rails.

What does she remember most from this late summer arrival in 1960?

Cyril, certainly. The rhythms of him, nurturing him and being a new mother. Holding him close to her. Taking care of him. Taking him with her everywhere. These come naturally enough to Dixie, but they require adjustment from Pocatello to New York. For one, Dixie's mother is not present—which means all the child-rearing magic a grandmother brings to bear, all the matriarchal collective memory, the hints and advice and the precious moments when a grandmother provides relief by taking the baby, even for an hour or two, all of that is absent, or at least removed to the degree of an expensive and therefore infrequent long-distance call. Neither is

Gary around to share the duties or provide much relief, not until late in the evening most nights when he's already too tired and needs care and rest and quiet to study his schoolwork, write his papers— just as much care and attention, it seems, as Cyril needs during the day. He's not only going to his classes but also working, with the university having helped him secure a job floating up and down the harbors and waterways of the city, performing seismic soundings and dredging soil samples to see what's beneath the whitecaps and the sludge: Is it dredge-able? How far beneath does bedrock begin? Are there old footings and pilings? It's work that pays moderately well, for a part-time position, and it fits within and augments his degree program. He's not just taking any old engineering degree, he says—it's not simple like it was for Dixie's father, basic engineering enough to get a good job somewhere. Instead he's embarked on highly specialized training that will make him into an actual, technical, scientific *geophysicist*. It sounds great, a big word. Gary pronounces it carefully whenever he says it. And he promises it will result in the security of a good job, a company job, maybe one that will let them all—Dixie and Cyril and all the other children they plan to have—travel to exotic places, mountain ranges and swamplands and, especially, oil fields where there'll be plenty of money to make as they help build the future of the petrochemical world. This future sounds convincing to Dixie, continues to sound just as convincing as it did when they were making decisions together back in Pocatello, but the offshoot is that Gary spends all his time on campus or on a barge with his instruments and meters. When he returns home in the evenings, he eats, studies, and sleeps. Though Dixie encourages him to hold Cyril, he rarely does.

New York moves by in fits and starts, and these first few weeks for Dixie stand out in her memory not at all. There's nothing much to worry about, nothing threatening once Dixie gets used to the number of people, the unfathomable but frantic purposes toward which they each stride, rarely raising their heads to look at one another, rarely acknowledging much of anything, other than their own decided paths and imputed progress.

Of this time, she does recall a particular trip—not the first, but one of the first half dozen or so such trips, soon to be routine—which leads her to the grocery-deli around the corner from the apartment Gary has rented. It's a one-bedroom apartment, really not much more than a studio room, a single window, a little kitchenette, one lightbulb in the ceiling (and a couple hooded lamps Dixie buys with the last of her personal savings, so that she doesn't have to sit with Cyril beneath that single glaring bulb all day and all night). Gary earns enough from his part-time internship to keep them in their flat, and to let them budget their meals for the week. Dixie takes some of that small budget, sometime during the first or second week after her arrival, just when monotony seems to be setting in, and she goes with Cyril to the deli to see what she might find for their dinner.

Though she has been in this deli before, and in a few others up and down the nearer blocks of their neighborhood, the prices still shock her. Likewise, the selection also shocks her. She can get Chinese spices. She can get all the fruits and vegetables and grains and cheeses, especially if she arrives early enough in the day. The cost means that she only ever buys half what she expects to need, not nearly enough to make a full week of meals. It just doesn't feel right to spend more, not at any one time. And, as an added benefit, the repeated trips give her a reason to venture out into the world rather than sit at home, or go for random walks in Morningside Park, along the edge of the Columbia campus area where Gary has, with good reason of course, decided they should live.

This particular day, Dixie gets in line after having selected her produce, her dry goods, her meal-making necessities. Three or four ladies have queued ahead of her, and three or four quickly fill in behind, so that the whole little aisle between the canned food and the up-slanting bins of fruits and vegetables seems to be docked with waiting women, each of them holding a basket full of their various requirements, half of them, or more, also with a baby on their hips, or a toddler holding a hand. In this tableau Dixie blends perfectly, though she realizes her clothes have a rough edge and a homespun feel to them that the women do their best not to notice, or glance at more than once. Dixie is a nonentity to them, and she's fine with that. None of them bother to say anything to her. None of them bother to strike up a conversation. They are all preoccupied. Even when their toddlers try to make eye contact or mumble baby-words, the mothers shush them back into line, back into harried silence.

All of these women in the store are white, all of them except the woman right in front of Dixie. Dixie hardly pays this any attention. The number of white people in any given line has never before been a thing she has spent much time mulling over or has ever needed to think about overmuch. She does notice how the woman to her front has smoky brown skin, dark brown hair too, curled beneath a flowered bonnet, but she looks at the woman with appreciation and a mild bit of curiosity. Dixie knows a few Indian women from the reservations near Pocatello, but this woman is different, and as she stands in line Dixie notices a fluidity in her movement, even in such simple things as standing still, the shifting of her weight from one foot to the other, that makes Dixie think of dancing.

The line moves fairly quickly, with the cashier eyeing up the goods held out in the baskets of the first two women. These women nod their heads, smiling at the grocer, batting their lashes a bit, and saying, "Yes, Frank, credit today, please."

"Credit it is, Darlene."

Same with the second: "Credit for sure, Georgette."

"Just send your Thomas around. Just send your William."

This is the pattern.

Easy as that. Dixie knows how it works. She's done similar back in Pocatello. She knows the grocer there, knows him personally, a cousin of her mother's. She knows the baker too, the butcher, the milkman, the handyman, and she recalls all of their faces as if merged together into a police lineup: the cast and crew of Pocatello shopkeepers. Dixie feels, at least up until this very moment, that the rules in Manhattan might not turn out to be much different. The grocer knows you, or learns to know you. The grocer takes your word, and the word of your husband, to settle up charges on a given schedule, weekly or according to whatever arrangement you agree upon. The system makes things simpler and faster than always paying cash. No need to worry about anything, anything at all, once it's in the hands of the men.

Dixie hasn't reached that point of familiarity yet, but she knows she will. Today she has cash enough with her, and she starts to get it ready, setting Cyril and her basket of groceries down on the floor, opening her purse.

The third woman in line, the dusky brown one with the dancing fluidity, presents her basket to Frank, even as Dixie feels a little flush of anxiety about fumbling in her purse. All this happens so quickly for everyone else. Dixie doesn't want to be the one to slow down the line. She doesn't want to be the one who trips up the system and makes the ladies waiting in the canned food aisle behind her experience any sort of delay.

The dancing movements of the woman in front of Dixie suddenly stiffen up though, as she places her basket in front of Frank.

"Cash," he says.

"I have it," she says.

"Of course, Mercedes. But I have to say it."

"I know."

Frank doesn't look at Mercedes as he removes each item, one by one, from her basket and lays them out on the counter beside his till. Unlike the quick glance into each basket that had been enough for the previous two women, he weighs the items and totals up the ounces and pounds. He does a bit of math on a sheet of butcher's paper, and he shows her a number scribbled out in sum. Mercedes—who does not have a baby or a toddler—says nothing, but Dixie sees the muscles under her jawline tighten. She opens her purse and starts to dig in it.

Frank's grocery is cramped. The line has grown longer. Dixie hears grumbling behind her and feels the warmth of shared embarrassment, shared suffering spreading over her: too many bodies in too near a proximity with one another. That and the pack-animal mentality of the line, which beckons Dixie to join it. This mentality seems to throb, to envelop the whole store. Even Frank, who has been pleasant enough, grows a bit anxious, looking up from his register to the line of ladies, all of them in frilly long-sleeved dresses, all of them seeming now to stand on tiptoe in order that they might watch Mercedes ahead of them in line.

"I don't have it," Mercedes says.

"You'll have to put something back then."

"Hurry up," says one of the ladies, anonymously far back in the line. The words come out just loudly enough so that they aren't a whisper. They are meant to be heard, maybe not by Mercedes, but definitely by the others in line.

Mercedes pauses, sizing up the things on the counter to her front. Dixie notices that all the items are very basic. There are no frivolities, not even any fruit. It's beans, flour, lard, and a little package of the grubbiest, grayest meat, a package Dixie had seen earlier while she searched for hamburger. The sight of it had turned her stomach and had almost led her to leave Frank's store to journey down the street a bit farther to the next shopkeeper.

As Mercedes pushes the package of graying meat to the side, another of the ladies in line speaks up: "Step aside."

And another says, "Don't delay us."

And yet another: "Make a decision."

Dixie feels Mercedes's anger as she sees her back stiffen. It's like a ballerina striking a pose ahead of the full orchestral chord. It's full of anticipation and forcible self-control. It's not a response, not yet, but it's preparatory.

The lady right behind Dixie, perhaps accidentally, perhaps not, nudges Dixie in the back.

Dixie tries to ignore it.

The nudge happens again, this time more pointedly.

Dixie does nothing.

Dixie doesn't want to join in. She feels the energy of the pack, but she doesn't want to be part of it. It's an anonymous and decidedly cruel energy, and Dixie wants neither of those things, not the cruelness—that's no part of her nature—and certainly not the anonymity. She craves just the opposite, not so much notoriety as true connection. Not so much fame as intimacy. What's more: Dixie's back has been hurting for a bit, since the train ride, or earlier. It's a funny thing, and it makes her wonder whether she's pulled a muscle. Or whether her monthly is going to come early or something. That's the sort of nudge this is, a poke directed from woman to woman, right in the tenderness of the lower back where it can't be ignored.

Dixie braces for another nudge, another call to join the group of white ladies, white and almost howling ladies. But instead, reaching right over Dixie, right over her shoulder, the woman behind Dixie taps Mercedes on the top of her bonneted head. "You heard us, don't pretend you haven't. Step aside if you can't pay."

"I'm done," Mercedes says. "I can pay."

"You've taken too long."

The woman, still oddly reaching over Dixie, right over her and almost through her, tries to take a firmer grip of Mercedes, scrabbling at Mercedes's head, her hair. Failing to find purchase, she pushes Mercedes down and away from the counter. Mercedes ducks, swivels her hips, but tries to stay facing Frank's counter, unwilling to directly confront the score of women behind her.

Dixie though, Dixie turns. She turns right around, making a decision without even knowing she has done so. If Mercedes won't face them, Dixie will. She can't hold her tongue, though something inside her says it might be wiser to do so.

She turns, steps sideways just a little so that she blocks the aisle more completely, putting herself between the dark-skinned dancer lady and the woman who has reached over and done the shoving. What's more, Dixie picks up Cyril again and holds his bassinet in front of her like a shield or like a grail, and the sight of the child there with his glassy, unconcerned eyes, his glassy, unconcerned smile—the avatar of all their efforts and longing, their purpose as housewives in this world of men—makes the collection of women in line draw back as if they are indeed confronting a sacred relic.

"Hi," Dixie says, smiling, trying to defuse things, trying to break the ice, doing exactly what she might do if a fight had broken out beside a saloon or in a church parking lot in Pocatello. "Hi," she says, "I'm Dixie Jane . . ."

"I don't care who you are," says the first of the women in line, not even looking at Dixie, not even returning Dixie's smile.

"No, no, you don't," Dixie says. "I can tell you don't. But you should."

Dixie worries about the wolf pack of women behind her, all of them looking at her, looking at Mercedes. She feels Mercedes behind her, not cowering but also not stepping up to join her. This doesn't bother Dixie, but it does make somewhat easier her decision regarding what to do next.

She turns around, with a bit of a flourish, mostly to give the women in the canned-food aisle the shoulder, but also to look Frank squarely in the eye.

"My name's Dixie," Dixie says again.

"I heard," says Frank, with classic Manhattan directness.

Dixie likes that. She feels like she and Frank might be able to get along, even though he's treating his customers differently from one another.

"Great," she says. "You're Frank, right? This your grocery, right?"

The man nods.

"Okay, Frank. I'm buying Mercedes's groceries for her. Except for this meat. Take this meat and throw it away. We'll buy the hamburger I chose instead. Please let me know how much."

Dixie sets her own basket to one side, taking the hamburger from it. She steps forward to the counter, brushing Mercedes's handful of two or three bills and her accompanying small pile of coins back over the surface of the counter a few inches in Mercedes's direction, pushing them aside. She puts her purse right in the middle of the space she has cleared and she makes herself big, squaring herself to Frank and giving the women behind her the full silence and immovable confidence of her pioneer-strong shoulders. (Dixie, of course, is the daughter of an engineer and a schoolteacher—Arlo and Gladys—and it's not from them she gets this abrasive edge. She probably doesn't realize it, not right then, but this is pure Paul, her "uncle," his energy, a part of her upbringing she'd rather not think she possesses. Even though she doesn't know what it is or where it has emerged from, she finds this edginess thrilling, as if she has exploded in place in the very center of New York, even though she's nowhere near the city's center.) It feels incongruous in the extreme, but it is anything but that. It's really, deep down, the first sign that she belongs here, belongs to the city. It's not that she's rude. It's that she's alive and in the fight.

She has enough money for the purchase, but only just enough.

When Frank takes the handful of dollars from her, and counts it, and gives her change in return, he leans forward and says, "That was swell of you, Ms. Dixie. Just come back in half an hour or so and I'll give you your basketful. On the house."

"Thanks, Frank," Dixie says.

"No, all the thanks should be for you," Mercedes says, taking the bag of groceries from Dixie. "Will you come to our house for dinner then? We will share this as dinner for both our families."

Dixie is glad about this. She hasn't made a friend in New York yet, but she thinks that Mercedes will become one. It's early still. It's too soon to tell. But as she walks out of the store with Mercedes beside her, leaving the crowded aisle of nonplussed white women behind them, they discover that they are headed the same way down the street together. More than that, they realize they live in buildings only a few doors down from each other, shouting distance.

"Neighbors," Mercedes says.

"Neighbors," Dixie answers, and she holds out her hand, fingers together, the same knife-edge as she remembers using so effectively with her Professor. Dixie knows what it means, the secret symbol of it for herself. She knows it is not just a formality. The gesture has taken on extra meaning. Mercedes is unsure though. She looks at the offered hand a little suspiciously, but then succumbs to Dixie's directness, Dixie's good cheer, Dixie's forcefulness, and decides to shake, offering little pressure, little firmness, but a definite grace and languor that fills Dixie with enchantment of a feminine sort she hasn't before encountered.

"That feels good," Dixie says, meaning not just the conclusion of their handshake but also the bit of electricity between them.

"Just like a man does," says Mercedes.

"Just like it, yes. Where I'm from, we do it sometimes. Men or women."

"Out west?"

"How do you know?"

"You sound like a cowboy, from the movies. Like a girl cowboy."

"I guess that's true enough," Dixie replies, seeing herself suddenly anew, like she is bigger and maybe a bit more mythical than she has thought, something more than just a lost little girl come to the big city, someone more than just Uncle Paul's pet project.

Mercedes waits for a second, then—not releasing her grip on Dixie's hand—pulls Dixie a bit closer and into a hug. Mercedes's body is curvy, warm, and pliable. She molds herself against Dixie even as Dixie straightens in the embrace. "Also, we should do as women do. We can do both. Hug and shake."

"We can. And should."

"Amen."

"Amen indeed."

The evening sky has flushed pink around them by then, lighting up the undersides of the trees so that their organic nature glows against the otherwise concrete and bricked-in angular channel of the street. The street has filled with the late summer warmth that comes in the evening, not so much from the sun itself but from the way the concrete remembers the sun, releasing stored radiance and stories of the day back into the air. Above this, a decided coolness wafts in from the water, down the canyons of the streets, and Dixie and Mercedes feel the contrast between the pavement's hoarded warmth and the air's freshness, a feeling that lightens the footfalls and the moods of all those who pass by them, baskets or briefcases in hand, people flowing, cars flowing past. Dixie does not feel or even very much hear the noise of the city, not right then, not as much as she had been feeling or hearing it in the past weeks. The noise of the city has been swallowed in the moment, and it feels nice for her to realize that it fades, that it is not omnipresent, not forever, not always there, not always an aggravation. Dixie does not need to put cotton in her ears.

"I'm serious about dinner," Mercedes says. "You will come here, tonight, with your husband"—Mercedes looks down at the bassinet then—"and your, uhh, baby, and we will have dinner together. This is just a temporary place for us while my, while my . . . spouse . . . goes to school."

Not noticing Mercedes's hesitation, Dixie says, "Yours too? Which school?"

"Columbia."

"Wow. They are going together then."

"That's amazing, maybe they will like each other as much as you and I seem to like each other."

"Maybe," Dixie says, feeling strangely good about the idea already. She thinks it should be an easy enough thing, with Gary so matter-of-fact he will certainly see the benefit of a friend, a set of friends, for both of them. But she's not so sure about his reaction to them, not as sure as she would have been before the encounter in Frank's grocery. The women in line have thrown her off. Their reaction to and treatment of Mercedes have thrown her off. Dixie has seen discrimination before, but mostly between white men and Indians who come in off the reservation to visit and debauch Pocatello's bars and stores. Dixie had chalked up the ill will and vitriol in Pocatello to a righteous reaction to drunkenness, to disorder, and to the tales of cowboys and Indians she'd been fed her whole life. Mercedes, with her flowing movements and her quietness, her perseverance and her very spare basket of groceries, does not seem the same. Yet, Dixie sees that she is treated the same. Without putting words to it, Dixie knows it has nothing to do with Mercedes as a person, and everything to do with the beautiful dusky brown color of Mercedes's skin. Dixie knows this, even though she can't quite put it into context.

Dixie would not have hesitated at all, without the encounter at Frank's grocery, but she realizes, right then, that she doesn't know how Gary feels about these things. Is he more like the ladies behind them in line? Or will he be practical and good-natured and do what the Bible says, in terms of loving everyone and especially neighbors, even if they are like Mercedes and Mercedes's husband, people of a somewhat different race? Dixie doesn't know.

Mercedes sees Dixie's hesitation. She cocks her head to the side a little and then says, "What I was saying about dinner, or what I meant to say, was that it'll be fine and nice if you come to dinner here, tonight, at our place in this neighborhood, but that I'd really rather invite you to our true home over in Park Slope. That's Brooklyn, across the river. Still part of New York, but a very different part. It's got more, umm, flavor to it. It's got more flavor and more of the spirit of us, me and my Gabriel. You'll love Gabriel. We will all meet. Dinner tonight, here, then? And dinner soon after in Brooklyn with the rest of the family?"

"Yes," Dixie says. "But only if you let us host you for dinner too, to repay the kindness."

They hug again. A quicker hug, a hug that is less the sealing of the start of their friendship and more a simple, temporary "goodbye until later." They have passed from strangers to friends, just like that, and have done so without the jolt of a braking train, without the jolt of an unexpected kiss. Dixie likes this. She feels the parallelism in it. She doesn't compare the Professor and Mercedes directly to each other, but she acknowledges the echo of experience that has reared its head, and she likes Mercedes even more because of that resonance.

Cyril's awake and has been watching all of this conversation. He's a quiet child. He never makes little burbling noises that seem to distract other parents, other moms. Sometimes Dixie wishes that he did. Sometimes she wishes that he would be a little more present. But his watchfulness, his quietude, nevertheless add to her burgeoning sense of confidence and clarity.

God forbid someone says something bad about Cyril today, she says to herself. *I just about took that lady's head off in the deli. And over what? An unpaid bill. God forbid someone were to really try to get under my skin. They wouldn't know what hit them!*

This idea fills Dixie up, so much so that she skips with it, empty-handed in terms of her grocery list, but filled with both the presence of Cyril and that of her new friend, Mercedes. It's a lovely feeling. A lovely day. The dirtiness of the street alongside her, the tipped-over trash cans, the occasional graffiti, the rust in the trusses of the row houses, their fence-stairs scaled with peeling black paint, all of this is gilded both in the sunset's warm colors and in the warmth of Dixie's rising emotion.

Dixie is so filled by all of this, in fact, that she doesn't notice the streak of smoke that shoots through the sky to her front, a slow-motion fireball that seems to split in two: one part diving downward, the other changed, slowed, but seeming to skip and jerk forward from west to east right over the horizon.

Above the ruckus of the New York evening, Dixie neither sees nor hears any of this. The crack and thump of the distant explosion goes unnoticed by her: only a better-tuned Manhattan listener, one who has learned to completely disregard all elevator noises, all jackhammers near and far, all braking trucks and honking horns, one who has trained his ear, or her ear, to only notice *difference*, only that person would hear it, and hear it they would, never forgetting.

Because New York, for all its indifference, loves trauma.

The two parts of this fireball cross the Manhattan skyline, contrails of smoke and debris indeed representing trauma for the city, an episode that makes time—heretofore placid and gliding along its rails—jump forward in a crystallization, a lurch, a definite oscillation of the atomic state, the quantum state. It makes everything, for all who were there, coalesce into a moment of known spin and direction, a time when everyone can identify where they were and what they were doing.

Dixie hasn't heard it. She hasn't trained herself (yet) to take notice. But most of New York does, most of the natives. Mercedes, a block away already, notices, and stops, and then runs the rest of her way home.

None of this breaks in on Dixie's consciousness. Instead she continues her walk home, her glide up the stairs to the flat she and Gary share, all the while with the knife-edge of trauma nearer than she knows. She scales the three short flights to her studio. Something is happening inside her, even as the trauma draws nearer through the outside world. Dixie enjoys a few more hours alone with the sense of "something happening," trying to put a word to it, a label to it, as she nurses Cyril and waits for Gary to come home, waits to ask Gary about whether, a bit later, he'd like to dine with her new friends, their new friends, Mercedes and her husband who goes to Columbia.

CHAPTER 6

Gary arrives.

The intervening hours creep by for Dixie. She doesn't mind. It's quiet. It's slow. It revolves around Cyril, who has had a bad case of hiccoughs all evening, perhaps something transmitted to him in Dixie's breast milk that he doesn't find easy on his digestion. Dixie has enough time and more to mentally catalogue everything she has eaten during the past day, just to give her a sense of what, if anything, could have caused the hiccoughs. She does this, focusing, while only intermittently letting her thoughts return to Mercedes, and by extension, to the Professor: friends, new friends.

When she hears Gary's footsteps outside in the apartment building stairwell, with louder and more direct steps confirming that he approaches through the little enclosed space of the hallway outside, she stiffens, stands up, and moves to the door. Gary opens the door to find Dixie right in front of him, right there blocking his way. She doesn't mean to be so up front, but today has been a day of body language, of positioning herself, and it continues, unbidden, as she greets her husband.

She's made him a seltzer water, on ice, his favorite. And she points it out beside his chair in the corner of the apartment. He doesn't drink, so it's seltzer she makes him, with a slice of lemon.

Cyril goes a little limp, a little cowed, a little uncertain, as Dixie hands him to Gary.

She eases Gary into his sitting chair, his spot in the windowed corner of the apartment where he has piled his books and his lined scientific graphing paper, his charts, and his bits of disassembled instrumentation, things he has brought home from the surveying job (which he doesn't have to work that night, Dixie knows) and also from the geophysical lab at Columbia, mostly keeping them and working on them because he loves tinkering with and understanding mechanical objects. If he has a hobby, beyond the duties of schoolwork and homelife and his seismic surveying of the harbor, his tinkering would be it. He even has a special set of glasses and a special set of tiny screwdrivers, the glasses affixed with a gemologist's loupe to magnify small wires and soldering, the screwdrivers to take apart, wedge, pry, knock, twist, and reassemble various items in this collection.

Dixie eases him into this chair.

She takes his shoes off.

She fancies up his seltzer, squeezing the lemon and then taking away the rind.

One of his eyebrows has arched. He seems aware that something is definitely afoot, but he hasn't said much of anything. Certainly, he hasn't asked Dixie what she's hankering after.

Dixie, for her part, checks the clock once or twice, trying to remember whether she and Mercedes had agreed upon a time for dinner. It's late, but not too late. The sky outside the lone window shows black, what sky they can see through the wedge of space that cuts between their apartment building and the neighboring construction, allowing a slim passage between pipes and hung laundry and the whorls of power lines, out to the world beyond, the western world—an allowance of sunshine late in the day, while early morning brightness shows first through that window as a reflection and a secondhand glow on the east-facing brick wall opposite their little room.

"We are invited to dinner," Dixie says at last.

"Really?" Gary says. His voice has a note of interest and amusement and even hope in it, promising signs. He doesn't look at his books. He doesn't pick up his gemology loupe or any of the scattered electrical components that weigh down his stacks of schoolwork and occupy the windowsill beside the chair. "When?"

"Tonight."

He looks out the window, then at the clock.

"It's eight o'clock."

"Yes."

"Too late."

"They're okay with that," Dixie says, not knowing if it is true. Then she really goes out on a limb, pretty much making things up as she says: "I explained it all to them, how you work late and have classes and—guess what?—he . . ."

"He?"

"I met his wife, but she told me about him. Don't worry."

"Told you what?"

"Wait a second," Dixie says. She takes a deep breath and comes closer to Gary, hoisting Cyril from his arms, nestling the baby against her once again, then lowering herself so that she sits on his lap, on one of his legs. She pins him in the chair, above him but forming herself against him. It isn't exactly fair, and Dixie knows this, using Cyril, and her gentle capture of Cyril, as well as some additional bodily nearness, to soften his mood, to elicit kind responses.

"Wait a second," she says again, "it's easy to explain all this but I was going too fast. I met a woman in the deli, in the line at the grocer's counter, and she and I started a conversation. Turns out her husband goes to Columbia too, and we're neighbors, and she invited us to dinner tonight. That's where the *he* comes from. I don't know him. Haven't met him either. There's nothing to worry about. I just thought you would find it interesting and fun to make social friends with a schoolmate, especially since the wife and I seem likely to become friends."

Dixie leaves out any sort of explanation about Mercedes's inability to pay, the discriminatory reaction she witnessed among the other shoppers, and especially any mention of her new friend's name or her distinguishing color. In fact, Dixie has started to think of Mercedes less in terms of color and instead has labeled and focused on fluidity as the defining characteristic, as if she wore her dancing heart as a sign, a token, right there on that lovely dusky outside layer. This has been there in the second or third deepest combobulation of her mind (under the cataloguing of foods that might make Cyril burp, or hiccough, and the constant wondering about Gary, his workday, his timing, his adventures, his life). It's been sitting there, forming up as a feeling about Mercedes, just like the image of the Professor has formed up, and continues to exist, with its tangles of gambling riverboats, unknowable academia, tall grayness, circus performances from yesterday, retold by Paul, all of it in Paul's voice, Paul's manner, and—not to forget the main thing, the main bit of mystery that clings to that encounter—the possibility of angels. That's a thing in Dixie's mind—angels with cotton balls in their ears. Angels with elephants and clowns and archaeology and Uncle Paul whispering to her in the darkness. Angels that Dixie can't think about, not too clearly, not ever clearly enough. Mercedes is there, real, right next door to her, but has already taken on this glow of being "set apart" or "set aside" much the same way that the Professor has. This makes Dixie more nervous than she should be when discussing things with Gary. It's like she's unveiling a secret part of herself but also like she's only willing to reveal that part under her own, limited and revocable terms.

She doesn't tell Gary any of this. And it works. It keeps things on as superficial a level as Dixie possibly can, given the stakes at play.

"Sounds good enough," Gary says after another, longish look at the clock. "I'm free tonight. You've chosen as good a night as possible, most likely."

"I know."

"And eight o'clock gives us a few minutes at least."

"Just a few."

"Where do they live?"

"Only a few doors away, right on our street here."

With a gulp of dismay Dixie realizes that—just like she hadn't asked about or been told the appropriate time to come for dinner—she hadn't bothered to determine Mercedes's exact apartment. Buildings are big, and that's new to Dixie. Buildings are big and mostly anonymous, especially the one Mercedes went into, probably fifteen or even twenty stories tall, compared to the lower and more manageable five stories of the complex where she and Gary have rented their room.

Dixie bites the side of her cheek in worry. Gary doesn't see.

"We'll do it," he says.

And that's good enough. Good enough for now.

She hugs him, and jumps up, throwing Cyril back into his arms. She's still wearing her day clothes, but she had already earlier in the evening opened her trunk, which she keeps in a corner of the apartment, and now she takes from it the nicest of her dresses, nothing fancy, but nicer than her average daily attire. It's black, with long sleeves. Dixie never wears anything shorter than her elbows—and it boasts a flowy, swishy fringe of green around her ankles and her neckline.

Normal things happen now, forgettable things in the routine of getting ready: Gary growing annoyed that they're late as Dixie puts on her "face," Dixie spilling milk on Gary's shirt as she hands him a bottle for their baby doll so that he has to change it after they at last have gathered themselves together enough to make a few first steps toward exiting their own door.

Fiasco complete, they finally arrive at Mercedes's building. They go in and there, in the foyer, Dixie pauses.

She doesn't know which floor. Even if she did, she still doesn't know which apartment among the several similar apartments it might be on that floor either.

She sees row upon row of names and numbers written on little white plastic tabs, each affixed to the front of a square mail delivery cubby, identifying it for the mailman. Dixie sees this and steals a quick glance at the nearest row, not enough to allow her to decipher whether she sees a Mercedes there—and truly, not many first names are written at all; instead the preference seems to be for the semiofficial P. Howard or J. Amundson or L.L. Dwight. This leaves Dixie at a loss. Not even the name Gabriel does her much good as a full first name, that of the man of the house, for there must be forty different versions of Truman, G. and Showalter, G. and Pogorelski, G. and Dixie has no way of knowing which of them should, in reality, be G & M—Gabriel and Mercedes. No one bothers with the woman's name, or even the woman's initial, at all.

Gary has placed his hands on his hips. He's hungry, most likely, and as a result of both hunger and her actions Dixie can also tell that he's annoyed. This makes her frantic. He's not moving. He's stuck in the center of the foyer, and she's dashing with Cyril in her arms from mailbox to mailbox trying to discern which name might be Gabriel and which, if any, Mercedes. Dixie squats, reads a name, then stands, and through her gritted teeth she smiles at Gary, trying to show him that everything is okay—it'll all be okay, don't worry, honey, don't worry, dear, it'll just be a moment—and then she turns and ducks down and looks once again for names on the next cubby or row of cubbies. Still, no hints appear.

Dixie says a silent prayer, even as Gary speaks over her: "We're half an hour late and don't even know where we're going. Let's just call it quits, whaddya say? Let's go get a sandwich somewhere, huh?"

"You're not mad?"

"Of course not. Why would I be? It's a lot to ask, starting out a dinner the first month we're here. We can take it slower. We'll have other chances."

"Oh, Gary," she says, though still ducking and reading the mailboxes. "You're so good to me. You're too good to me."

Right then a woman comes into the foyer from a stairwell at the back of the lobby area, tucked behind the cranky-sounding elevators that have been moving somewhere mysteriously near them, up and down, a vertical migration caught forever in single, solitary shafts. The woman approaches. At least Dixie thinks it's a woman, right away, instinctually, registering all the subtle animal clues of facial shape, smoothness of skin, fineness of bone; even her stride—though direct—has something womanly to it in the hips and the knees. Yet, the woman wears clothes very similar to Gary's: slacks, shined black shoes, a belt, a collared shirt with a tie. It's dinner attire.

Dixie asks a question, really not angling after anything except information about where her friend might live. She means to say, "Do you happen to know Mercedes?" But all that comes out, instead, is a one-word question, "Mercedes?"

"Yes!" says the woman in the man's clothes, inferring the full question, but answering—and giving off an impression—

76

completely different. She's obviously not Mercedes. She's a white woman, not Hispanic, and although it seems like she might have longish hair, she has for the moment pinned it up and slicked it back in a very commanding way.

Gary casts a meaningful look at Dixie.

Dixie shrugs.

"You must be Gary?" says this woman in slacks and dinner jacket.

"Yes," Gary says. He doesn't move or offer to shake hands. He should. But he doesn't.

The woman pays it no mind. "I'm Gabrielle," she says.

"Not Mercedes?" asks Gary, thoroughly confused.

"No," says the woman in man's clothes.

"But you are Mercedes's *Gabriel?*" asks Dixie, making everything worse rather than better.

"Yes."

"Who we're having dinner with?"

Gary is shaking his head at this point. He takes a step closer to Dixie, but Gabrielle has already beaten him to it. She's nearer to Dixie, and she has positioned herself between Dixie and Gary.

Strangely enough, Gabrielle is also shaking her head "no."

"First of all," she says. "Let's not worry about names, or anything like that." Turning to Gary, she says, "Mercy told me you go to Columbia, Mr. Hawley, and it's nice to meet you. We should talk about that sometime in the future. But for now, I've come down to tell you that we've cancelled dinner. At least dinner here. You've heard what's happened across town today, of course?"

"Heard what?" asks Dixie.

77

"I'm so confused," Gary says. "What's the crash got to do with anything? Who are you?"

"What crash?" asks Dixie, sending him a scolding look that she can't help but also flash in the direction of Gabrielle.

"I thought you knew."

"How could I know anything, stuck all day in that dark little apartment . . ."

"Wait, wait, wait," says Gabrielle, heading off what seems to be the start of a domestic difficulty. "I've got more to say about the crash. It's a big crash—"

"Yes, just like *she* . . ." The word *she* catches in Gary's throat, but Gabrielle nods and smiles and Gary continues, seeming only slightly perturbed. "Just like *he* says, a big crash, Dixie. A whole airliner, two whole airliners—one TWA and one United. They hit each other in the sky and both crashed. Bunch of people dead."

"Not just a bunch of people. Not just any people. They're *our people*," Gabrielle says, passing a hand over her face, which, like a magic eraser, causes the blood to drain away and leave behind a suddenly exhausted imprint. "That's what I'm trying to say. I stayed here, waiting to tell you we need to cancel dinner. Mercy is polite like that. She wouldn't leave you hanging even though I told her it wasn't important, not with everything else going on. But she insisted. Went on her own back to her family to see what she can do. I'm heading there now. That's where the crash was. Mercy's been there all evening. I fear for her, and of course for her family."

Gabrielle turns to leave, but then, as an afterthought, never expecting them to act on it, never expecting how Idahoans might take such an invitation, Gabrielle adds: "You're welcome to come with me, lend a hand . . ."

CHAPTER 7

That's how time jumps ahead, at least in New York City.

Events.

Big happenings.

Trauma.

A hundred or more dead as parts of one plane hit Staten Island, and the other, bigger plane drives a furrow through six buildings in Brooklyn—Park Slope actually, not just some anonymous and unknowable row of blockhouses, but right in the midst of a place filled with people, real people with real lives, real concerns, real joys and sorrows. In this case it's Mercedes's people. Into it all the official and unofficial services of the city rush: First, immediately, the informal networks of neighborly help, unexpected heroes pulling people free from debris, taking not just one but several trips into burning buildings for bodies, living and dead, children and old folks and even dogs and cats gone crazy, biting, scratching, frantic in the heat and suffocating smoke. And then after that, more formally, the official networks: police with their cordon lines, fire trucks, ambulances. There isn't a big delay (as in some neighborhoods), but that gap between crash and arrival of the formal "first" responders, that's where the regular folk step up.

They fill the breach and never leave, their legitimacy a matter of preeminence but also of necessity and willingness. It never even crosses the minds of the police to ask them to leave. Why would it?

The agreement there, between the formal and the informal networks, finds stasis quickly and then does not move much, an unwritten rule: once you're in, you're in. Everything else is out. Everyone else is out, unless they have a pretty damn good reason to cross over the barricades, to come through the police lines, to join.

That's where time changes, inside the cordon, inside the epicenter. The normal day in New York combines frenetic pace with a deceptively easy, morphine-drip slipping away of complete and utter gridlocked busyness. But trauma, near association with trauma, that's what makes time stop, or move into that gear that is sugar-syrup slow, outside the frame, a jerkiness in the continuum that produces minute-by-minute, moment-by-moment brilliance (and after which things sometimes recover in a similarly herky-jerky manner, with different people having different reactions, different needs, to bring them back into normal time after the event). Everyone experiences this at some time or another, unless they keep themselves completely protected from the world. Everyone experiences it, at least in small doses—moments that slow and stick and measure out the memory of a timeline that might be shared, but never duplicated.

This is Dixie's first such experience of New York trauma. She's never before been involved in the sort of exterior chaos where she must, without doubt, lean back and say to herself—*I'm not sure. I'm really not sure if everything will be all right now, now in the moment, or now over the span of the near future, when I, like so many others—like Gary, like Gabrielle, like Mercedes most of all—will have to process and deal with what we have seen and done.* Dixie doesn't know anything about this, but something inside her tells her it will be okay. She doesn't like to think about it, not too deeply, not with all her life having been worry-free up until this point, even her train trip with the Professor.

80

Nothing at all to worry about, there. Nothing to dwell on. She gets flashes of circus-story creeping in, but she puts those aside, telling herself—and meaning it—that she can handle this, she can handle the crash, she can handle the blood and whatever. This evening that should have been a plain, pleasant, sociable dinner with new friends, neighbors, she finds herself, and Gary with her, strangely joining Gabrielle, all of them in their dinner clothes to help where they can with the chaos in Brooklyn. It's touch and go, but Dixie faces up to it and wades in.

How best to describe this?

How best to describe the three of them—Dixie, Gary, and especially little Cyril—right in the middle of it all, pushed to the epicenter by Mercedes's personal connections, Mercedes's family, Gabrielle's relationship forming the bridge that brings them into that inner cordon of the informal and formal responders, a little bit late because of the kindness Mercedes had shown in making Gabrielle wait for them, so politely canceling dinner. Late but there all the same. Two politenesses bring them together: that of Mercedes, afraid to cancel on Dixie, and that of the Idahoans, who don't turn down the request for help.

"We're family," Gabrielle says to the police, "family of the wounded." He forces his way through the flashing lights at the edge of cordon into the area vectored around the crash.

The patrolman looks at Gabrielle, at Gary, Dixie, and especially at little Cyril, and then, with an eyebrow raised—*this is just crazy enough to be true, bringing an infant into a crash site*—he allows them to duck beneath his police line.

We're family, Gabrielle says as a ruse, but quickly this statement becomes nearer to truth than any of them understand. In their focus and their determination, they discard all the blankness and niceties of new friends, all the hesitations, all the formalities. They are informal, close, sweating, stinky, raw, sharing cups of water and even a flask of whisky (Gary's first, almost accidental, swig). They only pause in their efforts to gulp a little time, a few moments here and there of rest, of perspective, of stunned silence, like fish fighting for air at the surface of a barrel.

All of this comes through as a generality though.

All of this comes through in pastiche.

Certain things in the situation cannot be remembered, not clearly enough, never clearly enough, and certain things also cannot be forgotten—memories and moments that will reemerge for them each, vividly unwelcome, throughout many wakeful nights. (Dixie knows what this is like. She's already got a place in her secret heart for such memories, a somewhat sweaty place that smells of elephant spit and old peanut husks and Paul. She knows that she'll put the crash there, in that same place. And she thinks that is where the Professor, and his playing cards, and his talk of angels will also go, if it's not already there, and it'll be normal, good, nothing at all to worry about, nothing traumatic.)

Dixie helps during this time to staff a makeshift first aid room, tending cuts and bruises and worse injuries too, many wounded in shock, some suffering to such a degree that Dixie cannot comprehend the pain. She is one among many, one among a corps of makeshift nurses doing makeshift triage, helping treat the wounded, with all the multitude of them working through the evening, beyond exhaustion, wet with both their own blood and fluids and with the lifeblood and essence, sometimes burnt, sometimes oozing, that spills from and sops into the things (and people) they touch and treat.

Gary on the other hand rolls up his sleeves and enters almost arm in arm with Gabrielle into the thick of it, where fires still burn, returning at intervals to see Dixie, to check on Dixie, to let her know he is doing just fine, chin up, chest out, something of the war hero, the stories he's told of Korea showing in his eyes. His memories of this, and whatever hell it brings back to him, Dixie cannot know, can only imagine. His memories of this have their own circus-secret place in which to hide, to be hidden, but it's a very different place from Dixie's.

Because of their different vantages and the different but complementary ways in which they lend their strength and aid, the event becomes for Dixie and Gary both a shared experience and a partition between them, separate places he has gone and she has not, separate things she has seen and felt and he has not. Gary's memories and efforts are a rush of action. Dixie's action comes in fits and starts, like a severed vein pumping communal lifeblood, while also including a significant measure of endurance, suffering, and empathy. Things like these she recalls offering up from the depths of herself, there in the confines of the first aid room, there within a bubble that Gary does not experience and which he seems never really to try to understand.

The hours of helping and even, later, of cleaning and clearing up after this event has finally passed, the hours of all of this continue right into the middle of the night, right into the morning, until at last they all find themselves sitting together on a curb a few blocks from the crash site. It's a hell of a way to start a friendship.

Mercedes has not said much at all throughout the evening. She's lost a cousin. Four more family members remain missing, feared dead. Incinerated. Existing no more. Gabrielle has been the voice among them, the one talking. It's not anything important she says. In fact, everything Gabrielle says, as they sit there, is meant more to fill the air than to convey particular data, particular opinion. It's her way of making the uncomfortable silence more comfortable.

Dixie feels Gary next to her, throughout this, growing more and more tense. She squeezes his hand, tells him it's all right.

Dixie doesn't care for silence herself, so she sympathizes with Gabrielle. But she also understands her husband, like many

Idahoans. They've got little time for chitchat. They want words to matter. Dixie senses this, and she has a premonition of things going very badly, even before Gary decides to say something. Dixie has this premonition and that's why, with Mercedes withdrawn beside her, she squeezes Gary's hand.

But Gary can take it no longer.

"What are you?" he says, turning to Gabrielle.

They'd been working together, side by side, throughout the whole of the night. They've become, and Gabrielle has even said so much, like something of a family. It's a good thing. Or it could have been. As Gary speaks, Gabrielle—rightly so—appears taken aback by his question. Haven't they bonded? Haven't they gone past this type of question? Is Gary just unable to ask such a thing in any other way?

"What do you mean?" Gabrielle asks.

"I mean, are you a man or a woman?" Gary says, warming up, even putting an edge on his words.

"He doesn't mean that," Dixie says. "He doesn't know what he means. He's tired."

Mercedes stands.

Gabrielle circles around to her, behind them. Both of them standing as Gary and Dixie remain seated on the curb.

"That's just not what he means," Mercedes says. "He has misspoken. He doesn't know what he's asking. He's tired."

Gabrielle: "Mercy, it's all right."

"No. No, it's not." Mercedes is hot now. "I thank you for your help tonight and for the help in the grocery this morning too," she says, "but we don't need to be asked this question."

Gabrielle pulls Mercedes to him.

84

"No," she says, turning to her husband, her lover. "No, it's not all right."

With that, Mercedes pulls herself free of Gabrielle's grip and turns fully away from them, all of them, striding off down the sidewalk in the opposite direction of the crash, the opposite direction of her neighborhood, her family. It's as if she plans to walk all the way back to Morningside Heights, all the way back to their Columbia apartment, even after the night they've had.

Gabrielle shrugs, almost as if to say *sorry,* and then hustles after her. But he turns, and frowns, and shakes his fist at Gary, and Dixie winces, after all that, after the whole night together and the blood and smoke and burning smells. That's what they're left with, an almost comedic shaking of the fist, absurd, borderline otherworldly, a trompe l'oeil. That's what Gary's created for them. One bad question: first friends, up in flames, right at the tail end of perfect exhaustion.

This is a factual detail, this rough landing, this tearing apart of what seemed already to have been forged and solidified. Dixie hadn't thought about it yet. She hadn't processed it. But deep down she felt it and she knew this particular tearing apart would stick with her just like the death and life and the in-between states she had witnessed, in all their forms, these past few hours. She thought about how tenuous and uncertain everything seemed, about how many choices and chance encounters they'd have, here in this city, with people like Gabrielle and Mercedes. Was this the substitute for friendship, this passing in and out of each other's lives? Or was something more permanent soon to emerge?

Dixie thinks about this on the taxi ride back, as Gary sits silently, a bit sulkily beside her.

He even tries to bring it up again, with a trailing-away: "I just wanted to know . . ."

But Dixie ignores him.

The recollected facts of their night transfer from reality to memory only as mere representation, a succubus of the mind, made from mingled sensation and ripped-apart time. Even though the night contains a myriad of big memories, and important moments, even though Dixie is now left to wonder about Mercedes and Gabrielle, and about Gary and his capacity to love and understand, or lack of those capabilities, all these things form a superficial layer in Dixie's mind.

Beneath that, the most impactful occurrence, the most critical moment of all of it—at least for Dixie—is something she dredges up midway through the following morning out of what feels like a combination of her subconscious and her memory. This mingled bit of imaginative memory waits to spring itself into the forefront of her mind until long after she and Gary have made it back to their apartment, long after they have stolen a few minutes of sleep, heaped beside each other, tangled together in their dirty clothes, faces down on the bed that occupies the very center of the small cloister of their little studio.

Cyril starts crying.

Dixie wakes, as always, while Gary does not. Gary never hears him, never wakes for him. *What can Gary do, anyway? He can't nurse the child. What can he do, better for himself, or for us, than recuperate in his own dreams, process his own nightmares, emerge—I hope—normal again? Even though we both still have blood on us, both still have the smell of burning jet fuel in our hair, transferred to our bedsheets, clouding the room, what more can he do?*

Dixie wakes and rises from her bed and goes to pluck Cyril from his crib. On the way though, and only one or two steps from where she slides out of bed, Dixie bends over, her mouth filling with saliva and her head spinning. (She's got the sense of that *more important moment* full upon her, pressing her down, like she's being suffocated beneath a thick blanket. She struggles with that, and with bone-weary tiredness, and with the dizzy end of her own few minutes of sleep.) Cyril has woken. Dixie moves toward him, feeling all these feelings before suddenly and without warning the contents of her stomach heave through her mouth and her nose—and though those contents don't amount to much, since she ate almost nothing the night before, the vomit spreads with an acrid, acidic, bilious exclamation, an amoeba of organic matter, not quite living but still associated with and stinking like the slow decay of life.

Dixie doesn't pay much attention to it. She's been through a lot. She's seen a lot. And she isn't surprised that her body reacts in this way. It doesn't seem particularly important to her, not right then. Cyril is the only thing that matters in this moment, Cyril and the suffocating feeling of that *something heavy* that stays with her from her dream. Dixie goes to Cyril, extracts him from his crib, and then settles herself in Gary's chair, not caring that it is *his* chair, his special chair, his chair with the instruments broken down into bits, carefully arranged, the loupe eyeglass, the little tweezers and screwdrivers and tools, not caring at all. Not caring about anything. In fact, she just leaves her vomit on the floor. She tells herself she can deal with it later, tomorrow, whenever.

As she puts Cyril to her breast and as he starts to nurse, his crying tapers away to a whimper, a moan, and then nothing, nothing more than the rhythmic suck and chuff, the action of his little mouth and his little lungs. Dixie hasn't woken completely. The fog of her dream-state still floats around her, vomit or no. And as the rhythm of Cyril's noises fills her ears and her mind and her spirit, the fullness and thickness of the dream descends around her again, now a waking dream, confusing in its elements of dream-state and reality.

She's there, in this dream, returned to the epicenter of the makeshift first aid room. It's someone's bedroom. Or kitchen. Or both—just a studio like Dixie and Gary's studio. Just a dream that merges facets of kitchen and bedroom, studio and hallway and workshop and walls blown open wide to the wind and the stars. Dixie doesn't know exactly what she is seeing. She doesn't know whether she has returned into a facsimile of true experience or if she now sees a trickier amalgamation of many things, many scenes, many times. She doesn't remember reality too clearly. (Or reality, she thinks, is never really as clear as it pretends to be.) Around her in this dream-state gather all the other volunteers who joined her as nurses, each of them wadding up cotton and putting it in their ears. Dixie does the same, and quickly, for she feels something coming, something bad and noisome and alluring. The silence that descends, after the cotton has been fitted in her ears, provides relief, allowing her some space to maneuver, allowing her only to see, rather than to hear the sibilant, somehow grating sounds of this forthcoming, chaotic dream. There is a sound to it all, but it comes to Dixie like a heartbeat within a heartbeat.

Though Dixie can hear nothing in this dream, the visions she sees are bad enough. The nurses, each of them now protected by wads of cotton, go about their business, tidily, tidily, while around them in the dream-state of this evanescent room all the detritus of their makeshift nursing treatments gathers as well—bandages Dixie and the other volunteers created from torn bedclothes, buckets of water, vinegar for cleaning, bleach, broken bits of lumber from tables they're using to tie and splint legs and arms—all of this covers every surface, stacked up, sliding apart in piles, a glacier of it, a sea, a tectonic mountain. Beneath this move the bodies of the suffering injured, causing the mountains to fracture, the seas of bandages to swirl. Within, Dixie watches burnt and mangled bodies move, like fish in a barrel again, swimming through an ocean made of blood and cleaning fluid and the hot, putrid air of the Brooklyn evening, loaded with smoke and incineration, but also with stars and the swaying leaves of the city street, all seen through the blown-open walls of the building, the transparent walls of the city.

That's when *he* appears.

Her Professor.

He's there, in the midst of it.

He comes in among a fresh batch of the wounded—men and women on stretchers. These are some of the worst, pulled right from the bowels of the exploded building, burnt all up and down their hands, feet, legs, and faces, stinking with the reek of melted hair, moaning, or dead already, limp, and only there for Dixie and the other volunteers to triage, briefly, before finding more sheets to use as winding cloths, hand towels and handkerchiefs to cover their staring eyes. They are Mercedes's relatives. They are, in this dream, Mercedes herself. They have her eyes. They have her hair. They have her smile, where it is recognizable amid the tortured grins and the partial cremation of their ruins. When they move, even in excruciating pain, they move with lovely, dusky, dancer-like grace.

Dixie is looking at Mercedes rendered a hundred times over again, as if in a hall of mirrors, all of her faces accusing her of being white and unknowing and uneducated and newly arrived from somewhere safe and free and without worry. (There's nothing to worry about, nothing at all, Dixie, dear. Everything is fine here. It's just a circus, after all. Just a performance. You'll soon be back home where you belong and where no one needs to know about the sorts of things that happen to girls in the circus, okay?)

He's there, among them, among this multiplicity of Mercedes. He's there, her Professor. Not one of the wounded. He's upright. He's alive, tending them, helping them, just as Gabrielle and Gary are doing. All on his own he has brought this batch of wounded in, Dixie's not sure how, perhaps by magic, perhaps by making them all choose cards so that he might know which among the multitudes are worthy of a Four of Levitation, or an Ace of Disappearance, or whatever spell of movement he needs in order to lift, drag, carry, float, or dissolve and reconstitute them anew, straight from the fire into the Sisyphean care of Dixie's dream-vision volunteers. He's brought Dixie and her crew, with their plugged-up ears, a hundred different versions of Mercedes. Some they can save. Some they cannot.

This is bits and parts of reality, this dream, and all of it has been rearranged, of course. All of it has been scrambled, juxtaposed, made infinitely more confusing and more pleasing.

Dixie dreams this dream with Cyril at her breast and vomit on her floor and all the blinds of her little apartment pulled shut against the indifferent, unending, caring-but-uncaring, blissfully unaware (and inappropriate?) traffic of New York City outside. It is morning out there. It's a morning that Gary sleeps through, a morning Dixie had been sleeping through before Cyril woke her. Sunlight steals around the edges of the blinds, slants through the motes of dust and particles of vomit-stench that fill their little apartment's atmosphere. Dixie dreams this waking dream of her Professor even as she watches the steady presence of these slanting rays, her eyes wide open, like a mummy, or a queen wearing a mask at a coronation.

Hers is a death mask, a mask she uses to condemn her own choices, burying them deeply, pushing them down, away, down, away, so that they never will be anything to worry about. (Nothing has happened. Nothing worth worrying about at all. The show must go on, with its noise and lights and acrobatics. You'll put on your show face and no one will ever know the difference, will they, Dixie dear?)

Dixie watches this dream unfold.

Even as she knows the dream is made from bits of reality, she watches it unfold and then fold back on itself, changing, revealing new truths and new deceptions. She can handle it like that. The dreamscape gives her just enough space to maneuver herself, just enough separation.

It's a dream.

But it's also a memory.

It's a memory that her mind has destroyed and rebuilt, and—in that remaking—it has exposed a truth raw and pure: *he was there*. She knows it. She *saw* him, *sees* him. Her Professor was there amid the chaos. Among the things she could not see, right then, among the things she could not know, could not allow herself to dwell on and understand, right in that moment, he was *there.*

Dixie knows this. But she can do nothing. Not at this moment. Not at all, really, now that the incident has passed and remains only a memory for her to examine, looking backward through the lens of time and dream.

She can do nothing at this moment because she's in her bubble again, the closest, darkest, deepest, most troubling bubble of all— baby holding her down, Gary holding her down, vomit and closed blinds and the infinitely perilous nearness of the four walls of her studio apartment all holding her down, holding her in, the memory of the circus and of Uncle Paul always close at hand, threatening to emerge.

She can do nothing. Nothing except recite to herself the same mantra that helped her the last time she felt this sense of suppression. It's her only resort. It's her only salvation. And so she repeats these words, over and over, under her breath, until Cyril again decides to sleep. She repeats this mantra, quietly enough that Gary will not wake, but loudly enough that she hears it not just in her mind but also in her ears:

There's nothing to worry about. Nothing to dwell on. Nothing to harbor in your heart or in your mind. There's nothing to worry about. Nothing to dwell on. Nothing to harbor in your heart or in your mind. There's nothing to worry about. Nothing to dwell on. Nothing to harbor in your heart or in your mind.

All is okay, Dixie. All will be okay. All is okay. There's no need to repent. There's no need to be sorry. You've done nothing wrong. It was just a game, just a story he made up about elephants and clowns and acrobats and peanuts. There's nothing to worry about.

Nothing worth worrying over. Nothing to harbor in your heart or in your mind. The bodies you see are nothing. The vomit on the floor is nothing. The Professor, even if he was *there*, is nothing. Nothing worth worrying about. You're safe now with Gary. Safe with boring old Gary. Safe and far away from Pocatello.

Part III
Is It Ever Uncreated?

CHAPTER 8

Here's the thing.

The dream contains something else too, as real (or unreal) as the appearance of her Professor in the middle of that air crash chaos.

Sex.

It contains sex.

A lot of sex.

Sex of the sort a good girl like Dixie has been raised to avoid, to not think about, to never crave. Unbidden, uninvited, churned up from the depths of her body and her being amid the outwash, literally the upchuck, of all this emotion and memory, she experiences sex in profusion, in bombardment, in a moment that almost becomes a totality, an all-at-once overpowering event, happening everywhere, but also concentrated right on her and her alone during this crossover between her dream-state and her closeted, new-mother, vomit-stench reality.

Dixie has of course had sex before. Cyril was not an immaculate conception. But he had come along quickly, almost too quickly, so that the act of lovemaking had never become much more than a duty before her little nineteen-year-old belly swelled with him and the whole process got awkward and Gary stopped bothering her for it, content to watch her, and Cyril inside her, grow big and healthy. Dixie went to her marriage bed almost as pure as the driven snow (she'd done some "things" with Gary but had never done "it"). She didn't ask him if he also came into their marriage a virgin, but she assumed Korea, or college, or Gary's half decade of extra years, not to mention his half lifetime of additional experience, probably meant he had "done it" before. Dixie didn't really care. She doesn't dwell on made-up grudges over who might have been someone's first love, or first partner. She doesn't dwell on this and she doesn't expect him to have been an angel, only a man. When she does think about it she hopes it was beautiful for him, or at least fulfilling, whether it was indeed a first experience for him on their wedding night or if it happened some other time, some other place. She hopes it was beautiful and good and fulfilling for him; it wasn't for her.

When they had sex, that night when they got married, she took off the long train of her white dress, gauzy, an old thing handed down from Dixie's great-aunt Margaret, rumored to have been made of fabric that traveled across the prairie and into Idaho in a trunk belonging to Great Auntie Margaret's father's first wife. She folded this train up and placed it in a corner of the hotel room they had splurged on for their honeymoon. Then Gary undid the bindings of the corset that held her upper garments together. She remembers hoping, as his fingers fumbled with the cords and strings along her lower back and sides, that he might touch her skin, run his fingers up and down her rib cage as he gentled the corset away, that he might explore her legs, keep her standing there as he touched the outside, the inside, felt his way up along her knee, her thigh. She remembers the room being cold. She remembers a painful tightness in her chest, a prick of puckering first in one nipple, then the other.

She remembers a clown standing in the corner of the room, but she blinks really quickly then, and shakes her head, and it is gone, that clown-mirage, even before Gary finishes undressing her.

"Lay down," Gary says, without any of the touching she had imagined or hoped for.

Dixie does what he asks, stepping over to the bed backward and sideways so that she never takes her eyes off him (or off the corner of the room where the clown with Uncle Paul's face had appeared). He's shirtless already, his tuxedo folded on a chair, and this is nice. This is something Dixie can, and will, grow to like: his skin white like her discarded dress but well-muscled too, strong and puritanical, reminding Dixie of vinegar and bottlebrushes where his man scent collects in the hair of his chest.

She keeps her legs together as she lowers herself backward onto the sheets. She does this slowly, trying to project an image of seduction she thinks might be necessary, or at least appropriate, for the moment.

She only makes it halfway onto the bed.

She means to lever herself backward a bit, scooch herself more completely onto the top of the duvet cover, closer toward the center of the bed. She means to get more comfortable, to position herself among the few pillows that have been propped against the curving gray-painted iron headboard.

But Gary can't wait.

He steps to her, right up to her knees where they remain hooked against the edge of the mattress. He pushes her legs apart. He positions himself nearer, leans over her. She sees his penis standing up like a white-throated rooster crowing in the morning, sees it briefly and with surprise, before he mounts her while remaining uncomfortably positioned halfway between standing and kneeling, thrusting at her with his boney hips, his engorged member poking between her legs. As he enters her it hurts. Dixie winces. She had been ready for some pain, especially since other women—friends and relatives—warned her about it as they combed her hair and perfumed her earlier that day:

"It always hurts right away. Not for the man, of course, but for the woman."

"It's the curse of Eve, just like your monthly flow."

"You'll get over it soon enough, don't you worry, darling. Then you'll be a woman."

Dixie had heard all this, as she had heard snatches of similar conversation among women before, chatty women laughing in groups and gaggles. She had heard it and she thought she had prepared herself for it. She thought she knew and understood and would be okay with the whole process of it. But the pain surprises her by combining the searing sharpness of a puncture or a tear with a different and occluded pressure, or displacement, that feels like all the organs inside her, unaccustomed to company, suddenly expanded, then collapsed, contracting and repositioning without much or any advance notice. The heaving motion feels unnatural and guttural and, while not quite wrong, certainly was never a thing Dixie expected.

Also not expected: the brevity.

That first time with Gary lasts maybe two minutes, with the initial sixty seconds focusing itself around that searing, singeing sharpness, diamond bright in the center of her innermost parts, while the last minute, even as the initial sting normalized, most acutely focuses on her feeling the strange, unexpected pressure in the deepest parts of her belly, her stomach, her spine. Dixie remembers almost warming then, almost feeling something *different* at the very end of that pressurized harrumph of a minute. Maybe this *different* thing isn't better. Maybe it will never be better, she can't tell, but at least it changes a bit and gives her a hint of something other than just pain. Those last few seconds during the pressure-like feeling in her innards, she approaches the verge of change, though it stops. It stops because Gary stops. And it is over then, the whole thing over before it really reaches anywhere at all, and Dixie knows that she then held Gary's seed somewhere inside her, sticky and smelling of the sea. She doesn't mind this. She knows it is right and good and her duty as his wife, and so she smiles toward the cracked white hotel ceiling above her as she feels his pulse dropping and his whole self shivering and going limp. She doesn't think much about the *verge-like* feeling her body had started to focus on. She just appreciates the fact that she has found a husband like Gary, someone who will take care of her, make everything all right, and hopefully give her children in the near future.

Sex of this sort, that's what Dixie knows. Sex of this sort is the only thing Dixie has known.

Sex of this sort repeats itself almost every night for the next two or three months and almost without change—both in Dixie's memory and in the reality of that period of her life. Never again is it a wedding dress that she wears. It's normal clothing. But it's the same process and it's the same ending: disrobing, being ordered to lie down, a hasty thrusting half-on and half-off the bed because Gary just can't seem to wait, while the actual act never lasts more than four or five minutes, if that, and never brings Dixie any closer to knowing the *verge-like* feeling toward which she had been brought on her wedding night.

Two months, maybe three, then Dixie misses her cycle, Cyril starts to fill her belly, and Gary eases away from his demands, throttles back on the frequency of their encounters, stops expecting anything much at all. Sex decreases from a nightly event to every other night, to twice a week, and then to one or two uncomfortable incidents where Dixie cries because of the pressure Gary's big body, and his animal thrusting, force against the rounding lump of her belly.

That's the sex Dixie knows.

That's been her experience of sex.

But it's not what she finds in the middle of her waking dream, there with Cyril just having finished his meal of her milk, there in the little shrouded apartment room, dark and lonely despite the daylight outside and the snoring of Gary facedown, still fully clothed on their bed.

The dream Dixie has been having eases out of and away from its start in the crash site first aid station. It eases away from the bandages and blood and burnt hair and moaning of injured flesh. It loses any connection with Mercedes, with the plane crash, with Gabrielle, or with Gary. Cyril remains, which seems strange to Dixie at first. But later it makes sense. *He* was there, after all. And *he* has every right to reinhabit the terrain of a dream that she has patterned on a place and a time where he featured so surely and so completely.

She's on the train again.

Of course, she's on the train. Part of her has been on the train ever since she left it. Part of her has never left her train cabin, her dining cabin, her sleeping compartment (yes, sleeping compartment . . . though never mentioned or remembered during the worry-free moments of the ongoing illusion that is her wakeful life. Sleeping compartment: never a thing—not on her budget—for which she would have/could have spent money).

She's on the train again and the Professor is there.

The cards are on the table between them.

The Professor is telling Dixie about himself, just as she asked him to do, but she can't hear the words he says. She catches bits and pieces of the sentences, names mostly, the names of places filled with exotic spice and consequence: Kermanshah, Budapest, Glasgow, Cartagena. Dixie doesn't even know where these places are or what they might mean in the context of the incredible life-history the Professor has been providing.

She notices how his hair, thin and soft, seems to fall like the laurel of a conqueror over his forehead, like Caesar or Mark Antony. She reaches to brush back one of the stray strands.

The train brakes.

Dixie falls forward, sliding her hand down the Professor's back where she feels, unexpectedly, something other than the softness of academia's disuse. She feels knots and cords of muscle. She feels bone, but bone of the sort accustomed to cantilevering around strong joints. She feels sharp angles and warmth, unlike the chill she remembers from his oddly inhuman hands.

The train brakes, infinitely. Infinitely it brakes in Dixie's dream. It brakes slowly and with languor, and Dixie uses her slipped hand to force the Professor forward over the dining car table, toward her, even as the momentum of braking sends her across the table too, right into him, right up against him, where she has her face close to his, her lips ready for his, where she has made herself unavoidable. It's a circumstance. It's not anticipated or planned. In the real world, or at least the worry-free world of what Dixie remembers when she is merely remembering rather than dreaming, that's where this whole incident ends: a kiss she forces on him and he, at least a little, allows himself to reciprocate. It's a moment where they press their mouths together. Nothing more. Nothing to be worried about or to feel a need for repentance over. It's nothing worth mentioning or even, really, remembering. There's nothing *wrong* with it.

But in the dream, all the best sorts of *wrong* things now begin to happen.

And, holy bejesus (yep, that's the expression Dixie uses, silently in her dream), holy bejesus, the wrong things really *do* start to happen, right away and with a magnificent sort of clarity.

Dixie heats up. In real life, she can feel it. Her body temperature rises to such a pitch that she thinks about standing up from Gary's special chair, there in the slanting mote-light of their darkened midmorning studio apartment room. Dixie thinks about rising and putting Cyril back in his crib, now that he's once again sleeping, so that she can fan herself, cool herself down, and deal with the phenomena she's experiencing. But she fears that Gary might wake.

Or Cyril might wake. Or, even if neither of them wakes, she fears that the dream itself might disappear and prove itself unreal, just when it promises a handhold at the *verge-like* moment she's approached, once or twice since her wedding night, but has never really had the chance to explore.

The Professor returns Dixie's serendipitous kiss. His hand behind her head, he presses her hard against him, his face against her face, even as the train resumes its pace and the dining cabin around them returns to its normal volume of conversation—waiters chatting, patrons harrumphing at the interruption imposed by the brakes, glasses clinking as they are turned once more upright, laughter. The Professor returns Dixie's kiss and then he wipes the cards from where they remain scattered around him, whether on his lap or the table or the floor, spewing them every which way and providing some sort of closure to the whole fortune-telling intro he'd embarked upon. He's done with cards, this action says. He doesn't need them. He's done with prediction and investigation and the sussing-out of whatever phantom future he thinks Dixie might possess. He's ready for action, and Dixie agrees with him that action is the best possible solution, the best possible way to go forward.

They rise together, barely keeping their hands free as they run up and down each other's bodies, barely keeping them free enough to operate the levers of the dining car door, to flee the slightly shocked expressions of the other passengers who have turned to watch them, to steady themselves as they move, conjoined, conjoining, into and out of embrace and dominance, one but separate, with shared purpose but also tearing at each other, venturing across the threshold between train cars, over the gap, into the sleeping compartment, the Professor's sleeping compartment, which will—Dixie knows in the foresight of her dream-memory— become something of *her* car as well over the coming day or day and a half. She knows, she remembers it from her dream, that for the next sixteen hours she spends all her time there, every second of her time, all her time with *him*.

He kicks the door in.

He doesn't bother closing it, though it swings behind him three-quarters of the way shut just from the momentum his foot provided.

They're inside.

They're secluded, at least secluded enough to no longer care.

He puts fingers from each of his hands inside the collar of her traveling dress, two or three fingers on either side, hands turned outward, right along her collarbone, and he rips the neck of the dress wide, splitting the fabric along the seams, giving it another pull until it falls away from her chest and belly, letting it fall, letting it drape over the small, neatly made bed onto which he pushes Dixie.

He opens the fly of his pants and exposes himself to Dixie.

She doesn't have much experience at this, with Gary only ever having entered her where she might make a baby, but nothing about the next moments seems unnatural or wrong or unexpected, as she takes him in her hand, and in her mouth, manipulating him as he strips away his clothes. He's hard. He's standing upright. He's long and delicately veined and shaped in just such a way that all of Dixie's parts fit comfortably around him.

He turns her.

He's inside her from behind, but slowly, slowly enough. And they pause like that as the night flows along, unrumpled, still and untouchable beyond the shaking window of the train. The Professor's first slow motions move her like the wheels on the rails, steadily, inexorably forward, deeper and deeper, bit by bit. He speeds. She greets him and allows him. They stay like that for only a moment, enough for Dixie to think—*this is how long it usually lasts.*

Only, it's not over yet. Not by a long shot.

The Professor turns her again, sits her down, puts his tongue between her legs, up and down her legs, inside her and then out again, up her belly, back into her warmest reaches.

She scratches his back with her fingernails and this makes him arch forward, more pressure from his mouth against her groin. She leaves long red streaks on his cloud-white, slightly freckled skin. She runs her nails up his neck, along the base of his skull, behind his ears.

The *verge* approaches. Rapidly it . . . bam, there it is. She's on it. Like the crest of a wave, she's on it. She's over it. The next wave is coming. The wave after that. Into the troughs and up onto the summits, the waves flow beneath, inside, and through her. The train rumbles on, waves and waves of it, and then unexpectedly the railway curves so that some centripetal force throws her balance off in a most blissful way, reverberating with strength and steel, re-centering her, and him, adjacent to her earlier orgasm, as it races, downhill, thrilling. Like lightning bolts and earthquakes all at once she pulls him to her and holds him there while all the shivers storm.

After that, a moment of just breathing.

She thinks it is done but he has other plans.

He lays her down.

He takes his time now, pulling away the shorn bits of dress from her waist, getting her fully naked, shutting and then latching the door with a certainty and an ease and a timeless, continuing slowness. He finishes this and then sits on the chair opposite her, stripping away the last of his clothing. Without saying anything he takes himself in his hand. He's still erect. He motions toward her and tells her to join him on the seat, to be on top of him, to let him venture once more inside her.

This does not end. It goes on and on.

There are no clowns. There are no camels. There are no acrobats or elephants or peanuts or cotton candy.

But there is a ringmaster, this Professor Dixie has met in her mingled moment of dream and reality. There is a ringmaster and he's completely in charge.

In the dimness of the morning studio, with Cyril in her arms, Dixie remembers it and all the feelings, all of them—right up to and including the orgasm from his tongue—all of this returns so that she moans a little and feels herself warm and wet right there on Gary's chair, right there with Cyril on her breast.

It's wonderful.

Magical.

And totally unreal.

Dixie doesn't know what to do about it, the messes she has made—first her vomit and now her orgasm. But she doesn't really care. Not right then she doesn't. There will be plenty of time later to clean things up. Plenty of time to change clothes, to clean herself. She'll just sit now. She'll sit for a while and let the train pull back into its station. She'll let the morning turn to noon and Gary, sometime later in the day, at last awake, will find her rosy-cheeked and calm, somewhat exhausted, for sure, but calm and happy and only partly present with him.

CHAPTER 9

Dixie goes to Frank's grocery. Not just once, but again and again. It becomes her place (and that has very little to do with the produce, or the graying meat selection).

Dixie walks Cyril outside the building where Mercedes and Gabrielle live.

As autumn comes on, Dixie makes it a habit to take Cyril to the park just down the block, where she can see a good swath of the sidewalk in front of Gabrielle and Mercedes's place.

She catches glimpses of them, from afar, and one time Mercedes walks past her, though Dixie doesn't notice until too late, since, with the onset of the autumn's first chill, Mercedes donned a knit hat and a rain slicker, collar pulled high. She crouched so low, pulled so deeply into herself, that Dixie couldn't see her face, couldn't pick her languid dancing movements out of the outer garment's grayness, and therefore didn't realize it was her at all until she was gone, replaying in her mind the quickening of the shrouded figure's footsteps when she passed. That quickening seems to indicate that Mercedes saw Dixie. But Dixie won't let herself believe it. Dixie won't let herself believe that Mercedes could be so cold.

Dixie writes her a letter. Three letters actually, the first trying to rationalize things on Gary's behalf, telling them, Mercedes and Gabrielle—telling Mercedes, really, mostly just her, just Mercedes—that it was simple and uninformed curiosity, just a poorly worded sentence, just a situation Gary didn't know how to deal with, and that he was tired, so tired, as they all had been, implying that things should be forgiven. The second of those letters: more of the same, but also covering how much Dixie missed Mercedes and how much she hoped Mercedes was well, how much she hoped they might be friends, might spend some time trying to work on what seemed, before the horror of the plane crash, a friendship they both would enjoy. The third letter just admitted they were wrong, and Dixie thinks this one might go a little too far, even, putting herself on the line, attributing some of Gary's poor form to her own hidden curiosity, her own somewhat unholy need-to-know, none of which were things she felt at the time or now deeply believe to be true, but *are* things she's willing to consider about herself if it might help Mercedes come back. Not one of the letters receives a reply. And this makes Dixie feel as if she has been mistaken about the whole friendship thing, mistaken that Mercedes and she, even Gabrielle and Gary, could be social together, could be friends, could enjoy long walks, dinners, dancing. Dixie tries to shut it all down inside her.

Still, she finds herself at Frank's grocery almost every day now—not because it's a good grocery. Not because she likes the majority of the people there. Not because the food enthralls her, or the prices lure her. She goes because, first of all, she needs to buy food *somewhere*, and, second, she returns again and again to Frank's in order to re-create the moment of budding friendship she'd experienced with Mercedes. She wants that. Dixie wants the escape. She wants the conversation. Her own apartment draws in around her, dark and solitary for most of the day, dark and solitary and occasionally filling with clowns and elephants, and that's not Dixie's nature by any stretch of the imagination, to sit and sulk and deal with her demons, Paul's demons. Dixie needs some freedom, some wide-open spaces, and Mercedes—for that fleeting instant—had seemed like she could provide a spark of something, something brighter and more alive than even Idaho had been.

Cyril has started to coo and say words by this time, though only Dixie knows they're words. Dixie knows it's more than just babble. The "ma, ma, ma" means something, as it only gets babbled out when Cyril wants her attention or is looking at her. And the "da, da, da" (said equally as often to stray dogs in the park as it is to Gary) also means something, though Gary seems unable to hear it.

As Dixie is holding Cyril one day at Frank's, the ladies in line strike up a conversation with Dixie, or, maybe more precisely, they strike it up *at* Dixie.

She remembers them, of course. Maybe not the same ladies. Maybe not exactly the same ladies, but the same archetype. Dixie looks away from them, down at her shoes.

"Shy thing, ain't she?" one of them says.

"I'm not shy," Dixie fires back.

"Sure do look like it," the woman says, as she takes her basket and walks around Dixie, never minding that Dixie and Cyril had really been in line, one place ahead.

Dixie's a bit stunned. Dixie's a bit speechless. To save face, she pretends like she wasn't actually in line. She concedes this, as she works to gather her thoughts and her opinions and her next steps. She takes another pass along the canned food aisle, selects some beans, a jar of pickles. All the while her frustration solidifies and threatens to spill over into anger. Feeling this, and feeling wronged about the whole incident, she returns to the line—not to the end of the line, but to the middle, right where she had been queued before, right to the spot where the other ladies threw her off her game.

Certainly, Dixie means to tell them off.

She means to let it rip.

She means to hammer them for being so, so, so difficult and so dark and so humorless and so careless with other people's emotions.

She remembers how the woman, maybe this very same woman, had reached right over her shoulder in line to grab hold of Mercedes and try to tug her out of the way. Dixie is mad. Remembering how they treated Mercedes, she's mad. But a voice deep inside her says: *Don't* tell *them what to do. Don't* tell *them how to act.* Maybe it's the voice of her churchgoing youth, full of nice moralities and accommodations. Maybe it's the voice of Paul. *Don't* tell *them anything. Show them.* Show them.

This realization, this instantaneous 180-degree pivot in attitude and posture changes everything for Dixie. She realizes she can tell them off. She can choose to exact a bit of revenge for their meanness. But instead, she smiles, and puts forth her warmest welcome (despite an upwelling of alien tears in her eyes, right then), and bites back all her sense of injustice to say, "Ladies, I'm hosting a party Friday night. All the neighborhood is coming. Can I count you in?"

"What's the party for?" one of them asks. (Dixie doesn't know.)

"When does it start?" (Dixie hasn't thought about that yet.)

"Where is it being held?" (Dixie pictures her little studio and can't imagine all these women and their husbands inside.)

She's rolling with it though, she's rolling, and it feels good.

She leans back, and really lets the moment take her, so that with one mouthful, one giant gulp of hubris, she stakes herself to answers across the board: "We're hosting it, my husband, Gary, and I, at the Columbia ballroom . . . in celebration of his new job . . ." (Does Columbia have a ballroom, Dixie doesn't know, but it sounds possible. Better than possible, it sounds darn good. And Gary, a new job? She guesses so. She guesses they can play up the hydrological internship.) ". . . you're all invited. We'll have hors d'oeuvres and punch at six o'clock, music after. Bring your menfolk."

Dixie turns away, then, somewhat embarrassed, but one of them asks, as if jabbing her in the back: "Will there be invitations, so we can get in the door?"

"Of course. I'll bring yours tomorrow. One for each of you." Dixie sets down her little tote of shopping items and picks up Cyril, holding him like a shield. The women smile at him on the way out. They chatter amongst themselves as she steps through the door.

Only Frank shakes his head. And, frankly, it's a good thing he does, because—when Dixie comes back later, after having convinced Gary and made reservations at a room suitably in the shape and size of the ballroom she had imagined, and after she's hand-printed invites and gotten together a million other things— Frank remembers the exchange and finds himself somewhat sympathetic when she pleads for a bit of an advance on the groceries.

"It's a lot you're asking, little lady," Frank says.

"It is, yes," Dixie says.

"Weren't you the one who defended that Mexican girl?"

"Mercedes. And she's Venezuelan."

"Fine, whatever," says Frank. "I can do it. But on one condition..."

"Oh, okay, thank you, thank you! Any condition. Anything at all."

"This is going to sound a bit weird."

"Anything!"

"Let me see that baby of yours."

"Cyril?"

"Yes, that's his name then, Cyril?"

Dixie dips her shoulder toward Frank. She uncovers Cyril's face. She holds him close to Frank.

Frank doesn't say anything. He looks at Cyril. He looks at Dixie. He's got old eyes, rheumy, set deep under thick eyebrows so that they always seem shadowed to Dixie. His eyebrows raise. The lines at the corners of his eyes crease more deeply. It isn't a smile, but it isn't a frown either. It's accepting. It's okay. Everything is going to be okay. Everything is normal, that's what his look tells Dixie. That's what his look conveys. Don't worry about it, Dixie. Don't worry about anything at all.

CHAPTER 10

That's Dixie's first solution to New York City.

After her near miss with friendship, real friendship of the sort that seemed possible with Mercedes, her solution is fake friendship, forcing herself to find friends.

The party Dixie throws is a symptom of this.

For what it's worth, within its own context, it turns out to be pretty successful, circus-themed, with little elephant and monkey decorations, peanuts and crackerjack for hors d'oeuvres, all the waitresses in sequins and feathers. It's successful despite Dixie spending more money on it than she'd budgeted or agreed with Gary up front. She runs a tab with Frank for the food. She cashes checks before Gary has money in the bank. Still, whatever it takes is what Dixie decides she must do. As a result, all is ready when the big night comes.

The party goes down without a hitch. Though Dixie is nervous standing at the ballroom door, fifteen minutes before her invites suggested people arrive, she knows people will come. She has extracted promises. She has gotten reassurances. She is confident.

And come they do. Fifteen, twenty couples, maybe forty people in total. Friends of friends. Unknown folks, a good group. Colleagues from school. Advertising men with their advertising ladies. A local playwright. A college professor or two. A man who owns a small fleet of tugboats, some of which Gary's mapping team has rented. The couples laugh. They dance. They prance around the three red rings Dixie erected in the middle of the dance hall parquet, to mimic the rings of the circus. Dixie and Gary play host and hostess for the first time in their lives, with Dixie making Gary dress up as the ringmaster—coattails, bow tie, faux mustache, brill-creamed hair—and bellow out all the announcements during the party theatrically, a thing that suits his military marching voice. He does well at it (but not well enough: he's never quite Professorial in the way she wants him to be. He's never quite naturally *that man*). For Dixie it feels like playing house, like she's finally playing house the way she wants to, the way she's been taught—only she's doing it on a more grand and exotic scale. The success of the party leads to invitations elsewhere, to other events, copycat events where the hosts and hostesses choose similarly theatrical themes: tropical luaus, Siberian fur-coat freezer parties, Wild West and even baseball themes. Dixie (and Gary with her) at last integrates into the community in and around Columbia University, in and around their neighborhood—tacky, crude, socially striving, gossipy, but feeling un-isolated even as they keep to themselves in the wider spectrum of the city. The friendships they make end up lasting long, longer than Dixie expects, and they provide plenty of opportunity for the superficial things Dixie needs: walks in the park, bridge tournaments, trips upstate to little cottages on some Adirondack lake or another, crocheting club, all the little niceties that had been missing.

It's just what Dixie needs.

Just what she thinks she needs.

Or sort of.

It's at least a poultice.

It's at least a patchwork job that lets her feel like everything might be all right—with her, with Gary, with Cyril, with Paul, with her parents back in Pocatello, with Mercedes and Gabrielle, with the universe.

The distraction of these new friends does what *ordinary* is supposed to do. Lulling her, lulling everyone around her. And that would be fine and good, the simple way forward, except she's got a bit of an inescapable unordinariness to her now. And it won't go away. The memories of the plane crash won't go away. The dreams about sex won't go away. The visitations of Paul and the clowns, which she knows aren't from New York but still appear amid the New York landscape, mixed in with things, like they've been let loose from some box inside her, some portmanteau: these won't go away either.

There's plenty of life that happens in the next few weeks, with Cyril growing and all these clubby friends in clubby Columbia around and about and available. But what sticks in Dixie's gullet? What bothers her? What burr has lodged itself in her heart? It's not tough to guess what this is, because that mixed miasma of sex dreams and circus and Professorship and Mercedes continues, never quite as amplified as the first occurrence had been, nursing little Cyril, letting the rancid smell of her own vomit sit in the smallness of the apartment, letting the rays of midday steal around her as in the darkness Gary still sleeps and against that slanting light and fulgent shadow the shadows of the dreams cast themselves before her waking eye. The mash-ups of these things are never quite as significant, but they are still orgasmic. And they are the only such moments of pure, personal orgasm she has, with Gary never learning the art, never mastering (or even much caring for) the art.

Dixie can deal with these dreams.

She even welcomes them: they're both a launching point and a refuge when she and Gary have sex. She often lets the dreams take hold of her, bring her to orgasm if they're quick and powerful and delirious enough to operate within the boundaries of Gary's four-minute maximum.

But, even with this level of comfort, there are some troubling things that start to happen.

For example, starting out only a few weeks after the big crash in Brooklyn—when Dixie lost her chance at friendship with Mercedes—she goes through a dark period. Perhaps it is postpartum. Perhaps it is New York's dreary, salt-gray winter, stringing on and on. Perhaps she still experiences aftereffects and flashbacks from the crash itself, the memories of it, that haunt her. Whatever it is, Dixie's alien returns. She starts crying every day, and Gary tries to do everything he can to console her, all of it with no effect: he buys flowers, he takes her to dinner, he makes sure friends (their new bridge-playing neighbors and so forth) visit her at regular intervals during the day when he is away studying or working. He even arranges for a trip to Miami, just the three of them, Dixie, Cyril, and Gary, for a taste of the tropics—which cheers Dixie on the outside, and gives her a tan of the sort she's never had before, not even when running wild as a child in Idaho, but which also requires Gary, in concert with the local university and civil planning commission, to spend his days taking depth soundings of the Miami harbor. More work. More time alone with Cyril. None of this is Gary's fault. He's really a model husband throughout all of this. For the day and age, he's considerate, skilled, possessed with self-assurance, tall, handsome, and white. What more could Dixie want? That's what her friends ask her. *What more could you want?* What does she feel might be missing from her life, or what gives her cause to be dissatisfied; what makes the alien of tears rumble inside her and fill up the lower lids of her eyes, so that the hot saltiness in them spills over? What is Dixie missing?

111

She doesn't ask herself this.

She just cries.

And Gary tries to cope. He tries to heal. He tries to help her.

Finally, resorting to a long-overdue idea, Gary invites Dixie's mother to come to New York. He means this as a temporary thing, of course, because their apartment is only *so* big, and he figures that Dixie's mother won't love the city. He's wrong on both these accounts. She stays. She moves in. (Dixie imagines the house in Pocatello slowly filling up with her father's bits and pieces of engine parts with her mother gone, though in true Idaho form everyone pretends that nothing is amiss, that he's doing just fine back on the "ranch" and the separation from his wife isn't anything other than a good chance for her to spend some much-needed time with Dixie: a week or two to start, though—as time slips by, in that hustle of a New York way—the two weeks become four, the four weeks become twelve, and Dixie's mother remains even up to and through the point when Gary decides they must find a new, bigger apartment with a separate room for his precious mother-in-law. Dixie imagines her father alone, alone except for Paul. And she doesn't imagine what Paul does, during this time. Not at all. She shuts her mind to that.)

This is all normal.

This happens to everyone.

What isn't quite as normal is Dixie leaving baby Cyril, and her mother, and Gary, to spend a week at one of those Adirondack lakes "with some of the friends."

"Which friends?" Gary asks.

"Just one friend actually."

"Who?" He's not mad, just curious, and maybe a bit hurt, or alarmed, to find out that plans have been made without him in them, or without even consulting him. Dixie's been known to do similar things before, one example of which was her wild train trip eastward with almost no consultation or thought, but Gary believes that was just an episode, just a onetime thing, that Dixie had gotten lucky to arrive safely and have everything go okay for her. Gary has no knowledge of the events of that trip, other than Dixie's go-to line that there was nothing to worry about at all. It all went smoothly as can be and was a whole lot of fun, seeing America like that!

Gary isn't upset about this little "girls' vacation," as he starts to call it, but he is surprised when he finds out who she's taking it with.

"Mercedes."

"Mercedes?"

"Yes, that's what I said."

"Like Mercedes and Gabrielle?"

"Yes, but just Mercedes. No Gabrielle. Girls' trip, remember?" she says, with a bit of a cutting edge, cutting him off, reminding him of how he wrecked things by asking too many questions about girls and boys and girls who might dress like boys.

"Okay, fine," he says.

He has so many questions, but doesn't feel able, given Dixie's look of storminess, to ask them.

That's fine with Dixie. She doesn't want to answer any more questions, mostly because she's made it all up. She hasn't seen Mercedes at all. She hasn't restarted their friendship. She hasn't made amends. She's going to the Adirondack lake on her own, all by herself, because she wants to deal with this alien inside her, the tearjerker alien. She wants to rip it from her. She wants to strangle it. She wants to see, hear, feel it no more. And she wants to—no, she knows she needs to do it alone. Just herself. Some quiet and solitude perhaps, perhaps that will be soothing. But it's more about a battle scenario and a confrontation Dixie plans to have with her own innermost guts than it is about relaxation.

She can't tell Gary this.

Maybe she could tell Paul about this. Maybe she'd scream it at Paul, if she had the chance, if he came here, if he showed up by accident or something. Maybe she'd have the strength for that. But she can't tell Gary.

Still, she feels like she needs to tell her husband something, something more, just a little bit more, because right now he isn't convinced, and the last thing she needs from him—even though she loves him in all the ways she ever expected to love him—the last thing she needs is for him to come up to the lake, to get some misguided notion of saving her, to come there with open arms and a bouquet of flowers and a big hug, because that will only push the alien down deeper where Dixie can't reach it. It will push the alien down deeper and Dixie will have to fight it again, constantly, holding back the tears and stomping down the un-Dixie-like behavior that the alien forces her to exhibit.

She holds her stomach as she says this next bit, feeling again like she might vomit.

"Listen," she says, touching Gary's hand with a newfound tenderness (while at the same time remembering how on their first meeting Mercedes's handshake had sent a little thrill through her), "there will come a time when I think we can try again with Gabrielle. I know you didn't mean to ask him what he is in a bad way, but he took it badly. It's a precarious thing for him, for her. They're good people, and I want us all to be friends; still, right now, at this particular moment, they're not ready."

"Not ready for me."

"Not ready for you. Not ready for the two of us together. Not ready to try to go out together and be friends with those who are, as Mercedes says, *sapphic.*"

"Sapphic, huh?"

"Like Sappho, the poet, who loved women."

"They're both women then."

"Duh, Gary, come on!"

"Well, I mean, I knew that. I know that. I just don't quite know what to say about it."

And that was Dixie's escape valve. "Exactly," she says. "That's exactly why it'll just be me and Mercedes for a while, okay?"

Except it isn't.

There's no Mercedes at all. Not at the lake house in the Adirondacks, not ever for coffee, for friendship, for good times or bad. It's only Dixie.

She's comfortable with that, comfortable having an imaginary friend, in just the same way she's comfortable having imaginary sex dreams and in just the same way she's comfortable heading up to the mountains, to one of the other new circle of lady friends' cabins, for the alone time she needs to confront and fight the alien inside her. She's bringing her portmanteau with her. She's bringing her circus memories and her plane crash and the whole of the unremarkable ride she took on that train from Idaho to New York City. She's bringing it all with her and she's going to get rid of it. She's going to cut out its heart, that little alien inside her, and she's going to follow Paul's advice, what he said to her before she boarded the train in Pocatello: "The only solution, Dixie, is to bury it. You know what to do. Don't let it show. Don't let anyone know. Just bury it and be done and normal. That's the only way you'll be able to move on. There's no other way to run away. Not now."

CHAPTER 11

The trip to the lake is one of the oddities Dixie allows into her life.

The others, over the next three years or so, are similar in shape and form and sense. It's always Mercedes, imaginary Mercedes, who Dixie is going to meet. But it's never again as long, or as serious, as that whole week alone at the cabin had been. It's *alone time* (or friend time) on a different scale entirely, and it's about as random in its timing and its urgency as anything Dixie's ever experienced. She doesn't know when it will happen. She doesn't know why, at least at first, the need for this "alone time" seizes her. From the outside, it seems like it might be a refuge from dreariness, or a way to hide, but it's not. It's full of excitement. It's the most exciting thing she does, this being alone, this imaginary-friend escapism. She doesn't know what Gary thinks of it, though it seems he allows for it, leaves space for these excursions of hers, especially because they seem— on her return each time—to result in a better Dixie, a Dixie closer to the Dixie he knows and loves, a Dixie who is not fighting against whatever demon (or alien) has taken root inside her.

These aren't frequent occurrences. It's every few months, less often sometimes, sporadic, with long gaps and then sudden binges. Dixie thinks this is much like the struggle with addiction other people fight. After the week of combat in the Adirondacks, the next time Dixie sees Mercedes—which is the code for it, the code she uses with Gary and with herself—comes a long while in the future.

This is because, at the beginning, even though she feels the need for it now and again, Dixie fights it.

She thinks, because of the gargantuan effort she's made all alone at her friend's cabin on the lake, that she's completed the struggle. She thinks that she's won. She thinks she's equipped herself to live normally, and without any need either for imaginary Mercedes or for imaginary anyone. She thinks she's put the circus behind her. She thinks she's no longer hearing Paul's voice, his weasellike instructions for her, at every turn. More importantly, and more finally, she thinks she's equipped herself to live without the alien inside her.

At least at first—during those first months when she's in denial—she thinks that if she ever allows herself to use the Mercedes excuse again, the jig will be up. She'll breathe life back into her alien. She'll get off track once more. Gary will notice. Gary will try to intervene. She'll have to struggle, instead of enjoying all the new niceties and frivolities of the life she and Gary and Cyril are on the verge of seizing as Gary's studies continue to proceed at pace, or even a little ahead of pace (he thinks he'll graduate early). Dixie does not want to disturb this. She doesn't want to disturb the ease and fluidity of what seems to be their ascent onto the first rung of the social ladder in the New York of Columbia and the Upper West Side. It feels so selfish of her, to disturb any of this, to ruffle the feathers, ripple the waters. This isn't what she's been taught to do. It isn't the place a woman is supposed to occupy. She's supposed to be quiet, to go along with the program, to support and help and love and soothe and encourage. She's not supposed to do things for herself. She's not supposed to have an alien inside her, or if she does, she's supposed to deal with it quietly, never mention it, and keep her chin up. Working from this illusion, Dixie fights against the myth of her friendship with Mercedes. She fights for almost two years. For almost two years she refuses to allow herself to see Mercedes, to reuse that excuse and slip away to deal with what is happening inside her, what has been pushed down deep.

Cyril is a fully-fledged toddler and it's 1962 when Dixie next finds herself unable to control the urge to "see Mercedes again."

Dixie arranges a babysitter, as Cyril hasn't yet started kindergarten. She knows why she's going, she knows where she's going, but she's not saying. She doesn't need to tell anyone. She doesn't even really need to tell herself, or at least she doesn't need to dwell on it. Gary's gone, at work, and the impulse to be alone (to be "with Mercedes") comes upon her suddenly and powerfully.

She props Cyril in a corner, in the window corner where he likes to sit, and she waves goodbye to him from the door of the larger apartment she and Gary have been in ever since her mother visited. The door is down a short hallway. Dixie can see Cyril's face there, turned away from her a bit, unhappy with her leaving but unable to communicate what he's feeling.

She says to him, "Mommy's going to go meet a friend. Mommy will be back in a few hours, nothing more than a few hours, okay?"

The boy says nothing in return.

"You'll have fun with Auntie Marguerite?"

Cyril's head moves just slightly, as if nodding in agreement.

That's good enough for Dixie, even if Marguerite is running a bit late. Marguerite has keys to the apartment. Marguerite cleans. Marguerite does the dishes. Cyril knows her. Cyril knows to wait for her. Cyril is okay on his own, there in the apartment, if Dixie steps away to run an errand or two, to get a coffee. She has left him before. *It's normal. Everything is normal, everything is going to be okay, Dixie,* she tells herself.

In fact, as Dixie shuts the door, and as she steps into the stairwell outside her apartment's entrance, she hears Marguerite coming up from a few floors below. Dixie leans over the railing and calls out to her cleaning lady, Cyril's de facto babysitter: "He does fine with the bigger wheels, the smaller ones are just there in case."

This sounds dumb. Dixie knows it. The lady is perfectly familiar already with Cyril's toys. Dixie is just nervous, letting her energy out through her words.

"The little wheels are too small for his fingers and the holes are too small for his fat-nubbed colored pencils still," Dixie says. "But keep them out, near the highchair, just in case. Mostly, just feed him toast. Or maybe some peaches from the can that's open in the fridge. He can have milk too, and a little oatmeal before naptime at noon."

Marguerite reaches Dixie and nods at these instructions as if it is all crazy talk, but Dixie knows the woman is used to it, used to crazy mothers like her giving last-minute instructions when, in truth, Marguerite has seen it all, done it all, and is better equipped by far than Dixie to deal with any emergencies that might come up, any care Cyril requires.

Flustered, Dixie skips down the stairs, leaving Marguerite to unlock the apartment door all on her own. She's off to "meet Mercedes" at last. The excitement fills her heart with a fluttery energy.

She hasn't told Gary about this rendezvous.

She'll excuse it after the fact, she tells herself. It's all fine. He'll worry a little, but it's the one thing he won't probe too deeply. Or, she says to herself, "I could come up with a million other things Gary won't probe too deeply. He's stuck in his harbor-mapping and his instrument-fixing. But I like the idea of Mercedes, and I don't have to invent a story about her from whole cloth. It's already proven. It's already a thing. It's already mostly untouchable."

Are these noble sentiments on Dixie's part? No. She admits as much to herself. No. No, they're not good things that she's doing. But they're not bad either. Not inherently bad. It's 1962 after all, and Dixie's a modern woman, living in modern New York, and she could be making up stories for entirely more sinister reasons than to meet an imaginary friend (or to steal a few moments of alone time). For God's sake, half the women in her new group of Columbia friends have standing excuses to cover various *liaisons*. It's expected behavior. It's easy. It's a little wrong, but it's easy, all the same. No one will question it if Gary believes her cover story, or pretends to believe her and turns a blind eye.

Dixie knows this. She feels liberated by it.

She also knows where she's going.

She knows where to "find Mercedes" today. There's a physical and geographic element to the sensation of incurable loneliness that has taken hold of her. This sensation swooped in as the real harbinger of this excursion, just like for the trip she took to be alone in the Adirondack cabin. And it's the very same feeling, geographical, historical, eventful, that will take hold of her every time during the coming few years' worth of Dixie's imaginary meetups with Mercedes.

Dixie knows where she's going. She's headed to Jamaica Bay.

She's heard it on the radio: *ninety-five dead there*. A flight headed from Idlewild Airport to Los Angeles has rolled over off the runway and come down in the water. She heard it on the news. She heard it from the ladies in line at Frank's grocery. She heard it from Frank himself. And she knows she has to go. She has to go out to Rockaway where she can get close to the wreck. She feels herself called that way. She can do nothing about it. Or nothing that she's willing, at that moment, to force down and away, force back inside herself like she's been doing for the past year or two. Today she's got time. Today she's got Marguerite on the line to care for Cyril.

Today she's got an excuse to go, as long as Mercedes—or the mirage of Mercedes—can be invoked to conceal her true intentions.

It's an early March day, blustery, with the Atlantic seaboard making itself felt and heard, even at a few of the subway stops where the train emerges in Brooklyn aboveground before reaching the seaside itself. Brooklyn as a seaside village, filled with fog and sea-mist and fresh breezes, seems a bit odd to Dixie, a bit medieval perhaps, but the fog chills her and the smell of the salt water floods in each time the subway doors open. New York so often seems, to Dixie, as if it is turned in on itself, landlocked, not tied to harbors and oceans (though Gary, in his engineering certainty, his harbor-mapping focus, would never see it that way). New York, Dixie thinks, treats itself like it is a million miles away from everywhere, set aside but also the epicenter of everything else, so that the idea of nowhere can't be imagined. So that the idea of nowhere—which is easy enough to find in mountains or wilderness or looking at the empty spots on a map—doesn't even matter. Nowhere isn't ever an idea, or a concept worth exploring. It has no value, except in the memory of an Idaho girl who grew up with the specter of vistas and plains. Today, with bluster in the March air, even before Rockaway, as first the subway and then the bus pulls up, stop after stop, mile by mile closer to the ocean—or at least to the bit of the ocean squeezed between New Jersey and Long Island, packed with freighters and fishing boats and sailboats rejoicing in the wind—the opening doors of subway and bus allow the scents of big city and boardwalk, skyscrapers and ocean to mingle: popcorn, seaweed, concrete, marshland, mist.

At the terminus of the bus line in Howard Beach, Cross Bay Boulevard has been shut down. The crash site is far down Cross Bay, way out in the middle, and just west of the causeway's pilings. As the bus comes down Woodhaven and clears Highway 27, Dixie can see steam and smoke and an occasional tongue of fire rising from the spot, but she can't see the plane itself. The bus driver speaks to a policeman standing at a set of quickly erected barricades that block forward progress onto the causeway. The bus trundles backward and turns in the middle of the road, a seesawing maneuver that takes the driver several tries, plus the help of two or three policemen to hold back other motorists. They head down Woodhaven, going inland, circling all the way around Idlewild on the east side of Jamaica. Dixie thinks she's missed her chance to get out and see the crash up close, but the bus finally clears the east side of Idlewild and dumps her off at Rockaway Beach, making the journey longer by almost half an hour but giving Dixie time to think about the roadblocks she has seen, the way people have gathered to ogle at any open spot along the shore—on both the Howard Beach and the Rockaway sides—and how the gaggles of ambulances have pulled up, out of action, staged like a gory circus parade in each and every open space or empty lot, sometimes circling up together like they are making a defensive perimeter in the same way covered wagons once defended themselves on the Oregon Trail. None of the ambulances flash their lights. None of them blare their horns or pull up speeding and screeching. None have animals in them. None have clowns or dressing rooms for the sequined horse ladies. Not one of the ambulance drivers, lounging around the doors of their vehicles, wears cotton wads in their ears. None of them seem magical in the least.

The deadness and stillness and orderliness of all the emergency vehicles reflects the fate of the flight's passengers and crew. Unlike Park Slope, there aren't any wounded to treat. Unlike Park Slope, there's really no need to rush, or to triage, or to do much of anything except stare at the plume of steam and smoke that still curls skyward from Jamaica's marshes, a mile or more down along the causeway closer to Howard Beach.

It's late already. Not late in the day, but late in terms of the crash itself. Dixie feels like she's arrived too late. She's too late to slip inside the cordon. She's too late to be one of the first arrivers who are, like in the Park Slope crash, accepted among the chaos, organic to the chaos. She's too late to be much help. She's too late to see much of anything.

She joins one of the loose groups of onlookers rallying together along the interior of the roadway, the bayside shore of Rockaway, gathered there among scrub and loose gravel just to the side of where Cross Bay connects. After a moment of staring at smoke and steam, Dixie shifts her attention.

All the other onlookers continue to face in the direction of the crash. Like moviegoers oriented to the show, their faces are upturned. Like spectators at a circus, lit by the lights of the main ring as the trapeze artists come into view, dashing into the light, these onlookers lining the dreary edge of the bay wear similar expressions of disbelief and vacuity. Their features are silvered in similar light, like circus light, movie light, caught in the silver screen. Unlike them, Dixie turns her head side to side and then moves her body so that she faces at angles to the crowd, looking down-beach, up-beach, a black sheep, a lone wolf, the bent nail that will need to be hammered down—if from high above any gods of voyeurism exist who might be inspecting the scene, if from high above any angels guard her.

What is she doing?

She's looking at the other people.

She's looking from one face to the next.

She's drinking them all in, one by one.

But she doesn't see the thing she came to find. She doesn't see the person she came to find. Slowly she exhales, steps back to the bus stop, and—though many people exit as the next bus pulls up, coming to gawk along the shore—she is the only soul to board at Rockaway, heading back to the city.

123

What does Gary think of this?

Nothing. It goes by the wayside for him, if he even notices at all.

That's probably unfair to him. Why should he notice? He's perfect in so many other ways. He's carving out the life they want, the life they agreed on. If his young wife needs to go visit their less reputable former friends, if she needs to maintain that relationship, if she needs—like she's said once or twice—to go visit Mercedes where Gabrielle and she now live, back in Park Slope, then Gary doesn't really see the need to interfere. He tells Dixie this (and it hurts her just a little, that passive acceptance, that unwillingness to participate. They all could have been friends together—Dixie and imaginary Mercedes, Gary and imaginary Gabrielle).

Still, that's not perfectly fair to Gary either.

He rolls over in the middle of the night one night (he does this a lot, with Korea seared in his mind, seared there so that he cannot run away from it even when he's staring at the safe confines of their own ceiling). He thinks Dixie is sleeping but she has woken with him, though she lies still and watches the shadows on the far wall, her back turned to Gary, her whole body feeling him breathe, sipping in shallow and worried breaths.

"I understand a little bit," he says. "You probably think I don't. But I do. And it's okay."

She wants to say something then, but she doesn't. She doesn't know what to say.

"We're all lonely," Gary says. "We're all stuck with ourselves and we can't escape. Not even here in New York."

Dixie thinks about offering him some sort of escape: *Let's run away. Let's go to France or Louisiana. Let's make a cabin in the mountains where we can fight aliens together. Let's build a spaceship or a submarine.*

But she doesn't say this.

Gary turns aside, falls asleep. She can hear the down-welling drowning slowness that comes into the tempo of his breath.

Gary falls asleep again, but Dixie doesn't.

The summer of 1962 passes. Cyril turns three years old. The bigger apartment they've taken for themselves once again opens its doors for Dixie's mother. Her father, once again, does not come. On the outside, when they're not listening to each other in the darkness of their bedroom, all is as it should be in Dixie and Gary's world. No one talks about Paul. When Dixie's mother tries to pass on a few words from him, even innocuous well-wishes, Dixie leaves the room and goes to find Cyril, holding him to her as if his three-year-old body is still just the size and snuggly shape of the baby doll he once had been.

October of '62: Dixie and Mercedes meet again, this time when a boiler blows at the New York Telephone Company cafeteria. Twenty-three are killed. Ninety-four injured. Dixie and Mercedes roll up their sleeves and help, telling the police at the cordon line that they're nurses.

But still they don't see what they've come to see.

They look.

They turn their heads this way and that way.

They watch in the corridors of the Telephone Company's office. They seek among the faces of the throng of onlookers gathering at the sidewalk's edge. They put away their bloody gloves. They fold up soiled bandages and sheets before throwing them away, an act of finality for the event that doesn't resound with their own mission: they are watching. They are waiting. They are staying until the last minute just in case something happens toward the very end. They do the folding and the throwing away and the sweeping up of broken glass as a means to be helpful amid the trauma. As a means to delay that moment, their moment.

But they see nothing. *They,* of course, in the loosest, most abstract, imaginary sense.

Dixie and Mercedes try again right away that December too, with two more of their "lady dates," almost back-to-back, which worries Dixie a little. She's getting manic with it. Too much, too frequently, and Gary might very well start to ask questions again.

But she can't help it.

The impulse is undeniable.

The impulse is uncontrollable.

They slip into crowds of protestors when the newspaper people go on strike. They hope for chaos, but the situation at the newspaper office never really flares to epic proportions. It simmers, and works a deep knife into the industry, for months on end. There's plenty to do, but Dixie and Mercedes lose interest right away. It's not exactly the sort of thing that will result in seeing what they want to see. It's not shocking. It's not trauma. It's not going to produce the syrupy-slow passage of time that a real event might do.

They need something more definite, more single-episode. Something that will make time slow down until it is once again— like on the train, like after the Park Slope crash—no longer logical in its behavior. (Dixie asks Mercedes about this, her opinion on it, and Mercedes agrees 100 percent. It's one of their better conversations during these years of imagination and Dixie thanks Mercedes for it afterward, thanks her for her support and friendship and for always being there. It's nice to have an imaginary friend, especially one as agreeable as Mercedes seems to be.)

They modify their plans: they'll not meet up for just any old newsy event. Only the biggest things. The things that will matter and shock people. However, as much as Dixie wants to slow things down, they pinky swear to go out again, right away, for the city council meeting where Robert Moses's Lower Manhattan Expressway is to be voted on. Mercedes feels strongly about this. It matters to her. There's a promise of violence in the wings, but, again, just like the newspaper strike, nothing physical actually happens. People are frightened, people protest, and then they rejoice when the project fails. The LOMEX neighborhoods survive, leaving nothing for Mercedes or Dixie to do. Nothing to clean up. No slowing down of time to sugary-sweet syrup. No shock.

At neither of these events do the ladies see what they've come to see.

They return to their homes disappointed, but feeling, somehow, less alone. And that, if nothing else, keeps them together.

CHAPTER 12

"Going out with your friend again?" Gary says, one morning before he heads to class.

It's autumn of 1963. Gary's no longer a normal student, but a postdoc, working through his final semester, finishing his dissertation, something about how seismic waves move through different types of soil. Dixie doesn't know. She doesn't particularly care, except that it makes Gary happy and proud. He seems more comfortable with himself. He's started to wear thick-rimmed glasses, though he stays with his white shirt—long sleeves and a jacket in winter, short sleeves in summer—and his thin black tie. He's a throwback to the 1950s while much of the rest of New York has swapped out their prim and proper business attire for dressing more mod, Jackie O–ish, even the men in light jackets and panama hats and sometimes hair that touches their ears. Dixie wishes Gary would wear some color now and again. Dixie wishes he'd listen to Elvis. Dixie wishes he'd consider something other than a crew cut.

"Not Mercedes," she says, though she's not sure why. It would have been perfectly okay to say Mercedes and just keep that code word working between them. But she's doing something different this time, a little different, and so she goes forward with the truth, the new truth of this situation. It feels like time to mix things up.

"Peggy . . . Bill's Peggy. You know Peggy. She and I are headed downtown to watch them tear down Penn Station."

"You do weird things," Gary says. "But more power to you."

That's as far as it goes between them.

It's almost unreal.

It becomes too easy.

Dixie's lost some of the sense of responsibility that had at first surrounded it, some of the need to be careful and keep these ventures segregated from the "reality" of the rest of her life.

Looking back on it all, she knows she's made a mistake, confiding in Peggy, but she can't get out of it now. She opened her mouth, told Peggy about it, and now she can't retract her words.

"I do this thing," Dixie says one night, almost unthinkingly, as Peggy leads her from the card table at one of their friends' houses, whoever is hosting that night, out through some gauzy curtains to a balcony. It's autumn, a bit cold, but the balcony door is open to relieve some of the fug from the room. Peggy smokes. She's smoking now. It wafts with her as she leads Dixie outside. The smoking itself isn't strange, or any reason to go out into the cold of the balcony. Every person in the apartment's drawing room (other than Gary and Dixie) puffs away at cigarettes or cigars, women included. But this visit out to the balcony doesn't really revolve around smoking. The visit is a lady thing, a conversational interlude. Dixie has become more familiar with the expectations of episodes like this, gossip and confidences and girl-talk. She's ready for it. And so, safely out in the cold together, with the automated humming of an Upper West Side street clanking away several stories below them, Dixie leads off by chattering away at Peggy: "I do this thing, I want your opinion on it. I do this thing where I sneak away sometimes on my own . . ."

This gets Peggy's attention. She raises an eyebrow.

"Not like that," Dixie says.

Peggy puts her hand on Dixie's forearm.

"Honey," Peggy says, raising an eyebrow in disbelief. Then her tone changes completely, going dry and serious. "Listen," she says. "We've only got a minute before Bill comes looking for me. Won't leave me alone for an eyeblink it seems sometimes. Not since he found out."

"Found out what?"

"Well, you know . . ."

Dixie doesn't know, but she knows it'll soon become clear.

"Anyway," Peggy says, "what I want to ask you is about your friend Mercedes. Gary mentioned her to Bill. Bill said something about it to me."

"Oh," says Dixie, suddenly blushing, suddenly confused, suddenly realizing that other people know about and talk about her fake visits with Mercedes, her excuses to be out in the world on her own.

"Don't blush," Peggy replies, shaking her head and staring at her own feet. "This isn't a thing for you to blush about. It's my problem."

This is strange of Peggy, as Dixie knows her mostly to be a brash—maybe even annoying, maybe even *the most annoying*— member of their circle of friends. Dixie doesn't have much love for her, can really do without her, actually, but Bill and Gary have gotten close and there's no way for Dixie to uninvite them from their card-playing troupe, rotating their get-togethers between each other's apartments, without also accidentally uninviting herself and Gary.

"This is hard to ask," Peggy says, "but hear me out. I need a little favor."

"From Mercedes?"

"I think so."

"What?"

"I'm pregnant."

Dixie turns her head to the side, confused. She takes half a step back from Peggy. She feels the blood rush from her face. It hits her hard to hear these words, spoken aloud.

Peggy speaks quickly now and there's an edge of desperation to her words, a harder edge than the soft, fluttery sort of annoyingness that has so far in their acquaintance repulsed Dixie. "It's not his. It's not Bill's. Of course it's not—" She laughs. "If it was his I wouldn't be talking to you about it right now half-hidden behind these curtains, pretending like we're powdering our faces or whatever. Listen. I need to get rid of it. Can Mercedes help? I've heard that they do things like that out in the ghetto. That they know people. That they have places you can go, doctors who will meet you somewhere . . ."

Dixie is so confused. She wants to say: "Park Slope isn't ghetto."

She wants to say: "I haven't seen Mercedes in three years."

She wants to say: "Getting rid of a baby? That's wrong. That's just so wrong. Can't you just give it up? Have it adopted? Can't you simply convince Bill it is his? Can't you just do something, anything else?"

But she says none of these things.

That's how Dixie ends up, a few days later, standing next to Peggy on the sidewalk in Park Slope, looking around at what had been the crash site, all repaired now, all bustling and almost unscarred again (if you look closely though, you'll see some different-colored bricks where the patch-up jobs were done, burn marks on pavement, furrows beside the sidewalk). This is how Dixie ends up in Park Slope trying her hardest to not remember where it all happened and, at the same time, trying also to remember which of the houses belongs, or at least belonged, to Mercedes's family. Did Dixie ever go there? Did she ever even know which house it was? Does she have anything more than scattered, bloody, sexy dreams about the place? She's not sure. It all jumbles together and leaves her feeling lost in place and bewildered.

It's colder today than it was the night when somehow—escaping cards—she and Peggy stood together on their friend's balcony and didn't feel the biting New York wind, weren't oppressed by the New York autumn grayness, weren't dirtied by its streetscape and the close proximity of so much traffic—pedestrian, automobile, the fluttering of newsprint and garbage and whatnot.

This feels odd in all the worst ways for Dixie.

First off, the location: she's been here, on this street, of course. But it was blown up then. It was chaos. It was an alive and burning, echoing, everyone-running sort of place. Now it is normal again. And that's unnerving. To see it—admittedly two years later, and two years is a lot in New York City time—to see it not only back to normal but uncaring, forgetful, changed (but changed back into itself); to see it like this is like seeing a saw mark on the bark of a tree heal over, leaving no trace of the blade that cut it. This healing over, this suppuration, makes Dixie think of New York as a living, self-aware sort of creature. And, as such, Dixie taps her own belly, puts a hand on her belly, where her alien lives. She does this unconsciously perhaps, but also in acknowledgment of the way both things—the inside and the outside—seem to gang up on her, seem to force her into these situations. She remembers vomiting the first night she brought herself to orgasm, and her mouth fills again, just at that moment, with thin saliva, preparing itself for more.

The second sort of oddness though, one that comes with a sense of déjà vu, presents itself in the way Dixie remembers that she had never bothered to ask, on their first day of friendship, for

Mercedes's exact apartment address. She remembers how she led Gary on a fine chase, a frantic chase, trying to make a first friend but not knowing which floor, which mailbox, which place to go to. She remembers Gabrielle coming downstairs, greeting them, and Gary's reaction. She skips over the whole rest of that night. It's too difficult to parse. And she feels, wrapped up in that moment of introduction to Gabrielle, not only the moment of beginning but also the moment of ending, both things at once, both ends, all coiled together right there in Gary's very first reaction, which isn't a terrible reaction. It's a natural reaction. At this moment Dixie can see it in his eyes, in her memory of his eyes, how he is taken aback by Gabrielle and thrown on his heels, remaining for the most part speechless, which Dixie and Gabrielle and later Mercedes, when they meet up again after the crash and the triage and the slowness of that day and that night's passage of time, mistake for some sort of consent and comfort. It's not. It's Gary's way of being off-balance. He might be okay. He might land on his feet. He might trudge up wintery mountains and down through valleys of mud carrying his bazooka or machine gun or whatever in Korea, he might do all that just fine but still be unwell, still be off-balance. He's definitely off-balance in this montage of him that Dixie holds in her mind's eye. Dixie realizes she did not see it right away, and for that she blames herself.

Today she stands in the same spot again, although it is Peggy beside her. Peggy who seems, herself, off-balance. Peggy who is looking to Dixie for guidance.

Dixie is older and wiser now.

Dixie also doesn't have anything at stake this time (except perhaps for a secret hope she'll run into Mercedes, a secret hope that they'll reunite, a secret hope that makes Dixie's glances furtive, fleeting from Peggy's face, slipping from attentiveness there to quickly look up and down the sidewalks, in and out of the shops, just in case Mercedes comes around).

Dixie is older and wiser and it's easy for her to know what to do.

She picks an apartment house at random.

It's a street of brownstones.

The door has stairs before it, ten or twelve of them. An iron railing. A small foyer. A few postal slots. A corresponding number of doorbells. Dixie leads Peggy into this inner sanctum. She looks at the mail slots. Two have names on them. Two do not. She chooses an unnamed apartment. She rings the doorbell. She hopes no one answers. Her hope is justified.

Silence on the other end.

Bolder now, Dixie rings again.

Still no answer.

Peggy's eyes are hardened. She's not talking. She's just waiting, looking at the rosebud color of Dixie's painted fingernail where she presses against the brass-toned doorbell. Nothing. Nothing happens beyond the tinny sound of the distant ringing, the somewhere-inside buzzing of the doorbell.

"I'm sorry," Dixie says. "She must not be here."

"I see," says Peggy.

"We'll try again next week."

"Let's wait."

"I can't. I've got to get to Penn . . ."

"Bullshit. Penn Station doesn't matter. Not in comparison to my problem," Peggy says. She takes Dixie by the arm and leads her out of the apartment building, down the street just a few doors to where a small diner, with a row of swiveling stools against the counter and a red vinyl booth positioned up against the storefront window, gives them a good vantage from which to observe the apartment building, the randomly chosen apartment building, as well as the whole length of the street, up and down.

They get coffee as well as cream cheese on a bagel that they share.

Dixie checks her wristwatch, a present Gary got her for their third anniversary. It's set with rhinestones around the rim, really not her style, but it's everyone else's style in 1963, so Dixie goes with it.

The whole time, Peggy says nothing. It's uncomfortable silence. It makes the waiter behind the counter watch them. It makes the other customers look over their shoulders. Dixie should say something, but she hasn't got words. Instead, she looks beyond Peggy, at her but also beyond her, over her shoulder, down the street, across the intersection, keeping everything in focus but, by doing so, also ensuring that she focuses on nothing. The Brooklyn neighborhood becomes a blur. The Brooklyn noises become background to the silence.

It is out of that blur that Dixie realizes Peggy has begun to cry.

And it is out of that blur, right at the moment when Dixie reaches for Peggy's hand, that Mercedes walks past the window, looking right at Dixie, looking right into her face.

Dixie blanches.

But Peggy, through her tears, doesn't notice.

Nor does Mercedes notice. She seems oblivious to Dixie's presence. It's as if Mercedes's eyesight cannot penetrate the storefront window. Perhaps there is glare from the diffusion of the sun through the glowering sky, or a shadow from the autumn trees overlaying the glass, making it opaque, filling it with bright streaks from the sky or gray and brown and unwholesome algae- or army-green colors melting off the citified trees. Perhaps she sees Dixie but is just exceptionally unmoved, deft at hiding her surprise, or utterly unsurprised and uncaring. Perhaps she's too deep in her thoughts, or too focused on the nearness of her family's home, to observe the world around her (though, from what Dixie remembers, or has invented in her mind of Mercedes's better qualities, she dismisses this idea: Mercedes sees everything. Mercedes notices everything).

Perhaps the answer is that Mercedes just doesn't realize what she's seen, who she's seen, until later, replaying things in her memory and realizing that, behind the glass, Dixie's head swivels fully one hundred and eighty degrees, like part of one of Gary's repaired machines, a slow and calculated, gear-like rotation as Peggy on the vinyl-upholstered seat across from her cries.

Whatever it is, Mercedes does not stop.

"We should go," Dixie says, unsure if she'll follow Mercedes or not.

"Have you seen something?" Peggy asks, unseeing herself.

"No," Dixie decides. "It's just been long enough. I don't even know if Mercedes lives in this neighborhood anymore. They probably moved away. They probably live somewhere else now. We shouldn't spend more time here."

"But what will I do?" Peggy asks.

Dixie has an answer for her. Or makes up an answer. She's not sure which. She doesn't really care, to tell the truth. She's disgusted by Peggy's plan. Every time she thinks about it her own stomach churns. She knows it is wrong. She only goes along with it because she's certain—she's not sure why, but she's utterly certain—that nothing will come of this adventure in Park Slope. Mercedes isn't the type to know about, or give advice about, abortion. This thought is fixed in Dixie's mind, immovable and strangely horrible, almost saint-like in its repulsion. *Mercedes isn't the type. Mercedes won't help.*

We're just here because I want to see Mercedes and I want to go to Penn Station. This is all about me, Dixie says to herself. *I want to see and be seen.*

Though Dixie is ready to leave, Peggy remains fixed to her seat.

"I know what you should do," Dixie says.

"About the baby?"

Dixie nods, but doesn't explain. She just wants to move Peggy onward. She'll share the answer later. She'll use it as bait, as a bribe to get Peggy out of Park Slope, whatever it takes. The solution to Peggy's problem is there, right in the forefront of Dixie's brain, but she waits to spill the beans. She waits and uses a little bit of misdirection in the meantime.

"Come on," Dixie says. "I've got a secret."

"Really?"

"I started to tell you about it last night, but you needed to talk about your issue, so I held off."

"It's a man, right?"

"Sort of. But not really."

"What do you mean?"

"It's really more an angel. A man who is an angel."

"That sounds delicious," Peggy says, cheering up even though the words crackle around the last bits of salt from her crying.

"Yes," Dixie says, playing along, at least enough that she raises her eyebrows, pulses her lips together, gives off all the signals of coyness. "Yes, delicious indeed. But different than what you're thinking, dear."

"That's what we all say," Peggy says, now back to having that edge of bitterness.

"No, hear me out. I've never been with him. I've never even spoken to this man—" A lie, on top of a lie, or at least a dream-lie, Dixie knows, as the memories of the Professor in her sex dreams flood around her. "Here's why I think he's an angel. I go to weird things. You might have noticed . . ."

Peggy shakes her head "no."

"I go to weird things, do weird things. Like horrible things. The most horrible things I can find. Crashes mostly. A train crash was the first one—" . . . lie . . . "The train I took to New York went off the rails in Ohio, right after Gary started grad school—" . . . lie . . . "I saw him there, this angel man. That was the first time. Then a plane crash here in New York. Then when the boiler blew up at the telephone company, you remember that? The newspaper protests and strikes. I've seen him at all those things, but only ever out of the corner of my eye—" . . . a lie, again, heaping lies upon lies.

Dixie is burying herself. Lie after lie. Almost every sentence. Dixie makes up more encounters, puts the Professor into situations and scenarios where she had been trying to find him, makes successes out of her failures. She's telling a big tale, a story, that somehow, as she speaks it, makes more sense to her than the actuality of her lived experience. She hasn't seen the Professor again since the plane crash. She hasn't seen him at the boiler explosion, the Jamaica Bay crash, the newspaper strike, the Mr. Moses's LOMEX hearing. She hasn't seen him at all, except in her dreams. And the totally innocent, totally un-worrisome train trip from Idaho to New York, when she did see him, see him for real, in living flesh and blood, seems now, in this story, to have morphed into a horrible crash as well, become part of the pattern, simplified, that Dixie wants to share with Peggy. Dixie isn't sure how she's contorted everything, or why she's contorted everything (other than to make it easier for Peggy to digest). It's a good tale though. It's working. It's got Peggy by the throat. The pieces all fit into a digestible whole.

"That's why you want to go to Penn Station. To the demolition."

"It's like a crash."

"He'll show up?"

"Out of the ashes and dust. He'll walk right out and then right past us and I think you'll see him with me and be able to tell me whether you think he's an angel or not. I need you to do that, okay? I need someone else to see, someone else to believe."

"I'm in," says Peggy. "Count me in."

"But listen," Dixie confides. "He'll walk right past us. He'll pretend not to notice. It's like he's not of this world at all."

"An angel."

"What I need from you, Peggy dear, is for you to see him. And then, more importantly, I need your help so that he will see me. I want him to see me and acknowledge me and then, I hope, forget me. I need to be over it. I need to be done with it. I need to put it away and not let it out again. It's getting in the way with Gary. I need your help to bring it to a head and to end it. Okay?"

"Okay," says Peggy, as they leave the diner and head back on the subway toward downtown. "Okay, but I need your help too."

Dixie nods.

Peggy grabs her arm.

"I really need your help, with this—this thing in me," Peggy says. She touches her belly then, and the two women look at each other for a soul-wrenching moment.

Dixie nods again, promising, promising something she doesn't know whether she can actually do.

CHAPTER 13

It's a new era after Penn Station.

It's a busy few years for Dixie and Peggy. Dixie never lets herself believe that Peggy actually sees him, her Professor. That wouldn't be fair. That wouldn't be the way the game gets played, at least in Dixie's mind. She's not willing to share. She'll do all the other niceties. She'll be the faithful married wife, as well as the devoted mother as Cyril grows and goes to school and does all the amazing learning and thriving and loving and making pictures with crayons on stiff colored paper. She'll do all these things, but she won't share her Professor.

This whole series of events bonds Peggy to Dixie in a way that Dixie can't quite bring herself to understand. It's part gratitude, for sure, as Dixie helps Peggy with her little problem. And it is part mutual loneliness as well, a falling together of two young women in a big, lonesome city, women who have no other real recourse except for the company the other can provide.

Peggy swears she sees it, swears that she sees *him*. She swears that, in the very first moment at Penn Station when the workers start taking apart the structure—not with a wrecking ball like Dixie hopes and expects, but piece by piece, dislodging and bringing down the big old eagle above the front façade—she sees the Professor, Dixie's Professor. Truthfully, there are probably a couple dozen actual professors in the crowd. And there are probably a hundred or two hundred men who come close enough to the description Dixie has provided (though, of course, none of them with cotton wads stuffed in their ears; none of them with unread magic playing cards). Peggy swears she sees, almost meets, almost even talks to Dixie's Professor among the throng gathered around the crane and the workers who lower the eagle statue down to the sidewalk from its perch on the pediment above.

Dixie doesn't know how that can be.

She doesn't see the Professor.

She doesn't talk to him, or almost talk to him.

And she doesn't leave Peggy's side the whole time, Peggy who is still quietly crying now and again on their trip back from Park Slope, holding Dixie's arm just as if they are a couple, not so much unlike Mercedes and Gabrielle. At the very least their body language proclaims them bosom friends, friends who have known each other since childhood, rather than relative strangers thrown together in the mush of the city's social laboratory.

What can Dixie say though? What can she do? What power does she have to refute a moment that Peggy imagines and that becomes, in their friendship, a pivot point, an incident helping them inflect inward toward each other and begin the busy few years of Dixie's program of "being seen"?

It's the power of belief, of needing to believe in something. Dixie gives that to Peggy. It's the power of story, of crafting a shared sense of suffering. It's the mirage of the Professor allowing them to believe there is something more than their shallow lives upon which to fasten their energies and their imaginations.

"We need to go to these events," Dixie tells Peggy. "We need to go to all of these events, everything that matters. We need to do it together, okay?"

Peggy nods agreement.

"We need to do it together because we're the only ones in this whole darn city who can see this man."

"This angel," Peggy corrects.

Far from being brash, far from being annoying and nasal and somewhat slovenly in the way she had been throughout her earlier man-chasing days, Peggy simply acquiesces. Peggy agrees. Peggy reinforces. Peggy becomes the beta to Dixie's alpha. Peggy becomes the hairdresser, the clothing consultant, the handbag connoisseur, the travel companion and lady-in-waiting who Dixie needs on this new adventure of "being seen."

They have this shared story together. It becomes two ladies spying for angels, seeing angels in trauma. It becomes this so that the bond, the story behind the bond, doesn't have to be two ladies going to a cabin in the Adirondacks together, meeting a man with a black doctor's case full of tools, drinking half a bottle of rum, then biting down on a leather strap while he fishes an alien out. It doesn't have to be that.

Nor does it have to have anything to do with them, these two nice Columbia ladies, hauling an old trunk to Morningside Park and burying it there beside a park bench.

Story can be whatever they want, as long as it is something they share just as deeply. Story can be whatever they want it to be, and if they make it nice and pleasing and fun to think about, why, then everything will be okay. There will be nothing to worry about. Nothing for which to repent.

They are together in November of that year when JFK is shot (no one ever forgets this), though they have nowhere to go, nowhere to be out and seen in their grief and their participation. They just get dressed up and head down to Times Square. Dixie wears a somewhat shapeless swing dress, but in a bolder than usual color, russet like an Idaho potato. Peggy turns her nose up at it as if to say, *How will you ever be* noticed?

They attend rallies for the public-school boycott in early '64. Peggy's got her in a miniskirt, bright green, and a lemon-colored jacket. She almost can't help but be seen, she feels, like a billboard or a neon light, except that half of the other ladies in their mid-twenties are dressed in an identical manner, so many mannequins.

They venture to the World's Fair together. More importantly they do the antiwar protests, burning draft cards in Union Square— not for their husbands, who receive exemptions as scientists, young scientists sent to look for oil in Montana and Texas and the Middle East in order to aid the war effort, but for some of their students, younger friends who have joined their friend set. They're not the only women to attend, and not the only ones who put themselves in the same category, the same market to "be seen," as most of them remain on the lookout for men. Peggy and Dixie are, however, some of the few to actually get their fingers scorched a little. For this event they wear psychedelics, hiding the prints from their husbands, who would never approve. Dixie thinks that the best place to hide her outfit, after the fact, after wearing it, would be her big green portmanteau, her trunk, but she doesn't have it anymore. She doesn't have access to it, not easy access. So, she just takes the dress out to the woods, the little woods in Morningside Park, and buries it under the trees there.

They're at the July riots in Harlem in 1964, the opening of the Verrazzano-Narrows Bridge (they hope it will collapse, and that the Professor will appear among the detritus of iron and guylines that they imagine littering all the harbor between Brooklyn and Staten Island).

143

They go to Jones Beach after the crash of Eastern Air, and Peggy gets a chance to roll up her sleeves and dirty her hands. They both vomit together, catching it in Dixie's new (suddenly worthless) Etienne Aigner handbag. This mingling of bodily fluids has a bit of extra meaning for them, of course, after the Adirondacks. But that is never mentioned. The story doesn't go there. The story between them—and there's story plenty, words and words and words—has everything to do with these dangerous things they see and do, these moments they experience. It has everything to do with the phantom angel of the Professor in their lives. It never, never again between them involves a subplot about that cabin upstate.

Gary's making money now. It's his first real job but a big difference, a big step up from internship/assistant positions with the harbor survey. He's flying around the world. He's going everywhere and staying days, or even weeks at a time, and his salary allows them to move into a new flat, a proper one, he calls it, with a room apart for Cyril, a spare room for the next baby, and even quarters for a maid once they need one. Dixie's never had spending money like she does now. The New York grocery prices are not as intimidating. The handbags—like this one into which Peggy vomits—are a luxury, and make her feel guilt on a whole new level, but they aren't out of her reach. She even has a conversation with her mother about sending some money home, "helping them with the bills," she says.

This goes nowhere.

Even if they need it, which Dixie thinks is true, they won't admit as much. The only one who will say he wants money is Paul. And if she does send cash home, she knows her parents will give it to him. Then what? Then what will he do, if he has a little money?

Dixie feels guilty bringing it up, suggesting she send money, hearing the unspoken questions and concerns about what Paul might do, if there were money in the house. This leads Dixie's mind toward home, in both its good parts and its bad. And so, when her mother says, "You should come back to Idaho . . ." Dixie isn't surprised.

"Not to live," Dixie says, over the long-distance line, which is hollow and slow and tunnellike.

"No, not to live," Dixie's mother replies. "Just to visit. It's been five years and your father misses you. He should have come out. You invited him, and that was kind, but it's not his style. You should come."

"Just because he's stubborn?"

"Just because he's your father," she says, and after a moment, hesitating at first, she adds, "And because Cyril should see him and know him."

Dixie hears the ominous tone to this message.

"Is something the matter?" she asks. But her mother won't elaborate.

"Just come home for a while. A month. Or for the summer. It'll do us all good to see you."

She can't deny this. She can't protest too strongly, not with Gary gone for such long stretches himself, even knowing that some of his travel takes him "out west," near enough to Idaho that he could almost base himself in Pocatello.

"You should go by plane," Gary says. "Jet flights will take you right to Salt Lake. Then it's just a hop up to Pocatello on a prop plane."

"Prop?"

"Short for propellor."

"Oh, gawd," Dixie says, picturing the planes she's seen come into Pocatello, buffeted by the winds of the high plains, their wingtips dipping, their whole frame seeming like it might roll over and spiral into the earth. "Oh, gawd."

But the train seems worse to her.

"That crash you experienced in Ohio," Peggy reminds her, "that was a train. And then you were involved in the Park Slope crash even before we went out to Staten Island for Eastern Air. No wonder you haven't wanted to travel overmuch. You've seen it all."

"I'm thinking about a bus," Dixie says. And she means it. There should be no reason for her to fear. Dixie knows in her rational mind that literally thousands of flights happen, and even more train trips, without incident. But the finality, the catastrophe, the time between realization and an end, falling from the sky to the ground, she can't bear.

Also, she thinks, perhaps she'll see the Professor again, heading west himself, boarding the bus (or train, or whatever she takes) somewhere in that nebulous Ohio-to-Missouri flatland. Maybe that'll do the trick. Maybe that will help them meet again.

She makes plans for the trip, right when Cyril finishes kindergarten that spring.

Yet, before that, right on their own beloved Columbia campus, one of the bigger and more traumatic incidents unfolds. There, at the Audubon Ballroom where Dixie and Gary have gone for piano concertos and screenings of various faculty theater shows, fundraisers, awards banquets, etcetera, the activist and provocateur Malcom X is shot.

This is a moment more dangerous than most Dixie has seen.

Yet, Peggy convinces Dixie it is the perfect moment for baby doll dresses and little matching flats, done up in checkered but suitably solemn reverse-print black and white, crisp against the grayness (punctuated throughout by black, by white) of New York's February streetscape, each of them with a single blood-colored carnation pinned to their lapels. They're of course too late for the assassination itself (how were they to know such a thing would happen, right in their own backyard?), but by no means are they too late for the protests and the mass parade leading to the man's solemn funeral after the fact.

The two women work their way a few blocks deeper into Harlem to the site of this funeral. There they stick out, welcomed for the most part, or tolerated at least, left alone, left unmolested, but definitely outliers among the sea of somber black faces, most downturned, most cold, but some still carrying the anger and fire that X expected of them.

Together, they are white-skinned as lilies, innocent as lilies too (and checkered, Dixie above the waist, with a flat black woolen skirt below; Peggy below the waist, with a black turtleneck above), among the sea of black-coated, black-faced, weeping or angry mourners lined up, shuffling around the corner, all the way along the street to where X is being eulogized at Faith Temple Church of God.

They don't go in.

They don't think they'll be allowed. And, as much as they are moved (and fright is a powerful mover of feelings and alertness, fright for themselves, shocking them out of their aloneness momentarily, making them aware), they haven't come to Harlem to mourn. They've come to watch. It's respectful, but also a little ugly of them, ugly for them.

"Go home," one woman says to them from the confined line of citizens who wait to enter the temple. This woman cups her hands and shouts at them, loudly enough that her voice carries across the street to where Dixie and Peggy stand, curbside. The doors of the temple have Star of David windows on their front, and the whole thing looks like a movie theater, a church in a movie theater. A man with a long beard comes out through those doors, raising his hands, dressed in long robes and a high hat. Dixie has seen nothing like this before. He tells the crowd to remain quiet, to remain respectful, then he goes back in.

That's when Dixie sees him.

"There he is," she says, pulling at Peggy's arm.

"The Imam?"

"What's an Imam?"

"That man who came out. He's like a pastor for Muslims. What confuses me is the Star of David. You'd think a Jewish symbol on a mosque . . ."

But Dixie doesn't care about that. "No," she says. "No. I wasn't paying attention to any of that."

"Then what?"

"Up there!" Dixie points to a building just to the right of the temple. Rather than one or two stories, it's five or six. In a window midway up, midway in, a curtain flutters.

"Like the Kennedy shooter," says Peggy. "Like Lee Oswald. Whoever it was. There and then gone."

Dixie says, "It was him. The Professor. I'm surprised you didn't notice him, since you saw him last."

Dixie says this with a bit of ice in her voice, a bit of nagging jealousy, a bit of a challenge: *prove it* that you know who he is. Peggy ignores her. "What was he doing?" she asks.

"Just staring."

"Waving?"

"No. Just staring. Staring at me."

Part IV
Seeing into Sheds

CHAPTER 14

Dixie returns to Idaho. She returns to Pocatello. She returns to her father, and to Paul. With Cyril along, she braves it, boarding the jet after Gary books all the tickets and hauls all the bags she has packed down to the airport, handing them over at the counter so that they can be loaded in the belly of the plane.

"I'll come right away when I get back from Arabia," he says. "It'll be home base for us all summer. Boarding up the place here until the fall. You'll have so much fun."

Dixie doubts this, but she doesn't argue.

All the way back to Idaho, all the way to Salt Lake City, she's moody. She's not herself. Or, more truly, she's her new self, this New York City person. She's not sure when it happened, but she can see it, in reflection, in the people around her on the plane and in the airport, not right away, not at the Idlewild starting point of the trip—Idlewild which has just been renamed JFK—but certainly she catches the first glimpses of it when she lays over in Chicago, more so on the next stop in Salt Lake, the reflection of herself, how she looks and how she acts and how she is being seen by others. She's not smiling at the other passengers or the airline attendants. She's sharp with them. She's sharp with Cyril. She's preoccupied with her clothes, with her fingernails, with her magazine. She's not Dixie.

What's happened? she says to herself in the mirror of the women's bathroom once they touch down at Salt Lake, on the layover there. Cyril stands next to her, still young enough to come with her into the powder room, grabbing at her hands and playing with the knobs of the bathroom sink. Dixie mostly ignores him, but she does watch him out of the corner of her eye, making sure he is there. She watches him out of the corner of her eye looking downward in the mirror so that she sees him from two angles at once, reflected and in real space too, farther beneath her and in her peripheral vision. Dressed in his best clothes, there in the shiny airport bathroom, he seems more doll-like, more unreal than usual, and Dixie has a hard time not being annoyed at him, even though he is only five years old. Even though he represents most of her day, most of her daily, worldly concerns. How was she supposed to know—no one ever told her, not that she can remember, though she supposes it was just assumed, assumed all along—how was she supposed to know that a child would become everything to her, that all the world's expectations of her, as a mother, would focus on him? How was she supposed to know that, with his arrival, she'd almost become invisible herself? Invisible and subservient. Living through him. Living to teach him, to rear him up, to keep him healthy and fed and loved. That is her lot. She doesn't mind, except in this most glancing way, this sidelong look where she allows herself to question everything—what's real, what's not; what matters, what doesn't.

Cyril looks like a baby again. Just a doll of a baby. But Dixie knows he's not. She knows he's a real boy with real mischief, ideas, motivations of his own.

Dixie's got her purse out, a big tin can of Hidden Magic hair spray in hand. She leans inward toward the mirror, and she's going to coif the helmet of her hair, one or two strands of which have rubbed themselves into static disobedience during the half hour or so when she let herself close her eyes and momentarily rested her head against the terry-cloth fabric of her headrest in the jet plane's seat.

Will he even recognize me? Dixie asks herself, as she looks at the curled bangs, the dark hair, which—with Peggy's connivance—has been cut and bobbed at her shoulders so that it dashes outward, sprightly and fashionable. *Will he even recognize me and see the same girl who left Idaho just a few years earlier, without a care for any of these big-city New York trends?*

Will he even recognize me? she says to herself for a third time, thinking, on the surface, at the most superficial level, of her father. But that's not all she thinks of. Deeper down, there's her Professor too. Of course, that's who she is thinking of, all the time. That's her game. That's half the point of this journey, at least up until this very moment in the mirror. She's wondering whether he'll recognize her because half the point is to be seen by him. It's her and Peggy's strategy. And this is yet another chance to confront him, to put herself out there in a situation where he, their angel, is likely to appear, a situation fraught with all the memories of a previous journey, a situation where it has been proven, by past experience, that she should expect some likelihood of him appearing. Dixie is thinking about the Professor at this level of *being seen*. But she's also thinking of her father, superficially.

And somewhere, tangled up in all that, not really the same thought at all but certainly part of it, mixed up in it, uncomfortably so, there is the specter of Uncle Paul. Will *he* recognize her?

She won't really admit it.

She won't really let it come to the forefront of her mind. She won't form the words. It's easier to say to herself: *I wonder if he'll even recognize me,* and have those words reflect on the game she's been playing for most of these last several years, a game that has gotten rather serious and rather intense between the time when she left

Pocatello as a girl and, now, five years later, as she comes back a woman. It's easier to ascribe the worry that she feels, which is an aspect of *being seen*, to her dream-lover, to her imaginary beau, than it is to think about how it affects her father. Easier to do that than to think of Paul at all, to see him standing in the corner with his clown face when she lies down on her bridal bed. He wasn't there. He was something in her imagination, sure. But it's easier to keep up the game than it is to deal with reality.

Of course he'll recognize me, part of her says. *He doesn't see clothes. He doesn't see makeup. He doesn't see New York City manners, wherever they've come from, however they've taken hold of me. It'll be just the same as olden days. It'll be just the same as when you left, Dixie dear.*

Still, when the can of hair spray sputters and runs out, and after a shake or two of frustration—like she's trying to strangle it a little, or rattle out more of its vaporous juice—Dixie jumps as if the can has exploded, rather than run out of juice. This surprises Dixie (and Cyril beside her too). She is surprised at the vehement way she throws the can, aiming at but not hitting the waste bin in the corner of the airport bathroom. The can clatters against the tiled bathroom wall. It caroms away and spins to rest on the tiled bathroom floor. The whole room echoes with the sound of it.

In the quiet, in that moment between the throwing of the can and it rattling to a stop, Dixie feels Paul's hands on her. They touch her shoulders, her chest, her rib cage. One finger is on her chin, another finger in her mouth. Dixie should bite him. She knows she should bite him, but she doesn't. She never bites him. She's mad at herself for that. She's mad at her father too. She's mad at the hair spray can and at her new bangs and at the stories about clowns and horses and big top tents, stories she liked to hear because they meant an adult would be with her in the dark, at bedtime, even if that adult was wearing a clown-face mask. Even if that adult was Uncle Paul.

Dixie shivers.

152

Cyril looks at his mother. His eyes seem to say, *Mommy, are you angry?*

Dixie looks at him. She's still cross, and it comes out in her voice, even as she denies it, so that the sound of her words tells the truth better than the words themselves: "No, not angry."

Then she softens, bends down to him with her knees together, to the side, his body up against her hip where the pleat of her dress traces the upper part of her leg. She hugs him.

"You're nervish then?" Cyril asks, his pronunciation cute, but his perception too deep.

"Yes, I'm *nervish* I suppose. Going home isn't easy."

"We just left home though. We just left New York."

"But this was my home, where we are going."

"When you were small like me?"

"Yes."

"Why?"

"It's just where I was born."

"Why?"

"Because it's where Granny and Grandpa lived."

"Why?"

"Oh, god, Cy," she says. "You've got so many questions. Hmmm. Let me think. I know. I've got it. It wasn't Granny and Grandpa. It was their parents, years before. I suppose they came out here, out west, because they were trying to get away from all the people in the overcrowded east and make a life for themselves. Lots of people did that back in those days."

"But you and Daddy went back."

"It's different times now."

"You went back for Daddy's school?"

"Yes."

"He went back for his school, and you went back for him. And you took me with you."

"Yes."

"Because you needed to get away?"

This last question, Dixie doesn't answer. She doesn't even know if Cyril speaks it aloud, or if she just imagines it. She just stands, and takes Cyril by the hand, and starts to lead him out of the ladies' bathroom. A few other airport passengers have come in, have left, and they've given Cyril a good looking-at, how he's so earnest, so focused. None of the onlookers in this bathroom are too disturbed by his presence in the ladies' room. He's only five, after all. But they've looked at him nonetheless, sizing him up. His string of questions hasn't helped. He's supposed to be quiet, to remain quiet, especially in the bathroom. Dixie has taught him that. To be quiet around other adults. To be seen, but not heard. To never make Dixie answer questions or engage in conversation around other adults. It's important for Dixie to be able to have adult conversations, she tells him. But nevertheless, it seems to Dixie like he's been listening, and thinking, and coming to conclusions about the world, biding his time until, at this very moment, right here in the ladies' room, he's come into focus as being too old, too mature, at least for this act of accompanying his mom and holding her hand and standing innocently next to her as she sprays her hair back into place. Dixie tells herself she'll need to find a new system soon, or just trust that she can leave him outside sitting on a bench when she has to do her business. He's getting so big.

He's getting so big, and his next words, his next question almost prove this change, making all Dixie's insides clutch together, her knees buckling a little, with its perception. "You and Daddy went back east, just like Granny and Grandpa's parents went west, so that you could be who you wanted?"

Dixie scans Cyril's face. There's no threat in his expression. *How could there be?* There's no ulterior motive, no subtext to his words. He's just piecing together the threads of this journey, the reasons why he's had to travel in a jet plane all the way across the country. Mother and son, they are both exhausted. They are both *nervish.* They are both thrown off by the changes in air pressure and by the juttering of the plane as, a few minutes earlier, it passed through turbulence on the way down into the veil of the Rockies, approaching Salt Lake Valley.

After another moment or two, Dixie pulls herself together. She doesn't really answer Cyril. She doesn't mean to *not* answer him. She doesn't mean to prevaricate. But she's thrown off by the way his question seems to be two questions at once. Or a condemnation of sorts. *"You and Daddy went back east, just like Granny and Grandpa's parents went west, so that you could be who you wanted?"*—as if she wasn't who she wanted to be before she went to New York. As if the whole experience was, somehow, temporary, out-of-body, and unoriginal. As if her true self had been left behind and everything she'd done in New York (and on the uneventful train ride from Pocatello to New York, the totally normal, nothing-to-worry-about train trip) had manifested in pantomime, in masquerade, in knowing duplicity.

Dixie doesn't answer this directly.

She says, instead, "You'll love running around Pocatello this summer. It's so different from New York City. You'll be able to just run and run and run and it'll be good for your little mind, Cy. It'll be good for your body and your mind and your soul. You think such adult thoughts and you don't need to, not at your age. You need to run and be free, okay?"

Cyril doesn't respond to this. He's still holding Dixie's hand. He's still looking at her with eyes that don't judge, and don't prevaricate at all. He's still looking at her simply as if he waits to get to her answer, her real answer, for her to give him her real answer.

"It'll be good for you so that you don't have to worry your little head about big people questions," Dixie says at last, which is the most dissatisfying thing of all the things she's ever said, she thinks. It makes her sigh through her nose, and bite her lip, and—later— when they've boarded the little single prop plane that'll take them over the mountain from Salt Lake to Pocatello in the north, Dixie pulls out a little mirror from her purse and uses it to muss up her hair. She doesn't want Cyril to unthink these things. She doesn't want him to put away his amazing, penetrating thoughts. But, really, she also doesn't want them directed at her. She doesn't want to see herself, in the little handheld mirror, with her New York City mask on. She doesn't want to wear that mask any longer.

Cyril is asleep by then, so he doesn't see her mess up her carefully brushed and sprayed hair.

He doesn't see her cry a little, not recognizing Dixie anymore in the compact's silvery surface. No matter what she does, as she destroys the helmet of her hair-sprayed mass, Dixie from Pocatello won't return. She just ends up looking frumpy. She just ends up looking disheveled. She can't capture the old her. To anyone who sees her in the airport or has a conversation with her once she arrives, she can explain this. She can explain it to her mother, to her father. She can and probably will need to explain it to Paul. He'll be all over it. He'll have lots to say about it. He'll be sure to remind her that she doesn't look like herself, that she's a stranger, that she's all grown up, a woman. It's been a long, long journey, after all (not nearly as long as the train trip east had been, but nevertheless, she can act exhausted and frazzled and explain the way her hair looks; she can explain why her makeup has drizzled and blotched beneath her eyes without having to admit she let herself, at last, there on the plane looking at her reflection in the silvery compact, cry). She's coming home and she's all filled with excuses, nervous tics, images of what her father will look like and say, images of how her father will see her, how Paul will see her, how the Professor will see her: a fun-house mirror of self-reflection from which Dixie barely unentangles Dixie. A fun-house mirror where Mercedes is there too, imaginary Mercedes. And real Peggy. These are people she carries inside her, stories she carries inside, but ones she'll never explain, never even try to explain, to anyone in Pocatello.

Dixie flies to Idaho all full of tangled stories.

When they land though, it's just Granny who comes to the gate. It's just Dixie's mother, Gladys. Arlo doesn't come. Paul doesn't come. It's just the women, mother and daughter alone. And maybe Mercedes. If there is a time, a space, for just women, just women in Dixie's life, it's Mercedes who shows up there. Imaginary Mercedes.

Gladys gives Dixie's hair, the rat's nest of her hair, just one good glance and then writes it off. It's Cyril who says (when they get in the car and Granny fires it up, driving them across town toward Dixie's childhood home), whispering so that only Dixie can hear: "It's okay, Momma. I love you lots."

CHAPTER 15

What does it mean to *be seen*?

Why does it matter?

Can it be rejected as a human need? Can a person live simply as an ascetic, unseen, removed from everything and everyone around them? Can Dixie?

Dixie experiences two answers to this set of questions during the summer of her return to Pocatello. The first comes from New York City, where isolation and invisibility are a product of the crowds, the crowding, the blending of each individual into background noise, motion, chaos. The second comes from her father, who has taken up more or less permanent residence in his garage workshop, choosing isolation and invisibility even in the midst of family, even in the midst of the fabric of home and community.

He sleeps out in his work-shed most nights.

Takes his meals there.

"He's just gotten old," says Dixie's mom, when Dixie brings up this weird behavior. "Curmudgeonly."

Then a few minutes later she says, "Ever since Uncle Paul went away . . ."

"Uncle Paul went away?"

"To New York."

"Jesus," Dixie says.

Her mother merely nods. She touches the corner of her mouth. She looks toward the shed where Dixie's father is sitting already, working, grinding on some bits of machinery, even though it is the breakfast hour. Dixie doesn't know what she's thinking and isn't sure she wants to know. She's curious about her father, and sad, not for him, but for her mother, and for herself, missing him. And she's even more curious about Paul. *New York City?* That seems unlikely. That seems, almost, unfair.

Dixie tries to imagine why he's there, and she hears, in her mind, his voice saying something like, "Thought I'd just give it a try."

And then, "If it's good enough for sweet little Dixie, then it's good enough for Uncle Paul, isn't it? Shouldn't it be?"

The logical thing for Dixie to ask would be something like, "When? When did he move to New York?"

Or even, "Why?" (Though that would take plenty of thought from her mother, plenty of digging down, deep into the family history, and Dixie doesn't think her mother is prepared enough or capable enough of doing that kind of work, for herself or for her husband or even for Dixie. Especially not for Dixie. It'll all have to be Dixie, doing the work—though Dixie doesn't know what that work is, what it means, how to start . . .)

Dixie's mother can stand at the kitchen sink and see Arlo's workshop through the little window there, all the edges of which she has decorated with little glass bird statuettes and baubles, suspended on string, adhered to the window, perched on the window ledge itself, all of them throwing spangles of color around the kitchen. She's standing there now, as she says these few sentences, and she's looking out across their little fenced-in backyard toward the workshop. She holds a mug of tea in her hands. Opposite this, Dixie sits at the kitchen table, which means she can't quite see exactly what her mother watches, out there, but she knows her look isn't specific to anything anyway. It is a general stare, a stare no longer focused, no longer focused on her husband and his habit of isolation, a stare that has instead become, slowly, creepingly, a habit of introspection, a habit of being *in* a place but not *of* it. This is what drives home for Dixie the similarity between life in New York and life in Pocatello, the way they both allow or even demand that a person *not be seen.*

What does it mean to be seen? Dixie asks herself. But she doesn't have an answer to this question. Not right at this moment. Regardless, it feels like a partial victory to her, having the question itself, something she can grab hold of and explore, and so her spirits lift a bit and she's able to go about the business of being home while asking herself this question in each new (or remembered) situation that summer in Pocatello: *What does it mean to be seen?*

(She is also thinking, somewhere in the background of her mind, whether Paul has been watching her in New York. If he's been there, watching her, afraid to make contact, but watching . . . if she ever ponders the small, semantic difference—albeit with big psychic impact—between *being seen* and *being watched,* she doesn't let on about it. She spends the whole of the summer hardly thinking of Paul at all, even though all the places and things and times she remembers from her childhood are filled, if not with the memory of him directly, with the memory, at least, of his presence, his impregnation of everything in that environment.)

Dixie bides her time as she watches her father's isolation. She wants to talk to him about it. She wants to ask him about it. But she knows the moment isn't right. In this aspect, and in this aspect alone, she regrets that Paul is not available for her in Pocatello. He'd tell her what Arlo's issue is. In fact, she'd have a tough time avoiding him telling her. Paul would have a story about it. He'd have an anecdote. He'd have a reason—off base, most likely, inappropriate—a story that would, somehow, get under Dixie's skin and make her worry, like a thorn in the tender pad of her foot, for weeks.

Freed of all this—except for the specter of her father alone—Dixie does all the things she should do on a visit home: she helps her mother host various aunts for tea, various cousins and friends for dinner. Her father makes the necessary appearances at these events, though he is silent in a way that isn't so much the cattleman's silence, the pioneer's stoicism. It's the silence of nonparticipation. He makes appearances just frequently enough to prevent further questioning, from his wife, from others, but his presence is only maintained, it seems, as a shield for the greater solitude he's created. He's only there just as much as he needs to be in order to continue with his majority separation. Dixie watches him but continues with her life, with all the things she thinks and knows she should do while she's "home" in Pocatello. She does the social circuit her mother requires. She goes on visits to old friends and acquaintances. She organizes and helps with picnics. She brings Cyril with her most places, especially to see some of her old friends, all of whom have their own broods of children, their own worries and issues. It's a process of being seen, but only as an expectation, a social norm. Dixie maintains a light touch throughout the summer. She never engages deeply. She allows herself to be distracted. She lets the forms of interaction keep her a bit distant from any real connection (and in this way, perhaps, she's a bit of her father's daughter). Throughout all this she continues looking for her Professor, but not very specifically, not rushing out to any of the places or any of the events in a Peggy-like way to purposefully *be seen* by him. Things that happen in little Pocatello just aren't traumatic or influential enough, she thinks. Things that happen in little Pocatello just won't attract the interest of an angel, their angel, her angel. Because of all this, time for Dixie seems set apart, un-immersed as it can be, even in the midst of doing, doing, doing. Pocatello, Dixie knows, is not home anymore but serves her well enough as a place where she bides time, treads through time like it is water.

She's waiting for Gary, she says. Maybe they'll settle down here, she tells herself, tells her friends, her mother (unnecessarily raising her mother's hopes). She knows this isn't true. She knows it is far from the truth, both for her (with her fancy New York clothes left folded in her suitcase) and for Gary's world-traveling new line of work. Maybe they'll build a house, she says. Maybe they'll sell their New York apartment, the one they just bought last year, rather than continuing to rent. Maybe they'll sell it and get a place here with a picket fence so that they can send Cyril to school among the good, solid people of Pocatello, these children and grandchildren of pioneers and ranchers and escapees from the east. She says these things even though she knows they are false. The falsity builds an invisible wall for her between the reality of life in this small town, which exists at arm's length in front of her, tumbling along in its steady and somewhat oblivious way, and the inner life Dixie leads— which is still watching for her Professor, still waiting for Gary, and now, for the first time, missing its immersion in the pace and oblivion of big-city life.

Through all this, Dixie realizes she's got a secret way to break through to her father, an ace in the hole, a card she's held in reserve for five years, literally a card. She's got that Jack of Hearts. When Arlo had given it to her, she'd been locked in her first bout of combat with the alien inside her. She'd had a first experience of the alien, how it jerked forth tears from her in a way she couldn't understand. Dixie's father—man of few words at the best of times—never provided any explanation for giving such a thing to her. He never commented on it. He never explained its significance. He'd never promised, in words, to say anything about it at all, though his eyes and his slowness in giving it to her had conveyed the sense that there might be, certainly must be, a story behind it, a story he could, maybe should, in the right future moment, decide to share. The card had been a going-away gift, a thing he fished out from a jar on a shelf in the very same workshop where, now, he spends almost all his waking hours.

Dixie considers asking her mother about her father's near disappearance from life. *What's the matter with him?* She means to have a conversation about her father, before approaching him directly. But she doesn't. She wants to watch him a bit more, watch what he does when Gary comes to visit them in a few short days, providing the first punctuation to their summer.

In the meantime, she checks on the Jack of Hearts once or twice. Sitting on the edge of the bed in her old childhood bedroom, with dolls and lace doilies around her, she takes it out from her suitcase, out from a zipper pocket inside the suitcase, holds it, stares at the boyish face staring back at her, rouge on its cheeks. She rubs it with her thumb as she thinks, and the face shines with the oil from her finger, shines as if the wax on the surface of the card was made new. This isn't a clown's face. It's a prince's face. It's almost a woman's face. It has a different energy from any man she's met in real life. It has an energy much more like that of Mercedes. Or of Gabrielle. Gabrielle—that's it. Youth and beauty, and the way a woman might look like a young boy. Or a boy like a woman. Dixie feels she is onto something here, but she can't quite bring the idea into focus. She can't connect it to her father. She wants to. She wants to figure out the clues without asking him. But she can't.

After a moment, she puts the Jack back inside the zippered pocket of her suitcase where it will be safe.

Summer spins onward from its light green, end-of-spring start to its hotter, firefly middle.

With the approach of ticker tape and bunting, the smells of the Fourth of July holiday in the air, like popcorn and the sulfur-tinged fumes of fireworks, even as the nights stay warm there on the edge of the open, windy high plains, Gary does return. He's good about that sort of thing, keeping his word. He's steady, regular, well-rounded in everything he does. He's pretty much the perfect man, and Dixie knows that, with another round of visits to their Pocatello friends, he'll be seen and appreciated and she'll be the envy of the "in" crowd.

Gary brings with him a suitcase empty of all the necessities, absolutely no clothes or toiletries, but filled with little doodads and gifts from far Arabia. He takes the whole big bundle of it and sets it on the dining room table, right there amid the hubbub of his first few moments in the house, and hauls out a number of packages, varying sizes, all wrapped in plain butcher's paper or newsprint. These he lines up on the table. Dixie's mother is there. Dixie's Aunt Mabel (no relation to Paul). Dixie's father. Dixie herself, of course (with Gary covered in her lipstick, marked with it, little roseate blemishes).

Cyril is sleeping at the moment of Gary's arrival. Dixie whispers it to him, makes everyone whisper throughout the whole of the unwrapping ceremony—which gives the moment a hushed tension. As a result, Gary sets aside the biggest of the packages and says, smiling at everyone equally and craftily, "For when he wakes."

Dixie's mother smiles, somewhat nervously.

Dixie's father, huffing, takes the package—Gary doesn't protest, though Dixie does, trying to grab it back from him. He takes it and he leaves the house, walking his well-trodden pathway to the backyard shed.

Trying to liven things up, Dixie's mother claps.

Dixie's aunt claps.

Dixie, hearing Cyril stir from the bedroom, also claps, then goes upstairs, leaving her own present still wrapped.

Dixie's mother shoots a look first at Gary, then at Dixie's aunt as this happens. They are very different looks, each of them in quick succession. The first is clear: *anger*. But of a strange variety, because it quickly dissipates, as Gary shrugs and winces a little and mouths the word "sorry." The second glance, the one directed at Aunt Mabel, is much less definite. What flicker crosses her face: guilt? A guilty look? A worried look? It's hard to be sure. And when Dixie returns, just a moment later, saying "It's okay, he's still asleep," the women stay fixated on the gifts. Gary stays fixated on the gifts, opening them one by one: a big tea flagon in bronze with incised figures, mother-of-pearl inlays. A hookah for Dixie's father, which Gary demonstrates for the women without bothering to fill it with water or live coals, just sucking on one of the mouthpieces and explaining, with the hose held in one hand like Fred Astaire's dancing baton, how the whole contraption works, and how the cafes in Cairo, where he's spent some time, coming and going from drier and much more austere Arabia, are filled with these devices, coal boys coming around to keep the tray glowing, snacks being served amid trained monkeys and screeching macaws. He's got little packets of spice he makes Dixie's mother and Aunt Mabel sniff. He's got tobacco, coffee from Yemen and Ethiopia. He's got a big ostrich egg, the biggest egg any of them have ever seen, with figures of animals and palm fronds carved right into the milky-white surface of the shell. He's got all the things.

Dixie's mother clears the photos of Dixie and of their long-ago family vacation to Yellowstone off the mantel above the fireplace so that she can arrange all Gary's treasures in a suitable place of honor. Dixie's mother and Dixie's aunt fuss around Gary, asking him all the questions about his travels. Gary takes one of the kitchen chairs and sits on it, backward, jauntily, to entertain the matrons. And Gladys barely looks out of sorts at all, now that the worst has passed, now that Arlo has once again settled back into his shed, where it seems (at least in her accustomed perspective) he most belongs, and—importantly for them all—now that Aunt Mabel has not asked any questions about the situation in their house.

It's all okay. Everything is just fine. It's normal and even good and there's nothing to worry about at all. Dixie feels good, great, excited by Gary's homecoming.

Dixie's father comes back in.

His presence puts a stop to the festivities, though not an unnatural one. The women simply withdraw, starting to make lunch. Dixie goes with them to help, as is expected. But she sees her father and Gary having a conversation, a very direct conversation. Almost heated.

Then Arlo withdraws again. Dixie should be able, easily enough, to say something to him, stop him, something like: *"Where are you going, Dad?"* Perhaps this is the right time, the moment she's been waiting for, to discuss the Jack of Hearts. Perhaps she can get Gary to take a bath, a shower, unpack his real suitcase, the one with his clothes in it, so she can ask her father what is happening, so she can have this critical moment.

Before she can do anything, Gary makes a quick circuit around the room, almost like he is pacing, and then he follows Arlo outside to the shed.

Dixie goes upstairs.

She tugs on the cord of the blind that covers her bedroom window. It rolls up, like some sort of papery animal's tongue. Outside she can see the men in the shed, but only parts of them: Gary's leg in the doorway, the top of her father's head in the side window that looks over the uncut, knee-high lawn with the rusted corpse of their push lawn mower leaning against the fence.

Dixie unzips the pocket inside her suitcase.

She takes the playing card from it.

This feels like the time. The right moment: both men in the same place. No Uncle Paul to confound things. A good and honest talk with the most important people in her life.

She takes the playing card and rushes down the stairs, out into the yard. But, as she approaches, she slows. The closer she gets, the harder it is to move forward. She doesn't want to burst in upon them, or surprise them, or stop whatever conversation they're having. She's ready to interject. She comes to a stop outside the shed. She decides she's going to listen for a bit. She's going to listen and judge whether the moment is, indeed, the exact one for which she's waited.

She steps up to the workshop shed's lone window. She peeps through the window, unable to help herself. She's quiet in her approach, quiet and cautious in her peeping, and she's rewarded in this slyness by seeing, through that window, her father sitting on his workshop bench while Gary stands in the doorway of the shed with his arms crossed. Between them, on the workbench, is the package Gary brought home for Cyril. It has been opened. Its contents spill from the torn paper as if eviscerated.

Dixie has heard her father's voice far too infrequently these last five years to be anything but happy at the sound of it. It's crinkled and dry, and if Dixie didn't know deep in her heart that her father was, really, ageless and would never, ever think of getting sick and dying, if she didn't know that and have total trust in her perception of it, then she wouldn't like that voice one bit. She wouldn't like the sound of the old man in it, the wheeze, the dryness, the harbinger. Dixie's heard her father speak far too infrequently even since she and Cyril have been home. Just the fact that he is saying words—that he and Gary, even under tension, are having a conversation—fills her with happiness.

The words are not difficult to make out. The men speak loudly.

"You unwrapped it," Gary says.

"I don't know what you're trying to do," says Arlo, pointing at Gary, then at the box on the table. In it: a doll. A doll wearing traditional Arabic clothing, bright colored, bold patterned.

"Just a gift. Just something fun. Just something I found in the market in Arabia that I thought might be appreciated."

"But, a doll? Does it have to be a *doll?*" Arlo asks. He seems a bit deflated, as if he only momentarily could hold on to the fire of whatever anger had seized him.

"She loves them."

"Of course she does. But you shouldn't encourage it."

"Damn it, Arlo," says Gary, which is weird, Gary using her father's given name, not to mention Gary swearing. "You should know how much this means to her. You, of anyone, should know."

Rusted, oily gadgets and sprockets and doodads have been cleared from around the doll in the box in a broad semicircle, as if Arlo had swept the surface clean with his forearm.

Gary takes a step forward into the shed, not in a threatening way but in that Korean-War sergeant stance that brooks no argument, that looks at the world for only what it is. He has a bit of John Wayne to his voice when he says, "What happened between you and Paul?"

"What do you mean?" Arlo says, but he looks down, unable to hold Gary's gaze.

"I mean, a man doesn't invite another man into his life unless something significant has happened. A man doesn't open up his house and make a stranger part of it, a forever part of the family, unless something big has happened."

Arlo says nothing.

Gary continues: "A man doesn't live with and pretend all is okay with a man who has damaged his family, his daughter, all the things he should hold most dear. Why do you tolerate this person, even if he's gone right now? Why has he been allowed—"

Arlo raises a hand, shakingly. The tension in the air sprays out from that point, electric but uneven, the two men at such different stages of life and of health. But still, that tension exists. It's dangerous. It's maybe deadly.

Gary backs down. He looks at his feet. Then he looks back at Dixie's father, saying: "Arlo, I understand some of this. It is like this between me and the men I fought alongside in Korea, my squad, my platoon. We never lose that bond. Did Paul save your life? Did you do something and he saved you? Is that it?"

"I ran away from home," says Dixie's father, as if under a spell.

"I know. I know that already," Gary says, interrupting him, much too impatient for Dixie's needs, as Dixie has never before heard these words, or any other words about her father's childhood or adventures. In fact, Dixie has assumed all along—even after all those years ago receiving his gift of the playing card—that her father has never had any adventures, any adventures at all. He just doesn't seem the type for it. He just doesn't seem to contain any sort of story, or anything other than steadfast simplicity. He simply seems *unseeable* (except now, somehow, Paul's presence all through her childhood is coming through tied to her father, a possibility she has been blind to, has grown up with, has grown up inside of, looking from the inside out, a perspective that offers no perspective at all).

"I know you ran away," Gary says, now in measured tones. "You told me that last time we tried to have this conversation. I don't want to hear about the bloody circus though. I don't want to hear that mumbo jumbo that Paul couches it all in."

"The circus is important. It's the heart of the story, boy," Arlo says, trying to regain some moral superiority. He could simply refuse

169

to speak, but Gary is standing over him. Gary is angry. Gary has struck, without really trying, a most menacing posture, fully blocking the doorway, gradually moving forward toward Arlo so that Arlo leans back on the gray metal stool at his workbench.

Gary is silent now though.

Gary has no more words.

It's a standoff, at least until Arlo offers up one more tidbit, one more jot of information: "For a kid like me, a teenager stuck in Idaho, the idea of escape seemed to be the greatest thing imaginable."

"Escape?" Gary says.

"Yes. I think that is what draws everyone to the circus. Not the hairy woman. Or the strong man. Or even the elephants and lions and so forth. It's just differentness. A place other than where you are. A place where a kid can be different."

"But why is *that* important?" asks Gary. "Why, Arlo? What's that got to do with Dixie? What's that got to do with Paul? I need to know!"

"Because most people aren't happy where they are." Dixie's father says this, then pauses for a moment. Gary must sense that he intends to say more, because he doesn't ask another question, not right away. And, after a moment, Dixie's father does say something else: "Most people aren't happy where they are. And most people aren't happy, either, with *who* they are."

Dixie remains glued to the window of the shed, listening and watching, but something in her mind disengages. Something in her mind hits a big red pause button at this moment. It's not as if the conversation between her husband and her father stops. But she can't seem to process any additional information. Her mind checks out, puts up the white flag of surrender, switches into radio silence, so that even though her eyes still see two people speaking to each other—Gary picking up the box with the doll in it, trying to salvage the paper that Arlo has ripped—and even though her ears most likely still hear the words of their conversation, only slightly muffled by the windowpane, nothing of it registers. Nothing of it remains for her to remember and call out to herself, to replay after the fact. If it is remembered it stays buried deep in some subterranean vault of her memory. She can't recall the words or the substance of the rest of the conversation.

All she registers is surprise.

Her father ran away and joined a circus? Some sort of something happened that tied him and Paul and that circus all together? What about the Jack of Hearts? What did that have to do with anything? What was his gift of it meant to convey? What did he mean to tell her, giving it to her, when he presented it in farewell those several years ago? Why is he telling Gary about it now, telling him all this unexpected history, rather than ever having been able to tell her? Gary has asked him about it. That's the obvious answer. Gary has forced the conversation. Gary has been persistent. Gary has been angry. And Dixie has done none of those things. Dixie was, and is still, she thinks, too busy with herself, with her tear-provoking alien, with her baby boy, raising him up now into a young man, too preoccupied with her marriage, too busy musing over her Professor, too busy to worry about her own father and this story of his, this secret history, this past that somehow bonds him and Paul together.

Dixie doesn't feel well.

Right at this moment, nausea overtakes her.

She feels hot, flushed.

Her own father, a complete stranger. Paul, who has been both her friend and her bedtime companion, telling her all those stories of circuses when she was a child—CIRCUSES! It all swirls around in Dixie's mind and she does not know what to think. She does not know *how* to think. She can't think. She can only feel. And what she feels is very similar to the feeling she had after the plane crash at Park Slope, the feeling she had the next morning when she woke to feed Cyril: nausea, the need to vomit, and a total lack of concern whether she does, right there, in front of everyone.

If a mind can shut off and still think, or at least produce the vestiges and traces of thought, this is what Dixie does: seeing the sights and sounds but not resolving them into meaningfulness, locking everything up, not parsing meaning from the words her father and Gary speak. It's all too much. She knows she locks it up. She knows she is caught inside herself again. She fails to see how parallel the idea of the circus and the idea of a card-playing, fortune-telling, pinstriped hooligan Professor onboard a train (and again appearing at airplane crash sites and traumatic moments) might really be. She fails to see this parallelism, she fails to register it, and she fails to hear how tenderly her father says Paul's name, the few times Gary drags it out of him. She fails to hear her own name. She fails to understand what Gary is after. What he's digging after. She fails to recognize the importance of the Arab doll in this unwrapped box, catalyst to the heated conversation between these men. She fails to process all of this, but it is there, locked up inside her, locked away until a later day when she feels safe to explore it all.

Perhaps that is the point.

Perhaps her mind shuts down right then, because she is not ready to hear.

Perhaps her mind is saving her from the lure of certain mythologies, certain voices in the circus of the sea.

CHAPTER 16

At this point, there's a bit of a jump in the story, as there needs to be when laying out the better part of the life of someone as richly difficult as Dixie. It's back to New York City, of course, and back to friendship with Peggy plus the card-playing, afternoon-tea group of ladies. It's Gary now making, earning, good money, which means Dixie lives differently, experiences a different sort of New York than she had the first few years. Now it's fashion creeping in, changing as always, something to spend that new money on. But it is also the start of a nation's consciousness of war, debate over what America should be, in terms of defending the rest of the world from the dread of communism versus peace, peace at any price, and a peace-loving new generation, demanding that others be treated as equals and allowed their own ideas of self-determination. All these things (and much, much more) happen around the nation, and they happen in New York too, touching New York, perhaps even scraping it, glancing off it, illuminating it, but with illumination like the passing of a comet in the night sky, a thing that those in the terrestrial world observe and reflect upon and perhaps even fear (in their superstitious way) but that never really causes more than a ripple on the surface of the world in which they, these New Yorkers, live.

There are of course New Yorkers more worldly than Dixie, people for whom the city is a bastion and a home base, the core of their identity and their homestead, though they spend winters in fronded places like Miami or the Riviera. There are New Yorkers much, much less worldly than Dixie too: those who grow up in and never really leave the borough where they are born, except perhaps for a trip now and again to Coney Island, or down to exotic Atlantic City, or maybe up to Saratoga for a race. They are of a type mutually unintelligible but instantly identifiable to one another: you're so and so from such and such a neighborhood, I can tell by your accent, your ethnicity, your clothing, your cooking, your crew cut, your walk, your whatever marker of intracity otherness. These people are worldly, or appear so, but only within the bubble of the city, where—truth be told—there are worlds upon worlds, and Dixie's world is but one small and insignificant instance. New York is a big blending place, but also a conglomerate—not so finely mixed—of separate peoples all functioning together. Some, like Dixie and her family, come from outside. They are the ones who see it most clearly, contrasting with not only what they've known of the rest of the world, but more importantly with who they, themselves, happen to be. They bring their baggage of self and of place to the city: Pocatellos and Pekings and Portsmouths and Polands there to be ingested, accepted (or not), churned about, digested, made into an individual contribution of energy and being, a quantum trembling among the pulse and permutation of the city's pumping streams. Most of them have found cotton wads to put in their ears. Most of them no longer worry about the sirens all around them. Or the sirens inside them.

Can these next four or five years of Dixie's life in New York be summarized so quickly as that?

Can all the little changes and impacts be annotated, accounted for, noticed (like bits of comet breaking loose from that passing flare, skimming down to touch and enlighten the Gotham sky, perhaps impacting over and within the city itself)?

They can't be. Yet, they must be. Or at least some flavor must come through, otherwise Dixie and her story would appear, on the other end of those years, unrecognizable. Maybe a shadow of the character who entered the initial scene. Four years, even ones spent steadily sleepwalking through New York's frantic environs, four years will change someone, will leave scars and wrinkles and impressions. Stepping back far enough, blurring the eyes so that the whole pastiche of time, during this era, this half-decade, blends into itself and reveals only its highest highs and lowest lows, the important thing that appears is stability. Not too many things change. The world outside Dixie morphs: from Malcolm X and marches on Washington to bell-bottoms and Woodstock, Vietnam, moon landings, the Summer of Love, MLK Jr. and RFK assassinated. All these things happen around Dixie, around the world, around New York, but they don't happen directly *to* her.

Even the big events in New York barely mark her.

She returns from that summer in Idaho in basically the same state and same shape (spin and direction, eh?) she reached at that moment of amnesia and indigestion outside her father's shed, peeping through the window. The rest of her time in Idaho becomes a repeat: more of the same sociality as its earlier phase, more of the same or similar rounds of friend-seeing, relative-seeing, picnics along mountain streams, etcetera, etcetera. Added to this also though, and with a bit of a sinister air to it, is this element of Gary and Arlo (and Paul!). This may have been going on for some time, the attempts by Gary to get to the bottom of things. But now Dixie notices it. More and more she notices it, even as the regular things of a regular summer home in Idaho continue to happen. Dixie notices. And she now remembers, re-remembers, similar conversations from the past. She notices the tension in Gary—it had always been there, since the beginning, right there on the outside of his army-sergeant face, but she'd written it off, looked beyond or through it. Now she sees it every time he walks into the room. He's uncomfortable among them. He's on edge in the house

175

of Arlo and Gladys (and Paul). He contains it but it simmers. And so, with this realization waking in her, she (and Arlo, and Gladys) do not really mind when he departs. They are spared additional such confrontations when Gary leaves again for his next business trip.

The summer ends, eventually. It's a sad enough event, leaving home, heading back to New York. Sad enough for everyone involved, including Dixie, but not sad enough that her alien again roosts inside her.

When Dixie returns to her New York home she does so with her ears plugged up, those cotton wads reinserted. She's happy to see Peggy again, happy to return to her card-playing ways, happy to forget about the possibility that important things might be happening everywhere else, outside, and everywhere else, inside, inside her family, as Gary continues his world travels and Cyril grows and her parents molder in Idaho, and, ohhh gawd, lest she forget about it, as Paul apparently makes a new life, some sort of new life, somewhere nearby, near enough even though New York is a city full of separate, interlocking worlds. Paul is here. Paul has been here awhile. Paul is up to something, she fears. Shadowing her. Escaping with her. Through her. She's not sure what he's doing, or why. She can't think about it too much, though she watches. She watches for him to show up. She is far, far away from the sort of self-reflection that could tell her, if she practiced it, that her very act of non-reflection and noninvolvement in questioning herself is itself a decision, an event, an important thing. More than that, it is a trend, another way that Dixie pushes the most important issues down deep into herself and covers them over, like a portmanteau buried in a leafy New York park. Dixie lets that summer of her return home to Pocatello bury itself in the happenings of New York life, and she allows herself to think of it all as a nothing, another nothing, just like her first train ride from Idaho had been. Nothing to worry about, nothing at all. She allows New York City's flow to overtake her and she allows her rhythm with Peggy to resume.

There's the Beatles at Shea Stadium late that summer, right after they return aboard another jetliner and right before Cyril starts kindergarten (what will the teachers think of him? Dixie warns him to be "normal" among the other kids, to hold his questions to himself most of the time, to store them up and save them to ask her, or Gary, when he gets home each night). Dixie goes to that Beatles rock 'n' roll concert, a great place to *be seen*, Peggy tells her. But nowhere does she uncover evidence of either trauma, the slowing of time, or her Professor. Nowhere does she see Paul. She catches no glimpse of either of them, even if they are out there, the two of them, one with cotton wads in his ears and maybe his older-style pinstripes now looking fashionable again, as John, Paul, George, and Ringo wear their fancy-collared slim-fitting suits. Dixie loves the new music of rock 'n' roll. She loves screaming—it recalls for her the sensation of freedom she felt as the train rushed toward her on the Pocatello platform, making her hold her bonnet to her head and lean against her big green trunk for support, a quickening of her heartbeat, an unavoidable rush approaching her and overwhelming her from outside herself. That same rush, that same wildness, that same threat of falling forward into oblivion, and that same pull, conflict, and sense of choice, represented by the steadfastness of her roots (back then by the grounding element of her luggage piled up next to her, plus baby Cyril in his bassinet; now by her growing apartment, her growing circle of friends, and Cyril growing too), these things conflict but also support one another. They are opposite elements of a teepee, leaned inward over her head, enclosing her, making themselves steady in their juxtaposition.

Dixie also notices, for the first time in her life, that she's older than some of the other concertgoers who have come for this performance at Shea Stadium. She's in her mid-twenties now. And the mob of Beatles fans has a more youthful tone to it: teens, younger twenties, mid-twenties folk who haven't already started families, who haven't done the whole college thing, who haven't put down roots. Dixie fits in still, visually, but only just barely. And Peggy, who comes with her and who hasn't aged quite as well—

177

drinking every day and smoking and not having taken a long vacation to refreshing Idaho all summer—Peggy draws some questioning, unpleasant looks from the crowd around her, nothing threatening but just a distance and a divide, the definition of the cultural gap forming between this younger generation and earlier ages over such things as rock 'n' roll, free love, and politics.

Maybe this is the moment that starts to plant a seed of doubt in Dixie's mind about her theory of *being seen*. Maybe it's a moment of actual self-reflection. Maybe Dixie realizes that their strategy isn't quite the be-all and end-all it had seemed. No words form around this. But nor is it pushed down as deeply as, say, the perfectly marvelous, nonthreatening, non-worrisome events of her train trip from Pocatello to New York, those few years earlier. (Nor is it pushed down as deeply as the perfectly marvelous, nonthreatening, non-worrisome events of the Adirondack cabin where she dealt with her alien, with Peggy's alien.) In terms of its heaviness, its importance and gravity, this issue of *being seen* with Peggy floats above that. It floats above her father speaking to Gary in the shed too, at least above the last half of the conversation she overheard, the part she can't and won't remember. All she hears, all she remembers of it is her father's voice sounding tired, thick, maybe even ill—like he is nothing more than a shell of himself. The moment floats above the big plane crash where Dixie and Gary and Mercedes and Gabrielle nursed and tended and rescued the wounded from the wreckage of disintegrated plane components as well as from the rubble and fire of that Brooklyn neighborhood's demolished and burning buildings. It floats even above Dixie's imaginary friendship with Mercedes, which she has largely now forgotten and replaced with the real, but passive (present but unaffecting) friendship of Peggy and their little cloistered Columbia-wife circle.

Maybe *being seen* isn't the thing Dixie should be doing.

She has this sense. She even has words for it, and she means to talk to Gary about it—though she's not sure how—or talk to Peggy about it, though she doesn't want to put extra distance and discord into their easy rhythm of togetherness. She doesn't want to disturb this relationship, even if it isn't all it could be. Dixie remembers the first of her months in New York when she knew no one except Gary and Cyril and therefore spent most of her days alone. She doesn't want that, so she readily trades silence on the issue of *being seen* for companionship.

In 1966, with Cyril bundled off to first grade, Peggy and Dixie make it to a few big events, nothing special really until that fall.

There's a big fire in October across from Madison Square Garden. They watch that but do not see the Professor.

In November, they go to Truman Capote's black-and-white ball, not as invited guests. They aren't that upwardly mobile. They aren't that *cool*, as the new expression seems to have it. They simply stand outside and watch Capote's guests come in, each of them being announced at the stairs to the Plaza Hotel even though almost all of them are masked: Tallulah Bankhead, President Kennedy's mother, Rose, Gloria Vanderbilt, Babe Paley, Harry Belafonte, Ralph and Fanny Ellison, Lynda Bird Johnson, Frank Sinatra, the Maharani of Jaipur, Italian princess Luciana Pignatelli. A few hundred of the most noteworthy people, mixed in with some of Capote's Alabama friends plus a few of the kind and hospitable people he met during the writing of his latest book. He's flown them in from Kansas for the most head-spinning, dizzying night of their lives, these uncomplicated people who hosted him and helped him, and they provide a counterpoint, a leavening to the star-studded night that makes it all seems so much more democratic.

Peggy and Dixie stand outside together for most of the time these guests arrive, watching big cars open their doors. They bask in the glory of the evening as they wear their own imitations of couture ball gowns, Peggy's white, Dixie's black. They stay on the curb like this, right there where they can see the lights of Central Park and the long aisle of Fifth Avenue with its stores and storied sidewalk lit to the south, a palatially residential sleepiness to the north along the edges of Central Park. They watch the arrival procession at least until that November evening gets too cold for them. Then they walk around the corner, along Fifty-Seventh, to find a bowl of warming soup and cups of cider, sitting together in a diner on the same side of a padded vinyl bench.

"I think this was the wrong type of thing for us," says Dixie. (These are the words she's stored up and has been meaning to share, with Peggy or with someone, anyone.)

Peggy frowns, starts to say something in defense.

Dixie waves her hand, cuts Peggy off. "Don't get me wrong. I loved it. It's just—what?—what are we trying to do here?" She's thinking of her Professor, how she hasn't seen him again for so long, despite all her intentions. She's thinking too of Paul. And how all the time now, whenever she's out on the town, she finds herself watching for him too, but not with the same pleasant, almost magical expectation.

"Be friends," says Peggy. "We're trying to be friends. We're succeeding at it. What more do we need?" To her the Professor is but a pretext, a fun myth, a ghost they chase, a reason for a togetherness-inducing activity that has become an end unto itself.

"We're trying to *be seen*," Dixie answers, a bit sharply.

"Well, we couldn't have come to a better place. This was *the* place. This ball. People will be talking about it for weeks!"

"No," says Dixie. "I mean, yes, sure, they will. But I think we're supposed to be doing more than that. Or at least I am."

That's as far as the conversation goes though, that night or for any of the next several years, this waning portion of the 1960s. Dixie has the words. She wants to share what she's feeling. But it doesn't work when she speaks. The words come out, but not the meaning.

Dixie pushes Peggy toward more traumatic events, not only places where they can *be seen,* but also, she thinks, places her Professor will show up. (Who cares, she tells herself, whether or not Peggy has forgotten him. Who cares whether Peggy ever saw him in the first place or just made up that whole story? Dixie doesn't care. In fact, it gives her a bit of comfort to think Peggy was never really in on the secret, that she was never really gifted with a vision of this man, this angel, who only comes around during the worst of times, when time itself, New York City time, slows down and changes to its syrupy worst. The idea that Peggy may not have ever seen her Professor makes Dixie feel more special, more singled out. It doesn't affect her friendship with Peggy at all. They chug on together, light and present, on that outermost edge of presence, throughout the coming years.)

Another year passes (Cyril in second grade, Peggy still smoking, Gary off on his adventures around the world, a week on, a week off, two weeks, sometimes more than that). There are the Groovy Murders, which get the town stirred up but don't provide much of anything for Dixie or Peggy to watch, to visit, just news to follow as the police find a couple of grifters who admit to bludgeoning an East Village hipster and his flower child girlfriend.

In 1968 they go to the scene, standing outside his atelier, where Andy Warhol has been shot. Perhaps they secretly applaud his lover, his protégé, this woman who wounds him but doesn't finish the job. She seems to them to be someone who could join their club, their voyeur experience, with a passion for stalking and a sense of being on the outside looking in. Not much more develops from this though. No Professor. No follow-up protests. No sense of time slowing.

The Columbia University protests that year provide a bit more spark. They kick off one week after MLK is shot. Harlem has been up in arms, understandably so. The whole country, it seems, feels as if the hair on the back of its neck stands on end. It's a national thing. But it's also a New York thing. Dixie and Peggy feel it.

They can't help but be involved in this situation—the protests happen right there in their neighborhood, right there twined up in their daily lives. They don't have to go anywhere to experience them. They don't have to put in any sort of effort to see or be seen. Their lives are physically and unavoidably part of the "scene." Gary (and Peggy's husband too) work for the university: Gary as a white-shirt-wearing, pencil-behind-the-ear, pocket-protector engineer, a throwback to what already seems an earlier age, the not-so-long-ago '50s.

The protests shut the campus down.

They focus on a gym the university wants to build.

Students seize two separate buildings: first the main administrative hall, and then, when the core of black activists kick out the rowdier white students, the white group takes over the main library. For the white students, the issue focuses around Columbia's involvement in war research. For the black students, it's about segregation, with the planned gym being called "Gym Crow"—an entrance for black residents of Harlem on one side of the building, barely a nod to the historical neighborhood it disrupts, and an entrance for the mostly white Columbia kids on the other side.

Gary offers up a vacation to the Adirondacks, just to get them out of town and out of the middle of the protests. This makes Dixie shiver, not just because her whole goal and purpose this past decade has been to watch for and hang around (she can't quite bring herself to say "participate") in such an environment as these heated protests, where she might see her Professor, but also because of the Adirondacks themselves, a place she now loathes.

"I got too much Adirondacks," she tells him, a bit slyly, "back that first year when I went up there with my friends, my girlfriends, you know."

Gary nods as if he does, indeed, know. But he doesn't. He doesn't know that Dixie went alone. He doesn't know what a struggle she had there, against her alien. He doesn't know and he doesn't ask, hasn't ever asked. He just lets it slide. He doesn't know that Dixie and Peggy returned, to deal in similar form with Peggy's alien. He doesn't know any of this, only that Dixie doesn't want to go along with his suggestion. Even though he seems cool about it, the suggestion, and his laissez-faire attitude, puts Dixie on edge. Dixie pictures him in the Pocatello work-shed with her father, *not letting it slide.* He has the capability to dig his heels in. She knows this, both from that episode and from smaller things in their lives together, small decisions as well as big, hard decisions. He doesn't usually shy away from tough things. Maybe she's tougher than her father. Or sneakier. Somehow she's gotten away with it, all these fictions about an alien, and about Mercedes, and about whatever it might be, whereas Arlo produced a reaction, a tougher Gary. She's glad he remains ignorant of what she and her alien fought about, back on that trip in the Adirondacks. But she's also a little hurt that he doesn't confront her, dig deeper, have a longing to let her share her secrets. He's become a bit of a stranger in her life, both one of her closest people and one of her most distant.

Gary tries again with vacation ideas. "Then Idaho. Back to Idaho for a while? Back to see your parents and friends at home again? I've heard your father isn't—"

"No," Dixie says, and she leaves it at that.

Every day for that week she makes a point of going to campus. It's easy enough for her. Cyril's school is on the other side of Morningside Park, right through the main quad of the campus and its halls. Dixie, or one of the other moms, usually walks with the kids. Dixie takes it upon herself to escort Cyril this week, every day.

Cyril is interested in the protests, of course, in a way that strikes Dixie as perhaps unhealthy for a third grader.

"Do you think they'll close school for us?" he asks on one of these walks, cutting through the South Lawn early in the morning. It's quiet, unlike in the afternoons when she picks Cyril up and the protestors have woken into their chants and slogans. They can see both Low Library, where the white anti-war group barricades itself, and the Hamilton Hall administrative building, where the black protestors hold speeches and rallies.

Dixie doesn't say anything, not right away, so Cyril repeats himself. "Do you think they'll close my school?"

"On account of the protests?"

"Yeah, like a snow day."

"No, I don't think so," Dixie says. She's looking at the buildings though, feeling their morning quietude contain a threatening sort of self-possession.

"That's too bad," says Cyril. "I'd like to spend some time with you in the park."

This makes Dixie stop in her tracks.

She turns to face Cyril. It's a bit savage, but she also grabs him by the arm: "In the park? Which park? Why do you say that?"

"Morningside Park. Geez, mom, what's the matter?"

"Why do you say that?"

"Because it looks fun."

"What does?"

"You, stopping there. I can see you from the window of Ms. Levin's classroom, after you drop me off in the morning. I thought you were waiting for me to come out and have a picnic the first time

I saw it. Are you having a picnic? Can I join you one of these times you go sit there? Is it fun?"

"I'm just sitting there," Dixie says, a little lamely, a little stunned.

"Okay," says Cyril, but he does so with a knowing veil clouding the light behind his eyes. Dixie thinks this "okay" contains just a bit of sarcasm to it, a taint of sarcasm, a nasty tone as if his whole attitude is far too grown-up, far too infected with New York acerbity—even if he is only in the third grade.

"Don't talk to me like that," she says.

"Like what?"

He's honestly hurt and confused by Dixie's response. And Dixie softens as a result. She thinks: *I must have imagined it. He just wants a day off from school. He just wants a picnic with his mom. He wasn't being sarcastic after all. He wasn't condemning me. He doesn't know. He doesn't know why I stop there, in the park. He doesn't know what I'm doing. He just guesses. He just likes the idea of skipping school.*

Her eyes remain a little wild though.

Her fingers still clench Cyril's shoulder, even as he pulls away, angling out of her grasp, stepping back.

She makes amends. "Do you want to skip today?"

Cyril's eyes widen.

"You'd let me?"

"Maybe."

He squints at her, probing for a trap. "Why? So I can sit with you out in the park? So we can go to a protest?"

"I was thinking maybe a zoo trip, and a slice of pizza."

"Okay," Cyril says, and there is no trace of acerbity in the word anymore. He's back to being a kid again, a normal third grader who wants to eat pizza, play sports, and skip school.

Dixie doesn't go sit on the park slope anymore, near the bench and the concrete waste bin where she has, almost without thinking, without computing her actions, indeed been taking a few moments every morning after delivering Cyril to school. This day is her last, at least during this spring of protests, at least during this age when Cyril needs to be chaperoned to and from his elementary school. Dixie stops. But forever after she maintains a picture of herself, formed through her imagination and her interpretation of Cyril's words: the view from his classroom, Ms. Levin's classroom, probably through a cloudy, cobwebbed window, bright construction paper artwork from the whole class of kids framing it, a view out over spring-bleak Morningside Park, where in the distance Columbia University keeps its exclusive bastion, and in the foreground, more important to Cyril and yet just out of his reach, his mother sitting on the ground by the trash can, by the park bench, cross-legged on the wet spring ground facing away from the protests, rather than toward them. Facing toward the little wooded hillock behind the park bench.

Dixie doesn't think that Cyril's view, or his eyesight, are so acute, so penetrating, as to notice her crying there in the mud where she sits on such days. But she knows it. She knows that's what she does, each day there. And the idea of Cyril seeing her crying, in that particular place, is tough for her to shake from her mind.

Part V
Concrete and Allegory

CHAPTER 17

It's not possible to say, with any conviction, that "things calm down" for a while that year, 1968, in New York City.

Maybe it's just Dixie. Maybe it's just Dixie who calms down.

Maybe it's just her, stunned a bit, diverting herself from Cyril with his skipped school day, allowing herself to pretend he did not ever see her sitting in the mud just a few feet off the sidewalk in Morningside Park.

The rest of frantic 1968—all its upheavals and social churn, the slow burn of Harlem in those days and that age, with such momentous consequences that she should have been out there, immersed in it, watching for her Professor—all of it starts, for her, to slip away again into sameness, that lulling and hectic sameness that is the way most New York City days squander themselves.

The fallout from MLK's death continues throughout summer, fall, winter. Columbia University and Dixie's neighborhood nearby remain on edge. The streets stay restless, but with promise somehow apparent in them too, the promise of protest organization, of passion, of change in the wind, of youth.

Nixon wins the presidency and declares victory from the Waldorf Astoria in Midtown.

187

Lew Alcindor—later known as Kareem Abdul-Jabbar—sits out the Olympics and teaches basketball camp in Harlem instead. Tommie Smith and John Carlos take off their shoes to protest black poverty and mount the victory podium after their 200-meter dash with their hands in the air, fists forward, lifted for Black Power.

A school strike keeps Cyril at home for thirty-six days that autumn. (Dixie answers all his questions, all day long, throughout that odd start of fourth grade.)

Bobby Kennedy is shot in Los Angeles, with a wake at St. Patrick's Cathedral in Manhattan three days later where Dixie and Peggy go to mourn with many thousand others (and, of course, wearing their best black dresses, watch from beneath subtle veils for their Professor).

At none of these events does the Professor make an appearance. In fact, except that it has become a matter of form, a matter of habit in their joint ventures to discuss the Professor and to *be seen*, Dixie would rather not think of that man, or think of that episode of her life, at all. She has almost shed him. She has almost learned not to care. Her dreams of train crashes and plane crashes, of entangled bodies (blending with the entangled miasma of her body and his body, that man, her Professor, in an inappropriate, unreal, and worrisome, worrisome vision), have become less and less powerful for her, less and less frequent.

At one point Peggy says, "Don't you just feel it getting stronger?"

"What?" says Dixie, actually having been—at that very moment—thinking about how the urge to dream and to reexperience the heat of that specific sort of dream has, for the last weeks or months, begun to fade. "What is getting stronger? What do you mean, Peg?"

"Your urges."

"Urges?"

"You know. For sex."

"No." Dixie says this simply, innocently enough, truthfully, but also quietly.

Peggy seems to not hear this. She barrels forward. She's got something to say and, darn it, she's going to say it. "I remember my auntie telling me I wouldn't ever enjoy *it* until I hit thirty years of age. That's what she said. Until then I'd just have to grin and bear it, or take what enjoyment I could find. I mean, I've *always* enjoyed it, at least when it's not with Bill—"

Dixie laughs obligingly.

"But I know what Auntie means now. I can't stop thinking about it."

"When do you turn thirty?"

"Last year . . . but shush about that. Bill and everyone else think I'm still twenty-nine. So, we'll have a party in a few weeks, okay, the big three-ohhh."

They laugh about this. They laugh about Peggy's "needs" getting stronger, God forbid. But all the while Dixie thinks it is going in reverse for her. No more has she been subjected to waking dreams so powerful that she can't move, can't bring herself to rise from her chair (remembering the suffocating dark of the little one-room apartment where she first lived in Morningside with Gary and baby Cyril, and where she was overcome, the day after the plane crash, by an orgasm welling up from her waking dream-state). It's been eight years. Things have faded, and the charade of chasing *her* Professor has, for the first time, started to wear thin.

This is why Dixie resists, at least at first, when Peggy calls her one night that following year, the twenty-eighth of June, 1969, to be specific.

Dixie sits in the living room. The TV is on. They're watching *Gilligan's Island*, which has lately become Gary's favorite show. He's home from whichever faraway place he had been visiting. "Too hot in the summer, we're calling off the drilling and sampling until the temperatures moderate," he said, by way of explanation, when he showed up a few nights earlier somewhat unexpectedly. He tells her he'll teach at the university. He'll prepare for the next expedition. He'll be home this summer a lot more than Dixie has grown accustomed to.

He doesn't move away from the TV, or Gilligan, when the phone rings.

He has no interest in telephones.

He knows that the only people who call are Dixie's friends. And, although there are quite a few such friends, it's usually Peggy who calls.

Yet, despite that apathy, this time as Dixie heads toward the kitchen where the phone sits in its peach-colored cradle with its peach-colored cord coiled about it, he turns his head and says, "You ever think about how different it would be if you and Mercedes stayed friends, rather than giving her up for Peggy?"

Dixie wants to say—*You didn't approve of Mercedes. You didn't approve of Gabrielle. You asked that one dumb question. Ruined it all.* She wants to say—*That's not what happened. I didn't give her up. You scared her off. You and your one dumb, insensitive question.* But she can't. She can't say this. She's sort of caught. She remembers—she well knows—that an imaginary Mercedes had been her excuse for almost two full years, the two worst years of Dixie's aloneness. She remembers that she led Gary to believe in a continuance, an ongoing friendship, a "girl thing" that he never was able to join, for one reason or another. It had been a truce between them. Gary allowed her to have her imaginary Mercedes, never investigating it too deeply, never inviting himself along, never planning events again

190

where they might meet up as "couples" like they did, and do, with Peggy and Bill. Imaginary Mercedes had been a thing, a rationalization, an excuse that allowed Dixie to go out to Jamaica Bay for the TWA crash, to go out to the boiler explosion in the cafeteria, to go out to all of those things for the first couple years of their time in the city. Imaginary Mercedes had allowed her to be less alone. Imaginary Mercedes had been a very real crutch, a lifesaver.

The phone rings, not just once or twice. Before Gary's comment, the phone had already reached that number of rings: once, twice, verging on a third time. As Dixie stops, and prepares to say something in response to her husband, the phone continues, normally enough, except that now it fills a big emptiness, the pause that has fallen into the space between Gary's words and Dixie's wordlessness.

"I know you weren't visiting her," Gary says.

The phone keeps ringing.

"It was pretty obvious," he says.

The phone has reached five or six rings. It seems to be threatening to stop, obtaining that magical number of patience the caller has: five, six rings, seven.

Dixie exhales, very loudly, and then decides: she ignores Gary. She takes the last steps away from the TV, toward the phone. She plucks the phone from its cradle and says, "Hey—can I call you back in a minute?"

"There's a riot down in Greenwich," says Peggy. "Meet me outside in ten."

"I can't."

"Yes, you can. He will be there. I can feel it this time. It's the big one. It's the one that'll make him show himself again."

"Peggy . . ."

"You're going out?" asks Gary.

Dixie puts her hand over the phone's receiver. From the kitchen she raises her voice, not really meaning to, but Gilligan is laughing in the background, Cyril is sitting at Gary's feet with his little toy Martian ray gun in his hand, making zooming and shooting noises, and Dixie feels like she has to yell just to be heard. She has to yell to carve out space for herself.

"I'm going out, yes," she says.

"Ten minutes," says Peggy.

"Okay," Dixie says. And she hangs up.

"We'll talk about this later," she says to Gary, as she grabs her jacket from the peg in the hallway by the apartment door.

"We don't need to," says Gary. "I know you were going through hard times. We don't need to talk unless you want."

This makes Dixie pause again. She appreciates it, this acknowledgment. She felt threatened by it at first, the way it cropped up unexpectedly mid-ring, mid-Gilligan. But she appreciates how Gary brings it to a close like this. He's told her what he needs to say. And he's finished it by allowing her to make the next move, leaving space for her, which makes Gilligan, and Mercedes, and Peggy, and the Professor, and everything except for Cyril and Gary and their home together suddenly seem much less important.

"I'm not sure," Dixie says, truthfully enough. "I'm not sure whether I need to talk about it or not. Let me think."

"Okay," says Gary. He's quiet, settled, unconcerned. But his eyes follow her, as she flutters toward the door. If a person were to compare him and, say, Odysseus, the heroic quality of perseverance might seem obvious. But the story, the story each of them occupies, varies in passivity and purpose. Is this heroism, to accept and allow Dixie so much space, over so many years wandering lost?

Dixie shuts the door behind her with a slam that is not anger but is, for certain, hurry and excitement. This injection hits her too suddenly, this speaking of Mercedes's name by Gary. Dixie hasn't heard Mercedes's name said aloud in five years. She's certainly thought of Mercedes, even after and amongst all the make-believe escapism in which Mercedes so prominently figured. She's thought of real Mercedes, hurt Mercedes, Mercedes who moves with a dancer's grace and the duskiness of autumn leaves. But Dixie hasn't heard the name spoken aloud. And she hasn't heard Peggy so excited about a conflagration, about a riot, an event, a moment of trauma. She hasn't heard Peggy so directly invoking their Professor, as she has tonight. The whole cross fire of these circumstances has the hair standing on Dixie's forearms, her heart beating hard in her chest.

Peggy waits street-side in front of the building.

They catch a cab.

The passage southward toward the Village is quick, at least at first, following Riverside Drive along the Hudson. Then it slows, and stops, and doesn't move forward at all once they turn inland around West Fourteenth Street, heading toward Greenwich. There are crowds out and about. Police vehicles. People milling. Folks walking their dogs and doing so with slouch hats and ratty fatigue coats and corduroy hippie style. It's a different place, different by far from the vibe of the places Dixie and Peggy inhabit around Columbia, or what they see when they venture a few blocks away into either Harlem or the Upper West Side. As these ladies disembark the taxi, a few blocks out from what seems to be the epicenter of the disturbance, they feel awkward, exposed, as if at any moment the people around them might break into beat poetry and the two of them, unequipped to hear, let alone understand, might have to hike up their proper but slightly antiquated dresses, plug up their ears against the incessant rhyming of the beats, and wade in, whether they're ready or not. Will they make it? Will they be accepted among this throng? They've got no idea what they're getting into, as step by step the scene becomes weirder and weirder, further and further from their comfort zone.

As if to address this, Dixie says, "How'd you hear about this one?"

"I've got friends," says Peggy.

"Of course you do," Dixie says. "Like me."

"No, not like you. I mean—" Here Peggy makes her wrist go limp. "I mean friends like this."

"Faggots?" Dixie feels bold saying this word. She doesn't do so with any scornful intent, but it's more a challenge to Peggy, more a naughty and unnatural word for her to call up from the edge of her vocabulary.

"Yes. I do. I do indeed."

"You do not."

"Do too!"

"Who?"

"I can't tell you. For obvious enough reasons, I can't tell you, or anyone. Been sworn to secrecy in these things. But just trust me, there are people you know who move in such circles. Maybe not faggots or queers themselves but associating with them, you know, experimenting, part of that crowd, they say. Friends and acquaintances of mine and Billy's. Double life–living sorts of people. Respectable people. They tell me things. They come down here, nights and weekends. It's where they can be free, they say."

"They tell you this?" Dixie asks.

"Yeah," says Peggy. "Sort of. Or I heard it."

"Gossip. I don't believe a word. You're a gossip."

"I am not."

"You are."

"I think it's true. Why wouldn't it be? They've got to come from somewhere. We wouldn't have this whole neighborhood here in Greenwich full of this sort of thing if they didn't come from somewhere."

Dixie can't argue with this. She remembers how Gabrielle and Mercedes were right there, living among them, not really hiding, but living in plain sight, going to school, to university, having a life, acting like a married couple, nearly man and wife. Dixie doesn't see anything wrong with it, not outright, not like so many preachers and people back home might have told her or might believe in their own hearts. But from what Dixie has seen there isn't much harm to it. They don't seem to be doing harm to anyone, certainly not to their own eternal souls, whatever that might mean, or to their present happiness. They seem charmed together. In love. And not quite as lost as the rest of New York, even though Mercedes had to deal with reactions to her presence in Frank's deli, brown-skinned and lovely as she was, dancer-like lovely, and probably also experienced the same thing, or worse, every time she and Gabrielle went anywhere together. God only knows what Gabrielle has had to deal with, invisible to Dixie as she, or he, goes about daily life being that more manly person.

It's pretty late that night, the night of the twenty-eighth of June, 1969, when Dixie and Peggy push through the crowd toward where the epicenter of this protest swirls, puckering the masses of people as if everyone is being sucked inward by a whirlpool. They're at Seventh and Perry. They can hear chanting. They can hear police sirens. The people linger, most in no hurry to move forward or to leave, gathering thick in the street, groups and gaggles, standing together, walking inward toward the chaos like Dixie and Peggy, looking around corners and pointing, some yelling, some gesturing, most just watching. Light flickers off the front sides of buildings, the inward-facing sides, the sides toward the center of the conflagration. Dixie and Peggy allow themselves to be pulled inward along with others in this crowd, venturing farther down Seventh until they hit the Christopher Street crossroad. From there they can see the full length of Christopher eastward: a crowd gathered in and overrunning the space of a small triangular park, a police line formed up in front of a bar, a bit of a shady-looking establishment with the windows boarded up and a blinking vertical marquee sign that reads: stonewall inn.

They've arrived at just the right time.

They've arrived in the middle of the chaos, the middle of the "moment."

The paddy wagons are pushing through the crowd, sirens on, engines running, pulling up curbside in front of the Stonewall. Inside the cordon of police, a few officers, some in plain clothes, some in uniform, have started to shuffle handcuffed people from inside Stonewall one at a time into the gaping maw of the first police wagon. It's a mafia joint, of course, as so many of these shady places are. The first few they bring out are, accordingly, the "business folk," mustachioed and swarthy. They are marched with arms bent behind backs: Italian, eyes cast downward, pretty dark five-o'clock shadows, well-groomed greased-back hair, the stereotype Dixie's seen in all the movies. That's normal enough, Dixie supposes. Like a drug bust or closing a gambling den. But it's not the end of the spectacle. Not by any means.

To the cheers and jeers and taunts of the encircling crowd, maybe two hundred, three hundred people at this point, the police next begin to lead out the patrons of the Stonewall themselves, also one or two at a time, just as they had done for the mafiosos. Except now there is a big difference. Now the fun really starts. Some of the patrons are transvestites, men in their mothers' dresses, smooth-shaven or bearded, Adam's apples or effeminate. Some are women, butch or prim. Some are gay, well-dressed, in expensive suits or dirty hippie clothes, a vast and colorful assortment as if, every time the door of the Stonewall opens, Dixie and Peggy do not know what to expect. Many, though not all, of the people the police lead out from the Stonewall use this as a platform, a parade: they flaunt, they flutter, they play to their audience. It's funny, and brutal, and nervous and exciting and unreal all at once.

Dixie laughs along with the crowd. She boos along with the crowd.

Peggy laughs too. Peggy boos.

They're having a grand old time.

They're in the midst of a gay riot, the makings of a gay riot, and they don't know what to think of it. Compared to the protests of the Columbia students, this seems much less serious at one moment, much more of a carnival, before suddenly turning ugly— bigoted and ugly and destructive—in the next. The scene has a million faces. It's a fun-house mirror, frightening and fabulous at one and the same time.

To Dixie's extreme horror and gratification, the scene also contains that seed of a moment in which—like the train ride from Idaho or their work at the crash site in Park Slope—time itself begins to slow, become syrupy, and step out of its New York rhythm. She feels it happening. She looks up, up and away from the front door of the Stonewall Inn, where the parade of arrests continues, growing more tense and edgy, and she starts to scan the crowd.

Is he here now? That's the thought that fills her mind. *Is he here and, if so, what does that mean? What's going to happen?*

Dixie makes a full 360-degree turn, bodily, as if she is an atom alone on an unhinged trajectory among this whirlpool of accompanying molecules, all being sucked inward, inward, while she watches, and spins, and holds her ground, her place on the periphery, her moment as a participating observer.

That first pass fails: she doesn't see him. Maybe she doesn't see him at all, ever, but just feels him, feels that he is there, watching her, watching the slowness of time, asking everyone who has drawn a card from him whether they are willing to gamble a little. *Take a card*, he's saying, somewhere, to someone.

Dixie doesn't see him, her Professor.

Dixie doesn't see her Professor at all, not on that first reconnaissance of the crowd. However, a moment later, next out the door, swinging a handbag and hitting the policeman who holds her wrist, yelling out—

"He touched me. He touched me where I shouldn't be touched!"

—next out from the Stonewall is none other than Mercedes. Real, live Mercedes. Not an image. Not a function of Dixie's imagination. Older. Darker-eyed. But Mercedes, no doubt.

She swings her handbag. She hits a police officer. She is pushed to the ground, yelling. And the transistor of the crowd's schizophrenia, its vacillation between humor and horror, switches definitely in the direction of horror, of anger. Bricks fly. Someone climbs a streetlight and drops bodily onto the roof of a police cruiser. The crowd surges forward. Dixie cries out, yells: "*Mercedes, Mercedes!*" But whether Mercedes hears her or not, Dixie cannot tell. She catches a glimpse of her friend, of the patterned and very normal, very feminine dress she wears, as the doors of that first paddy wagon close behind her. A second wagon quickly pulls up behind it. Its doors open. The first wagon plods through the crowd, not easily. Rioters rock it back and forth on its springs. People, protestors, stand in front of it until it bumps them. Moving at only a few miles an hour, not really geared up to hurt anyone, still trying to de-escalate the situation, the police push forward, taking Mercedes with them, Mercedes and maybe a dozen others, mafia and queer, gay and straight, children—street children who hang out at the Stonewall, selling themselves for booze and drugs—as well as older men and women, all of them alike, unalike, blended together like a quilt. Blended together like New York.

She's gone. The police wagon is gone.

Mercedes is gone.

Dixie pulls at Peggy's arm. "Let's go," she says.

"Wait," says Peggy.

"My friend is in there," Dixie says. "We've got to go get her. We've got to spring her loose. Pay her bail. Whatever it takes. We've got to follow them down to the precinct station."

"Wait," says Peggy.

"I can't," says Dixie. "I've waited too much. We've got to go."

"No," says Peggy. "We need to wait."

It's only then, with Peggy pulling Dixie back into the scene, back toward the chaos, that Dixie sees the chorus line form, maddened protestors facing off against the line of police, each of the Stonewall's remaining patrons taking the next person by the shoulder. They're upset. They're crazy. They're standing their ground. They're brave and they've got a special angle, like a superpower, a special vision for how they'll confront the world. It's a scene replayed a million times on campuses and at marches and sit-ins around the nation—for women's rights, for Black Power, for peace—but now for the first time in this community, which has hidden for so long, has hidden but is now standing up. They are standing up to the police, to the power, and they're doing it in their own unique way.

The line of protestors forms so that it faces the police ring barricading the Stonewall. The line forms shoulder to shoulder, arm in arm, hand in hand, and the conjoined people begin to kick in cadence, in unison, in beat, in true chorus-line fashion, just as if they are at the Moulin Rouge or Atlantic City. Some wear dresses. Some wear slacks. Some strip off their pants and go bare-legged or shirtless.

And there, among them, right at the very center, arm in arm with Mercedes's own Gabrielle (who, just as Dixie remembers him from those five or six years earlier, wears a very well-tailored suit), arm in arm with Gabrielle is the Professor, cotton wads in his ears, doing the high kick in the center of this protesting troop.

Dixie thinks, just for a moment, before Peggy does eventually lead her away from this crowd, taking her as she asked to the precinct station at last, that she sees the Professor look at her. She sees the Professor look over his shoulder, never breaking his grip on the man or woman to one side or the other of him. He just turns his head, and smiles, and at last, at last, *he sees her.*

The Professor sees Dixie.

Dixie sees the Professor.

Dixie sees and stares and suddenly, like a veil falling from in front of her eyes, she sees just who the Professor is. Not a ringmaster, but close. Not an elephant tamer, but close. Not a pretty lady riding on the back of a sequined steed. But close. Close. Close. All along, too close.

He's Paul.

And he's here in the city.

He's been here all along, watching her.

Part VI
Three Ellipses

CHAPTER 18

First ellipsis: abortion.

That's what this alien stuff is about. Standing out in the street in front of the Stonewall Riot, Dixie throws up.

No one is quite sure why, not even Peggy.

No one but Dixie. She knows why.

Suddenly she's there, in the Adirondacks, all on her own. She has unlocked the cabin door with the key she'd gotten from one of the friends, same circle as Peggy, but before Peggy. Just a nameless lady who circled around them, knew them, knew what was up.

Dixie's alone when she does this, this first trip to the cabin. She spends the evening alone. She brings a bottle of wine, and a bottle of whisky, just as the instructions said. She drinks the wine, most of it, while watching moonlight on the water of the lake through the screened-in porch. She sits in a rocking chair. She rocks and it makes noise, a lonely noise. Birds and bats and insects buzz around outside the screened porch, keeping her company. She is drunk enough when the lights of another car come flooding down the long gravel driveway of the cottage, drunk enough that she cannot stand easily from the rocking chair. She staggers. She puts a hand on the screened window of the porch and feels it give way against her weight, tearing and letting some of the tension of the in-rushing mosquitos come free, free, as if they are also aliens waiting to be liberated inwardly.

She feels the bump of the baby in her abdomen. It's not alive. She can't think of it as alive.

The man who comes into the cabin, past Dixie where Dixie holds the mudroom door open, has a pale light to him, absorbing and reflecting the lone gray bulb above the garage in the back of the cabin. He gives Dixie a Queen of Disappointment, a card with a stoic woman studiously not looking at the wilted scimitar in her hands. It's ornate. It shines like it has been gilded by the moonlight. It is not a card she would have chosen for herself.

Above, in the night sky, a cloud threatens the moon but does not eclipse it.

Dixie follows the instructions.

She finishes the bottle of wine. She uncorks the whisky, takes a swig of it, and holds it forth to the masked doctor. He uses it to wash the sharp ends of his fingers and his tools. He is a mosquito. He is an alien. His fingers are as cold as the Professor's fingers had been, that first time Dixie touched them.

Dixie lies down on the couch and clenches a rag between her teeth, spreads her legs, lets the doctor tie her legs to the couch, bind them gently and softly. It's all over in a few minutes. It's all over in a few eternities. Dixie screams into the rag and bleeds into the furniture and spends the next two days limping around the porch and kitchen and bathroom, then cleaning up the blood as best she can before she heads back to Gotham.

It's the same when Peggy comes to the cabin.

It's the same man, the same instructions, albeit with two bottles of wine.

This time, Dixie's there too, so Peggy doesn't have to be alone. Dixie knows what it is about. She's experienced. She does not need Mercedes or anyone from the "bad" part of the city. She brings a bag into which they put the drunken remains of the moonlight.

Second ellipsis: trunk.

Dixie first buries the trunk with just her baby, her remains of a baby. She can't bring herself to simply dump it in the woods as the doctor suggested. She can't bring herself to flush it down the toilet or feed it bit by bit to the fishes in the lake. These are all possibilities. The instructions say so.

But Dixie knows what she wants to do with it.

When Peggy goes north to the Adirondacks for her own alien expedition, Dixie brings a bag just for the purposes of the particular benediction she now intends to repeat. She brings a bag and catches all the bits and pieces and makes sure they aren't flushed or fed to fishes or tossed out to the wolves and whatnot in the woods.

She makes Peggy come with her.

Peggy doesn't want to.

Peggy is done with it. Two days of recovery, cleaning away the blood and the memories, and then Peggy wants nothing more to do with it, no memorial, no nothing.

But Dixie makes her do it.

Dixie makes her come out to the place in Morningside Park, a few feet from a park bench and a big iron waste can bolted to the sidewalk. She makes Peggy take a shovel and gloves and come with her to dig up the trunk, that green portmanteau that had helped

Dixie move her life from Pocatello to New York City. The two ladies, the two best friends, they dig up the trunk together, open it, and put Peggy's alien in there right next to Dixie's older remains.

A smell comes from it that makes Dixie gag.

A smell comes from it that causes Peggy to turn away.

But there is also a look in Dixie's eye that suggests, to Peggy, everything will be okay, everything will be all right. There will be nothing to worry about at all, nothing to fret over, nothing to feel bad about, if only the two of them hold this secret and this secret place tight in their chests—only every once in a while throwing up in public when something like a Stonewall Riot should in future happen. Something that rips away all the pretending and all the pain and shows one of them or the other what their raw insides look like.

That smell.

And the specter of Paul there, Paul as the Professor, Paul as himself in this chorus line kicking up his heels. That smell and Paul are quite enough for anyone, even someone as brave as Dixie, to expect themselves to endure. We should not marvel that she threw up, then and there, with the smell and the memory of Paul so present and inalienable.

Third ellipsis: Paul

Oh, Dixie can't think about Paul yet.

She just can't.

He's there by her childhood bedside in a blur. He's there in the house where she grew up. He's there as a fixture of Pocatello.

But that's all he is.

He's there by her bedside singing circus songs to help put her to sleep.

He's got one hand on her shoulder, another holding a book of cleverly drawn circus animals, like Dumbo but dirtier, all of them somewhat similar to playing cards. That jester's jauntiness. Those hollering fools.

Paul's got one hand on her shoulder, whispering in her ear, and another hand under the covers between her legs.

He lives in Dixie's house.

He's Dixie's uncle, accepted by them all.

He's part of the family.

He has changed her diapers.

He has wrestled with her, bathed her.

He has watched her when her parents have gone out to the movies or up to the mountains camping for a weekend. He has watched her when Arlo only wanted to work on his machine parts in his little machine garage.

That's all she can think about, Dixie, right now, when she sees Paul become the Professor, when she sees the Professor unbecome himself, lines blurring, opening open. Dixie sees him with a full deck of cards spreading out on the table between herself and Cyril, all those many years ago on a train from Pocatello to New York City.

"I'll keep you company on the journey, Dixie dear," he tells her in that letter left among her peanut butter jelly sandwiches. "I'll be there for you, watching you, just like an angel would do. When you get lonely, I'll be there for you, and for Cyril."

Part VII
New Professor

CHAPTER 19

In this matter of self-examination, this new decade of self-examination, a starting point for Dixie might be to admit that she does better dreaming, or dream-remembering things, than she does with in-the-moment reality, at least for big-ticket items in her life. That's probably obvious by now, though not to her.

Case in point.

The little things she deals with well enough, this next year.

She and Gary move to Dallas, Texas, a few weeks after the Stonewall Riot. It's like landing on Mars after at last acclimatizing to New York City. Immediately it gives her perspective, to see the city differently, to look back and to like the city more, to enjoy it from afar, to reflect on it a bit (maybe that's what she needs for herself too, perspective: But how can she obtain it, when trapped always inside herself?). She's floating along in this. She's pulled along in Gary's wake. And that's fine. It's fine. Everything will be just fine, Dixie.

In Dallas she finds herself, despite what she still feels is her natural charmingly rural, western, and sunny-tough disposition, all of a sudden viewed by others as a cold and overly direct New Yorker, storming into places, forgetting the niceties of "hi, hello" and "God bless your heart." Even forgetting on occasion to smile. She gets to see New York reflected in her own behavior, her hurry, her manners.

As this new life in Dallas begins, Dixie realizes it isn't the same as New York. For instance, one such encounter when Dixie realizes she must slow down, a woman—again in a grocery, though this time a Tom Thumb supermarket rather than a little deli like Frank's— approaches her, and smiles (Dixie smiles in return, catching herself distracted and flat-faced). The woman offers her hand to shake. It's a hand clothed in a white glove that reaches almost to the elbow. This is 1970, mind you, and the glove looks positively antebellum to Dixie. This Texan woman's hair extends skyward in an enormous beehive that also feels, to Dixie, as if it were mimeographed from the '50s. The woman doesn't notice Dixie's glance at the galling height of the beehive. She doesn't notice the way Dixie seizes her limp white-gloved offering and shakes it with particular vigor, as if it is a small animal and Dixie a terrier who has proudly caught it and has decided to stun it with back-and-forth thrashing.

The woman smiles. Keeps smiling. Then she says, "Darling, have you been saved?"

"Saved?" Dixie looks around the Tom Thumb at the blaring block-lettered posters proclaiming sales of this and that, savings of gobs and wads, cents and dollars. She's understandably confused. "I think I got thirty percent off these frozen green beans," she says.

"No, no, silly," says the woman. "God—bless—your—heart. I mean, of course, you see, your salvation. Of your eternal soul. Have you been saved by Jesus?"

Dixie handles this just fine.

She puts down her grocery basket and walks out of the Tom Thumb, hand over her mouth to hold back laughter. She'll finish her shopping later. She needs a break now. As much as the cattiness of the ladies harassing Mercedes at Frank's deli got beneath her skin,

Dixie—now older, now wiser—won't let this do the same. She steps away. She gives her wits time to gather. She gains some perspective and composes herself. It's a minor thing. But it's a step in the right direction, really.

"Good lord," Dixie says to Gary that evening. "God—bless—my—soul. I've never even thought of needing salvation."

"It's an evangelical thing," he explains. "They've got a lot of them here."

"What are evangelicals?" Cyril asks, which surprises Dixie and leads her to explain a few things to him. He's old enough to know. And it's a good conversation between them, mother and son. Gary, like usual, stays out of it.

All this is normal, and fun, and the type of growing pains that happen to any family, the type of bonding experiences that come with change of place, and culture, while reinforcing the solidity of the family itself, showing how the quirks of personality in such a mobile little nuclear group withstand changes in scenery.

Life in Dallas is like this. Normal on the outside. A perfect mirage of exactly what Gary and Dixie expect it to be. What isn't normal, at least not in Dixie's experience so far, is the way the rest of that evening, and really anything—at any time—that goes beyond the veneer of normality, quickly diverges from the normal. Dixie can handle the normal. She's got trouble though, whenever she dips her toe into the deep end.

That evening, for example, Dixie can't wait, can't wait, can't hardly think of anything else (see what creeps in there, that Dallas vernacular already, that "hardly"), can't hardly think of anything else beyond getting Cyril to finish his homework and tucking him into bed, getting Gary situated in his little garage laboratory with his gizmos and seismic meters, so that she can have the kitchen to herself, the kitchen with its lifeline phone back to New York City. Dixie is tethered there, in a way she wasn't ever tethered to Idaho.

Sure, she called her mother every now and again from New York, looking for treatments for diaper rash, colic, how best to fold and put away bedsheets, ways to remove stains. She never talked to her father that way, over the phone, about things little or big, except when her mother forced him on holidays and special occasions. So, phone calls like this hadn't been a habit. They aren't a carryover from her first move, Idaho to New York. The tether of the phone line, its existence and its effect on Dixie, forms the bedrock substance of this feeling she has, this feeling that, just scratch the surface of normality and, woof, the whole thing becomes massively abnormal, painstakingly peculiar, very much suspicious and—she's tempted to think—false. Except it's the phone line to New York that feels real. And the rest, the charade of Dallas and even of her home life with Gary and Cyril, is the mirage.

Most surprisingly about this tether: it isn't Peggy she longs to call. It isn't Peggy she longs to connect with. It isn't Peggy from whom she seeks near daily reports on New York's happenings or with whom she wants to share the humor and the oddity of her supermarket salvation experience.

It's Mercedes.

Real Mercedes, not make-believe Mercedes, invented Mercedes, Mercedes who was an excuse to leave the house, an excuse to pursue the voyeurism of trauma.

This need to speak with Mercedes almost every day falls squarely into the category of Dixie's blindness to big things. All the other things in Dixie's life she deals with well enough. All the little things amount to an easy, slippery slope that makes her life seem to whisper away. The need to speak with Mercedes falls into the same category as the cotton wads in the Professor's ears, as the week alone in the Adirondacks, as the history of her father (and Paul) with the circus: an oh-we-skipped-some-important-things-because-Dixie-can't-deal-with-them-right-now sort of category.

Backing up, this is how Dixie's thirties are going to unfold for her, a different sort of story. That whole last decade (her twenties) simply jumped from event to event. From trauma to trauma. Dixie was looking for syrupy-slow time and the appearance of someone who would let her *be seen*. Now, suddenly, she's got someone who really *sees* her and it proves to be a unique and new and thrilling experience that is utterly different for her, an utterly different sensation than life with Gary, utterly different from the sex dream thrill she got when she chased the Professor. Utterly different than being watched, for sure. But, oddly, it's also somehow, on some level, exactly the same. It's a thrill. And it comes most strongly as Dixie fights against displacement and fights against isolation. It's a creation of her own. It's a thing she has used to fill the void—though she can't quite see it for such, not yet.

Here's how the rekindling of a real relationship between Dixie and Mercedes begins: that night, after the Stonewall, Dixie and Peggy post bail for Mercedes.

They bring her home to Gabrielle.

It is such a marvelous night: the dancing, the protest, the chorus line, the swinging of purses, the retreat of the police. It is such a night of coming around, full circle, that Dixie still feels like she is circling.

As they journey across town in Mercedes's company, Peggy asks all the questions, not even framing them with more sensitivity than Gary had done. But now the questions fall on ears better disposed to hearing them, Mercedes's ears, for at this moment Mercedes is grateful. She is open. And she isn't—like that night of the plane crash in her Park Slope neighborhood—mired in grief and shock and anger and exhaustion.

"Yes, I love him," Mercedes says, in answer to one of Peggy's questions about Gabrielle. "I love him even though he's difficult sometimes. So hot tempered. So quick to take offense."

"Yes, I call her a 'him,'" Mercedes says in response to Peggy's follow-up. "It's natural. That's who he is."

"No, he's not anatomically a 'he,'" she explains.

"Yes, I like sex with him. A lot," Mercedes admits. The ladies, all three of them, laugh.

Then they're silent for a moment. Each of them thinking their own thoughts, though all of a substance, all more or less flowing along the same mental and emotional (and sexual) pathways.

After a moment, before Peggy can ask another question, Mercedes anticipates her and cuts her off, saying: "When I first met him he wasn't a *he*. Not yet he wasn't. We were both just like me. Two girls in dresses, skirts. We had a math class together. He helped me with understanding the English. I'd just arrived from Caracas. He'd been here at school awhile. I was better at math. He was better at English, though that didn't last too long. Anyway, that's when we first kissed. Over the math book, studying together at the kitchen in my mother's apartment."

"But he went to engineering school?" Dixie asks. "Wasn't that more suited for you, if you're the math person?"

"Engineering school. Any school. It's more suited for the man. It is better for the man," Mercedes says, without seeming to regret it. "I still do the math for him, just fine, though I make him kiss me each time!"

Dixie remembers all this, even as she dials Mercedes this evening to tell her about salvation. She's nervous as she goes to the kitchen. She can hear Gary comfortably ensconced in their garage. There's a whizzing noise from one of his tools. A clunk. A tinkling. It sounds productive, and Dixie imagines the devices of his hobby, his repairman hobby, enmeshing him in wiry, semi-living arms. If she were a reader of science fiction she'd be thinking of robots and Gary in their grip. Either way, whatever the image, she labels Gary as safely out of the way. She does not see, or notice, the congruence, the generational congruence between husband and father, these echoes re-created at various phases of our lives: a garage, a shed, a separation. Dixie is too nervous to think about such things. And anyway, it's one of those deeper things, deeper than skin deep, deeper than the surface of being seen. So she doesn't go there. She can't go there, not without opening a whole can of worms she just can't deal with.

Dixie shouldn't be nervous, calling Mercedes. Sure, Gary knows that she talks on the phone to New York every night. He even knows it is Mercedes, rather than Peggy, who Dixie calls. But that doesn't mean he needs to hear Dixie. It doesn't mean he needs to watch her. It doesn't mean that he needs to see how nervous she is, every night about this time, how she blushes.

Cyril, she has checked on him twice already, first time bringing him a glass of water as a pretext. He isn't yet asleep, but comfortable, reading, and he says "thanks" to his mother without looking up from the golden-paged halo of his reading light, his quilted covers pulled up to his chin. He's bigger now, longer than a mere child. He's eleven, still with a high-pitched voice. Still hairless on chin, under his arms, his mustache. Still innocent-eyed. But not for long.

Dixie is nervous about him, that's for sure. And for all the reasons. Preteen years being what they are, plus moves from city to city, region to region, most of the time do not go well for kids Cyril's age. But he has taken comfort in books. He has continuing comfort in Dixie. He has the same from Gary too, though with a bit more distance, a bit colder and less personal. He's a good boy. He's solid. There's no need to worry about him. No need at all.

Dixie is nervous for him for all the normal reasons, of course, even though he's so well kept. But, in the specific instance of these nighttime calls back to New York City to share things and hear things from Mercedes, this nervousness about Cyril comes from an entirely different place than a mother's worry for her preteen son. *Cyril understands everything too well.* Always, he understands things too well. That's what Dixie is worried about.

She isn't ready for that.

Not yet.

Cyril might be a perfect mirror for her to learn the things she needs to know of herself, these questions about the blank spaces from the decade of her twenties. But Dixie isn't able, or willing, to use him in that capacity. Not yet.

Her son simply inspires a sense of willies in her.

She checks on him once by bringing him water, a second time by opening the door of his room just a crack. The lights are out. The book has been put aside. She hears him breathing and feels contented by the regularity of it.

Their Dallas house sprawls: a classic ranch layout, bigger than anything she ever imagined she'd own—big double garage, big living room with a fireplace sunken two gentle steps down from the rest of the floor. Gary works for an oil company now, full time, leading an exploration and mapping crew. It's good money. The house is in a good neighborhood—big trees, leafy sidewalks, a solid school—and it is slung low and solid like a bunker against the bit of hillside Gary said he needed to combat Texas's otherwise endless expanse of flattened plains. Gary found them a good neighborhood, a lone hill neighborhood, and he bought a house made of stone that sprawls over something like half an acre of property, enough for a swing set, plans for a swimming pool in the backyard once summer arrives, and maybe even a dog.

There's no dog in the house now.

Just Cyril in the earliest stages of sleep.

Cyril inspires nervousness because he understands things too well and Dixie knows, though she won't think about it directly or in absolute terms, that her calls to Mercedes don't really have much to do with needing to hear about what's happening in New York, the events, the traumas. Nor does she really need to talk about Dallas. Nor is chitchat about family really the issue.

Dixie might start out innocently enough. She might start with one of these topics.

She might say, "Tell me, Mercy dear, about this Black Liberation Army we're hearing about. What's the deal with that?"

Dixie's thinking of the Professor, on one level. But of Mercedes on another level. The two blur together. It's a good thing for Dixie. A good blurring. It helps Dixie move through the simple pleasantries of having a conversation, while also, in her mind, preserving a deeper layer, important to her because Dallas, and her housewife existence, doesn't always have that sort of stimulation.

Dixie might start off the conversation each night on the phone with something like that, inquiring about New York events with the keenness of an expatriate, missing her old "home." Or she might relate something revelatory about Dallas, like this day's salvation in the supermarket.

But the thing she won't admit to herself, and that she's afraid Cyril will in his mirrorlike way discover, uncover, understand without the slightest hint from her, is the deeper thing, the deepest thing, which—like all the deeper things from her twenties—Dixie still cannot name, still cannot say aloud. As much as she's repressing this, the very act of feeling nervous, of checking Cyril's bedroom, rechecking it, of listening for Gary to be deeply occupied outside, all of that, all of it represents a first sign of self-awareness. It's like a seed unfurling upward toward the light, still with earth attached to its fresh green stem. Self-awareness hasn't yet shed the husk of its shell. It hasn't emerged all the way from the earth. But it is coming. These are the harbingers.

Their discussion of the BLA goes nowhere. Mercedes says that Eldridge Cleaver has fled to Algeria, or Cuba or something. This proves utterly disinteresting to them both. It's news. But it's *so* distant. It's not why either of them are on the phone.

"Today a woman in the supermarket asked me if I had been saved," Dixie says.

Mercedes laughs. And that's better. That's closer to the goal. Behind her, in the auditory background of Brooklyn, other noises fill the crackling distance that cuts across the phone line. There are the car horns Dixie expects. There are the sounds of laughter. Rarely does Mercedes take these calls alone—she's back living with her family, her extended family. She and Gabrielle have had a split, probably a temporary one. These things seem to happen to them a lot. Dixie doesn't know why. She's afraid to ask. She's waiting for Mercedes to tell her, to volunteer the information independently. Dixie's in a spell and she doesn't want to accidentally break it.

"Why would anyone ask if you're saved?"

"Gary says it's an evangelical thing."

"You're not evangelical?"

"Heavens, no."

"To us Catholics, you all seem the same. It seems to me like Protestants get saddled with our Catholic guilt but have no way to rosary your way out of it."

"Except for getting saved by Jesus, apparently."

Dixie doesn't know what she's saying. She doesn't know why she's saying anything that she's saying. She's just producing words from her mouth in the hope that Mercedes will laugh again, or, barring that, will remain on the phone a bit longer. She doesn't care

215

two figs about salvation or about what the ladies in Dallas think, do, believe, or scoff at.

When Dixie and Peggy post bail for Mercedes, they take her home to the apartment in Brooklyn where she and Gabrielle are, at that time, living. For the whole subway journey Mercedes seems shaken. Understandably so. She has just been arrested. She has just spent time in jail. And Gabrielle was nowhere to be seen, nowhere to comfort her.

She insists that she needs no help getting home, but still, she seems shaken. She seems not herself. Silently, with not much more than a clandestine nod of assent between themselves, Peggy and Dixie agree to get on the subway with her, to go all together, to accompany Mercedes from Greenwich Village outbound to Park Slope, to see her safely home in those very early hours of the morning after waiting interminably in the police headquarters for the sergeant to post up the paperwork for the bail, for the clanking keys to be brought forth, for the doors to open and Mercedes to come out, black-eyed, bruised, her makeup everywhere. She holds in both hands, like a relic she intends to preserve forever, the purse that Dixie saw her swing at the cordon of policemen, holding it delicately in front of her, disbelieving almost, and looking down at it contritely, a whole different Mercedes from the one who had been pulled out of the Stonewall kicking and cursing in Spanish.

They help her reach her home.

They send her up the elevator to Gabrielle, to Gabrielle and her apartment, the one they share together, at that time, before whatever causes this most recent separation.

Then Peggy and Dixie pause for a moment, standing in the lobby, the little brightly lit, faux-marble-tiled lobby, replete with post office boxes, with packages strewn around in the darkened corners, panels of warped wood oddly glued over the marble, layers of rehabilitation, and light from three bulbs evenly spaced, uncovered, in the ceiling above.

"What do you think of all that?" Peggy asks.

"She's been a friend for a while."

"Not since I've known you."

"True," Dixie says, though the admission of that creates a weird harmonic in her mind. She thinks Peggy is hinting at something, or trying to get her to talk about something, but she can't quite place it.

"How'd you meet?" Peggy says after a moment.

"That plane crash."

"You're crazy." Peggy turns as if to leave. "You're crazy and I love it. You hardly know this person. You've hardly seen her in eight years, so you say, and here we are, posting her bail and dragging her back out to Brooklyn . . . just think: I was the one who had been claiming to have secret gay friends!"

"She's not gay."

"At the Stonewall?"

"Well—"

"And this Gabrielle?"

"Her, ummm, husband, yeah."

"A woman, right? Mercedes wasn't lying about that."

"No. She wasn't lying."

"Gay," says Peggy. "Gay, gay, gay. There are gay men and gay women, Dixie. It's called l-e-s-b-i-a-n-s."

"Goodness," Dixie says, shushing Peggy, waving at her with her hand as if to say, *Not so loudly! They might hear.* Perhaps this is leftover

217

hesitation from Gary's ill-timed, ill-formed question on the night of the crash—Dixie can't remember clearly enough. She's even begun to doubt that the plane crash, the night of triage, seeing the Professor there, her Professor, and then the sex dream, she's begun to doubt whether any of it was real. *Who rushes into a plane crash with friends they've just met, gay friends, lesbian friends no less? Who does that sort of thing?*

But the shush works.

It stalls Peggy.

It creates a silence in the marble-ish warped-wood lobby of Mercedes and Gabrielle's apartment building.

They hear steps on the stairwell adjacent to the old clankety elevator. They turn to face the stairs.

On the phone, from Dallas, Dixie wants to say something about this. She wants to say something to Mercedes along the lines of: *Do you remember coming back down to see me, that evening a few weeks before I left New York? Do you remember? What made you come down? What excuse did you use to get free from Gabrielle then? Was he even home that night? Why didn't he go post bail for you himself?*

All the questions.

Dixie has them in the forefront of her mind, right there on her tongue, which is a good thing, a sprout from that seed reaching toward the golden-white sun of truth and self-reflection. She has all the questions right there to ask, but she only says something insipid, like: "Tell me again about Brooklyn."

They hear steps on the stairway, Peggy and Dixie, and they turn to face the stairs. This puts the door of the lobby behind them, so that they are sandwiched between the sounds of the stairwell and the sounds of the outside world (Dixie remembers this clearly, a little crystallization, a little bit of syrup-time, as if her Professor is appearing right then, or as if wads of cotton have filled her ears, leaving them muffled and itchy). The sounds of the footfalls ring inside this world, descending, descending the stairwell, then bursting forth through the darkened stairwell door.

It's Mercedes. Of course it's Mercedes. Every time Dixie remembers this, who could it be, except Mercedes.

"I forgot to say thank you," she says.

She holds out her hand to Peggy. The women shake hands, very civilized. "Thank you," Mercedes says again. Peggy simply nods agreement, a little stunned perhaps. A little amazed.

On the phone, connecting Dallas and New York, Mercedes is telling Dixie about Brooklyn. She's saying inane things. It's pleasant. It's what Dixie wants. It's exactly what she wants. Dixie can both listen to the words and drift away, dwell on and in the moment that she remembers from earlier. She doesn't interrupt. She knows the dangers of interrupting, the way the ambience of the Brooklyn background will disappear once Mercedes hangs up the phone, the way the suburban Dallas night, with its leafy whispers and its only occasional rumbling of a car down their fenced-away street will disturb and distract her from the next hours of having to be all alone, by herself, thinking, thinking, pondering, being, trying not to remember.

In Brooklyn, back on the night of bail, Mercedes finishes shaking Peggy's hand. "Thank you," she says for a third time.

Then she turns toward Dixie. She places her hands on Dixie's shoulders, firmly, conveying the definite and unmistakable sense that a handshake will not suffice.

"The Black Liberation Army," Dixie says, out of nowhere, a train of thought wrapping back on itself, cutting things in half, threatening to end the call.

"What?" Mercedes asks.

"I heard about them. I heard about them and I want to see them. It was my thing, you know, all the time between when we first met and when I left last summer. I'd go see things like that."

"Why?"

"I don't know, I guess. Or maybe I do know. I'm not sure."

Mercedes still has her hands out, holding on to Dixie's shoulders, preventing them from shaking hands like she and Peggy had done. She's holding Dixie firmly, which is surprising to Dixie. Except for that one moment coming out of the Stonewall, and maybe the decisiveness of her evening, that horrible evening, in the aftermath of the plane crash at Park Slope, Dixie has thought of Mercedes as being soft, accepting, yielding, the yang to Gabrielle's yin.

"I want to kiss you," Mercedes says. "As thanks."

Dixie remembers this. Or almost. It's right there on the periphery. She can't let herself fully remember it. She can't allow herself to submerge in it, especially not with Mercedes on the other end of the line, a thousand miles away but also right there in her ear.

"What I'm trying to say," Dixie says, "is that I'd go to things, in New York, because I was looking for someone."

"For whom?"

"This Professor guy."

"A lover?"

"Sort of. Yes. It's complicated."

"It always is, dear."

The *dear*, said with the lilt of her Venezuelan kindness, her warmth, the inflection of a roll and a relaxation in the "r." It gets Dixie every time.

"Okay," Dixie says, back in the echo chamber of her memory, back in that antechamber of Mercedes and Gabrielle's apartment building. "As thanks, okay. I'd love a kiss."

Dixie thinks it will be on the cheek, like a sisterly thing, but it isn't. She closes her eyes, an eyeblink only, and finds Mercedes's lips touching her own, their mouths together, and Dixie surprises herself by not pushing away. She's unable to. She's frozen, not in shock or coldness, but in warmth, transfixed, rooted—these are better words than frozen, unless frozen evokes the warmth of frostbite, the numbing and throbbing, unabating heat of limbs and cheeks and deep inside places coming back to life from the cold. Dixie even opens her mouth, turns her head sidewise, thinking of Gary suddenly and then letting Gary fall away too, like last year's clothing, like the leaves on last year's trees, like last year's cocoon.

"Wow," Peggy says. "Shit."

And a moment later, as the kiss continues, Peggy softly adds a reinforcing "Holy shit."

That's where the memory ends.

"What I'm trying to say," Dixie says, starting again, starting over, even though it hasn't been going too badly, their call, their conversation, nothing has been going too bad really, starting with the Black Liberation Army, then going into Brooklyn and background noise and the Professor. It's all headed the right direction. None of their chitchat, their pleasantries, have caused Mercedes to stop. None of it has created a roadblock or a reason to get off the phone and return to the stifling Dallas darkness and Dallas silence, Dallas salvation. "What I'm trying to say, if it's all right with you—"

"Of course it's all right," Mercedes says. "I've had lovers too."

"No, I'm sorry, I don't mean to go down the road of telling you..."

"But you should."

"And I will, sure," Dixie says. "But what I mean to say is that I think I should come back to New York, just for a while, a week or two, to visit."

Mercedes is silent.

This is a bad sign.

Or so Dixie thinks.

The line is silent.

It stays silent.

Dixie starts to panic.

"What do you think?" she says. "It's not like I would have to stay with you or anything. I can stay with Peggy. I can stay with Jules or Camille. I've got other friends I can see and stay with. I can get a hotel. It can be whatever it needs to be. I can stay wherever. It's not that."

"No," says Mercedes. She's calm, but there's an edge in her voice. "It *is* that. And you *should* come. You should stay with me for sure. That's what we need. And then you can tell me all about what made you look for this Professor person everywhere in New York. We'll find him together, okay?"

"Okay," says Dixie, finally exhaling. "I'll arrange it with Gary and let you know as soon as I have made a respectable plan. I'll arrange it with Gary and it will be all right, normal, nothing to worry about. I'll take care of everything. It will be okay. I can't wait."

There's a little thing, though, about New York.

It's pretty easy to forget that Dixie and Gary up and left New York—what, four weeks, five?—after Stonewall. It's pretty easy to blame that on Gary's job. It's soothing to end up in Dallas, in the

222

salvation of those leafy green suburban streets. It's quiet. It's uncomplicated, or at least differently complicated.

It's easy to miss New York, once Dixie is away.

But she's cut a little tumor out of her story, here. She's conveniently tucked another something away, as if she has buried a trunk, a portmanteau, inside herself where the dots that don't connect go to die.

She can throb with expectation around Mercedes.

But she can't quite shake the image of Paul and the Professor being one and the same, kicking away there in the chorus line of the Stonewall Riot. Living it up. Loving it. Having been there, in that same place as Mercedes, when the police busted the joint. One of the regulars perhaps. Or an angel for them all?

Dixie has known Paul followed, at some point, to the city.

She doesn't let herself think about when that might have happened.

She doesn't let herself think about the mirage—she calls it a mirage, whenever it pops into her mind—of Paul and the Professor merging into one person. They are separate people still for her. They are separate, one an angel she has pursued, one something else entirely.

She cannot think through it, look at it, this yin and this yang. But it's there. It's there, all right. And it sweetens and sours the plans Dixie makes to start this new experience of New York: the experience of a New Yorker who has moved away but comes home, time and again, to immerse herself in it.

CHAPTER 20

"I love New York," Dixie tells Gary a few months later. "And I want eventually to go back and live there."

"You do?"

"I do."

Gary isn't as surprised at this as his question seems. He's just sorting out the math, the possibilities. He's been buying Dixie tickets back to the city, once or twice each month these last few months, so she can spend time with her "friends" there. He likes to joke that it's "about as expensive as the long-distance calls." He has done a good job coordinating between her trips and his, so that they overlap in Dallas a week or two each month. And they spend that time with Cyril, intensively, a rhythm they've all grown accustomed to.

"This ticket though," Dixie says, with her finger over the long scrap of paper that lies between herself and her husband on the kitchen table. "Can we change it out?"

"For what?"

"For Idaho. I need to see my dad."

"Are you taking Cyril with you?"

"No."

"Your dad's not well?" Gary asks. He puts down his newspaper and stands, circles slowly around behind Dixie so that they are both facing the same way, out into the yard where the excavation of their swimming pool has finally started, the earth laid bare by a big yellow scooping machine that now stands idle in this Texas June rain shower. Water from the rain pools in the flat expanse of grass, slips down the little hillock against which their stone ranch house nestles. When the rivulets of runoff hit the edge of the pool-scar, red clay and roots exposed to the heavens, they dash downward, one moment perfectly still in the flat grass, the next cascading, a mesmerizing effect even against the muddy swamp-water bottom of the gaping hole. Gary reaches for Dixie's shoulders. He flexes his fingers as if he is going to rub a knot, massage a knot from her neck, or her back. But as she shrugs and tightens up, he pulls his hands away and crosses them over his chest.

"He's not well at all," Dixie says. "I don't want Cyril to see him die."

"Everyone dies. All the more reason to go with you and say goodbye," Gary says, pragmatic as always. "It's a good lesson."

"I suppose."

Dixie is still resisting this. Gary can feel it. "Is there another reason you don't want him there?"

Dixie turns on him then. She's been crying, so her eyes are swollen. She looks horrible; Gary seems to understand this, and his motion toward her, as well as his hesitancy in touching her, reveals the allowance and the space and understanding and silence permitted by a long-standing and solid love. "I think I'm just being possessive. Jealous of them," Dixie says. "Jealous of my father's last bit of time with us. Isn't that ridiculous?"

225

This is close.

This is a good attempt at self-reflection, self-examination.

But it's not quite right.

She remembers the card her father gave her before she went to New York that first train trip so long ago. She remembers two summers ago, packing it up, bringing it with her in the expectation that she'd find a moment, during that long vacation at home, finally to ask her father about it. She remembers how she felt, discovering her father and Gary talking, openly talking, discussing things Dixie had never been brave enough to bring up, and then she remembers forgetting the rest, being unable to hear, process, store, comprehend. Dixie knows she should not feel jealous about that, but she does. And she feels like she needs a redo, at this last possible moment, one she undertakes alone: no Cyril, no Gary. Just her. Just Dixie and her father.

It isn't like Gary hasn't had a chance to finish that argument from the woodshed, get the details, get the goods—whatever they might be. Dixie could just ask her husband then, couldn't she? She could just ask Gary what the hell the circus was about, why Paul brought it up so often when she was a child, why her father got mad at Gary for bringing a doll back for her from his travels abroad. She could just ask her father, Arlo, the same questions.

At one point Gary, a few years earlier, even suggested that he make a trip to Idaho alone in order to "sort things out about Cyril and circuses and so forth."

That had produced a really frightfully rapid and unexpected reaction in Dixie.

"No!" she'd said, yelling it, suddenly with her voice strained and a single vein popping out on her forehead. "Nope. Not letting that happen. Sorry."

"It's like you're mad at your father," Gary answered, startled himself.

"It is, isn't it?"

But that's as far as the conversation went. Dixie just ended all idea of Gary ever going to Idaho to spend time alone with her parents. Her mother could never tell why. Gary could never tell why.

Cyril, for his part, never once asked about it, never seemed to have a need to head back to Idaho, to see his grandparents. He had become sort of ethereal—a presence, but one detached from the world.

And that's where it ended, this discussion about either Gary or Cyril going to Idaho with her or without her. That's as far as Dixie took it.

Not so this time. She's more explicit.

"I want to go on my own," Dixie says. "I want to have time on my own with my father."

"I'm disappointed," Gary says, then, looking up at her from under his brows, he says, "Cyril will be disappointed too, I'm sure." (This is a loaded sentence. Gary bites his lip as he says it. Dixie isn't sure why: she's been clear with him. No Cyril. Not this time.)

But Dixie takes a different approach. She's got an idea. She says: "Maybe you should take him somewhere?"

"A diversion?"

"Father and son time. Take him to Disneyland. Take him to the Amazon or on a fishing trip."

"I don't know how to fish."

"Gary!" she says, louder than she means to. They both turn to look at Cyril's bedroom. But the door doesn't open. No sound comes from it. They both visibly relax, lowering their voices, though the subject remains tense.

"You know what I mean," Dixie says.

"I do," says Gary.

"And you could do with some time alone with your son, anyway."

Gary winces as she says this. He seems to gear up to say something harsh, bracing himself frontward toward her like she had seen him do in her father's workshop shed. Bracing himself for a fight. But, after a moment, he draws back a bit, puts on a soothing voice. "No need to be critical."

"I'm not. I'm just stating a fact."

There's something in the air between them, neither of them making eye contact, both of them still staring out at the yard, at the filling-up swamp of their swimming pool.

"Dixie?" says Gary.

"Yes?"

"This is going to sound weird, but don't take it weird."

"I won't. I've seen weird. I've known *weird*. Whatever you say can't be even close to the types of *weird* I've seen." Dixie is a little manic here. Her eyes are wide. She's thinking of Mercedes. She's thinking of Gabrielle. She's thinking of the Professor walking out of a burning crash site with bodies floating beside him, rescued bodies ready to triage.

"About Cyril," Gary says. "About Cyril . . . I totally understand. I totally get what you're doing, why you need him not to come with you to Idaho, at least not this time."

"Really?" Dixie says.

Gary exhales. The tension floods out of the room. Gary puts his hands on her shoulders at last, and says, "You can't have him listening and watching. This is a moment just for you, just for you and your father. I think it is good for you. Cyril doesn't need to go everywhere. Eventually it will need to be just you, okay? It's hard, but true. Just you, you and your father."

Dixie goes to Idaho on her own in the end. And she's ready to speak with her father, ready as she'll ever be.

But she doesn't get away from Dallas, or Gary and Cyril, scot-free.

Not by any means.

You can't expect to have a Cyril, watching, listening, right from the first in his bassinet, and go off to Idaho on a somewhat important moment. You can't expect that, given these circumstances, no sort of blowback will happen—especially now that Cyril is almost a teenager, almost at that stage (or perhaps this is the first indication of that stage) of life in which pushback, and boundaries, and setting himself up as his own person, independently, have such force. In short, Dixie doesn't escape— even with Gary trying to occupy all of Cyril's time planning a two-week adventure to Machu Picchu. She doesn't escape Cyril's perceptiveness, his way of finding just the right moment, just the right word.

"I know what you think. I know what you think about Grandpa and the circus. Dad's told me some of it. Grandpa's told me some of it," Cyril says, coming into the bedroom as she takes a break from packing her suitcase for this journey home. She's a little tired, a little fraught with the expectation of the words she needs to say to her father. She's not ready for Cyril. She never is. Or she's too ready, allowing him to *be* places he shouldn't be. In fact, at this very moment, she's got the playing card in her hands, the Jack of Hearts.

She's looking at it but she's not even thinking of her father at all. She's thinking of Cyril. More pointedly, she's thinking about how she told Mercedes about Cyril, about Cyril's weird way of *being there* amid all the moments, watching, listening, coalescing things that he shouldn't grasp, knowing things that just seem too private, too personal, too hidden. It's weird and uncomfortable and Dixie is not sure if it is like that for every parent with their children, or if Cyril is truly special in that regard, special in an uncomfortably precocious way. It's like he appears, and speaks, and is most present in these strangest moments of Dixie's self-reflection. He's a mirror of a child, a waif, an insubstantiality. Dixie hates herself for thinking this of her own son, but that's what fills her mind as she looks at this Jack of Hearts. That's what fills her mind as Cyril enters and starts to talk to her.

Her mind skips away, escaping.

She and Mercedes are in a hotel room in New York, somewhere in New York. It's midmorning. Light slants through the blinds, plays on the far wall of the room, traveling down the wall like a finger tracing the contours of a new liaison. The covers of the hotel bed swirl around their two bodies. Pipes in the walls make ticktock noises, winter-heating noises, that go a long way to filling the silence that is otherwise only interrupted by the ragged edges of their combined breathing.

"I left him, you know," Dixie says. She's admitting this, and also a bit wide-eyed about it, like she's discovering it out of her own depths, right in that moment.

"When?" Mercedes asks. She's sleepy, only half-listening.

"When we were at the plane crash helping you. I left him. Don't you remember? The four of us—you, me, Gabrielle, Gary—the four of us sitting on the curbside when Gary opened his big mouth and wanted to know why Gabrielle dresses like a man. It was just the four of us. Just the four. But Cyril had come with us that night.

And he was there throughout all of it. Only, you see, I forgot him. I forgot about him. I left him. I got so caught up in what we were doing that I left my own son somewhere. Some of the medical people, the emergency people, they took him and kept him and fed and changed his little diaper and then found us afterward."

"I remember that," says Mercedes, as if it was a big moment, at the time, but one she hasn't thought about for a long while. "I remember sitting on the pavement with just the four of us. I don't remember your baby there. I only remember him from the line in the market when I first saw you."

"See, the thing is," Dixie says. "The thing is that I don't remember it. I hadn't remembered it. Not until he brought it up with me the other day. I didn't, couldn't remember—or I never really admitted to myself—that I had left him all alone during that turmoil."

"But how could he remember it at all?" Mercedes asks. "He was only a few months old."

"That's the thing," says Dixie. "That's exactly what I'm meaning to tell you. He's weird like that. It's not natural. He was just a baby."

Mercedes sits up straight in bed. The sheets fall from her chest, and Dixie lets one of her hands stray along the curved and dusky contour of Mercedes's stomach, up along the underside of her breast. Mercedes shivers. But her eyes are angry, the flashing anger of the heated moment that Dixie has started to know and love. "You should not call your own son weird. You should not call him unnatural."

"But he is. He's different. Special. And it's a tough sort of different to deal with, as a parent."

"Like a magic?"

"Like magic, yes."

That's where Dixie is, when Cyril walks into her bedroom. She's holding the playing card her father gave her. Her mind has traveled far away but also circles here, so close to home, as if by replaying this very memory she has summoned her son to come to her and speak inappropriately spot-on words.

Dixie feels combative toward him. Maybe only because he started the conversation so bluntly himself, she feels a need to be prickly toward him. She blurts out the words: "What is it that you think I think about Grandpa and the circus?"

"I think you are putting your own issues on him," Cyril says.

"What issues?"

"Love issues. Forgetting issues." Cyril is mad, in that teenager sort of way. Confused, trying to sort things, sort his world, resorting to anger. Dixie points this out. She tries to tell him that he's making things up because he's hurt about not going to Idaho. She tries to explain how important the trip to Machu Picchu is for Gary and him, to spend that time together, but the message doesn't sink in.

"Grandpa is going to die," Cyril says. "And you're going to ask him all the wrong questions."

"I am?"

"You are. Because you're only dealing with yourself right now."

"What are the right questions?"

This calms Cyril down, unexpectedly so.

"Really," he says. "Really you want to know?"

"I do. I've spent my whole life, or at least the last decade of my whole life, running away from the right questions."

Cyril sits on the bed beside Dixie. He takes the playing card from her and puts it into her suitcase, into the inside zipper pocket of her suitcase from which he had taken it a few years earlier during that

232

summer trip in Idaho, taken it out and brought it with him when he and Dixie stood together outside the work-shed window, peeping on Gary and Arlo, Cyril eavesdropping alongside Dixie on a most private conversation between his father and his grandfather. *Maybe he remembers the parts I haven't been able to think about. Maybe he will be able to explain everything to me. Wouldn't that be nice?*

"Well, for one," he says, "Grandpa got in some trouble."

"During the circus?"

"Yes. And you should ask him about that. And how Paul was involved."

"Uncle Paul?"

Cyril nods in confirmation.

"And what else should I ask about?" Dixie says.

"Magic powers. The magic powers he learned in the circus."

Dixie can't help it. She laughs at this.

"No," says Cyril. "He showed me."

"Grandpa showed you?"

"Paul showed me."

Dixie first pictures Cyril and her father together in the machine shed, as far away from magic as anything she can imagine, everything mechanical, greasy, rusted, wrecked. Then she pictures Paul, Paul by her bedside, reading to her about the circus. She sobers. The laughter dries up. She can't bring herself to imagine a conversation between Cyril and Paul. "I'm sorry for laughing," she says. "But that's the sort of thing grown-ups say when they can't tell the truth to a child."

"I know the difference between truth and make-believe, truth and lies."

"Maybe now you do. But you were five years old back then. Neither Paul nor your grandfather would have told you all the bad stuff. They need some way out of it, and that's why he said he had magic. That was just an easy way to explain things. Anyway, that's what I've got to ask him about, the tough parts. As much as you believe in all this talk of magic and stories about the circus, I'm the one who has got to ask the hard questions about that time. You know Uncle Paul isn't really our uncle, not *my* uncle? He was just a guy who hung around our house when I was a kid, hung around and bothered us—"

"I know," Cyril says.

"You do?"

"Grandpa explained," says Cyril. "Grandpa lost the magic. But Paul hung around because Grandpa let him. Grandpa owed him. He saved Grandpa from the trouble."

This makes better sense to Dixie than any of the alternatives. Still, she has her own theories and her own need to verify them. And even though she's only ever seen Cyril deal in cutting, hard-edged, incisive truths, still she doesn't believe him. Or, perhaps she believes him but can't yet bring herself to believe Paul was somehow getting into Cyril's brain. When had they spoken? Hadn't Dixie, hadn't Gary, gone to such great lengths to keep Paul away from their son?

"What sort of trouble was Grandpa in, back in the circus?"

"You know," Cyril says.

"I don't."

"You do. We were both there, listening at the window of the shed. But you're good at forgetting things, Mom. Grandpa told me that. He said, 'Your mom is the best person I know about forgetting things, especially if they have anything to do with magic.'"

"I'm too practical, is what he meant."

"But you don't remember what he told Dad about the trouble?"

"I don't remember that at all, dear."

"Hmmmph," Cyril says. He stands, and goes to the bedroom door, and is about to close it when he turns back to her and says, "I don't find that funny at all."

He's not mad.

His eyes just look at her sadly, that flickering of teenage angst and energy flow.

He's not mad.

He just shuts the door and disappears.

Cyril doesn't say another word to Dixie until they're at the airport, Gary ahead a step or two, carrying Dixie's luggage to the counter for her trip to Pocatello.

"I'm sorry, Mom," he says. "I shouldn't have left you in the bedroom like that."

"It's okay. I know you miss your grandfather."

"I'd like to see him again. Maybe after Machu Picchu?"

"Maybe."

Cyril takes Dixie's hand at this point, stops her, and makes her turn and bend down to him. He's twelve, almost thirteen, and starting to get his growth, so Dixie doesn't have to bend too far, not anymore.

Cyril stops her and makes her bend down so that he can whisper in her ear: "What you need to ask Grandpa about, Mom, is right there on the playing card. That's what you need to ask him about. It's his card, not yours. You never gambled. He did."

CHAPTER 21

The 727 bounces and bucks and Dixie doesn't like this one little bit. She thinks a drink would be in order, something to soothe her nerves, although she hasn't been much of a drinker, just a bit of wine with the ladies now and again is all. But now seems to be the time. And that's what she gets, a bad airline white, tasting like vinegar and honey stirred up in turpentine, served in a plastic cup. She takes a sip and then sets it aside. She's never learned to feel comfortable flying. Every time when she books a flight, she calculates: Is this the right one, the one that will land me safely where I'm going? Or . . . the wrong one? The one when something happens? A goose gets sucked into the engine. (Or a playing card.) Lightning strikes a wing. A mechanic has forgotten to tighten a crucial lug.

Or . . . hijackers? Because that's a thing that happens now. Skyjackers with pistols, barrels aimed at pilots, knives pressed against a stewardess's neck, maybe, against her cheerful gulping jugular. *Come fly with me!* Dixie has seen pictures in the papers, on TV.

It could happen. Palestinian terrorists. Black Panthers wanting to go to Cuba. That man who said he had a bomb, held people hostage, got his ransom, and parachuted out of the jet. Or the crash in Park Slope. Just two planes colliding midair when they had at one point been tracking through the sky, all innocuous, but unknowingly headed toward an improbable intersection.

Looking around, it doesn't seem like any of the passengers in seats to Dixie's left or right are hijackers. Businessmen. Families and kids. One older gentleman flirts with a flight attendant as she leans over his seat and hands him a drink.

A drinkable drink would be good, Dixie thinks, and she pushes the call button for her stewardess.

The plane drops again, like a falling elevator, and Dixie feels her stomach rise and plummet, leaving an emptiness in her chest, a vacuum. She draws in a deep breath, wanting to fill it. She does not like feeling empty.

"Nervous flyer, honey?" the man next to her asks—a businessman, she guesses, his face broad and red and his neck ballooning where the collar of his white shirt constricts it. He's already had a few turpentine concoctions of his own, likely of a stronger variety than wine.

"Not really," Dixie says. She doesn't want to join into a conversation with him. She's been trying to avoid it. She already knows that he doesn't see her. Not really. He sees someone else, some Dallas housewife, except she's aware she doesn't exactly fit the part—not nearly enough beehive, and too much dark clothing, too much modern New York and Guggenheim about her. Still, he's got her marked as someone he can talk to, tell all his stories, whether she wants to hear them or not, and the truth is, she doesn't. She doesn't want to hear them. She just wants to look at his glass, decide what he's drinking, as it seems he's an expert, and order the same from the stewardess.

Oh, my wife . . . oh, my job . . . Dixie imagines him saying.

"Flying's a hell of a thing," he says. "Sometimes I look out at the clouds and feel like I could live in them. Like they're solid." He laughs. "Or I'm not."

For a moment Dixie meets his eyes, and they're not what she expects. They are sad and pained and weary, and she thinks, maybe I *do* want to hear his story. Maybe it's something important, something I missed, something I might have forgotten that I need to know. Maybe none of these intersections, between two random planes in the sky above Park Slope, or between people, people from Idaho and New York and Dallas and God knows where, maybe none of them are random. Maybe they're all managed. Maybe they're all fated?

Why hadn't she chosen a card? Why hadn't she gone that extra step with the Professor, back all those years ago when they rode the cross-continental train together?

The fat businessman smiles and turns away, staring out his window toward his semipermeable clouds.

Dixie leans back in her seat, hearing the rush of the cabin air, the muted roar of the engines, and—because the fat man already owns the view out the window—she stares at the patterned fabric on the seatback in front of her. That's when it happens: time slows down, syrupy slow, spreading around her and through her, warm and sticky, and it feels both pleasurable, that spreading warmth, so languid and smooth, and also as if she could surrender to it and drown, trapped in its sticky weight.

The back of the airplane seat in front of her, that nubby industrial fabric. It reminds her of something. The colors aren't right, but the texture. The texture is what makes her stare. *The couch,* she thinks, *it's the same as the couch in the Adirondacks cabin, that's what it is.* That couch hadn't really matched the rest of the furniture, which was older, rustic, wood with faded cushions, a couple of camp beds. In contrast, that couch seemed like something a young couple would get for their Greenwich Village apartment, Scandinavian lines and sturdy fabric you could put your heels on and not destroy. Dixie had spent a lot of time sitting on that couch, especially when it was too cold to go outside and stroll around the lake. She'd read, some of the time, from the shelf of books and magazines in the cabin—the kind of collection that just accumulated over time, with a sort of randomness to it. Books like *Peyton Place* and *The Second Sex* and *On the Beach. Guerilla Warfare*, by Che Guevara. Five-year-old *Reader's Digest*s and *National Geographic*s mildewed at the edges, while inside them anthropological articles on Africa gratuitously showed slick black skin, tattoos, painful piercings. Pages sticking together. More recent copies of *Life* and *Time*. A battered board game and a few puzzles.

They'd taken the train, the Laurentian, Dixie and Peggy had. They'd taken it to Prattsville, and from there a hired car to the cabin. The train ride had been beautiful, the Hudson River Valley dressed in the remains of its fall colors, lakes glimpsed between trees. Solid brick houses clustered in little towns. Clapboard porches. Hills giving way to mountains. Peggy hadn't appreciated it though, and she'd spent her time pacing to the vestibule to smoke. Dixie supposed she could understand and sympathize with Peggy's case of nerves, considering what they were going to do.

Nothing would happen that first night at the cabin. Nothing at all. They ate sandwiches and drank what they considered to be classy martinis, at least for their present circumstances (they were younger back then, and inexperienced still in the making of martinis): a little vodka from an old jug they found on one of the shelves in the kitchen pantry, some Canada Dry, and each with a green olive from a jar Peggy brought with her, thinking—as the old wives' tale goes—that she might need to drop it, shatter it for appearances' sake if ever in public any seepage, any untoward liquid, coming or going, needed to be excused away.

Books and conversation growing old, as the first day together in the cabin ticked and tocked away, Peggy making a half-hearted attempt at starting a giant jigsaw puzzle depicting the Eiffel Tower. She dumped the puzzle pieces out onto a crooked-topped table in the cabin's main room. Then she spent the first five minutes debating whether it was, actually, the Eiffel Tower, or Big Ben, a totally inane but distracting line of thought.

They hadn't spoken much, that whole ride north. Nor the whole of that first day alone together in the cabin.

There wasn't much more to say. Or, if there was, it would all be too painful, too awkward, too immediate for the transience of their situation, the gravity of their actions.

The doctor had been scheduled to come tomorrow.

Dixie wasn't keen to remember the next part, not because she witnessed it—of course she wasn't going to watch Peggy on that bed, lying on clean white sheets. That was a surprise. To find clean sheets in the cabin! Dixie wasn't going to watch her. But she did help set everything up, covering her from just below her shoulders to the tops of her thighs, then standing outside the doorway within earshot, ready to jump into action if needed. She did assist after, and it wasn't so bad. She brought Peggy some tea and, later, soup. She stripped the soiled sheets, stuffed them in a pillowcase and deposited them in a hamper on the mud-porch, as instructed. Someone would take care of those later. It seemed someone was always there, or soon to be there, invisible but present as a force to watch over them, a secret society watching, helping, taking care from a safe and unattributable distance. Dixie wishes, looking back on it all, that it could be just women. That women could take care of women, have the knowledge and power to do so, make choices for themselves. But always there would be, will be, husbands, lovers, doctors, priests and clergy and legislators involved. Until most of them are women—maybe not *most* but at least *enough* of them—until then, these sorts of seances, of alien-excommunications, must happen at isolated lakefront cabins, if a lady has money enough. Or elsewhere, worse places, if she does not.

Dixie thinks about this and she thinks about her subsequent friendship with Peggy too, how Peggy every day after that followed her around, any day Dixie could spare, enthusiastically buying into Dixie's search for the Professor, supporting Dixie's pursuit of disasters and soirees and protests, places where they might be *seen,* events that would slow down time enough for Dixie to actually grasp it and fully live in those moments, little bits of her life that she pointedly remembers, that she can fully remove from inside her, that she can take out and look at and turn over in her mind so that she can almost feel the contours and realness all over again. Events that aren't blanked out. Events that aren't blurry. Events that might—she thinks back to when she was still just a young twenty-something mother—lure the Professor back to her. This time in the Adirondacks with Peggy, it changed their relationship. They had been equals before. But once Dixie arranged things for Peggy, once she did that, and stayed for Peggy the whole time, and took care of her, then Dixie had the upper hand. She didn't want the upper hand, but she got it. Something shifted between them, with Dixie dominant in their relationship and Peggy playing a happy, supportive second fiddle.

Now, sitting on the plane, looking at the nubs of the fabric on the seat in front of her, thinking how that fabric matches the fabric of the couch in the cabin, Dixie gets the whole blurriness of the Adirondacks event all at once, and not sequentially, but encapsulated: it comes back in a smell. The smell of blood.

She doesn't particularly want to dwell on that now, not with the plane still in the air and the real possibility of crashing any second hanging there before her. She doesn't want to breathe too deeply either, whether in memory or in reality, as the fat man's scent of booze and body odor gets into her nose even with the shallowest of breaths.

One thing that's not too surprising, under the circumstances: since Gary moved them all to Dallas, Dixie doesn't stay in very close touch with Peggy. They talk on the phone, every once in a while, but not the way she and Mercedes talk. There's no connection there, not really; even the syrup-time of their past shared trauma voyeurism doesn't bind them together all that tightly. Beyond it they don't have much in common.

They don't have much in common at all.

Or, not much that Dixie can really think about.

The thing they *do* have in common . . .

Dixie doesn't want to remember that.

She doesn't want to remember that at all.

She doesn't want to. And so she doesn't: it remains just one trip to the Adirondacks. One trip with Peggy. One blurry trip.

It's as simple as that. A black place in her mind that stays black and doesn't get looked at, looked into, thought about. A place much like her father's workshop shed: black, grayed out, invisible to her except when she really concentrates—and she rarely allows herself time or the mental space to do that. It's better that way. Better for Dixie. Better for everyone.

Next to her, the man has gotten out a deck of cards. He cuts the deck in half and shuffles them, the sound of the cards, that fast, hard *brrrrrp*, like fabric being ripped in half. It startles Dixie.

It must mean something, she thinks. It has to. She turns and stares at him. He is not the Professor. There is nothing about him that might be considered similar—not tall, not imbued with elegant boniness, no Roman emperor hair, certainly no cotton balls in his ears.

But his eyes. Is that what she saw, when her gaze first connected with his at the onset of the journey? Not just sadness and weariness but *familiarity?*

"Do you tell fortunes?" she blurts out.

He chuckles. "Fortunes? No. A little gin rummy sometimes."

"Oh." She hesitates. She hesitates because this could be several things: the Professor in disguise. A sad, lonely businessman flying to Boise. An angel. Who knows?

Dixie feels naughty.

Maybe it's the acrid wine.

Maybe it's the elevation.

Maybe it's the memory of Peggy in the cabin, trying to run away.

"Would you mind if I pick a card?"

The businessman's head draws back a fraction, turtle-like, emphasizing the bulbous pouch beneath his chin. He is most unprofessorial. He is most un-Roman. "Sure," he says. "Why not?"

He fans out the cards, his hands quick and elegant, like he's done this many times before. That gesture, so assured, so familiar, that practiced flourish, the cards in the shape of a peacock's tail—

He looks up from under his brows at her. "You want to draw one? Or is this something you have to think about?"

Apparently, it is. Apparently, it is something Dixie has thought about before, a lot. She hasn't wanted to make a bet, she doesn't gamble—she still doesn't—but what occurs to her now is that she and the Professor never discussed the terms of the bet, the stakes. She'd simply assumed that drawing a card meant some kind of agreement, some possibility of loss or gain. That a transaction lay at the heart of the matter. *Everybody bets,* the Professor had said, and now Dixie thinks maybe, back then, the newest of mothers, that she had misunderstood the entire game. Maybe it wasn't a game at all. Maybe there were no stakes. Maybe it was just a simple statement of fact. *Everybody bets.*

There are a million thoughts in her mind all at once. *You bet every day, don't you? You bet that the person you marry won't leave you alone. You bet that your husband won't notice you sneaking around. You bet that your son isn't listening from his cradle, or from across the playground, or in the coffee shop when you're chatting with the girls, just an infant but weirdly aware. You bet he will be safe climbing the godless jungle up to some remote Peruvian ruins in the Andes. You bet that it is okay for him to see his grandfather, or not. You bet that his uncle won't tell him bedtime stories about circuses. You bet that it is okay to be selfish about this little journey, this possibly last, final journey and conversation with your own damn father.*

And you bet that whatever he has to say to you isn't something you wish you'd never heard.

"You okay, hon?" says the businessman in the airplane seat beside Dixie, still with his cards splayed out between them.

Dixie shakes herself a bit and allows the tiniest giggle to escape her lips, because she doesn't want the man/the Professor/possibly an angel to think she's having problems, to know she's having problems. Everything's fine, isn't it? Perfectly fine, and nothing at all of any consequence is happening, nothing to worry about, nothing at all.

"Just silly," she says. "This all reminded me of something and I got lost in thinking about it. Gathering wool, that's what my mother used to say whenever I'd do that."

Trying to disguise the depth of the breath she takes to steady herself, Dixie reaches out and draws a card. Swivels her wrist to turn it over.

"So what'd you get?"

Dixie looks at it. It has no number. Just a man staring at her. The Joker, perhaps. "I don't know what it is," she says.

The man looks at the card. "Huh," he says. "Looks like this one doesn't belong to the deck. I don't know. Says 'Nemo' here."

"What's that mean?"

"I don't know."

The man takes the card back, compares it to the deck, shakes his head in confusion, then crumples the card up, folds it up, and places it into the pocket on the back of the airplane seat at his knees.

"Must be a problem with the pack," the man says, searching through the rest of the deck for oddities and finding none.

"Do you know if it means anything? Or what it's good for?"

The man shrugs. "Never seen anything like it before. But it rings a bell with me, back from my prep school days when they made us read Latin till our eyes bled. Nemo. I think that was what one of the Greeks called himself when he didn't want to give away his name. In the *Iliad* maybe. Or the *Odyssey*. I don't know."

Part VIII
Circus-like

CHAPTER 22

When she gets home—that is, to the house where she grew up, no longer home, but perfectly *Not Home,* no longer home—it's dark. The porch light's on and there's one light on in the kitchen. The house feels empty. You can sense it sometimes, even before you walk in, when no one's home in a house. Certain people create an absence that can be felt like a weight lifted from the premises, like the shutters and curtains have all been thrown open to let in the light, like the house might float away because it is no longer ballasted.

Dixie doesn't think of her mother that way, not really. She didn't mind her company back in New York. And she thinks maybe she understands something about her mother now, or more accurately, she's willing to think about it now. Her mother had wanted to get away from Pocatello too. Like Dixie, she couldn't do it on her own, but she lacked a Gary to set her up there, wherever *there* might be— Russia perhaps, the Maldives, Arkansas?—and she had to wait for Dixie to establish the beachhead.

She'd wanted to get away from Dad, Dixie thinks. Not enough to leave him entirely. But enough to be on her own, or at least to be regarded as a slightly different person, away from her identity, all consuming, as Arlo's wife.

Why didn't I want to think about that then, when I was a child, when I first moved away? Dixie wonders. *Why did I not want to think about my mother?*

Her mother is not in the kitchen, where the one light in the house burns.

Dixie turns on the faucet and positions a tall glass under the stream of water. The glass is made of plastic. It's the kind of thing you use on a picnic, opaque plastic with a pattern of white-and-yellow daisies printed on it. It's the kind of thing that didn't exist in this house when it was Dixie's home. Plastic is a novelty, a change, a corruption.

Dixie sips. After the bad, sour wine aboard the airplane, the water tastes metallic and refreshing.

The kitchen, she notices, is yellow and white, like the tumbler. The color of daisies. There is an oven mitt and an apron printed in white-and-yellow flowers—a trivet on the stove and a spoon holder patterned with daisies as well.

Is this new? Dixie wonders. Had she just not noticed it before? When had her mother adopted daisies as a badge of identity? Had someone given her a gift once, the trivet perhaps, and the motif just multiplied from there? Does her mother even *like* daisies? She'd never mentioned it to Dixie. Dixie can recall nothing of the sort.

Dixie turns her gaze to the screened-in back porch. It too is decorated in white and yellow, some of which has been faded by sun and cold and dust. An ironing board, a watering can, flats of tinned vegetables, and a sack of fertilizer.

Beyond that is the backyard, still overgrown with grass and weeds and daffodils, the push mower shoved up against the rotting fence. The shed is there too, lit from within by a single work-light.

That's where she finds her mother, pulling a box off a tilting shelf, the cardboard of it softened by age. As Dixie comes into the shed, her mother is just in the process of rather roughly slinging it onto the oil-stained, splintering workbench, approximately in the same place where Arlo had unwrapped the doll present Gary brought from Arabia, two or three years earlier.

Dixie looks around. There are trash cans heaped with rusting coffee cans, screws and nails and metal parts she can't identify.

"Mom? Is he dead?"

She blurts out the words without really thinking, except that he must be for her mother to be doing this already, throwing away his things.

Her mother straightens and then softens into some form of a greeting. "No. He just let all this stuff pile up and get out of hand, that's all."

Dixie looks around her father's shed, seeing now that it's being emptied out. All of her father's bits and bobs and doodads going into the trash, though a few items Gladys has placed in packing boxes.

"Why are you doing this now?" Dixie asks.

"I'm thinking of making it a gardening shed. I'm thinking yellow, white accents, a stencil of daisies, to freshen up the place. I'm tired of having all this junk lying around." Dixie's mother flings a hunk of metal pipe into the trash. "He's never going to do anything with it anyway." Then she bursts into tears.

Her father is in the hospital. It happened sometime that same morning, probably when Dixie was in the air, maybe while she was drinking sour wine and drawing cards from the sad businessman.

"One thing goes, and then another," her mother says in the car, as Dixie drives. "You know how it is. Or maybe you don't. You're still young. Too young to understand that, I suppose."

Her mother is right, she doesn't know. But she has at least a sense of what it might be like. She thinks about drawing that card, the Nemo, the one that looked like a Joker, a random insert in the deck, and she remembers the feeling of it slipping out between two other cards, plastic-coated cardboard on plastic-coated cardboard, everything sanitary and safe. She thinks: *What if this is some fundamental architecture of the universe I've disturbed? Some small, meaningless object that's actually holding everything together?* She had pulled it out. She had selected it. And now that it has been loosened from the pack: one thing goes, and then another. A plane falls out of the sky. A Professor boards a train. A husband spends weeks and weeks away hunting for oil and tectonic plates. A man, or woman, goes on an odyssey without ever allowing himself, or herself, to hear what is happening.

"Will he come out of the hospital?" Dixie asks.

"Not likely," her mother says.

They are close to the end of visiting hours, the nurse says, but they can go in and see him for a few minutes. The hospital room is dimly lit, filled with hushed whooshes and beeps. Her father lies in the bed, tubes in his nose, in his arm. His face is the color of wet cement. His eyes are open, but Dixie doesn't have the sense that he's really awake.

Dixie lifts her hand as if to touch her father, touch his wrist, but at the last second she thinks better of it, pulls back, and folds her hands one on the other. She says: "Daddy?"

He nods. His eyes are focused on something above her head. "That elephant," he says. "That elephant was really something." He pauses, forehead creasing in a frown, eyes focusing on a further distance. "It was so sad. All alone. Elephants should not be alone."

"Come back midday tomorrow, he's likely to be more awake," the nurse tells her. So that's what Dixie decides she'll do. She drives home with her mom. Climbs the creaking stairs to the small bedroom where she had slept as a child. Her old bed is still there, the faded quilt that always smells vaguely dusty still covering it. She strips off her travel-sweaty clothes, puts on the Chinese silk pajamas that Gary had brought home from a trip to Hong Kong, dark blue with white piping that always make her feel a bit like Mary Tyler Moore in *The Dick Van Dyke Show*. Laura Petrie, that was her name, Mary's character. That's who she feels like.

Dixie lies on her side beneath the sheet and blankets and quilt, pulling the covers around her neck. It's cold up here, colder than she's used to nowadays, between the sometimes oppressive steam-pipe heat of their New York apartment and the forced central heat (or stifling summer) of their new Dallas house. She curls inward, like a shrimp, feeling translucent and vulnerable beneath her shell of blankets and quilts.

Tomorrow, she thinks, *I'll be able to talk to him. Tomorrow I'll check one of these puzzles off my list, at last, at last, at last. I'm going to ask him about the circus. I'm going to ask him why it matters, why Paul told me so many little happy but uncomfortable tales as a child. I'm going to ask him what he did there, what he and Paul did, and what he's been hiding. I'm going to ask him everything.*

That next morning, after having a cup of bad coffee and a piece of toast, leaving her mother to the sorting of her father's shed, Dixie sets off on a walk around her old hometown. She has the sense that perhaps she'll find something she lost, something she left behind that day she ran sobbing to the train station, holding Cyril wrapped in his blanket against her breast, wanting nothing more than to escape.

Pocatello looks so small after New York. The modest downtown with its fading brick buildings, the little park she used to play in as a child. She remembers things like that, in general terms. "I played there." But she can't really remember the details. What had she played? Tag? Cowboys and Indians? What? The unspecific nature of her thoughts, her memories, bothers her. She wonders if she has something wrong in her brain. She wonders why it is all cloudy, the gray and black places invading even—or maybe especially—these childhood places. She knows she has been here, here and there, everywhere in the town, running, biking, playing on certain swing sets, climbing certain trees. She knows these things in her mind, but she has no definite recollections, no tastes, no sounds, no smells, no viscera. Everything has lost its color over time. *Is that just what getting old does?* she wonders.

She walks and walks and walks, stopping once to buy a Coke because she's thirsty, coming at last to Ross Park, or close to it anyway. Train tracks separate her from it. She remembers Ross Park, the high lava flows to the east, the Portneuf River to the west, the train tracks running alongside it, the grass an incredible emerald green. There was a zoo there, she recalls, with bears and bison and wild cats.

She doesn't go into the park. There's a line of freight trains on the tracks that separate her from it, and she doesn't have time to figure out where to cross them. She needs to head back to her parents' house, to her mother sorting screws and gizmos and whatnots, and from there to the hospital. To her father. This walk has been, or was supposed to be, a way to mount some courage, to gather her thoughts and her energy and her perseverance. But she turns back at Ross Park only feeling confused and a bit frightened by the lack of specificity in her memories of the place.

She walks along the river now, thinking she'll follow it back through town. Every once in a while she catches a whiff of something nose-wrinklingly foul. Sewage. No wonder no one plays in it, no wonder no one plays in the river, she thinks, and what a shame. Never did when she was a child either. She has a flash of a memory, something so quick it almost escapes her, but her hand reaches up to snatch it from the air, and it's this: standing on a bridge over the river, the stink overpowering her, thinking, *I should just jump, sink to the bottom and let the shit cover me up. Let the water cover me up.* This is a memory. A flash of memory.

The violence of it, the surge of rage, of self-loathing, takes her breath away.

How old was she then? Thirteen? Fourteen?

Why had she felt like that? She can't put her finger on it, but it is there, in her brain, real. Real as anything.

She's disturbed by the memory, but also, strangely enough, elated. It's a memory that comes with sensory detail. It's a memory that comes in full color, full smell, full sound. In a flash, it comes back, much of it, her on that bridge looking at the icy, stinky water. It's a disturbing memory but it is real and it makes her feel more confident in her own mind, her own past. She touches her stomach, one hand cradling her stomach, as if she is hungry, empty, emptied, and then, turning away from the river, she leaves.

When she gets home, her mother is frantic. "Where have you been?" she shouts. Her face is red, her eyes darting. "We need to go to the hospital. We need to go *now!*"

"Okay," Dixie says, at first thinking, *Well, she could have called a cab if she was in such a big hurry*—but then it hits her, the reason for her mother's dramatics.

She doesn't want to ask if her father has already died.

Her father's room feels different now. Dixie can't put a finger on why. Still the same hushed quiet, the beeps and whirrs of medical machinery. As her mother sits at the side of his bed, her hand resting on his, Dixie starts to have a sense of what the difference is.

Her father still breathes. His chest rises and falls. His eyes are half-open. But he isn't there at all. He is truly gone. He is gone already. A stroke. An aneurism. Something like that, the doctor tells them. He could recover. He could. But Dixie sees it in her father's ceiling-ward gaze: he's gone.

Dixie parks herself in the remaining chair in the cramped room. It is hard and wooden. Her body starts to ache almost immediately, but there is nowhere else to sit. She watches her mother's vigil at her father's bedside and wonders: *What should I do while my father is dying?*

She wishes she'd brought a book. Who could say how long this might take? And none of the questions she'd wanted to ask would be answered now. All of the things she had wanted to say to him would be left unsaid. All of the clarity she craved would remain unclear.

As soon as she has that thought, she wonders, *What things?* What had she wanted to say to her father? What had she wanted to ask him?

She can't remember even that. She had made a list the other day, but it's gone now, gone into grayness. Not important, really, done away by her father passing into this last stage of incommunicado.

He wouldn't have the answer to the riddle of the Professor, Dixie's Professor. He wouldn't have the answer to Mercedes, Dixie's love for Mercedes, her fascination with Mercedes. He wouldn't be able to tell Dixie why she is so restless and unsettled much of the time.

Or why she needs to be *seen*.

Or why, beyond that, she has been having these troubles *seeing herself.*

He won't, wouldn't even if present, be able to tell her anything about any of that. He'd only have old dusty stories that Dixie would still need to unravel.

Maybe it's better she knows nothing of them.

Maybe it's better that he takes them to his grave.

She watches one of the monitors. She doesn't know what the numbers mean, what they might be measuring. One marker goes up. Holds there. Plummets. Repeats. She thinks for a moment that it charts her father's erratic breathing, which seems to start and stop, as if he must gather himself to draw in the next ragged breath. But his breaths and the moving needle don't seem to match up.

Her mother hunches over in her chair and rummages through her tote bag, pulling out a disordered pile of yarn and knitting needles.

Dixie finds this interesting and a little strange. Her mother is not a good knitter, at least not that Dixie remembers. Dixie can't recall her mother ever knitting during the time she spent with them in New York. Knitting is just one of those things women of a certain age *do*, Dixie supposes. Whether they like doing it or not, it comes upon them, seizes them, manual activity to still the mind. *Idle hands do the devil's work*, isn't that the old saying?

She watches as her mother attempts to detangle and organize the mess of partially knitted yarn and as she then gets her needles into position. What is it she's making? Dixie wonders. It's a sort of rectangle, the colors a mix of blues and yellows. A scarf? Socks? A hat?

"What are you making?" Dixie asks.

Her mother shrugs. "A pot holder. I guess."

After a while, Dixie needs to stretch her legs. She needs to pee. She needs to do *something* other than watch her mother knit and her father die.

She rises from her uncomfortable chair. "I won't be gone long," she tells her mother.

The knitting needles click. Machines beep and exhale. Her mother nods. Dixie watches her a moment. She seems smaller than she was not too long ago, the skin beneath her chin loosened like a deflated balloon. Dixie has an impulse to wrap her arms around her mother, to give her a hug, but they aren't hugging people, by and large. They aren't touching people, except when necessity overtakes them. (Or, perhaps, in those worst childhood nights, when being told circus stories at the bedside.)

"I'll be right back," Dixie says, slipping from the room.

Down the hallways there's not much to see in the hospital, really. Glimpses of sick people in darkened rooms. Doctors and nurses walking in and out of those rooms, consulting clipboards. At one point she sees a young doctor leaning against a counter, chatting up a nurse on the other side of it, and for some reason she fixates on the doctor's cheeks, the beard starting to come in as though this was the end of a long shift. Dixie can almost feel that bearded cheek against her own. She wonders why she is thinking of this, of physical contact, in such a time?

She finds the cafeteria. It's small and smells of ancient chicken soup and stale grease. She realizes she hasn't eaten since breakfast, but she's hard-pressed to work up an appetite in this place. A cup of coffee, she thinks.

The coffee tastes as though it has been sitting on a burner for hours, scorched and rubbery. Even pouring in cream and sugar doesn't help it much, but she sits at an empty table and sips, not yet ready to go back to that hospital room and her father's dying. She should, she knows. What if she misses it?

But then, so what if she does? He's already gone, slipped away from this world. Does the moment his heart stops beating really mean that much?

You should be there for Gladys, she thinks, calling her Gladys in this, this most intimate and private of moments. Rarely Mom. Rarely that much affection. She can't claim to understand her mother, but she thinks she loves her. She has no reason *not* to love her.

She hears the scrape of chair legs against linoleum. She doesn't look up right away. She doesn't want to. Her gaze lingers on her coffee, on the swirling, speckled patterns the creamer made on its surface. *That creamer can't be good for you,* she thinks. *What's it even made of?*

When she does look up, she takes in the man who has sat down at the table next to hers.

He's positioned himself so he is facing her at an angle, giving them space as well as an unobstructed view of each other.

The man's flesh clings more tightly to his bones, that's one thing she notices, but time hasn't sat as heavily on him as it has on Arlo, or even on Gladys. His eyes are that same green, only slightly faded, his dark hair silvered but cut in that same near crew cut that conforms to the lines of his skull. The way he sits, legs stretched out, slightly hunched as though he's about to throw a pair of dice, she can almost see him as he once was, pack of cigarettes rolled up in white undershirt sleeve, the ghost of the younger man superimposed on the older, coming in and out of focus like a badly projected movie.

"Paul," she says. "Uncle Paul."

"Daisy? That you?"

She feels her skin pimple and crawl. "Dixie," she manages. "It's Dixie."

He smiles, showing his crooked, tobacco-and-coffee-stained teeth. "Well, that's what I said, wasn't it?"

"No, you said . . . that's not what you said."

"My apologies then. I'm a little distracted. As I imagine you must be." He rises. A little wizened now but still with that wiry monkey energy she remembers. Quick as a blink he pulls out the chair across from her, right at her table, right across from her, and he sits in it, on it, languorous and alive with his strange static energy at one and the same time. "I'm so sorry about your daddy. I never thought I'd see Arlo in this state. I thought he'd outlive me by eons."

Does he really think that? Dixie wonders. Or is it just one of those things you say when your friend of nearly fifty years is dying? Looking at him now, radiating that dark glittery energy, it seems to her that he's grown stronger as her father has grown weaker, that all these years Paul has absorbed her father's energy somehow, leaving him faded and withdrawn until his world existed only in the four walls of his little shed, the same shed now being dismantled by his wife, bit by bit, piece by piece.

"How's life been treating you, then, darling?" he asks. "I heard you ran away to New York."

"I heard you ran away to New York too," Dixie retorts. "I saw you, actually."

Paul simply nods, like a courtesy.

After a moment Dixie manages what she hopes is a casual laugh. "Ran away, I didn't run away. I went to join my husband. Gary. You were part of that whole decision, Paul."

"I argued against it."

"Why?"

"Just wanted to keep you safe."

"Safe from Gary? Safe from what?"

Paul doesn't respond. He just looks down at the floor between his feet.

Dixie finds herself in the unfamiliar position of wanting to defend her husband. She takes in a deep breath. She sits up straight. "Gary's done well. He's a geophysicist. He does important work—he travels everywhere."

"Does he now?" Paul stares at her, his eyes suddenly hard and gemlike, his smile stretching over his stained teeth. "So, what have you been doing with yourself, being left on your own so much?"

"Raising my son," she says, hoping that this puts an end to the conversation. She doesn't want to talk to him anymore. Doesn't want to hear his insinuations or look at that coffee-stained smile. She can just imagine how his breath must smell, the stale coffee and cigarettes and bits of old breakfast stuck between his teeth. He's very unprofessorial.

"Your daddy ever tell you about the time we tried to do the *Odyssey*, in the circus?"

Dixie shakes her head. She's ready to get up and make her excuses, except they wouldn't even be excuses, because she really should get back to her father's bedside and continue watching him die.

Paul must sense that she's tensed up and ready to bolt. "It's a funny story," he says. "And now I'm the only one that knows it. Or very soon I will be."

Dixie feels frozen in place. Because of course she has to hear it. Because of course there might be a clue in it. And beyond that, if this was something that Paul and her father shared . . . someone else should have that knowledge. Someone else should carry the story, but not Dixie. Not Dixie's memory. Her memory can't be trusted. It's all gray and black, big holes in it.

She does not much want to gain wisdom from Uncle Paul. She's starting to think Uncle Paul might be the devil, and maybe that was something she knew once and had forgotten too. She wants to suggest that Paul tell the story to Cyril. Cyril remembers everything. Cyril processes everything. But this thought catches in her throat. It catches hard, and Dixie remembers herself, at Cyril's age, subjected to stories of the circus each night when her parents were gone and Paul ended up, almost by default, being the one to tuck her into bed. Paul the babysitter. Paul the storyteller. Paul the only one who knows, any longer, what Arlo had done in those long-ago circus days.

"Well, it's like this," he says. "Our ringmaster wanted to do it. He was a strange guy. Talked educated. Spoke some foreign languages. Said he did, anyway. Maybe he was just spouting gibberish for all I know. We used to call him the Professor."

Now Dixie's not just frozen, she's encased in ice.

"He had this idea for something different, he said. 'We'll make up for our material deficiencies with an epic narrative.'" Paul laughs. "Can't believe I remember that, word for word like that, with his tone and his highfalutin manner and all, but it's exactly what he said. What he meant was, we were a shit circus. Pardon my French. We hardly had any wild animals, just that one old elephant and a tubercular chimpanzee. Our clowns were dead drunk most of the time. The bally broads, the kinkers, they weren't the best. But we'd do this crazy story about Odysseus returning home from the wars, we'd dress up the horses and the elephant and that chimp and have them play the monsters and such, have kinkers on a cloud swing and trapeze for your witches and gods and Sirens, put all that together and it would turn into something grand. That was what he said. 'Grand.'"

Paul laughs again. It sounds like sandpaper on cardboard.

"So was it?" Dixie asks. "Was it grand?"

"What do you think?" Paul is still laughing. "It was a goddamn disaster. A drunk clown spooked one of the horses. The bally broad fell off and crashed into the cardboard rocks. The chimp dropped a load and threw it into the front row, the bull's trumpeting and stomping its foot, the natives are screaming, and your daddy's running around like he's on fire, grabbing my shirt, yelling, 'What do I do, what do I do?' Meanwhile the Professor's got me tied to the mast, me as Odysseus, can you imagine? Me, an utter no one. Why am I at front and center? And, anyway, in his grand theatrical style, he's out there in front of the audience, striding around, going on about resisting the call of the Sirens. Funniest damn thing I've ever seen, if I wasn't half-scared out of my mind that the elephant might trample me."

He reaches out his hand, and his fingertips are a whisper away from hers. "You sure I never told you this story? The best thing about it all, though: we might consider them heroes, those Greeks, but they loved each other. They loved each other in a way that men love each other. You get me? You understand? The way Greek men loved other men. That was the part the ringmaster really wanted to practice. That was the part our storybooks don't want to talk about. That ringmaster, he tied me up to the mast. He tied your father up to the mast. He made us the heroes. And, right there in that ring, right there in front of that piddly little crowd, forty or fifty paying people only in some Podunk town, right there he pulls out his fancy elk-horn pistol and shoots himself in the mouth, brains everywhere, top of his head blown off and yet his body is still standing there for three, four seconds before it falls apart, and your father—it was his turn to be tied up, you see. He couldn't look away. None of us could look away and it took the cops, the sheriff of that little town, damn near an hour to get out there and start cleaning up the mess. Damn near an hour where we all just stood there, sat in the stands, looking at that sad, sad spectacle: ten years of wandering with that circus and it all ends with the ringmaster dead by his own papery-white hand."

Dixie doesn't want to hear this. It isn't a circus story. It isn't a nice story at all. It's probably not true. It's just the way Paul says things. It's just the way he tries to get under her skin, saying gross and terrible things.

Paul's got her hand in his now. He's stroking the back of her fingers. She jerks her hand away. "You touched me where you shouldn't have. You made me touch you."

Dixie does not know where the words come from. She didn't purposefully think them. They just appeared in her throat and forced their way out.

Uncle Paul barely flinches. He holds himself utterly still. His smile never wavers. His eyes hold hers.

"You're remembering things wrong. You always did have a poor memory."

No. No, she is not. For once she is remembering things right.

"You did," she says. She stands up, rage coming from some deep place in her belly, compelling her to rise.

Uncle Paul just laughs. "You were a hot-to-trot little thing. I was just showing you what you really wanted. I was just carrying on the tradition of the circus, darling. Arlo could never let it go, never let me go, not after what we'd shared together."

When Dixie gets back to her father's room, a nurse sits with her mother, speaking in hushed tones. Her mother nods, once, twice. The clicks and beeps continue. Her father takes in a deep, rasping breath. Then, nothing.

Is that it? Dixie wonders. Is he gone?

No. He breathes in again.

The pause is longer this time.

The nurse rises. "We're just outside if you need us," she says.

Dixie sits down in the other chair.

"Well," her mother says. She gently clasps Arlo's hand. The two of them watch Arlo breathe for a few minutes. A long inhale. A longer pause. At length, another breath.

Finally, Gladys picks up her knitting. She finishes two short rows before Arlo takes his last breath. Outside, in the hallway, Dixie can see Paul standing there, slouching against the wall, but she pays him no mind. He is nothing. He is no one. He does not deserve to come closer to her, or to her father. Certainly not to Cyril either. Not anymore.

CHAPTER 23

For a while she can push the scene with Uncle Paul out of her mind. The grief helps with that. An animal thing, red and raw and overwhelming. It comes in unexpected waves, unexpected because she had not thought she would feel her father's loss so acutely, if at all. She'd really come home less to bid him farewell, and more to ask him questions. She'd come home more for herself than for him. They'd spent so little time together since she'd fled Pocatello with Cyril, and he'd been so withdrawn when they did, with her anyway. Not so much with Cyril. Arlo had been friendlier with Cyril. He had tried to be a grandfather.

Dixie realizes she's going to need to tell Cyril about Arlo's death, explain it to him, explain what death is, what it means. She needs to tell Cyril about his granddad passing. But she has no way to reach Cyril and Gary in Peru. They are already traveling to Machu Picchu by now. They are already in the mountains, in the jungle. She'll have to wait for Gary to call.

There's paperwork to sign. Arrangements to make.

Back at her parents' house, Paul sneaks up on her now and again. She thinks she glimpses him sliding through the entrance from the mudroom to the kitchen, thinks she hears his chuckle coming from the top of the stairs. She pushes him away. She does not have time for this now. She wants him to leave. She wants him to go back to New York—

Wait. No, she doesn't. She doesn't want him anywhere near New York. New York is hers. She doesn't live there anymore, not permanently, but she doesn't want him anywhere near it, near her, near her real home.

She tells him this.

She tells him she doesn't want him in New York, doesn't want to think of him in New York. Doesn't want to run into him there. Doesn't want the Stonewall polluted by his image merging and unmerging with the idea of the Professor there, in that kick line, embracing all the wonderful syrup-slow time of the riot.

"But you're the reason I came there," he says, not exactly sneering at her. He's being truthful, and it's a bit pathetic to see. "I only came out there because of you and then I liked the place. More to do. Pocatello was seeming, to one like me, a bit small. I only came out there for you, Daisy."

"Dixie."

"Darling."

Dixie storms off at this, not having gotten anywhere.

She storms off, but she's got nowhere really to go, not with the funeral arrangements being made. Not with her father's burial to be undertaken.

Her mother spends the next few days mostly sitting on the recliner, watching TV and knitting the thing that might be a pot holder. Her frantic sorting of her father's possessions has stilled. It is as though she has nothing left to do. Nothing left to do at all.

"I can't see much point in having this funeral," Gladys says to Dixie. She has the footrest extended, her legs stretched out in front of her covered by a camp blanket. Dixie sits catty-corner to her on the couch. *Hawaii Five-0* is on the TV, at a volume where it's more background noise than something you're paying attention to. The TV is nearly always on at her parents' house, Dixie has discovered. "Not sure who would even come."

Paul would come, Dixie thinks, and she knows she never wants to see him again, except in a coffin. She'd fled the cafeteria after he'd said those things. But dwelling on it a moment longer, she feels a coal of cold fire in her belly, a rage she's been tending to for years, tamping it down all this time without knowing why.

You were supposed to have a funeral for your father, weren't you?

"Dad still has a few friends in town though, right?"

Gladys shrugs. "A few. He stopped seeing people much the last couple years."

"We should have one. It's the right thing. It's normal and natural and needs to happen."

"I don't care."

Gladys's face is inscrutable. Does she really not care? Dixie honestly can't tell: Is her mother indifferent, or does she too have a hidden fire? If she does, then for whom or what does it burn?

"What do you want to do, Mom?" Dixie finally asks.

"About a funeral?"

"I mean, in general." Dixie looks around the house, at the faded upholstery and wagon-wheel lamp and dusty *National Geographic* magazines stacked on the bookcase. The magazines make Dixie think of the Adirondacks. They make her remember things, flash on things. And for Dixie that's always a complicated moment: happy she is having memories at all but frightened of the content. "What do you want to do now that Arlo's gone?"

"I don't suppose it matters. I can stay here. The house is paid for. I have your father's pension and social security. It'll be enough."

Dixie absolutely does not want to make the offer, except that a part of her does. The part that is still trying to solve the puzzle of herself and thinks that maybe, just maybe, her mother has a piece or two.

And maybe she cares, a little, about her mother being by herself in this sad house with its proliferation of fake daisies.

"Why don't you come and stay with us in Dallas for a while? You know we'd love to have you."

And maybe she's telling the truth. Maybe it would be nice having someone else in the house, with Gary gone so much and Cyril busy at school and with his friends.

"I don't know," Gladys says, but Dixie can already see a little more light in her mother's eyes. She wants to, Dixie can tell. Because Dixie has always been her mother's way out of this narrow life she's living.

The phone rings. Easier for Dixie to grab it than her mother, reclining in the La-Z-Boy. When Dixie picks up the receiver there's a hum and then a silence, some rapid, faint Spanish, a clicking, and then a different hum at a higher pitch.

"Hello?"

"Dixie? That you?"

It's Gary. Gary calling from Peru. It's strange, but hearing his voice in this moment fills her with a kind of happiness, and it's been a long time since hearing Gary's voice has caused her genuine and spontaneous happiness. She knows the happiness is wrapped around a core of sadness, that it won't last, that it might never happen again. But at this moment, it is good to hear his voice. He is solid, rarely too high or too low.

"Yes. Yes, I'm here with Mom. Where are you?"

"Cusco. Gonna take the train to Aguas Calientes tomorrow and then on to Machu Picchu from there. I stayed an extra day in Cusco. Beautiful town. All kinds of Spanish colonial architecture, and most of it built right on these amazing Inca foundations that don't crumble in earthquakes, but dance. It's amazing. I have a mind to make a study of it, figure out how they do it, and all without mortar, just precise-cut joinery between the naked stones. You'd love it, Dixie. I'm sorry I didn't wait to take this trip with you."

"Yes, well . . ." She's not sure what to say or how to say it. "Dad died."

There's a pause on the other end of the line, a pause still filled with sticky static. "I'm sorry. I knew he wasn't doing well, but I didn't think . . . do you need me to come home?"

"No," she says. "We're managing. I'm just . . ." She feels a sudden sob rise in her throat. ". . . I'm just sorry I kept Cyril from a last visit with his grandfather."

The line crackles and hums. "Who?"

Gary's voice sounds far away. Well, he is in Peru, after all. Amazing to think they can talk to each other across such a distance, really.

"Cyril. Is he close by? I should tell him."

"Cyril?" Gary finally asks. "You want Cyril? You mean your doll?"

267

CHAPTER 24

There's nothing else to say about Pocatello.

Nothing else to say about Dallas either, really.

Just two loose ends, and they're both in New York City. Dixie's stunned a bit, her head whirling, and the only place she knows, to knit things together, is New York.

Dixie buys a ticket at the airport for a flight that leaves at 5 p.m. She'll be in the city before midnight. That feels significant to Dixie.

She has time for a drink in an airport bar before she boards her flight, and given her nervousness about flying, a drink seems like a good idea, so she orders a gin and tonic, a proper grown-up drink. The bartender in the little diner bar in the Pocatello airport pours heavy, and between that and the lack of food, by the time she's boarded her flight, buckled in, waiting on the tarmac for everyone to board and then to push back from the gate, by the time all that happens she starts feeling woozy. It continues even as the plane taxis to the runway, pauses like a sprinter waiting for the starting gun, gathers itself and leaps into the void. She still hovers between consciousness and dreams.

She feels the lurch skyward and those dreams take on strange and cartoonish contours: the circus, Dumbo, talking animals, a stork. The baby circus elephant, large ears making him an object of ridicule, but his mother loves him regardless. And as the balance tips toward dreams, she is this mother, waiting for the stork, and as the stork comes, closer and closer, she sees that it is not a baby elephant, nothing like that, it is a red and wrinkled infant, and the stork is no longer a stork, it is shadows of black wings and the frigid air beneath them, and the baby it drops off in her lap is now a shriveled thing, black around the edges, its gaping mouth uttering a perpetual hissing snarl.

I do not want this, she thinks, *it is not mine. I did not ask for it, it was forced upon me. I cannot bear it.*

The baby snarls and she hears it, she hears it loud and clear because she has—in this dream—forgotten to put the cotton in her ears and silence all these voices, these memories.

Though she spends the flight in a fever state, the time passes quickly. She arrives, touches down, debarks the plane into JFK's elegant, astounding TWA terminal, the Grand Central of the Skies, all swooping curves and light, like a gigantic white bird sheltering its passengers beneath outstretched wings.

From there she takes a cab, all the way to Brooklyn. She's running low on cash, but she'll figure out something. She hopes she'll figure it out, for she hasn't told Mercedes she is coming. She doesn't know how she'll be received.

But she knows where she's going at least. She keeps Mercedes's address and phone number close, in a tiny address book tucked in her purse. The address has been scratched out and written over several times, due to Mercedes's moves.

269

The taxi driver pulls up in front of the address Dixie has given him. She's never been to this brownstone before. The last one Mercedes occupied had been torn down—"that city planner, wanting to remove all the 'undesirables' from our neighborhood," she'd complained on the phone.

Dixie has never been here and yet it looks familiar.

There is the brownstone. It is almost the same as the two that flank it, and parts are identical but there are differences, if you really stop and pay attention.

Which, for once, Dixie does.

There is no black tin cornice topping Mercedes's building. The bricks above the last row of windows are a lighter color—newer.

She should ring the buzzer now. She should not linger. It is after 11 p.m. and this neighborhood seems as if it is not always safe. It's not Columbia, Upper West Side. It's Brooklyn in the bad days.

Dixie stands outside the brownstone but for some reason cannot quite bring herself to push the button. What if Mercedes isn't there? What if she is there, but doesn't want to see Dixie out of the blue like this?

Dixie paces away from the entrance. Not very far. Just to the corner on the other side of the brownstones. A vacant lot, choked with weeds and trash: a stack of old tires; a busted-up club chair, stuffing bursting out of the seat.

Against the side of the building, Dixie sees a glint of metal. A sliver of silver, illuminated by the streetlight on the corner. She moves closer to it.

The metal hunk protrudes from the rubble of the vacant lot, as if some portion of it had reached out toward the sun. The part she can see is at least three feet wide and nearly two feet high, studded with rivets. It is pitted and scored and burnt, streaked with black.

She can just make out a few faded words: "Fuel . . . Structural limit . . ." and some numbers.

She does not want to think about what this is, but she knows it with certainty.

Shivering in the dark, Dixie retreats to the entrance of Mercedes's brownstone and presses the buzzer.

Mercedes sounds surprised to hear Dixie's voice, surprised but not sleepy. "You're here? Please, come up."

Dixie climbs the three sets of stairs to Mercedes's apartment, her roller bag thumping now and again against the step as she ascends. By the time she reaches Mercedes's door, she is slightly out of breath. She hesitates at the door for a moment, thinking, *What if I've made a terrible mistake? Why have I sought out Mercedes? I'm not . . .*

She *isn't*, is she? Those times she ended up in Mercedes's bed, she was just confused. And overwhelmed. And in need of something real. Real touch. Smooth skin against skin. Warmth. And yes, quickening pleasure.

She draws in a breath and raps softly on the door. After a moment, she hears muffled footsteps, and then the door opens.

There is Mercedes, wearing a kimono robe, her black hair tumbled around her shoulders. "Dixie," she says, opening her arms for a quick hug. Dixie wants to drop her suitcase and her tote and hug her back, cling to her, but she doesn't know if that would be welcome or if it's even what she wants.

As she takes two steps over the threshold, she sees Gabrielle sitting on the sofa.

"Oh," Dixie says, "the two of you. Both of you."

271

She shouldn't be surprised. How many times have Mercedes and Gabrielle broken up and gotten back together over the last ten years?

And yet . . . the last time she was here . . . when she and Mercedes whispered and slept together in that uptown Manhattan hotel . . .

Dixie gives her head an internal shake. No. This isn't meant to be. She's meant for someone else. Some*thing* else. Maybe there isn't a "someone" for her.

There is no Cyril.

"Would you like something to drink? Some tea? A glass of wine?"

There's a squat bottle of Lancers Rosé sitting on the coffee table in front of the sofa. "Sure," Dixie says. "Wine. Thanks."

After Mercedes pours Dixie a portion, they settle in matching armchairs across from each other, their worn patches covered by decorative tea cloths. Gabrielle remains on the sofa, nearer to Mercedes. He wears a men's pajama set and smoking jacket. She, Mercedes in her kimono, the two of them sitting up straight, facing Dixie, make Dixie think of mismatched bookends that are somehow still a pair.

"So," Gabrielle says, "what occasion has brought you to New York, Dixie?"

Gabrielle's voice is clipped and strong, a cadence to it like a bugle call.

Dixie stares into her glass, unsure of what to say. It is not Mercedes she's come for, it seems. Instead, it's an excavation of sorts, a rummage through some closed-off closets of her memory. A search for a child who doesn't exist.

"I'm trying to sort out a few things," she finally says. "I'm trying to remember—" Finally she looks up. "We didn't speak for years."

Mercedes slowly nods. "Yes," she says. "I regret we lost so much time together. I regret I was so slow to forgive."

"Why did you need to forgive me?" Dixie asks. "Because of what Gary said? Because of . . . ?"

"What you did, it was not my place to forgive you." Mercedes sounds almost angry. "It was not my place to judge. I understand that now. But at the time . . . I was more hurt by your assumptions."

There is something in that closet that wants to get out. Dixie can feel it beating its fists against that closed door.

"My assumptions?"

"When you needed the abortion, you came to me. You assumed because I am not white, because I am some kind of 'exotic,' to you, because I live in Brooklyn and not Manhattan, that I could help you. You hardly knew me and yet you assumed such a thing. I thought, then, that you must not think of me as a real person. I didn't know what to do. I was mad. Asking for that kind of help, when you—"

Dixie hears this. She forces herself to listen. It's what she's here for. It's why she's come home.

When you needed the abortion . . .

This is not making sense. This is not how things went. "It was Peggy . . ." she begins.

"I am Catholic," Mercedes continues. "Abortion is an anathema to me. A sin!"

"God knows it's caused enough trouble between the two of us," Gabrielle says.

Mercedes nods. "It has been hard for me to accept. Very hard. I still wish . . . but for some women . . ." Her voice trails off.

"I've saved women's lives," Gabrielle says. "That's what she doesn't want to say. But she knows it now. She knows that there is

273

no real equality for women as long as they can't control their own bodies."

The line sounds like something Gabrielle has said many, many times. In fact, Dixie thinks she's heard him say it before. The thought solidifies into a memory—she *remembers* Gabrielle saying it. She remembers it. Upstairs, in a brownstone not far from here and over ten years ago. Sitting on a couch like this one . . .

"Are you all right?" Mercedes asks. Her voice is tender, concerned.

"I'm dizzy. I think I need to lie down."

The day of travel, the gin and tonic, the wine, the dream about Dumbo turning into a hissing shrivel, the memories pull her to the earth, an irresistible magnetic force. She thinks, *I will just curl up on the floor right here.*

Instead, Mercedes and Gabrielle help her to the couch. Mercedes takes off her shoes, smoothens the hair from her forehead, and Gabrielle returns with an old soft quilt and covers her with it. Dixie finds herself weeping, her shoulders shaking, and she's still not sure why.

"Can we get you anything?"

"You didn't do anything wrong."

Eyes squeezed shut, she remembers this: the warmth of Mercedes's welcoming smile fades as though someone had closed the damper on a potbellied stove. And then, Gabrielle rising from the couch, walking the two steps to where Dixie sits, placing a hand over Dixie's hand that clutches the arm of her chair. "She can't help you," Gabrielle had said back then in that dream-memory, "but I can."

Most of all, Dixie remembers the warmth of Gabrielle's open palm, resting on the back of her hand.

The couch in the Adirondacks cabin, the nubby industrial fabric that was just like the back of the airplane seat she found herself staring at the other day. The board games. The mildewed *National Geographic*s. The time she'd spent there.

"We have a place," Gabrielle had said in that dream. "And a doctor who will go there. It's safe. You can rest and recover. Take as much time as you need. Bring a friend along if you'd like. I know it's hard. It shouldn't be. You're not doing anything wrong. We shouldn't have to go through this because of what some man did to us."

Dixie appreciated the offer to bring a friend, but she had gone alone. She had no friend to bring, not at that time, not yet. But that changed soon after. And because of Gabrielle and Gabrielle's cabin, she had known how to be a friend to Peggy when Peggy also needed one.

It hadn't been that hard, for the most part. Not that much blood. Some cramping a few days after. Nothing serious. Just a curious emptiness. For all the times she'd been told it was wrong, she thought she should have felt much worse than she did about doing it. Wandering along the lakeshore, leaves crunching underfoot, she'd thought mostly about the illegality of it, that she'd broken the law by getting rid of the growing clump of cells that would have become a child.

The Professor's child.

That child was not Cyril, she tells herself now: I did not kill my own son. She knows this as certainly as she knows anything, for Cyril could not have been conceived on the train trip, that train trip from Pocatello where Dixie just didn't need to worry about anything at all. That would have been impossible.

Cyril existed before she left Pocatello for New York, she reminds herself. She'd carried him with her on the train. Hadn't she?

275

Cyril is real, she tells herself. He is. Or was. Because he was there before any of this craziness. He was there in Pocatello. Paul had told her about him. Paul had known Cyril. Paul had talked about, and to, Cyril. Paul had encouraged her with Cyril. It was like their secret. Their secret together. Paul had encouraged her with Cyril, to love him and hold him and swaddle him and care for him just like a little baby, just like the little baby she couldn't ever keep.

Dixie drifts off. More fever dreams.

Cyril isn't real. He's just been there for her these past, what, eleven years? Cyril isn't real but what has she been doing? Who has she been fooling? What has she been up to? And, why Paul? Why Paul at all during any of this?

Dumbo soars in the dream. He's got ears that fold back like the aerodynamic wings of a fighter plane. He's got a mean look in his eyes, bloodshot now. Don't anger the elephant when he's learning to be a grown-up, learning the hard lessons a grown-up must learn: separation from Mom, being tricked by other adults, being read stories by an almost-uncle as he tucks you asleep and slips his hand inside the waistband of your pajamas.

Mercedes and Gabrielle leave Dixie to sleep, and she mostly does, waking now and again to toss and turn before settling back into slumber. She thinks they come to check on her, once or twice. She remembers opening her eyes to see Mercedes standing there, and later, Gabrielle, who with unexpected tenderness shifts the quilt to make sure Dixie's stockinged feet are covered.

When the morning sends its gray New York light into the room, Dixie hears Mercedes and Gabrielle in their tiny kitchenette, speaking in murmurs. She smells coffee. That alone is enough to prompt her to sit up, rub the sleep from her eyes, and run her fingers through her tousled hair.

Mercedes brings her coffee and sits in the chair opposite. "How are you doing?" she asks.

"I'm . . ."

How *is* she doing? Dixie doesn't know.

Her father is dead. Her son does not exist. Her marriage seems vague and flimsy, two people tied together for no real reason. Held together by what, exactly? Custom? Habit? Shared belongings? Nothing better to do?

Who is she without those ties, those deeper ties? Without a son, without a marriage, what has she done? She's tried to be *seen*, and for what? She doesn't know who she is. If she were to see herself, she fears she wouldn't even recognize the outer form, the shell, let alone the inside of her, with this huge yawning expanse of grays and blacks in her memory. Who *is* she?

Slowly, quietly, she says, "I'm better, thank you. You're too kind. Both of you." She sips her coffee, which is strong and rich with thick cream. "I have some things to do, I guess."

What those things might be, she still doesn't know. But New York called her, ten years ago. It calls her still. It brings her back. Not smiling at her, not directly. It's gray and cold and full of hustle, remorselessly so, but it keeps calling, it keeps calling, it keeps calling.

If her life is a riddle, the answer to it must be here.

She takes a shower, cleans herself up, changes into fresh clothes. "You're sure you are all right," Mercedes and Gabrielle say to her several more times, in various ways. Dixie is not at all sure. But there's nothing they can do to help her. Not this time.

"Would it be okay if I leave my things here?" she asks.

"Of course," Mercedes says. And then she hesitates. "But . . . you will come back for them, won't you?"

"Oh, sure," Dixie says, with what she hopes is a nonchalant wave. "I don't want to impose on your hospitality. I'll get a hotel tonight. I just have a few things I need to do first."

She will face the city today. The answers are here, somewhere. She knows they are.

She puts on her most sensible shoes, then gathers up the things she will take with her: her over-the-shoulder purse, a light cardigan.

Mercedes and Gabrielle walk her to the door, the two of them arm in arm, widening their circle for a moment to gather Dixie up in it. For a moment, Dixie feels their warmth, their love, and the tears start to trail down her cheeks, because she does not know if she will ever see them again. She realizes that she loves them dearly. But it's time to go.

They break apart. "Thank you," Dixie says.

"You'll be back tonight? For your things?" Mercedes asks, not hiding her concern.

"Why, yes. Of course. I think so."

Dixie reaches for the doorknob. And has a sudden thought, about what she needs for this journey.

"Do you have two cotton balls I can use, by any chance?"

CHAPTER 25

New York in spring.

The wind is still raw when it comes up, the chill hasn't left the air, and Dixie is grateful for her button-up cardigan. But the sky is blue everywhere among the gray concrete and the red brick. Spring has begun to arrive, announcing its presence in fresh, tender green leaves, in tiny flower buds and tentative blooms.

This is what Dixie focuses on. Not the piles of garbage and rotting old couches and spring-sprung mattresses littering vacant lots, or the graffiti on the soot-stained walls. Not the mounds of filthy, blackened fabric that now and again resolve into a person, wearing too many layers of old clothes, sitting on subway grates, talking to themselves. Not the sharp-edged young men lingering on stoops, giving her the eye. Not the men in suits, the women in dresses with big round glasses and poofy hair, all hustling toward Manhattan.

Dixie focuses on spring.

She has rarely walked this kind of distance in New York. She's never walked from Brooklyn to Manhattan. She's taken cabs and the occasional subway. But she thinks there are no answers to be found in cabs. And even with the chill, spring is too delicious, too full of life and beauty, the sky the kind of blue that promises warmth to come.

At length she comes to the Manhattan Bridge.

It has never occurred to Dixie before to cross the East River this way. As she ascends she thinks, what a beautiful view! What a brilliant idea, to see the towers of Manhattan, all that promise and mystery and life waiting across the water. She shivers in the spring air, a delicious shiver of anticipation: he's out there somewhere, and she's going to find him. Today she's going to find him. She must.

Cyril isn't real. But the Professor is. He must be.

Or else, what has everything meant, these last ten years of her life? What has she been doing all this time, if both of the pillars of her life were nothing but a dream?

The bridge itself is choked with cars and taxis. She has a path to walk but wishes she didn't have to share it with all that automotive honking and exhaust, or the badly muffled engines, the yellow taxis everywhere. Others who walk seem mostly poor: shabbily dressed, jackets with collars upturned against the wind that blows more prominently up along the bridge's height. Well, of course, she thinks. People don't walk if they have the money to drive, or taxi, or take the train or the bus. The walkers: they are the lowest level of them all, or else just slightly crazy, health nuts, or environmentalists. New York has all the different types. Dixie sees them and catalogues them among the poor who have no other choice.

The bridge itself seems a bit shabby. Peeling paint. Rusting bolts. Beneath her, a subway train clatters and roars, rattling the deck, a vibration she feels after its passing in the iron and steel beneath her feet, in the guardrail that her hand grasps to steady herself. In fact, the bridge seems to tilt a bit to one side, weighed down for too many years by all those subway trains, not really designed to carry such loads for so long.

Fine, Dixie tells herself, it's fine. One foot in front of the other. She will get where she is going if she just puts one foot in front of the other.

Twenty minutes later, more or less, she enters the fringe of Chinatown.

She heads west. She knows it's not safe to the east, where Chinatown blends into the Lower East Side. Even during the day, she knows she should not walk in that part of town by herself. She's heard stories of streets controlled by gangs. Seen bombed-out and vacant buildings once or twice from behind the window of a cab: the 1970s doesn't look like it'll be kind to Chinatown, even though the place has, somehow, a bit of silver-screen glitz to it, the uptick in frantic behavior noticeable even when compared to the rest of New York, riotous.

She lets Chinatown envelop her—the signs she can't read, the language she doesn't understand (even if she *could* hear it clearly), the unfamiliar cooking smells, the splashes of red-and-gold paper plastered on walls and doors. She feels, if not a part of it, safer here, in the comfort of these crowds.

It's when one of these crowds parts, heading in different directions like the splitting of an amoeba, that she sees a white man emerge from a butcher's shop, holding by its neck an entire cooked chicken. The man stuffs it into a bag. He is tall, the glimpse of his profile resembling an emperor on a Roman coin, and he's wearing, of all things, a burnished old top hat. He has a frenetic energy to him. He has brown teeth that make him look British, or like something from the circus: not quite reputable, not quite new or clean.

The Professor. Her Professor.

He turns for a moment, catches Dixie's eye. Winks. And then disappears into the throng of people on the sidewalk.

"Wait!"

Dixie knows what to do. She knows this is the chance she has been waiting for, preparing for, the whole of these many years.

She runs after him.

She pushes her way through the crowd. She elbows, ducks, shimmies, first along the sidewalk and then out into the street, the gutter, between cars, whatever seems the fastest and surest line to take in closing the distance between them, now no more than a few dozen strides. She's grateful that the man, her Professor, is so tall, so angular, and wears a top hat to boot. That hat bobs ahead in the throng, accentuated almost to comic proportions by the fact that almost everyone else on the street, on the sidewalk, is Asian, Chinese—small and wiry and as homogeneously different from the Professor as any crown in New York could possibly be.

He's headed up Canal Street, out of Chinatown. Dixie can see, can almost feel how the crowd around him thins, seems to disappear, allowing him to stride ahead unimpeded while she's still stuck, just like she's in molasses, just like she's in syrupy-slow time while his time accelerates.

Turning sharply toward the building on the corner of Canal and Lafayette, he looks over his shoulder, beckoningly, steel-gray eyes connecting with Dixie. He doffs his top hat, as any well-mannered man should before entering an enclosed space. There's a set of steps leading downward. He descends. He goes down into the subway, right there on Canal and Lafayette, right into the Canal Street station.

He goes down and perhaps a minute later Dixie follows, a minute that is an eternity when chasing someone like this particular someone, whom Dixie has been chasing so long.

She sees him boarding the train.

He's wearing a duster, long and looking like it might be waterproof even though it also seems a hundred years old, something straight from Dixie's Wild West ancestors, her pioneers, or those dead-eyed men she remembers from the cattle yards in Pocatello. He's less a gambler, less a riverboat coxcomb, and more a high plains wanderer tonight, top hat and all.

"Wait," Dixie says again, as the doors of the subway car begin to shut.

She's forced to jump on a car several behind the one the Professor boarded. No problem. She'll just move car to car, through the sealed doors, the open grinding passage over the tracks, all in darkness. She'll just proceed forward, saying *excuse me* and *sorry* and all the niceties to the people she disturbs. She'll even smile, maybe try to change them, one by one, these New Yorkers who probably need a good dose of Dallas salvation.

She gets through one car, then a second car. The door of the third car is jammed. It won't move. It won't open. It won't budge.

She's stuck.

She can see him, right there, one car farther on, holding the chrome-plated ceiling bar, swaying as the car sways, as it speeds up and slows down.

Dixie looks behind her, contemplates backtracking, contemplates climbing on top of the car once she's in that open dark whooshing place, climbing on top and like a worm—for fear of decapitation in the darkness, fear that some rusted beam or stalactite might strike her—like a worm flattened to the roof she'd inch forward until she can slide down between the jammed door and the (presumably open) door of the car in which the Professor stands.

They've passed Bleecker and Astor. It's Union Square now when he turns, and looks at her, and points at the cotton in her ears, giving her a big hokey thumbs-up signal, very out of character, before he steps from the car.

She hustles to the door.

She steps out of her own car, out onto the platform.

She expects to find him there, waiting, but it's Keystone Cops: he's gone. He's back on the subway. She doesn't know. She can't tell. She's frantic, looking this way and that way.

A man plays saxophone, beside him a three-headed dog. The sound of the notes disappears for a moment, or maybe forever. Dixie can't tell if it is the onrush of the subway, or if it is the cotton in her ears, blocking everything out, making Orpheus in the alcove of the station into a perfect picture of passion, blowing, blowing into the mouthpiece, fingering the dull golden keys, tilting the bell lip forward, backward, as the music comes out and goes nowhere, or everywhere, everywhere except into Dixie's mind.

There's the hem of the duster, his duster, her Professor, telltale, going upward into the sun, out of the chthonic realm, up into the cold blue spring air. He did not reboard the subway car. He went up. Up and out.

They're street-side at Union, emerging into sunlight together but staggered. He's still ahead. He has hailed a cab. He climbs in. She flags another cab to follow. Keystone Cops and mythos, pathos, the missed connection, this should be happening in the rain! It should be in black and white on a silver screen. But it's also a spring day. A perfect spring day that wouldn't, just wouldn't work as film noir.

The Professor leads her on a merry chase: *Follow that car! Follow that taxi.*

Looking back at her, or across the lane, through the distortion of another car's windows. He watches her. He points to her ears. He gives her the thumbs-up.

She sees him in her mind's eye back on the train, that first train ride, the two of them together somewhere in the Midwestern cornfields, undressed, above her one minute, below her another as they tumble and ramble and wreck each other (none of that worth worrying about, it's all okay, all normal and okay and everything will be just fine, Dixie, fine).

It's not his child.

She's got Cyril already. Cyril can't be his.

The Professor isn't real. Was never real. He must have just been a dream, a figment of her girlish imagination. Cyril could not have been his child. She knows it. It'd be easy to think it was, or is, Gary's baby in her belly. It'd be right, a thing to celebrate, a child of their own to sit in Cyril's bassinet and curl at Dixie's breast just as Cyril had perhaps done, was doing during that trip . . . what a sight she must have been, she reminds herself, critically, looking at herself now from the outside, from above, as if she is an angel hovering over herself. What a sight!—nursing a glass-eyed, unblinking doll there in the train car, cooing at a doll with a porcelain face, putting a doll to bed, taking a doll to Frank's deli, forgetting a doll in the train car when she goes with the mysterious stranger, this man she'll call the Professor, back to his sleeping car, leaving that infant, that faux infant, that crutch, all alone.

Leaving Cyril alone just as she did during the plane crash in Park Slope.

Who does the baby belong to?

Dixie knows.

Dixie's not saying. She's been sworn to secrecy. Sworn by her own father: "It's a thing we can't talk about, Dixie. We'll get you help. We'll make it go away."

And all she can do then, that first time, back in Pocatello, is cry. Cry and take comfort in the doll her dad buys her as a crutch, a gift, a crutch, a locum tenens, succubus.

That's him, that's Cyril. He's there in the Professor's arms, cradled, being held out to her across the lanes of traffic. Everything stopped, smoggy, chugging, bringing down the blue sky in a haze of brown.

They're going north, ever farther north, right up Park Avenue, up into the ritzy blocks, past the Plaza Hotel, statue and fountain in front, all of which Dixie sees from afar, just a glimpse down the long canyon of buildings, along with a hint of the spring-green trees in Central Park's southeast corner.

Northward, northward, Keystone Cops, tag, a romantic end to a romantic film, only one that involves no certain characters, just vapors and images vibrating in Dixie's dark and gray mind, her missing spots. One minute the Professor holds Cyril. The next it's Gary, there, returned from Peru, ready to discuss things, ready to ask her the hard questions about why, after all these years, Dixie is thinking about and inquiring after that strange old doll she carried like a crutch, a crutch, a succubus, a shell.

Dixie's got Mercedes there too, in this fugue. She's kissing her, but ever so politely, on the hand, the white-gloved hand that Mercedes pulls off, rips off, not her style, substituting a bandana, a sequined slipstream of a samba dress. Dixie doesn't know what they wear in Venezuela when they're dancing, but it projects as slinky, maybe fruity, musky for certain. And suddenly the whole taxi is filled with the brightest feathers, tropical feathers. When they clear, she's lost the chase. The Professor's taxi has pulled away, but he's no longer in it.

He's out. He's striding, top hat held to his head, duster jacket billowing behind him. He's strong, young, masterful, paper-white and wrinkly all at the same time, and he's exactly the same as Dixie

286

remembers him from the train: mutable and skeletal both, commanding, Caesarian, immortal. That's the word: immortal. He hasn't aged at all. He's an angel for sure. A figment. A ringmaster who knows what Paul, and also maybe Arlo her father, who knows what they had done. He is an angel ringmaster professor man, thrown together from words she remembers Paul telling her bedside as he nibbled her seven-year-old ear. He's an apparition made from facts gone wrong.

He's gone. He's inside a building.

Dixie motions her cabbie to stop. She pays him. She goes to the door of the same building the Professor had entered but the door requires a ticket to go in. The entrance guard points her to the ticket booth. Behind glass, there, like a museum piece or a fortune-telling Zoltar from Coney Island, sits a woman with a beehive, big blush spots, blue eyeshadow. She files her nails, maybe her teeth. She has a three-headed dog at her feet, which Dixie can see, right through the solid concrete of the ticket-booth wall, last bastion of the chthonic.

"Two dollars," the lady says, passing a stub beneath the windowpane.

Dixie gives the woman money, a handful of misshapen coins, then takes the ticket and runs.

She doesn't know how much farther The Professor has gotten, how much more of a head start, or disappearance, he's been able to get away with in the interim, during this delay. But she fears the worst.

She fears she's walking into a circus. She knows this museum: the Guggenheim, with its gentle curvatures, its disorienting Frank Lloyd Wright perfection, its inside-the-big-top beehive interior, heading ever upward, ever upward in the splendor of whitewash. She expects peanuts, popcorn crackerjack, the smell of elephants (or at least one flying ace of a young Dumbo). She expects horses and trapeze artists, kinkers and ballerinas and kids sitting on the spiral balconies with their feet over the edges, laughing and booing and ahhing and oohing. She expects chutzpah, organ music, the smell of hay and mud beaten into brick in the heat and humidity beneath the elephant's chains.

But what does she get?

Silence.

A library-like *silence.*

No one is in there.

Or if they are, they can't hear what she hears. They can't see what she sees. She takes a few steps into the space, into the center of the open cavity, the swirling white center, in and down a bit, down some steps, past the cordon where—on busier days, days when people actually visit this void—a line might have formed.

She stops in the very center.

There, even with the cotton wads in her ears, a voice like the Voice of God pulsates from the eternity of the masterwork's ceiling, just whiteness there, just forever, a skylight, yes, but a disappearing one that opens into the infinite and absolute.

She's stunned.

She puts her hands to her face, holds her face as if it is about to float away.

She twirls around.

Taps her shoes together like she's on a yellow brick road.

And indeed she is.

She's lost it.

She's lost all connection.

Except for him, her Professor, two tiers of the spiral above her, looking down, standing there among the ghosts of the circus children who still dangle their legs so dangerously over the spiral's edge. He's there, looking at her, and whispering so that only she can hear: "It's probably time for you to know."

"Paul, why are you here?" Dixie asks. "Why am I chasing you?"

Her uncle sweeps his arm out wide. His circus cape flares so that the red silk interior lining makes her blink with its brilliance.

He's wearing his ringmaster suit beneath that cape, a velveteen jacket, striped white-and-black pants, the same rumpled top hat, and a mustache, thick and long and blacker than any of the rest of his hair, which is and has always been light and feathery, perfect for a laurel or crown, just as Dixie remembers.

At the start point, lowest along the spiral, a placard says: odysseus in modernity: an exhibit.

Paul sweeps his arms out wide to show her where the gallery starts, pointing out for her edification the first pieces in the series, each of them identically sized, identically spaced, so that they seem to be windows into another world, ten paces apart from each other but interlinked. A whole gallery of circus posters: that gregarious and burlesque font, those garish colors, the bombastic announcements—odysseus! troy! lotus eaters! amazons! Poster after poster.

And there he is, just as she feared she would see him, her father in a clown's makeup playing the part of Penelope to Paul's hero, weaving at her loom all the while Troy burns somewhere distant over the wine-dark sea. He's an epithet unto himself, her father. He's in a poster. He's captured. He's unmistakable. He's tied to the mast when he must play Odysseus. He's dressed in a wig. He's wearing rouge. He's smiling. He's got his hand over Paul's mouth. He's got his hand in Paul's hand. He's just what Dixie feared he would be, knew he would be, and it's okay. Everything is okay now,

Dixie, there's nothing to worry about. It's just your dad from long ago, here in a modern art exhibit about ancient Greek warriors in the Guggenheim, all of it being narrated by an angel in a top hat. What could possibly be wrong with that? What could there be to concern yourself with, in such a situation?

This is what you wanted to know, right? the ringmaster whispers. *This is what you couldn't ask him, not when he was alive and young, not when he was dying at the end.*

Dixie walks up the spiral, slowly, slowly, taking in each of the posters one at a time, pushing her way among the invisible bodies of the other patrons, gathered in groups, admiring this or that image, this or that authentic mishmash of text and color and bits of her father's past. She stops here and there—the Professor always a bit ahead of her, as if he is sweeping the way clean—stops to look closer at something: Is that Paul? Is that an orangutan? Why can't she hear the boy with the popcorn and crackerjack calling out to sell his wares?

Why is everything so muffled? So silent?

The lights seem to flicker as Dixie steps forward toward one of the posters, drawn toward it.

It features a deck of playing cards: Jack of Hearts, Joker like Odysseus.

From up ahead the ringmaster calls to her—Paul calls to her: *You can be my Penelope. You've waited for me all these years.*

These are messages from the gods, artwork of a stolen moment that no one ever painted, a guided tour by the Creator himself, if the Creator had a creepy sense of bombast and the smell of buttered popcorn.

There's the elephant as Polyphemus, one-eyed and able to lift up Paul's men, one by one, pretending they are succulent sheep.

There's the kinkers doing Circe.

The monkey flinging poo.

The whole thing coming down in a crash, an embarrassment, and the ringmaster (duplicated here in art just as he is in life, ahead of her, urging her onward) here in this poster going around killing off the suitors at last, disbanding things, shutting up the circus because they failed, they all of them failed. Selling off the canvas of the tents, the train cars used to load and move the animals and the gear. And then shooting the horses out in a slot canyon near Pocatello where the ringing of the shotgun along the canyon walls felt like a descent into all cataclysms all at once.

The shooting of the horses. Then, in front of that sad last little crowd, putting the gun into his own mouth while Paul, and Arlo, both of them tied to the mast and unable to do anything about it, unable to hear, had been forced to watch and witness.

These are the paintings, the art pieces, none of them literal, all of them modern and fractured and figured so that the eye of the beholder could be allowed to see exactly what it wants (and needs) to see.

These are all of the images, arranged like windows from the inward center of light to the outward (and nonexistent) history of a myth.

These are the images, described faithfully, as faithfully as can be, listed here. The images Dixie sees and digests and tries to understand.

There's only one more. One last image, way at the top, at the end of the spiral gallery.

This one the Professor holds for last, stands in front of it, blocking it from Dixie's view until she approaches and takes his hand (icy feeling, ethereal), and they turn together to look at it. This is the triumphal piece. This is the big payoff for the show. This is what everyone has come here to see, after all.

It's Paul, as Odysseus, wily and cloaked like the beggar of the ultimate scene, all the bodies of the suitors dead around him. And Dixie's father, Arlo, as Penelope. And they are caught in the moment of lovemaking—caught in that highest and most solemn and, in the parlance of that age, unnatural degree.

That is the bond that doesn't break.

That is how Paul becomes Uncle.

They are making love, and doing so on a bed of Persian-esque carpet laid in layers over the lid of an old green portmanteau.

Dixie stands there, understanding it all because she knew all along. She'd always known. So had her mother, of course. They'd all understood this. They knew. But they pretended not to. She doesn't know where to go, what to do next, or whether there is, anymore, anything left at all, of her, certainly not of Cyril, of anything.

"Penelope," says the ringmaster, the Professor, Paul (turning to face her, even though Dixie still stares at the framed poster, at its gilt edges, overdone, enraptured). "You have been my Penelope."

"But that only works if I wait?" Dixie says.

Paul nods, ageless and frightening.

Dixie thinks about it.

For a long moment she thinks about it. There's a sigh inside her, a letting go, a realization that—for all these years—the thing she thought she wanted wasn't what she wanted after all. It's not him she's been waiting on. It's herself. To see and know and hear herself as the hero of her own story, the wanderer returned, the wily one, the steadfast center of an epic. She doesn't need to be his Penelope. She has been that already, waiting, watching, trying to persevere. Trying to forget the baby he'd forced on her back when she was just a child, back there in little old Pocatello. That was Cyril—the consolation prize for a girl old enough to conceive, old enough for an old man's rape, but not yet old enough to disentangle a doll from a death.

She has been his Penelope.

But she doesn't need to continue that.

She can be her own Penelope.

And her own Odysseus.

With that thought like a beacon—a light above and behind the lights of the Guggenheim or the magic of her guide, this angel— with that thought liberating her, she takes the cotton from her ears.

Paul backs up, seeing something in her eyes as she turns to face him.

He backs up, away from the wall with the circus posters, away from Odysseus. In doing so he loses some of his magisterial quality. He loses some of his power. He shrinks, or seems to shrink, and the red satin lining of his coat loses its luster.

Dixie sees him for what he is: pathetic, aging, a normal but perverse man, a tortured soul, a damaged being.

She feels a twitch of compassion toward him.

This holds her.

It prevents her from charging toward him, barreling into him. Yet, she continues to fix her gaze on his face. She's inscrutable. She is godlike herself, in this moment.

She screams.

It's thunderous. It's amplified by the spiral of the Guggenheim's highest floor, as if the whole building had been designed as a downward-pointing megaphone, a way to call to hell.

She screams.

Paul, the ringmaster, the Professor, takes one more step backward. The railing is there, lower than he expects. He doesn't mean to—he probably doesn't mean to do it, he hasn't planned this, you see, he hasn't thought about it as a performative act, a handgun in his mouth at the penultimate moment of performance—he doesn't mean to fall from that height.

And Dixie, as far as she remembers, doesn't push him either.

It's just a scream.

It's all right. Everything will be all right, Dixie.

That sound of the Siren's voice has simply called him down at last.

ABOUT THE AUTHOR

Benjamin Buchholz is the author of the novel *One Hundred and One Nights* (Back Bay Books/Little, Brown), the nonfiction book *Private Soldiers* (Wisconsin Historical Society Press), and two poetry chapbooks: *Thirteen Stares* (Magic Helicopter Press) and *Windshield* (BlazeVox Press). He is also co-author, with Sam Farran, of the memoir *The Tightening Dark: An American Hostage* in Yemen (Hachette). His short stories have appeared in Storyglossia, Hobart, Mad Hatter's Review, and Prime Number Magazine, and been anthologized in the Dzanc Press Best of the Web collections. His nonfiction has appeared in Military Review, Infantry, and The Writer. He has served as a foreign area officer and U.S. Army attaché in Oman and Yemen, and lectured at Princeton University. He holds a BA from the University of Wisconsin-Madison, completed the Omani Royal Air Force Staff College in Arabic Language, and holds an MA in Near East Studies from Princeton University.